EXIT WOUND

Andy McNab

BANTAM PRESS

LONDON • TORONTO • SYDNEY • AUCKLAND • JOHANNESBURG

TRANSWORLD PUBLISHERS
61–63 Uxbridge Road, London W5 5SA
A Random House Group Company
www.rbooks.co.uk

First published in Great Britain
in 2009 by Bantam Press
an imprint of Transworld Publishers

A CIP catalogue record for this book
is available from the British Library.

ISBN 9780593059524 (cased)
9780593059531 (tpb)

Addresses for Random House Group Ltd companies outside the UK
can be found at: www.randomhouse.co.uk
The Random House Group Ltd Reg. No. 954009

The Random House Group Limited supports The Forest Stewardship
Council (FSC), the leading international forest-certification organization. All our
titles that are printed on Greenpeace-approved FSC-certified paper carry the FSC logo.
Our paper procurement policy can be found at
www.rbooks.co.uk/environment

Typeset in 11/14pt Palatino by
Falcon Oast Graphic Art Ltd.
Printed and bound in Great Britain by
CPI Mackays, Chatham, ME5 8TD

2 4 6 8 10 9 7 5 3 1

Mixed Sources
Product group from well-managed
forests and other controlled sources
www.fsc.org Cert no. TT-COC-2139
© 1996 Forest Stewardship Council
FSC

PART ONE

1

November 1988

The twin props of the Dornier Do 28 Skyservant went into hyper-scream as we lifted from Tempelhof's rain-lashed runway and climbed steeply through the West Berlin gloom. There was normally room for a dozen or so bodies in these things, but not in this one. The seats had been stripped out and the four of us had to sprawl on the cold steel floor.

The aircraft pitched and yawed like a dinghy in a gale. Gripping a rib of the bare fuselage, I pulled myself up to a window. Either Dex was trying to keep us below the cloud cover or failing to get above it. The West glowed and twinkled like a giant Christmas tree down there. A neon Mercedes sign seemed to throb on every other rooftop. The nightclub district was virtually a firework display. If we got back from this job in one piece, perhaps we'd go there and let off a few of our own.

The Luftwaffe had Do 28s coming out of their ears, and most of their flights out of Tempelhof, the Americans' main military airfield here, were milk runs. They took off from the island of West Berlin several times a day and followed one of the three air corridors across the Soviet-occupied East to reach West Germany proper. Nobody gave them a first glance, let alone a second, and that was the way Dexter Khattri and his seven-month-old ponytail liked it. His aircraft was going to be making a slight detour.

I felt like I was being spirited into occupied France to help out the Resistance. Going by the creaks and rattles and the rush of cold air into the cabin from all the leaks in the airframe, SOE could have used this very plane – the noise was so loud I thought the door had slammed open. I'd noticed rain leaking round the jamb after it was closed, so it was obviously loose. Maybe it had finally blown off.

I folded another turn into the bottom of my beanie to give the back of my head some padding. Then I pulled up the zip of my black Puffa jacket the final centimetre and braced my back and feet against the floor, knees up, hands in pockets. If they'd made matching Puffa trousers, I'd have opted for three pairs.

The Dornier lurched again and my head rolled on the protective woolly band. Dex was swinging us left and right. This time I didn't want to look out of the window in case I saw why.

It could be that we were weaving between the tower blocks. I pictured the local kids' faces pressed against their bedroom windows, wondering what the fuck was going on. Red Ken said that was what had happened last time. Dex had stuck a torch under his chin, Hallowe'en style, and given them a wave. They were probably still having nightmares.

The Berlin Wall was intact, but only just. It still boasted mines, dogs, electric fences, machine-guns on fixed arcs, everything the Communist regime needed to stop its citizens leaking West, but nowadays even the guards wanted to jump ship. Everybody knew it would be over very soon, one way or another. Only a year ago, Ronnie Reagan had stood at the Brandenburg Gate and delivered his 'If you seek peace, Mr Gorbachev, open this gate! Tear down this wall!' speech. But for now they were still the bad guys – and Dex and the three of us under Red Ken's command were about to cross into their airspace.

My headphones crackled as Dex quipped: 'Not far now, chaps – home for tea and wads before first light, what?'

The aircraft plunged to rooftop height. He gave a little chuckle. 'You can cross radar off your worry list – I think we bought that last week.' The chuckle became a laugh. 'If not, I hope you're wearing sensible shoes. It's a long walk home.'

As if the bone jokes weren't bad enough, Dex treated us to the first few lines of his old school song. His cut-glass accent provided the icing on the whole SOE cake. ' "Jo-lly boat-ing weather, / And a hay har-vest breeze, / Blade on the fea-ther, / Shade off the trees . . ." '

He went up a couple of dozen decibels. ' "Swing, swing to-ge-ther, / With your bo-dies be-tween your knees . . ." '

The Wall might still be intact, but Dexter Khattri wasn't. The guy was as mad as a box of frogs. No wonder his girlfriends came and went as quickly as his thought patterns. Dex spoke like Prince Charles on speed, which sounded strange coming from an Indian. But then again, my arse had been stung by more vindaloos than his ever had. The closest he'd ever got to the land of his forefathers was driving past a Bollywood video shop on Southall Broadway.

Dex's past-the-shoulder ponytail was his latest attempt at seeing how far he could push the envelope with the RAF head shed. This time he'd decided he was a Sikh. No wonder he was the only pilot I knew who'd remained a flight lieutenant for fourteen years.

Since we'd got back from helping out the *mujahideen*, Dex had been criss-crossing the Iron Curtain in Cessnas, Dorniers, helicopters, whatever it took. They said he'd flown more people out of the East than Aeroflot. He loved his life just the way it was, without responsibility. The only thing that pissed him off about the military was that he had a death wish and it

9

hadn't obliged. He was always too lucky. I hoped it stayed that way tonight.

We were crossing the Iron Curtain to the Communist prison camp that called itself the German Democratic Republic to make contact with a KGB agent. 'Vladislav' was going to give us the guidance system of a new generation of Soviet ballistic missiles. We were going to give him a big bag of cash.

2

We swooped between two tower blocks. I knew Dex wouldn't be able to resist whipping out his torch again. He probably wasn't going to get another chance.

With the Cold War in its death throes, the Warsaw Pact boys were holding the mother of all closing-down sales. Every KGB agent – like the one we were about to meet – had turned into Del Boy Trotsky. They were auctioning off apartment blocks they didn't own in Moscow and St Petersburg. Generals were using entire infantry battalions to shift heavy plant for sale at their Western borders. Some army conscripts were even being rented out as slave labour by the high command. They still had a quarter of a million troops fighting in Afghanistan, but no matter what the Soviet PR machine claimed, they were getting their arses kicked big-time over there.

Red Ken, Tenny and I had spent most of '86 running around the mountains with the men in beards. The Regiment dropped every bridge that came within reach so the Russian armoured convoys couldn't move around the place. Then we built IEDs to blow them to pieces if they did. Dex was busy doing supply runs for the *muj* when he wasn't ferrying us.

Even in those days, the level of Soviet corruption had been outrageous. Dex brought back shed-loads of brand-new

Russian weapons and equipment that had been sold by their high command. Most of it ended up being used against their own twenty-year-old conscripts. These kids were dropping by the hundred every day.

Now the entire Soviet bloc was in meltdown, the East Germans were going for it big-time. They were flogging as many military secrets as they could get their hands on. Even the Stasi, the state secret police, were doing a roaring trade in secret documents. Anything to bring in a few dollars before the whole system went to rat shit. The West encouraged it. Once the Wall fell, a new world order would have to be fought over – and if we didn't grab as much technology and intelligence as we could while the going was good, there were plenty of other buyers in the queue. We had to know what kit was about to flood the market so we could build better stuff to defend against it.

Red Ken and Tenny had been seconded to Brixmis, the British Commanders-in-Chief Mission to the Soviet forces in Germany. They'd needed another body for this particular job and had given Hereford a call to see if I was available. These two were tighter with each other than with me, but we'd always liked working together.

Brixmis was set up after the Second World War to foster good working relations between the occupying forces in the British and Soviet sectors. The French and Americans reached their own agreements with the Russians. For some reason the Brits were allowed as many liaison staff in the Soviet zone as the other two missions combined. Maybe they liked the PG Tips.

Red Ken had served twenty-two years in Para Reg and the SAS, and his face told the whole story – although his roll-up habit must have contributed something to those deep crevasses. He'd spent the last three years driving about in his matt-green Opel, taking pictures of tanks and helping defectors across the wire, but was getting out of the Regiment after this tour. He claimed he had no plans beyond sitting full-time on the terraces at Barnsley FC, but I knew he was talking bollocks.

Tenny was also from D Squadron. He was taking over from Red Ken, but for how long, nobody knew: when the Wall crumbled, so would Brixmis. He was about thirty, very smart and hard. You'd have to be, growing up with a hairdo that looked like a rusty Brillo pad. 'Tennyson' wasn't a name you normally heard shouted across an inner-city playground, but his drop-dead gorgeous fiancée seemed to like it, and I guess that was all that mattered.

Tenny had always been a star. After university and a spell in the OTC, he decided he wanted to hang out with squaddie lowlife rather than do what he should have done – become a doctor or lawyer or something that lined his pocket. Tenny had been going places. He had golden balls. We all knew he was destined for better things. For me, being in the Regiment was the best I was ever going to get. For him, it was just another stepping-stone to global domination.

'"Jol-ly boat-ing weather, / And a hay har-vest breeze, / Blade on the fea-ther, / Shade—"'

'Shut the fuck up!' Dex was doing Red Ken's head in.

Dex threw the aircraft into a tight right-hander. I had to throw out an arm to stop myself sliding across the cabin.

'Now, now, Red – manners. You guys should like it. The music was written by a Rifle Brigade chap at the North-West Frontier. I think his name was—'

Red Ken had had enough. 'Shut the fuck up, crap hat!' To Para Reg, that meant anyone who didn't wear a red beret.

These two had always been like a couple of fishwives. They bickered 24/7, but couldn't do without each other to bicker with.

Dex's tone suddenly changed. 'Border crossed.'

Down below it looked like someone had taken an axe to the

Christmas-tree cable. Even the navigation lights had been doused.

'Over the sterile zone.'

A Bronx growl filled our headphones. 'I can see that. Just tell me when we're going to goddam land.'

Tenny kept his voice low and controlled before Red Ken had a chance to tell our American friend where he could shove the Special Relationship. 'It's OK, Spag. We'll get you there, don't worry. We can't do anything right now apart from lie here and let Dex get on with it.'

I'd met Conrad Spicciati three days earlier and known straight away I didn't like him. It wasn't just because he was small and so overweight he looked like Humpty Dumpty – he didn't know how to behave with us. For a low-grade CIA agent he had a Pentagon-sized swagger. We had to take the piss. Dex started calling him Spaghetti. Ten seconds later we'd shortened it to Spag.

It got him so worked up his porn-star moustache was in a permanent twitch. He kept stroking it with his thumb and fore-finger, possibly to calm it down. I wondered if he'd grown it especially for the job. But I didn't give it much thought. As far as I was concerned, we'd get this shit done and never see him again.

He sat with his arms locked around a black nylon sports bag in the dull red glow of the aircraft interior, gripping it like he thought we were going to mug him. I probably would have done if I'd thought I could have got away with it. The bag contained Vladislav's twenty thousand US dollars. It didn't sound like a lot for a bit of top-secret kit, but it would have been a life-changing sum to me.

Tenny needn't have worried. Dex ignored him. '"Bang, bang, Chitty Chitty Bang Bang . . ."'

Red Ken's and Tenny's shoulders heaved in unison.

Spag bellowed into his headset that nobody sang on his goddam watch.

Biggles segued straight into 'Those Magnificent Men In Their Flying Machines'.

Odd smudges of very East German light appeared – dull and yellow, not the fairground stuff their Western mates went for a few thousand metres away. We called them *nein-watt* bulbs.

Red Ken cut in: 'OK, that's it, enough. Let's switch on.'

3

The Dornier dropped the final couple of hundred feet. My head bounced off the steel as we hit the ground and bumped along the field.

When I sat up I could see a line of small fires through the windows. Benghazi burners – normally small pots of petrol and sand, but probably mud here. Everywhere east of the Wall was ankle-deep in the stuff. The burners would have been laid out in an L, Second-World-War SOE-style. The base of the L was the threshold; Dex needed to land as close to it as he could to ensure he had enough grass to rattle to a stop. The long stroke gave him wind direction.

Spag was already up on his knees, headphones cast aside as if he had to jump and run under fire. He struggled to keep his balance at the same time as he hugged the bag to his chest.

Red Ken waved him down. 'The crap-hat has been watching too many war films.'

Tenny convulsed again with laughter.

Spag didn't like it. He stayed on his knees, ready to leap out and take on all-comers.

Red Ken wasn't finished. 'Who does he think he is? He's a pencil-neck CIA desk jockey, not the fucking Terminator . . .'

Tenny rested a hand on Red Ken's shoulder. 'Give him a break. This is his first time. And he's American.'

After Spag's thirty-odd years as a desk jockey, he wouldn't be auditioning for the job of Arnie's stunt double any time soon. He looked more like the new cartoon character I'd been watching on the American forces' network back in Berlin, Homer Simpson.

The Dornier slowed. Dex taxied to the threshold, swung the nose round so he was facing into the wind again, and closed down the props. 'Just like the old days, chaps – the four of us together in the middle of nowhere. At least we don't have to start spouting Pashto.'

Spag headed straight for the exit and scrabbled to get out.

Red Ken caught his arm. 'No rush, mate. If we've got a drama waiting for us out there, we'll find out soon enough. We need to take everything slow and calm.' He swung the door open.

My nostrils were hammered by the stench of shit.

Tenny saw my face screw up in the dull red light. 'Human fertilizer. Nothing gets wasted round here.'

Red Ken set off towards a thin torch beam that suddenly pierced the darkness.

Vladislav's contact appeared out of the gloom. His fresh boot-marks met Red Ken's in the frosty dew. They'd done a lot of business during his tour, but this was their biggest deal yet. They hugged like old mates and jabbered away to each other in German while Tenny checked our comms with Dex.

I didn't know the contact's name and didn't need to. Tenny and Red Ken were here to look after Spag, and my job was to look after them. I tightened my grip on the two-foot steel Maglite. There were rules to this game, and one of them was that Brixmis went unarmed. If you were caught with a gun, you got shot, simple as that.

Apart from my torch, the only kit we had with us was the radio in Tenny's day-sack and whatever Red Ken had in his. A couple of sharp rectangular shapes jutted against the thin nylon. I didn't know what they were and I didn't ask. If I'd needed to know he would have told me.

Our biggest weapon was secrecy. No one knew where we were, apart from those who absolutely had to. The KGB and the Stasi had no reason to be out here, sliding around in the shit. And if they were waiting to round us up with dogs and AKs, we were sterile.

Dex stayed in the cockpit. He tended to stick out in this part of the world. He'd be pissed off that he'd had to close down the engines. It was good for security, but bad for us all if he couldn't get them restarted. That was how he'd got caught last time. He'd ended up being traded for a couple of newspapermen caught spying for the East.

The RAF rule was that he should have taken off again and come back in when Tenny called for a pickup. But Dex didn't like doing that. He never had. He said it made him feel like he was running away.

4

Apart from the gentle whispers between Red Ken and the contact, it was quiet.

Red Ken's German was far better than mine, but that wasn't saying much. I was still at eighteen-year-old-squaddie level. *'Pommes frites ... Bier ...* Taxi...' was pretty much my limit, with the occasional *'danke'* and *'bitte'* thrown in. If anything else I wanted wasn't on display – so I could point at it and shout – I had to go hungry.

Spag stormed up to them, both hands still gripping the bag. 'Shouldn't we get moving?'

Tenny carried on checking comms. He'd send Dex a sitrep when we were at the meet, and another as we left. If we didn't report in, it meant a drama at our end. If he didn't acknowledge, it meant one at his.

I moved closer to the group. The contact was in his fifties. He ignored Spag. He dug in the pockets of his leather overcoat and pulled out a pack of F6.

Red Ken waved a hand. *'Nein, nein.'* He flipped open his day-sack and dug out one of the mysterious rectangular packages, a carton of Benson & Hedges.

The contact beamed as he ran his fingers along the cellophane. When Red Ken threw in a cheap disposable lighter, his early Christmas was complete.

It was too much for Spag. 'Jee-sus, let's get going here! We stopping for tea and cucumber sandwiches, or what?'

Red Ken was close to decking him. 'We'll go when we're good and ready.'

Tenny stepped between them. 'We wouldn't be here if it wasn't for this guy. If he wants to wait and smoke, that's what we do.'

He shook the contact's hand, triggering another stream of waffle. Tenny nodded. His German was excellent too.

'We have to hold back a while. We have to give Vladislav time to make the RV. He wants to be there before us to check it out. And he has something he needs to discuss with Red before we move.'

Spag wasn't having any of it. 'Fuck him. He'll be history when this whole pile of crap collapses.'

Red Ken offered the contact a cigarette from his own pack and they both lit up. Both drew deeply to help their creases along. The tips glowed and the smoke mingled with our breath. Red Ken glared at the American. He wasn't playing. He showed every sign of being prepared to stand there until they'd smoked the whole carton.

Spag spun on his heel and stormed back to the aircraft.

5

I stood alongside Tenny as the other two kippered their lungs. My eyes were constantly on the move, checking for lights or other giveaways.

Tenny checked his day-sack was secure. 'You still coming to the wedding?'

'Wouldn't miss it for the world.'

Even with his hair, Tenny had managed to trap the most beautiful woman on the planet. I was sure she'd been designed in a test tube. She was smart and funny too, a teacher at the girls' prep school in Hereford. I was more than a little jealous of the great life he had ahead of him.

'I've been thinking about going back to the Green Jackets after this tour. Janice and I are going for kids ASAP. I want to see them grow up, be a proper dad instead of spending years away. What do you reckon, Nick?'

I hesitated. I might have shared food, sleeping-bags and even body lice with him, but I was the last person to ask about family stuff. 'Don't know, mate. Big decision. They offering a commission?'

The day-sack was secure and he hauled it back over his shoulders. 'Yep, seems like a good deal. Stay in, but still get to be a family man. Well, as much as you can, eh?'

I nodded as if I knew. 'I'd go for it, mate. You'll be a general by the time I get within reach of sergeant. I'll be your driver if you want.'

The other two finished their cigarettes. Red Ken picked up the butts and put them in a pocket of his day-sack. 'Right, let's get on with it.'

Tenny grabbed Spag and we crunched across the field towards the contact's vehicle.

'Listen in.' Red Ken walked backwards so we could hear him clearly. 'Stasi have been sniffing around this guy. They know something's happening. Normally they want a kickback on the cash – or they have something to sell. They didn't offer him anything, so let's keep switched on.'

Spag bristled. 'You saying we got trouble? You saying we shouldn't even get in the vehicle with this fuck?'

Tenny cut in before Red Ken exercised any more of his diplomatic skills. 'We're here because of you. It's you we're taking to Vladislav. If you don't want to go, that's OK. Give us the cash and go back and wait in the plane.'

The Americans were buying the guidance system. We were only there because the deal was happening in Brixmis TAOR (tactical area of responsibility).

Spag gripped the bag as if it was his child. 'I'm not leaving this goddam money with anyone.'

'So our task is still to connect you with Vladislav. If our assessment is that we get in the vehicle, we get in the vehicle.'

We'd arrived alongside the most knackered Gaz van left in the Eastern bloc. It was trying its hardest to be a VW Camper, but looked more like a flat-pack wardrobe I'd once tried to put together without the instructions.

Red Ken and the contact jumped in the front. I got in behind with Spag. Tenny took the back row.

The windows were steamed up and cracked. It actually felt colder inside than out. It smelt like the old boy kept chickens in it. I pulled my beanie down over my eyes, put my hands in my pockets, and curled up as best I could on the ripped vinyl.

The drive along the pot-holed road was as bumpy as the landing had been.

Spag blew into his cupped hands. 'How long till we get there? What are we going to do when we arrive?'

Nobody answered.

'Red?'

Silence.

'I demand to know what's happening, goddammit.'

Red Ken finally turned in his seat. His head and shoulders were wreathed in smoke. 'Another twenty minutes.'

Spag glared out of the window. He was way beyond his comfort zone. I'd have preferred to be tucked up in his warm office in the US embassy, too.

The contact muttered something and he hit the brake.

It got the American flapping big-time. 'Jee-sus, what the fuck—'

Red Ken raised his hand. 'Shut up. Nick, Tenny – stand by. Spag, you'd better get your head in gear and keep your gob shut.'

Through the misted-up windscreen, all I could see was the strobe of blue lights.

Spag had his head in gear, but it was the wrong one. 'Why are we still driving towards it? Why aren't we in reverse?'

Red Ken ignored him. All his attention was fixed on the road ahead.

6

It wasn't a marked police car but a bog-standard Wartburg with a blue light on its roof. The front was tilted off the ground like they'd driven up an inspection ramp. The two lads flagging us down were dressed for winter. Both had big furry Russian hats. One was in a three-quarter-length sheepskin, the other in a long leather trench coat. Their street shoes were up to the ankles in mud, which was probably why they looked so pissed off.

'Stasi.' The contact confirmed what I'd suspected.

I stayed sunk in my seat as the Gaz came to a halt. Tenny mumbled from behind: 'What's going on, mate?'

Red Ken didn't have time to answer. Spag was flapping. 'Don't stop! They'll kill us! I'm ordering you.'

Red Ken smiled through the windscreen. 'Nick, Tenny – stand by. We'll sort this once we're out of the vehicle. I see two so far, no weapons.'

I gripped the Maglite in my right hand, with the shaft up my forearm. You're better off out on your feet than sitting in a wagon. Once we were in the open air, I'd be ready the moment Red Ken kicked it off.

The closer the voices got, the tighter I gripped. My eyes strained at the tops of their sockets. The two Stasi seemed to be waving us out of the wagon, with the confidence that comes from no one ever fucking you about.

Red Ken's fingers closed round the door handle.

The contact wound down the window. Cold air rushed into the wagon. His breath billowed as he spoke.

I heard the word '*Zigarette*'.

Then: '*Ach so – Englische Zigarette?*'

I pretended to come awake, and looked around dozily. Red Ken was sitting there, beaming friendship and goodwill.

Spag was close to hyperventilating. The knuckles gripping the bag gleamed white.

The contact opened his door and got out. The Stasi in the sheepskin arched an eyebrow as he studied the cigarette in his hand, but he accepted a light. Then he spotted the cheap disposable, and his hand grabbed the contact's wrist.

He muttered something and the contact laughed. '*Ja, ja, natürlich.*' He handed over the entire pack, and then the lighter, before gesturing to Red Ken for the carton on the front seat. They got it – as well as the one still in his day-sack.

Sheepskin stuck his head into the cab. 'Brixmis? Brixmis, *ja?*'

Red Ken shrugged and gave him some waffle. He sounded very authoritative, which got Sheepskin sort of nodding. The other one walked all the way round the van, peering in through the windows.

A local. Brixmis. The pieces were coming together in Sheepskin's head. He shouted down at the contact.

Red Ken shook his head and answered for him in English: 'We have no money – no money.'

Sheepskin drew down his pistol. His mate Leatherman was a split second behind. He pointed the barrel at the contact and screamed into his face.

Spag shat himself as Red Ken screamed right back: 'No fucking money, we got no money.'

Leatherman came round and joined Sheepskin. They were

getting angrier and more agitated. A very bad combination. They both pointed their weapons into the van.

Red Ken was calm. 'Just stay in the wagon. If we get out now, they'll shoot.'

Spag sparked up. 'I've got money. I've got money.' He held the bag up high.

Sheepskin pushed the contact aside and lunged into the cab. He leant over the driver's seat and grabbed the holdall. Leatherman kept one eye on us and the other on the bag. Both were very happy with what they saw inside it.

They turned and shouted at the contact. Fingers were pointed at their vehicle and then at us.

Red Ken opened his door. 'Nick, Tenny – out. Leave everything in the wagon. Don't piss them off. I'll tell you when.'

7

As we walked up to their vehicle I saw what the problem was. The antlers of a huge stag stuck out from under the front bumper.

Sheepskin stood on the road with the cash while his mate took the wheel.

The four of us slipped and slid in the mud at the back as the driver hung out of the window shouting orders. The exhaust fumes caught at the back of my throat and made my eyes stream.

Red Ken was in the middle. 'Nick – the driver. We'll take the money. On my word . . .'

One final push and the front wheels rolled over the carcass and reconnected with the tarmac. The engine revved as we stamped shit off our boots.

As Sheepskin headed past us for the passenger door, Red Ken yelled, 'Go!' He and Tenny lunged at him. I moved to the left of the car as the contact made a run for it. Leatherman poked his head out to see what was happening. The middle three fingers of my left hand fought their way into his mouth and twisted sideways, like I'd hooked a fish. I gripped his head with my right and pulled hard, as if I was trying to land him through the window. I couldn't see his weapon.

He screamed at me. My fingers were soaked in his saliva. His hands came up to try to grab mine and he ended up wedged in the gap. Seconds later, Tenny arrived and gave him a couple of boots to the neck. Leatherman shrieked. I kept hold of him as Tenny opened the door and grabbed a weapon from the passenger seat.

I let go. Leatherman's head hit the top of the window frame. He fell forward onto his hands and knees, trying to cough his Adam's apple back into place. Tenny kicked him down into the mud.

Red Ken had Sheepskin on the ground with a weapon in his neck. He shouted to the contact to retrieve the cash.

The blue light beat into the darkness.

He turned to us two. 'Get them in the boot. If they fuck about, drop them. Tenny, cut the blues and follow.'

We did what we were told, pushing, kicking, shouting, pointing their pistols at them. Seconds later we were back in the Gaz, Tenny in the Wartburg behind us.

Red Ken was breathing hard. I knew he was angry. He tried to control himself, but it wasn't happening. He turned and jabbed a finger at Spag. 'All you had to do was sit tight and *shut the fuck up.*'

Spag took a breath but decided not to answer.

Good move.

The muddy bag was back on his lap.

We drove in silence for another quarter of an hour before turning down a farm track. A collection of barns stood off to the right, rough old things knocked up out of concrete blocks and corrugated iron. One or two bits of rusted machinery had been abandoned to the elements.

The contact followed the track round to the back, stopped and killed the lights. Tenny pulled up beside us.

Red Ken went over to him as the rest of us clambered out. 'Hold these fuckers here. We do the deal and we leave. They'll find their own way out of the boot.'

Tenny shook his head. 'Better let them breathe. The exhaust is cracked and the fumes are getting everywhere. It'll kill them.'

'OK, give 'em air until we're finished. Then we'll close them in again.'

He lifted the lid. The two crushed and suffering bodies were coughing up their lungs. They tried getting out, but Tenny punched them back in.

The contact led the rest of us towards the nearest barn.

8

I kept a few paces behind the other three, as cover. My boots sank up to their laces in stinking ooze.

Spag tried to recover from looking like a dickhead. 'It was right to hand over the cash. They could have killed us.'

Red Ken checked stride and rounded on him. Their faces were inches apart. 'Listen in, twat – they were going to kill us *because* they'd got the money. Now wind your fucking neck in, let's get the deal done and leave.'

We worked our way past a dark, mud-covered Trabant, up to its hubs in shit. I saw the prolonged glow of a cigarette tip through a gap in the barn wall. Whoever was on the other end of it was sucking hard.

The contact headed for the door. 'Vladislav?'

A solitary *nein-watt* bulb dangled from the rafters. Its dim light only just reached the floor, but I could see the shit gleam on Vladislav's boots. The KGB man was another egg-on-legs. He could have been Spag's brother. Mrs Dumpty had been busy. His trench coat was so long it nearly touched the ground. He took a step back to reveal a battered canvas suitcase at his feet.

Spag barged past Red Ken and the contact. 'OK, what you got? Show me.'

Vladislav caught his drift, unzipped the suitcase and threw back the top. Spag snorted from excitement or exertion. Either way, he should have stayed behind his desk.

Vladislav dug through a pile of old shirts and pulled out what looked like a long-legged metal spider. When he held it up to the light, I could see it was some kind of circuit board with wires coming off it in all directions.

He stood back and let Spag inspect the goods. 'It's intact. I have much more on offer if you are interested.' His English was good.

Spag held out a hand. 'You got a pen?'

Vladislav fished about inside his coat. Then he knelt to empty the bundles of hundred-dollar bills into his suitcase.

'Don't you wanna count it?'

'I know you will be back for more, so why would you try to cheat me? If you have, I'll go elsewhere.'

Red Ken leant over to me. 'These Russians will do just fine, whatever happens to the Wall. There's no ideology here, mate. It's every man for himself.'

Spag's eyes gleamed. He finished writing on one of the wrappers. 'Come direct to me. We could do some serious business.'

He stood and they shook.

There were shouts from outside.

I started running.

9

I cannoned into a body at the door. My face rubbed against sheepskin.

Red Ken yelled from behind me, 'Leave him!'

I pushed against the coat, not even raising the Maglite, just squeezing past as Red Ken took him.

There were two bodies by the rear of the car. One was staggering to his feet. The other lay still. The upright one wore a long leather coat. He turned towards me and lifted his arm.

My vision tunnelled. All I could see was the weapon I was running towards. The barrel headed my way in slow motion. I felt nothing but the thump of my heart as I got within striking distance.

The Maglite came down on what I could see of the pistol and his hand. He buckled, but not enough. The weapon didn't fall, and neither did he. I connected again, this time to the right side of his neck.

I kept hitting, kept hammering his head, his neck, his arm.

A round kicked off inside the barn, then a double tap.

I slammed the Maglite down again and again on the target's head, jumping into the air to get that extra bit of momentum, until I heard the crack I wanted and felt warm blood spurt against my face.

He dropped into the shit beside Tenny.

I used the Maglite for the job it was designed to do – to find the weapon in the mud and guide me back to the barn.

'Red! Red!'

'Clear this end.'

I turned back, dropped to my knees beside Tenny and ran the Maglite beam over his face, searching for signs of life. 'It's OK, mate. You're breathing – means you're still winning. Got to turn you over. Take the pain.'

A gunshot wound to the gut. I grabbed his shoulder, log-rolled him and looked for an exit wound.

'It's fine, mate – it's still inside you.'

The only good thing about a gut wound is that it isn't as painful as anywhere else on the body. There aren't any nerve endings there. If there were, it would hurt to eat. As long as no major organs were hit, Tenny could live for a day, maybe two, without treatment.

I pressed my beanie against the entry wound. 'Keep it there, mate.'

Spag loomed out of the darkness with Vladislav. They both headed for the Trabant.

Red Ken had other ideas. 'Get in the fucking van – now!' He and the contact weren't far behind, hefting Sheepskin by his arms and legs. They dropped him into the mud next to his mate. The Trabant rolled out of the farmyard and Spag pushed himself into the Gaz.

One look at Tenny, and Red Ken binned whatever plan he'd had to hide the Stasi boys. 'Fuck 'em. Let's go.'

We loaded Tenny into the Gaz and the contact pressed his foot to the floor. I got on the radio to Dex.

Tenny was less worried about his guts than about what had happened.

'It was so quick. I sparked up the radio to give Dex a sitrep and they went for it. I—'

Red Ken placed his hand on Tenny's forehead, like a father

with a sick child. 'It doesn't matter. Getting you back is all that does. Not long now, mate.'

Spag just sat there with his bag of tricks on his lap. I didn't blame him keeping out of it.

When we reached the field, Dex's props were already turning.

PART TWO

10

Lincoln
14 April 2009

Judging by the number of lads packing the bars around the cathedral, the funeral was going to be a big one. I recognized a few of the faces knocking back the pints as they sheltered under awnings and patio heaters.

I pulled up my jacket collar, and not just against the wind and rain. I was hoping they didn't recognize me back. I didn't want to be pulled into any of the groups and have to waffle about jobs and families and how much hair we'd all lost. I'd only get agitated. I wanted to be here as much as I had to be here, but I couldn't stand the garbage people spouted at reunions. Maybe I was just jealous of them for having normal lives. There were a couple of lads I was looking for in the sea of faces. They were the only ones I wanted to waffle with.

'Oi, Nick!'

I turned. He wasn't one of them. I didn't know the guy from Adam – except that I don't remember Adam eating all the pies. He was surrounded by other beer bellies and red faces, throwing down the pints like they were still nineteen-year-old squaddies. Many were thinning on top; some were bald or grey. All of them were bullshitting about how great it's been since they got out. Great house, great car, everything's gravy.

Some wore their Green Jacket blazers and ties over crisp white shirts and neatly pressed slacks. Others were in their best suits. Me? I was in a Tesco shirt, washable trousers and cheap leather jacket. Most of them would have been lorry drivers, security guards, painters and decorators, firemen or policemen. That was what normally happened with the lads. The odd one would be on the circuit, fucking about in Iraq or Afghanistan, but today it really didn't matter who or what you were. The one thing everyone had in common was that they knew Tenny.

Tennyson had spent the best part of a year sorting out his gut before marrying Janice and taking up his commission in the Green Jackets – which had become the Rifles in the next shake-up. He never did make general, but was promoted to full colonel in command of media ops at Camp Bastion in Helmand province. It was a plum job, making sure reporters and news crews got where they were needed, and managing the PR output. Until he got zapped again, this time in the head by a 7.62mm short from an AK.

The voice called again: 'Nick! Nick Stone!'

I still didn't have a clue who he was, but shook his hand anyway. I didn't have much choice: he'd gone for it big-time. He pumped my arm so vigorously my shoulders shook.

'Good to see you, mate.'

Maybe he'd had more hair the last time I'd seen him.

'Graham – Graham Pincombe. How you doing, mate?'

Still none the wiser. 'Ah, yeah, fine . . . mate . . .'

My brain whirred into hyperspace as the very thing I was trying to avoid started to happen.

'What you been doing with yourself? The last time I saw you . . .' At last his hand released mine and for some reason headed for the tip of his nose. 'Ah, yeah. Germany – remember when we were on exercise in Germany?'

No, not a clue. 'Shame about Tenny, eh?'

'Yeah.'

'What exactly happened – anybody know?' I scanned the group for a face that might give Mr Pincombe some context.

He shook his head. 'He kept wanting to go out on the ground with the rifle companies. I heard he was next on the list for a cabby on the Javelin. That's when he got zapped.'

I smiled, and he smiled back. We both knew what that meant. The Javelin anti-armour rocket was a great bit of kit, and there was always a queue of guys wanting to have a go. Originally designed to take out tanks, it was now anti-personnel, anti-car, anti-bicycle, you name it. No job too small. And over long distances, too. Its optics and second-generation thermal-imaging technology could see in the dark or through rain and smoke. It was an infantryman's dream. Once you'd acquired a target and locked it on, you kicked off the rocket and that was that. Most brilliant of all, it cost seventy-six grand a pop.

Everyone wanted to lob the military equivalent of a Porsche at the enemy. There was a list, and everybody put their name up. When it was your turn, it was your turn, whether you were an eighteen-year-old rifleman or a forty-eight-year-old colonel. If there was nothing between you and a target up to 2,500 metres away, it kicked off and flew line-of-sight, with pinpoint accuracy. If you had a moving target, say a car, you could select top attack mode and the missile went up into the air, climbing 150 metres before striking down to penetrate the roof – just as it would do to a tank, hitting it at the point of least armour protection.

Pincombe took a mouthful of Stella. 'He got up onto the wall, took aim, and was just about to kick it off when . . .' He supplied the impact site with his finger. 'Taliban round, straight through the launch unit and into his nut. Simple as that.' He wiped his mouth with the back of his hand and came out with the predictable, 'At least he died the way he would have wanted.'

No, Tenny. I bet you didn't, mate.

A photographer walked past and took a couple of shots. All he got of me was the back of my head.

A bell tolled. Shoppers stopped and nodded at the drinkers. They all knew whose funeral it was. The local media had made it a big deal. I doubted a rifleman would be getting the same attention, or his local cathedral.

I turned away as another flash kicked off. 'I've got to go and meet up with a mate before we go in. See you there, yeah?'

'You going to the wake?'

'Nah, haven't got time. Besides, I'm driving.'

The bit afterwards was what I hated most. That was when the storytelling started. Everyone would swap memories of Tenny's awesome talent with anything from a PlayStation to forty-kilo dumbbells – just how he would have wanted it – but also of his courage and compassion, which he would have hated. Then, at round about the five-pint mark, everyone would start admitting to each other how shit their lives really were. Divorces, child support, mortgages . . . and a longing to return to the days when no one gave a fuck, except about each other.

Graham Pincombe went back to his beer, and I still couldn't place him. I walked down the hill, took a left and paralleled the main road to avoid any more pubs. I followed the line of guys, wives, friends and everybody else Tenny had collected over the years snaking along the pedestrian walkway towards the cathedral.

11

I was early, but I could already see that by the time Squaddies Reunited rolled out of the pubs and got themselves up the hill it was going to be standing room only. Lots of guys were in number-twos, their best dress. Boots and medals gleamed around me. Off to one side, I spotted a bugler blowing nervously into his mouthpiece to keep his lips up to the mark. It was a huge responsibility, playing the Last Post. If you fucked up, it was the only memory people took away with them.

'Oi, lard-arse . . .'

I spun round. 'Pikey, mate – how's it going?' I had to keep my voice down to control how happy I was to see him.

Pikey had joined the battalion back in the late seventies, the same time as me. We were both scabby seventeen-year-old riflemen. He was South African and, I soon discovered, a total nightmare. For the first six months I couldn't even understand what he said. All I knew was that every time I went down town with him, I woke up the next day with a hangover and black eyes.

For this lad, fighting was recreation. Provoking a brawl and getting filled in was his equivalent of going to the pictures. I couldn't believe what I was seeing now. One, he was still in the army, and two, it was now Major Pikey. He had more medals hanging off his chest than a Soviet general on May Day. And he still looked as fit as a butcher's dog, the fucker.

I grinned. 'Should I say "sir"? Well done, mate!'

A group of senior officers filed past. Any rank above full colonel confused me. I'd never understood all that scrambled egg even when I was in. The American system of one to five stars was easier on the brain.

Pikey whispered, 'It's a fucking nightmare.'

I thought he was talking about the promotion.

'I'm on rear party. I'm the lad who has to go and give the families the bad news. I've got four kids myself and two of them are older than the last two we buried.'

A couple of the scrambled-egg brigade nodded at him and he nodded back. 'I go and break it to them but they're the ones making me cups of tea. Even reading the eulogies, I start to crack up, man. Just send me back out there, I can't hack all this. My youngest, the girl, every time the mobile rings she flinches. She thinks it's someone else in the battalion who's got zapped.'

My eyes followed the officers as they took their reserved seats in the first three rows on the left. Tenny's family filled the opposite side of the aisle. Near the back of the church, a guy who'd just come in removed his raincoat to reveal an immaculate dark grey suit and well-pressed shirt. Pikey had also seen him – and noticed me noticing. 'Who's he?'

The closely cropped hair, clean shave and glowing ebony skin made him look like a Premiership footballer from Senegal. 'No idea.' I turned back to Pikey. 'I didn't even know Tenny came from up here. All the time you're with someone, and it never occurs to you to ask where they come from . . .'

'That's because it doesn't matter where you come from, man. It's where you are that matters.' He slapped me on the back. 'Good to see you, mate. Now I've got to fuck off and sort out the bearers.'

42

His George boots clicked off down the aisle and I squashed myself into a seat at the end of the very last row. I liked being at the back. It had something to do with my schooldays. People can't see or hear you there. And I'd be able to ping everyone as they came in.

I picked up the order of service. Tenny stared out from the cover in his Green Jacket kit and, for some reason, a moustache. Maybe it was part of the uniform. Whatever, he looked very much the colonel. But some things never changed. I felt myself grin. His rusty Brillo pad hair was still trying to fight its way out from under his cap.

Dex, Red Ken and I had told him that when he was prime minister we all wanted a peerage, something that would set us up for life. Tenny promised he would, if only to make us shut up: Lord Ken of t'Pit, Lord Dex of Cards, and Lord Stone of Stony Broke.

The smile left my face. It couldn't disguise the grief I felt that someone like him, a man with a future and a purpose, had got zapped – while someone like me . . . well, I just plodded on.

Another flurry of toe- and heel-caps clicked along the flagstones as a group of officers and warrant officers made their way to the front pews. Then Dex and his girlfriend appeared, looking sharp in their immaculately tailored outfits. He was decked out in a black suit, crisp white shirt and thin black tie. She was in a short black dress and very high heels. Even her hair was jet black, in honour of the occasion. She still had her sunglasses on.

I recognized Dex straight away, even though he'd shaved off all his hair. It looked like his new thing was Buddhism. He didn't see me. He was too busy feeling pleased with himself – every squaddie within a fifty-metre radius had leant across to cop a good look at his companion, elbowed his neighbour in the ribs and muttered what a lucky bastard he was.

Just a few paces behind – and dressed just as sharply – strutted the roll-up king. 'Nicky boy, all right, son?'

He gave me a quick wink and carried on going with the flow. 'The do . . .' He raised an imaginary glass. 'We'll see you there, yeah?'

I nodded and grinned. These were the only two I wanted to spend time with today.

12

The lads at the back were packed shoulder to shoulder. Those who hadn't been able to make it that far had to jostle for room on the cobblestones outside. The bugler fidgeted in one of the side chambers, now nervously flexing his lips. A dozen or so rows in front of me, Dex and Ken stood for a hymn. I could just see the shiny top of Dex's head now and again when those behind him moved. The choir was really going for it, and so was he. Ten years of starting school with chapel every morning probably got you into the swing of things. The tall bird next to him didn't seem to share his gusto. Now she'd removed her glasses I could tell she was bored out of her perfectly shaped skull.

The only thing Dex seemed to have changed was his hairdo and the ribbon on his chest. He'd won the DFC in Iraq four years ago, just before he got out of the RAF. Dex's dad would have been really proud. When Hitler marched on Poland, Dex's dad, the seventh son of a maharajah, was just graduating from one of the poshest private schools in India. The moment Neville Chamberlain declared war on Germany, so did the Viceroy. He didn't consult the Indian Army, of course, but that's colonialism for you. Thousands rallied to Lord Linlithgow's call, and Dex Senior's headmaster, an Old Etonian, made sure that when all his lads left for England they carried letters of introduction to an old schoolmate of his, an air vice marshal in the RAF.

Dex's dad took to the skies over London and Kent in a Hurricane, and if he was anything like his son, he'd have flown with a white silk scarf sticking out behind him on a coat hanger. After the battle of Britain, he fought in North Africa and Burma, winning the DSO and ending his career as a group captain. He stayed in England, made a fortune, inherited a couple of others, and sent his only child to Eton in honour of his old headmaster. The only downside to the Khattri story was that Dex's dad must have been as mad as he was. When he died, most of the cash went in death duties.

The Berlin ponytail had been about Dex keeping the RAF on their toes. He said his dad had flown in a turban and kept a spare in his flying jacket in case he became a PoW, and he was keeping up the tradition. The high command couldn't make up their minds whether he was honouring a sacred tradition or taking the piss, and that suited him just fine. He'd liked to keep people guessing.

The madness and the hair weren't Dex's only claims to fame. He was such a fine athlete that he beat all-comers at the 100 metres when he was at Eton – despite having had to stop and put his massive dick back into his shorts after it popped out in all the excitement. Sports Day had never been the same there since.

Red Ken had gone totally grey, and the extra creases in his face had moved him on from basset hound to deflated barrage balloon. His nickname had originated during the miners' strikes in '84 and '85. His family had been down t'pit for generations. His dad and two brothers had fought the police from the picket lines. Red Ken, along with quite a few others from mining families, had refused to meet Maggie Thatcher when she took time off from haranguing Arthur Scargill to visit Stirling Lines.

The great and the good from the MoD trooped up and gave their addresses, then a couple of Tenny's sisters got to their feet. One of them read a poem, the other extracts from letters he'd sent from Afghanistan. There wasn't a dry female eye in the house, apart from the tall one's, of course. I even saw a couple of guys' hands go up and brush away a tear.

The big moment came. The six pallbearers, all bulled up in their number-twos, moved up the aisle at a slow march. Pikey was one pace behind. The bugler got his lips in gear. Every man and his dog kept their fingers firmly crossed.

As the hymn finished, the coffin was slowly raised from its cradle. Pikey stood at the head, his hand touching the wood. He guided its ascent onto six shoulders with a combination of reverence and precision that had us all reaching for the Kleenex now.

The cathedral fell silent. There was a muffled sob from the family seats, then the squeak of perfectly synchronized boots as the crew carried their heavy load. With Pikey leading, Tenny was marched slowly back down the aisle. The first mournful notes of the Last Post sounded across the nave. Every head swivelled as the coffin passed. Immediately behind it, the family huddled together, supporting each other as they walked, followed at a respectful distance by the lads with the scrambled egg.

Janice looked as beautiful as ever, and so did the teenage twins. Their mother pushed one in her wheelchair and a much older man pushed the other. They wore identical long black velvet dresses that didn't quite conceal the sheepskin-padded straps that held their ankles. They had bibs around their necks to catch the saliva, but nothing could stop their heads moving rhythmically from side to side. Tenny and Janice's perfect world had collapsed around them when the girls were born – but their care had become the only thing that mattered.

As the coffin reached the courtyard, the bugle call faded. It had been note perfect. The organ sparked up, which seemed to be the signal for everyone to exchange a few hushed words.

The cathedral began to empty from the front. Red Ken and

Dex filed past. Red Ken gave me another little nod and gestured discreetly to meet outside. Dex didn't seem to understand protocol. He grinned from ear to ear as the tall one slid her sun-gigs back on, and gave me a big slap on the shoulder. 'Great, wasn't it? Splendid selection of hymns. I wouldn't mind the same when I crash. Looking forward to the wake.' He made a coming-for-a-drink? gesture.

I nodded and waited for my turn to leave.

By the time I got outside, the hearse was pulling away. Everyone in uniform saluted the coffin and the people in three black limos leaving for the private burial.

Then the mayhem began.

'Great service, wasn't it?' they all bellowed to each other. But unlike Dex, who'd meant it, they were just going through the motions.

A voice piped up behind me that would have done the Tetley Tea Folk proud: 'I'd rather have a shite life than a good service – that right, Nick?'

I turned and now I could smile. 'How's it going, Red?'

'Better than it looks as though it's going for you, son. Look at you – shit state. Get yourself a decent suit.' He produced a pack of Benson & Hedges.

I shook my head, pointing at the disappearing black limos. 'You'll be hitching a lift in one of those any minute now, if you keep on with that shit.'

'Good to know you still care, lad.' He put one in his mouth and coaxed a flame from a purple disposable. He nodded across the cobblestoned courtyard. It had started to glisten in the light drizzle. I pulled up my collar and we started to walk.

'How you been, anyway?' he said. 'I haven't heard much about you since you left.'

'This and that.'

'The Firm, Dex said.'

'Only when I first got out. I binned it. They hated me anyway.'

He laughed. 'They hate everyone, lad. You want a lift up to the do?'

We'd reached the road. Red Ken pressed a key fob and the indicators flashed on a long silver Merc.

'Whoa, you haven't done badly!'

He grinned as he opened the passenger door for me. 'Better than most. Still way behind Tenny, of course.'

I nodded. 'But he never made prime minister.'

'He still owes us our fucking peerages.' He waved to a couple of lads who recognized him, threw away his half-smoked B&H and opened the driver's door. He got in and played about with his seatbelt.

We nudged into the traffic as the one big wiper silently removed the rain. I sank back into a world of black leather. The Premiership player in the dark grey suit was standing back from the crowd, watching the Merc disappear. 'How're Chrissie and the girls, Red?'

He concentrated for a moment on the road as we wove through groups of mourners wandering oblivious to the traffic because they were too busy waffling to the mates they hadn't seen since the last funeral they'd all been to.

Finally he shook his head. 'She binned me. The youngest is in the States. The other married a hairdresser and fucked off to Australia. Can't blame them. Fuck-all left in Brown's Britain, is there?' He continued before I could even draw breath, keen to change the subject. Fair one. 'What about you? Remarried? Kids?'

'Nah.'

'So it's just you on your own, is it? Nicky No-mates-and-no-money?'

I smiled. 'Yep, just me. Who's the woman?'

'In the sun-gigs? Cinza. Not a clue why she's with him. Maybe she saw him in his running shorts. She works in London for some Italian fashion mag.'

The one-way system was blocked. It would have been

quicker to walk. The Merc finally glided into the car park opposite the drill hall.

'What do you do, Ken? How do I get one of these?'

We climbed out into the drizzle and jogged towards the queue at the open door of the nineteenth-century Territorial Army building.

He grinned. 'Same as you – this and that.'

'Must be a better bit of this and that than I've been fucking about with. I've been on the circuit now and again, daily rates.'

'Still got your house?'

I shook my head. 'Renting – a studio flat in north London, near Tufnell Park.'

He slapped me on the back. 'There's fuck-all wrong with you, is there? You need to sort yourself out, mate. Get a roof over your head and a good woman under you.'

We filed in. The bar was doing a roaring trade. The bowls of peanuts on the veneered tables were already nearly empty.

'There they are.'

Dex and Cinza were standing by a table on which sat two fresh pints, and Cinza was clearly trying to work out what the hell was happening – why all these people were drinking and shovelling peanuts down their necks like there was no tomorrow.

13

Dex put down his G-and-T and held out the two pints. 'Here you go, chaps.' He toasted each of us with a clink of his glass and then presented his friend. 'Nick, I'd like you to meet Cinza.'

I raised my glass. 'Hello.'

Cinza had a mineral water in her perfectly manicured hand. 'Now I have met two of your friends, Dexter.' Her accent was as cut-glass as Dex's – and about as sincere as the Queen's. 'Shall we go soon? I have a dinner this evening and—'

'No, Chinni – three.' Dex lifted his glass. 'To Tennyson.'

We toasted him, but there wasn't even enough time to get my glass back on the table and my fist around what was left of the peanuts before Cinza started having words with Dex about their travel arrangements.

Red Ken leant towards me. 'Tenny was getting out after this, you know. He got zapped the last week of his tour. Nightmare, eh?'

'I always thought he'd be in until they kicked him out or carried him out.'

Dex had been chewing the slice of lemon from his glass during the negotiations. Cinza finally lost patience and got on her mobile. He turned to us. 'Actually, we persuaded him to come in on a little venture of ours instead.' He turned back and interrupted her call. 'Chinni, darling, I'll drive you back in plenty of time. Just a while longer to talk to old friends.' He kissed her cheek as she waffled away in Italian, then turned and winked at us. 'She'll be fine. So hot-blooded!'

She certainly was. As she closed down her mobile she stormed off in the direction of the door, with Dex trailing behind. 'Darling, just a few more minutes . . .'

Red Ken took a gulp of Stella, then stopped halfway and watched how the men in her path reacted. It was like the parting of the Red Sea; their eyes followed her every move. He lowered his glass and wiped the sides of his mouth with his finger. 'We all did our time, lad, and what have we got to show for it, eh? Fuck-all, apart from a regimental tie or a padded coffin. Once you're dead or out, who gives a shit about you? So fuck 'em, I say. Steak for them, burgers for the likes of us – I've had enough of it. Time to have some of the prime beef for ourselves. The same goes for Dex – and the same went for Tenny too. He only stayed in because he had to provide for the girls. Old soldiers just fade away? My arse – we have plans.'

'Plans?'

'Can't tell you, son, unless you come in. I'm glad you're here – me and Dex were hoping. The three of us had kept in touch.' He smiled. 'Not like you, you shite. We need a third man now Tenny's gone.'

Dex reappeared, a little out of breath and with one cheek even darker than usual. 'She loves me really – I think.' Cinza had obviously treated him to a good slapping. He palmed the small beads of sweat from his shaved head. 'I'll call her tomorrow.'

Red Ken tutted like a disapproving dad. 'Loves you? You only met her yesterday. Fucking soft in the head, lad, you.'

Dex couldn't disagree.

'I asked Nick here if he fancies coming in as our number three.'

Dex slapped me on the shoulder with one hand as the other reached for his drink. 'Would you like to take Tenny's place in our little wheeze?'

I checked Dex and Red Ken. They waited, glasses in hand. 'Wheeze?'

Red Ken glanced round the room. 'We can't be talking about anything here. You going back to that squat of yours in Tufnell Park? How you travelling?'

'Train.'

'Come with us.' Red Ken jerked his head at Dex, who had started singing along with the jukebox. 'He'll be coming too, now he's lost his lift.'

I followed the two of them through the door. 'As long as Dex ain't driving.'

We were soon heading south towards Peterborough and onto the A1. Dex was at the wheel. I should have kept my mouth shut. He was driving like a lunatic, of course, as if this thing had wings instead of wheels. Red Ken and I were both strapped in at the back. I kept my attention firmly fixed on the traffic in front of us, catching Dex's eye in the rear-view from time to time. He was smiling away to himself, head bouncing from side to side as he hummed a tune.

Red Ken also had his eyes riveted to the windscreen, ready to adopt the position when Dex finally achieved his death wish. 'Let's kick this off, then, shall we, lads?'

Dex nodded and grunted. Or maybe he was rapping – it was hard to tell.

'This is what we've got, Nick. We're going to steal a shed-load of gold. I'll tell you where from once you say you're in. Don't worry, it's not a bank, more like a warehouse. We've checked it out. We know we can make entry, and have a good route out.'

'How much of a shed-load?'

Dex turned his head round just a little too much for my liking as the speedometer nudged ninety-five on the dual carriageway. 'Three metric tonnes – but two tonnes of that is structure. It ends up as a thousand kilograms of the yellow stuff.'

Red Ken had got his BlackBerry out and was already online. He tuned in to bullionvault.com and turned the screen towards me.

'Structure?'

The screen filled with charts and Red Ken held it closer. 'You'll find out if you're in, won't you? Now, the price of gold this minute is thirty thousand, six hundred and fifty US dollars per kilo. That's already up six hundred a kilo today.'

He came out of the site and started on the calculator. I didn't have to bother with the mental arithmetic. I knew it was going to be buckets.

Red Ken's extra-large thumbs pounded the keys. He had to start again as they hit too many at once.

'Six days ago, Nick, the price was twenty-eight thousand, six hundred. So ... Right, here we are ... We're now looking at—' He shoved the BlackBerry back towards me. 'Thirty point five bar.'

I looked at the calculator. He was right: 30,500,000. 'A few zeros ain't going to make me jump in. I need to know where it is, what it is, who it belongs to, how you plan to do the job, and where the gold goes afterwards.'

Dex's laugh came so suddenly and so loudly it made both of us jump. 'We knew you were our man. Just like the old days!' The laughter stopped, and I wasn't sure who he was talking to next. 'Well, not exactly, come to think of it. I'm not doing it for Queen and country any more, I'm doing it for me. So really, it's—'

Red Ken sank back into the leather. 'Dex, shut the fuck up, will you?'

I still wasn't getting the questions answered. 'Lads, I need to know what I'm getting into here.'

'I want to tell you. I'd lay the cards out, but there's someone else involved. I got to talk to him first.'

'Who?'

Red Ken sat back up and turned to me. 'Nick, it's a tough call, I know, but I can't tell you, not yet. You know the score. Listen, the reason you're here is because we need you and we trust you, so you got to trust us.'

'Sorry, lads, I'm not getting into anything I don't know about. I'm not going to be part of it until you—'

'Chaps!' Dex's hand was off the wheel. 'This is all getting rather boring. Nick, the job is in Dubai. It's a pair of gold doors that Saddam had made in the UAE for his palace in Basra. But, of course, they never made it into Iraq, did they? They're just sitting there, ready for an extension to put them on.' He laughed at his own joke. 'The gold won't even be missed. No one knows the doors exist – and is the UAE going to jump up and down when they disappear and let the world know they were dealing with big bad S a year before the invasion? Not on your nelly! It's a victimless crime. It's not like we're mugging someone's granny.'

'That's all well and good, but we'll still have to sell the shit. How much are we getting out of that thirty and a half bar?'

Red Ken wasn't happy with Dex, but so what? 'Forty cents on the dollar.' He tapped away on his BlackBerry. 'That's twelve and a quarter bar.'

Dex laughed. He was probably already walking round the Ferrari showroom in his head.

'But who's buying it? Where's it going?'

Dex was now driving as if he was in one. 'That's the thing we don't know, old chap – and, quite frankly, I don't care.'

Red Ken nodded. 'Nick, we're the only ones who are going to look after us. It's time for some steak. What do you say, mate? Twelve and a quarter bar three ways – and a bit for Janice and the kids.'

Dex was studying me in the rear-view. He winked. 'You

know it makes sense, chappie. You look as if you could do with the world's biggest leg-up. The doors are even flat-packed for us. Six crates, six by four by two. It'll be like loading up at IKEA.'

I turned back to Red Ken. 'You really going for it?'

'It's all planned. Two weeks, wheels turn. You need to be with us, mate. It's what Tenny would have wanted.'

'Lads, it sounds too good to be true. If anyone else came to me with this I'd think they were pissed.' I sat back while they waited for an answer. 'You're not selling it to me, but I'm in.'

They exchanged a big smile.

'But the only reason is because you two have shit for brains. I'm coming to look after you.'

PART THREE

14

Dex studied the little plastic cup his G-and-T had been served in like it was something he'd found under his shoe. He finally gave it a squeeze and moved it to his mouth. He took a sip and turned in his seat to face the two of us in the row behind. 'Cheers, chaps.'

I returned the toast with a red wine that perfectly matched the shit-on-a-tray in front of me.

Kenneth Merryweather, as his cover passport called him, wasn't so enthusiastic. 'Yeah, cheers.' He dunked his bread roll in his wine and had a munch.

We still had half the seven-hour flight from Heathrow ahead of us. I'd been expecting us to be packed in like sardines, the price you pay for taking your golf trip on the cheap, but I was wrong. There were fewer than a hundred people on the aircraft. Nearly everyone, except Red Ken and me, had their own row of seats to spread out on.

'Empty planes out, full planes back.' Mr Merryweather was taking a lot of pleasure in how hard the recession had hit Dubai. 'There are more than three thousand wagons

59

abandoned in the airport car parks at any one time because of expats doing runners.' He shook his head. 'Lose your job, and those fuckers hold your bank account until you pay your debts – and lots of people are losing their jobs. It's better to get straight to the airport and fuck off before they get a grip of you.'

I'd never been to Dubai, and Dexter Khan had only ever transited through before the two recces he'd made with Red Ken. Tenny would have been fresh to it too. Red Ken and Dex had already prepared the ground on those two trips. As soon as we met the guy who'd brought Red Ken the idea in the first place, it was straight into the job.

Red Ken knew Dubai like the back of his hand. He had worked there on the BG (bodyguarding) circuit for the best part of a year. It was supposed to have been for much longer. Chrissie had even gone out and joined him. Whatever it was that had gone wrong in their marriage, I got the sense that Dubai had tipped the scales. I wasn't going to ask specifics. If he'd wanted me to know he would have told me.

Of much greater concern for me was the lack of information. Not just the little I had been told, but the little they seemed to know. It was unlike these two to go into something so serious without being in control. Something was wrong with this job, and something was wrong with these two to make them take such a risk. They'd thought it was a joke when I'd said I was coming along to look after them. It wasn't.

Dex turned to face us again. 'Tuck in, chaps – you'll need plenty of energy for eighteen holes.' He was a member of a posh club in Surrey and had brought his own clubs with him. He was even wearing a blue Pringle sweater and Burberry patterned slacks. Red Ken was dressed much the same, and unfortunately so was I. We looked like P. Diddy's entourage.

Three days ago, Red Ken had let me rant on about how much I hated golf. I couldn't see the reason for it except as an excuse for dickheads like Dex to wear clown outfits. To me it was a waste of land, sand, time, water and metal. Only once I'd finished condemning every golf player on the planet did Red Ken admit he also played – and that Dex had put him up for membership.

The worst news was that he had an old set of clubs he was going to lend me. Everything had to look normal. I couldn't be walking round with brand-new gear. We were three car-showroom salesmen, off to 'swing a few', as Dex put it, and maybe have some other fun. Dubai was awash with Russian whores, Red Ken said. One of the things Chrissie had hated about the place was prostitutes looking her up and down if she had a drink with her husband in a hotel bar. They'd thought she was invading their turf.

I'd looked around at our fellow passengers in Departures. One or two groups looked much the same as us. Our cover was good. Nothing could be discovered about us because nothing was hidden.

The four PMC (private military company) guys on their way to Kabul had also been easy to place, with their chunky Luminoxes hanging off their wrists with mini compasses on the straps, and high-sleeved T-shirts to show off their new biceps. The only air bridges into Kabul were via Delhi and Dubai, and I knew from past experience which airport I'd rather transit through. Apart from work, the only two things to do out there were watch porn and take part in Operation Massive: hitting the weights. The NAAFI in Kandahar sold more tubs of body-building supplements than Mars bars. But what really gave these guys away were the desert-coloured Bug Out day-sacks that everyone bought from the American PX. Every bit as much a badge, I supposed, as our stupid golf bags. They'd certainly looked back at Merryweather, Khan and Simmons the same way Dex had looked at his plastic cup.

The other two knew what they were doing when it came to drivers and putters, but I was on the five-day trip as a golf atheist. They were going to enlighten and convert me. There would be no talk of the job during the flight or at any time unless we were out of a building and on our own. Dubai might be Disneyland on Gas Mark Ten, as Red Ken called it, but the place was swarming with police informers. The government had an image to protect. They were even thinking about a law to prosecute locally based journalists if they hinted Dubai was being hit by the world downturn.

Besides that, first-class seats in aircraft had been bugged on European and American airlines as early as the 1980s. Industrial espionage was rife. It still was. We worked on the assumption that every seat was bugged on every airline.

Red Ken's plan had few moving parts. Keep it simple, stupid, was a principle all three of us knew worked, and as we were all stupid to be on this job it was a good one. We were going to play a round straight off the plane at six thirty. That was when we'd meet the man who'd organized it – organized it far too much, in fact, even down to the passports.

Red Ken wouldn't give any more details about who he was. 'He doesn't want you to know until you meet, son. He's a funny fucker like that. But he's going to make us all a lot of cash – so just wait.'

I'd been bombarding him with questions for days. For starters, why had Red Ken, Dex and Tenny been picked as a crew?

'Because we're good.' Red Ken was serious. 'There can't be any room for fuck-ups. That's what Special Forces are about – in and out before anyone knows. This isn't about running into a bank with sawn-offs and grabbing the till. This is about lifting gold that no one knows exists – it needs to be done covertly. That's your reason, Nick.'

I explored the chicken-something while Dex put on his headphones and laughed too loud at a movie.

Red Ken leant across the spare seat between us and gave me a nudge. 'He was like that when we came over last time. I even think it's the same film.'

The final of the two recces had been a week before the funeral. Tenny would have been on his post-tour leave, before returning to the battalion to go through the process of getting out – having massively boosted his pension.

Dex caught us laughing at him and pulled off one earphone. 'What?'

Red Ken pushed himself forward so his head was nearly between the rests. 'I was saying Nick should apply to your club.'

'You'd love it.' One earphone was still on his cheek. 'I'll introduce you to the pro and maybe we can get your game up. Then I'll—'

I reached between the seats, pulled back the earphone and let go.

'Very funny.' He broke into a laugh and then his eyes were back on the screen.

I bit the cellophane off my rectangle of cheese. 'I wish I was like knob-head Laughing Boy, not a worry in the world, just getting on with life and a dodgy G-and-T.'

Red Ken sat back in his seat and stared at the blank screen in front of him. 'That's not the way, mate. You got no one meeting you when you get back from the trip?'

'Like I said at the funeral, no one.'

'That's harsh. I'll have my girls waiting for me. The youngest, Charlotte, has just brought my first grandchild home for a second christening. It's a girl.' He ripped the end off a citrus handwipe. 'The Brits got pissed off over the fact she was going to get christened in Sydney. It'll be a great day. Looking forward to it big-time.'

15

We dumped our bags at the hotel and had a quick shower and shave. We had to look the part: no stubble on the car-showroom salesmen. The choice of hotel was perfect – near the airport and the golf club, and just short of the city proper. It had seen better days, but fitted our apparent budget.

Half an hour later we met up again in the foyer, golf bags beside us and spiky shoes hanging from the straps.

Red Ken turned down the concierge's offer of a hotel car. We could have been going to any of the eight or nine courses, so why give away a precise destination when we didn't have to? Hailing a cab from the main drag didn't turn out to be easy. It got to the point where Dex was thumbing hopefully at every 4x4 that passed. As if.

Red Ken had been smoking in the shade along with the rest of the social lepers. He took me to one side. The sun bounced off his gigs as he moved his head and grinned. 'You might not like who we're meeting up with this morning any more than we do, but it's too late to say no. Just think of what this gives us, Nick. Think about Janice and the kids. That's why we're here. Besides, you have to look after us two, right?'

Dex wandered back, dejected.

I laughed. 'Didn't they teach you cab skills in the RAF?'

Red Ken looked up and down the road. 'I'll show you how it's done in Para Reg.' He stubbed out his cigarette and stepped off the kerb. Of course a cab was approaching – that was why he'd done it. He waved it down.

We loaded the clubs into the boot and Dex jumped in next to the driver. He was an Indian in a white shirt and tie. Dex was going to blend in perfectly. 'Dubai Creek Golf and Yacht Club.'

There wasn't much else to say. We weren't going to talk in front of our new mate, even though the big thing for me was that we were on our way to meet the middleman for this 'little wheeze', as Dex kept calling it. He had his head buried in *Golf Clubs of the World* and was getting very hyper.

He turned and nodded with excitement. 'Par seventy-one, 6,857 yards.'

I nodded back as if I gave a shit. Red Ken smiled, but it faded as he looked out of the window at the throngs of Filipinos and Indian cleaners washing store-fronts. Cranes cut into the sky in all directions above half-finished buildings. The ones that had been completed towered above us. I'd never seen so much marble, glass and steel. Dubai looked like Hong Kong on steroids, designed by architects on LSD.

We peeled off the highway and hit the approach road to the clubhouse. It had been designed to look like an enormous white Bedouin tent, pitched in a sprawling oasis of green.

The cab drew up outside the main door and Dex jumped out. He busied himself with loading the bags onto a trolley while Red Ken left to look for the elusive fourth man of this crew. I was left to pay the taxi. That was one bit of cab skills they both knew.

A Land Cruiser drew up behind Dex while he was still unloading. The driver and passenger were two sun-dried women in their sixties. They looked like they'd been getting drunk in the city since Margaret Thatcher's era. They had all the golf gear on, down to the peaked plastic hats without the crown. Their jewellery jangled, but not as much as their accents. The driver left the engine running. One clambered down in a pink polo shirt, checked shorts and golfing shoes and shouted back into the wagon, at her blue-shirted friend, 'I'll get a boy.' She was Romford, born and bred.

She walked between the bonnet of her 4x4 and the rear of our taxi as Dex straightened up from the boot. She pointed at her wagon. 'When you've finished with those, our bags are in the back.'

I opened my mouth to object but Dex was too quick. He put on the worst Indian-waiter voice ever. 'Yes, memsahib.' He gave an exaggerated bow that was totally wasted on them as they disappeared into the clubhouse.

'What the fuck you doing, Dex? We got a job to do here, mate.'

He smiled and did the Indian shaking of the head to indicate yes. 'Getting in character.'

Red Ken came back in time to see Dex at the back of the Land Cruiser and me with the trolley holding our bags. Another Indian guy was waiting to drive it away. 'What's he doing now?'

I explained as we picked up the bags and headed inside. Red Ken steered me to a leather sofa while we waited for Dex. We watched as he deposited the bags with the women in the foyer. 'You know, this place is filled with so many obnoxious, incompetent fuckers, especially in senior positions. Back in the UK they wouldn't last ten minutes behind the counter at McDonald's, let alone in management.'

Dex waited for a tip. The sun-drieds ignored him.

Red Ken was living up to his name – come the revolution and all that. 'I bet those two have maids like everyone else here, running round doing everything but wipe their arses. They used to be Filipinos, but now it's Somalian girls. These people get a maid and they have total power over her. They keep her passport, even though it's illegal. They decide what to pay her, and even when she can have a break or a day off.

'Chrissie hated the way they were treated. Some of the Brit girls used to get on to her. They said she was too soft with the two girls who ran the house, setting a bad example by not treating them like shit.'

Dex walked away empty-handed but smiling. I realized he was singing. ' "Jolly boating weather . . ." ' His Indian-waiter accent was outrageous. ' "And a hay harvest breeze . . ." '

The Romford Two were sure he was taking the piss but they didn't know how.

Red Ken picked up his set and handed Dex his. 'You finished? Can we go and get on?'

Dex grinned and carried on singing. ' "Swing, swing together . . ." '

I followed them outside. We sat in the shade to put on our spiky shoes. As soon as we headed back out into the sun, I could see four buggies waiting for us. In one of them sat an egg-shaped guy, his little white legs dangling just above the buggy floor. His short-sleeved white shirt bulged above his smartly pressed red chino shorts and knee-length white socks.

'Spag.' Dex beamed. 'How are you, old chap?'

16

I tried not to look surprised.

Spag stayed under the canopy but a fat and hairy hand stretched out for mine as Dex and Red Ken loaded the clubs into the other three buggies. I clasped his stumpy sausage fingers.

'You look well, Nick.'

The same couldn't be said for him. The face under the peak of the cap had had too many visits to the food hall, and its owner had spent far too long sat on his arse. I couldn't see the eyes behind the dark lenses but I liked to think they were bloodshot. He still wore his seventies porn-star moustache, but like the hair growing out of his ears, it was greyer.

He let go of my hand and put his foot on the pedal. We followed and drew up at the first tee. Spag climbed out, pressed a blue tee into the grass and a ball on top. By the time he stood up again his face was red and sweating.

The other two were out of their wagons, staying out of range of his swing.

Red Ken nodded at me. 'We knew you'd be pleased.'

Dex watched with a hand over his eyes, waiting to see where this ball was going to end up.

Spag took a practice swing. 'We've got a good tee-off time

here. Nobody up our asses, listening in.' His club went back and whacked the ball. I lost sight of it in the low sun.

'Me next.' Dex selected a club and approached the tee. His whiter-than-white teeth gleamed as he grinned at me. 'It's a small world, isn't it?'

The whack as his club hit the ball sounded more solid than Spag's had.

As Red Ken took his practice swing, Spag came and stood next to me. 'Damn shame about Tennyson. Goddam Taliban, we should nuke 'em back to the Stone Age.'

I nodded to keep him talking.

'These guys wanted you on the job all along, you know – like getting the old band together. But nobody knew where to find you. Maybe Tenny getting killed was kind of a blessing.'

I looked down at him. I couldn't see his face past the peak of his cap. 'I doubt he'd see it that way. How did you find them?'

'Right here, on this course. Red was working here at the time. Then I tracked him down in the UK. I need guys I know, who won't sink under pressure. You still one of those guys, Nick?' He kept his eyes on Red Ken as he twisted his body, following the imaginary line his ball was going to take. He was waiting for an answer but I wasn't going to play his game.

'I need people who I know trust each other and know what they're doing – and more than that, who are mission-oriented. Nothing will get in the way of the mission.' Spag shooed away an invisible fly. He still wasn't getting an answer. Fuck him.

'Why aren't you on the ground with us?'

His laugh rang out a split second before Red Ken's club connected. The ball flew off at an angle.

'Bollocks!' Red Ken glared at him, but Spag was oblivious.

'Once out with you guys was enough.' The roar of an aircraft taking off just a K away drowned even the hum of traffic on the freeway. He had to raise his voice. 'That's for people like you. Like Red's burger theory – I'm a facilitator, I make things happen. You're the burgers and I'm, like, a tender sirloin.'

'How did you find out about the gold?'

'Kinda when Saddam got captured and interrogated.' He slapped my back with a smile. 'But that's history now. Today we start making the future the way we want it to be.'

'So how does that happen? Where does the gold go? You got the plane – that means there's others involved. Why don't we know about them?'

Once we lifted the gold we were taking it to an airstrip equidistant between Dubai and Abu Dhabi, used by both cities' VIPs. Aircraft could come and go without their famous or infamous passengers getting noticed, which wouldn't have been the case at the two cities' main airports.

There were others involved, of course, and he wouldn't tell Red Ken and Dex about them. It worried me that they didn't seem to care.

Spag looked at me through his gigs; no expression and no answers.

'Who's buying the gold?'

He displayed a set of nicotine-stained teeth. 'Know what? Red said you weren't that happy about the deal. But you're asking a lot of questions you don't need to know the answers to. That kinda gives me the shakes, Nick.'

'I like to know what I'm getting involved with, that's all.'

'If you need to know anything, go ask Red.' He nodded over towards the tee. 'It's waiting.'

17

Dex laughed at me as I sort of lined up my shot. The only time I'd hit a golf ball before, it had involved getting it through a windmill and into a clown's mouth. It flew way off to the left into a patch of wasteground. It made even Red Ken's look good.

Dex was loving it. 'Maybe your handicap should be thirty balls, not thirty strokes.'

Spag put his club into his bag and manoeuvred his fat frame into the buggy. 'Fuck it, who cares? It gets us moving and out of earshot. I've got plenty of balls, we'll just throw one out for him.'

We rattled over the immaculate lawns towards their balls. In the middle distance, yachts sailed past on their way down the Creek. Shiny steel-and-glass monoliths lined the drags like rows of giant dominoes.

Red Ken's had landed on a decent bit of grass. We parked in the shade of a clump of palm trees and he shaped up to it.

Spag was straight down to business. 'Red, you got anything new to tell me?'

'No. Today is about getting Nick up to speed. Same as we would have with Tenny. We then keep our cover going tomorrow morning. Prep in the afternoon, and lift tomorrow night. Make the RV and then back for one more round before flying back to UK.'

Spag pointed a porky finger. 'Enough with the bullet points – I need to know the plan, in detail.'

Red Ken selected another club. 'All you've got to know is that we'll be at the RV and we'll have the doors.'

The plane would be at the airstrip at 0130 hours Friday morning, and would stay on the ground for thirty minutes. Spag said air-traffic control had it logged in as a normal private flight, carrying out a drop-off.

I put my hand up. 'I have a question.'

Dex was out of his buggy and peering up the fairway like an explorer, throwing up bits of grass in the non-existent wind.

Red Ken and Spag said it together: 'What?'

'How do I get my money?'

Dex turned back, swinging a club from the bottom end. 'It's all sorted, chappie. Spag has given us all half a bar USD as a down-payment. Tenny wasn't too keen on having his share in advance, while he was still serving our noble Queen.'

Red Ken motioned him on. 'Oi, shit for brains. Get on with it.'

Dex enjoyed insults, but only from friends. 'So I've been holding his money, and that's yours now, of course.'

'Sounds good – but how and when do we get the rest?'

'Everything's organized.' Dex went to high-five Spag as he sat in his buggy but got nothing in return. 'This chap is going to transfer the cash into an EBT – employees' beneficial trust – within three days. It's the same vehicle those naughty bankers use to move their multi-million-dollar bonuses out of harm's way. Everything's good, everything's legal. And that's why we love you, isn't it?'

Red Ken had taken his second shot and it wasn't much better than his first. He hurled the club back into his bag. 'Dex is right. It's all legit, son. You'll have no funny money to deal with. If you take it into the UK, they're going to want to tax you

– that's how legal it is. How do you think I got my Merc? The system works.'

'But where's that money come from? Like the sirloin here just said, he's a facilitator. He makes things happen. So who's the Kobe beef – you know, the banker – coughing up a shed-load of cash just for us to be on the job? Haven't you bothered to ask? Lads, what the fuck's going on?'

Dex put his arm round Spag. 'Our chubby little friend won't tell us, and I, for one, do not care who our banker is. But this chap here, he knows that if our money isn't in the EBTs within three days bad things will happen. Don't you, old chap?'

Red Ken had recovered from his disappointment. 'He knows we'll find him.'

I was sure they would, but that didn't help me know what I wanted to know.

Dex slapped Spag on the shoulder and headed for his buggy. I had expected Spag to do his nut by now, but he kept his cool as we all mounted up and headed for his ball. I even saw him smile a little as he drove.

Once the four buggies were parked up around the ball, Spag was back on the case. 'Remember, the pilot will keep it on the ground for no more than thirty minutes. If you ain't there, the deal's off.'

'Load of shite. You'll stay there. Anyway, we've never missed an RV.'

My arse was getting sweaty on the PVC. 'We carrying weapons?'

Spag almost jumped out of his skin. 'What the fuck? No weapons!'

Dex pulled out a club for him, wanting to get on with the game. 'He's right, Nick. If we need them, we won't be doing the job correctly.'

Red Ken agreed.

Dex handed Spag a club. 'Here you go, Tiger. Let's move on. Got another seventeen holes after this one.'

Spag's shot flew straight and true towards the flag, just as a couple of grass-cutters, Indian lads with bits of cloth wound round their heads and necks against the sun, moved into view. 'Hey, fore! Get out the fucking way! Jee-sus, these assholes!'

Red Ken shot out an arm and gripped him. 'Wind your fucking neck in! These people sweat their guts out sixteen hours a day, six days a week – all for eight dollars a day. Dubai is being built by these slaves while all the fucking overweight local babies just whinge and whine.'

Spag pushed past to get to his buggy. 'Don't give me that bullshit. You don't think the Mexicans are treated badly in New York City? And you Brits had slaves living in basements for hundreds of years.' His tic had kicked off and the moustache started to twitch. 'Fuck, Red, you people built entire cities on the proceeds of the slave trade, so don't lecture me. Look at the positives. You have any idea what this country does for its own people?'

He started ticking off the benefits on his fingers. '*Free* education up to PhD level. *Free* houses when they get married. *Free* health care. Even their phone calls are free. Everybody has a maid, a nanny, a driver – you name it, they've got it. They don't even pay taxes. Shit, of course this is a fucking great place for Emiratis. Thirty years ago these people were living in tents, scratching around for water – and now look at the place.'

Red Ken's face was purple. He took a pace and moved it right into the American's. 'It's Disneyland.' He pointed at the workers sheltering under some trees. 'These fuckers' passports are taken away when they arrive, and some of them don't get paid for months. They've got families back in India, Bangladesh, Pakistan, wherever the fuck they come from, starving while they wait for money that was promised but never arrives.

'And do their embassies help them? They get jack shit from anyone. They can't even go home because they're in debt – they had to pay some greedy twat to get the job in the first

74

place. And nobody wants to do anything about it because everybody's making money. This place is shite, end of story.'

Spag shook his head so hard that sweat flew off it. 'You self-righteous asshole. You just don't get what this place is about, do you? Every Arab, Egyptian, Libyan, Iranian, whatever, they all grow up saying, "I want to go to Dubai." This place is showing the rest of the Arabs how a modern Muslim country works.

'They've got no fundamentalism here. On that basis alone, outsiders like you should shut the fuck up. You should be very worried if this model fails. It'll end up being run by the fucking Taliban. That's why the West turns a blind eye to how they treat their workers and all the other shit that happens here. So why don't you just get on with your job then go back to wherever makes you happy? Or will you be down at the workers' camps, handing out your share of the profits? I don't think so.'

Dex had taken his shot and was leaning on his club. 'Either calm down or go and get a room.'

Red Ken lit a Benson & Hedges and turned away.

Spag eased himself into his buggy and pointed the wheels back towards the Bedouin tent. 'Fuck you.' The electric motor kicked in and he drove off. 'Just make sure you're on time.'

Dex patted Red Ken on the shoulder with his club handle. 'So when are you up for director of Liberty? That Shami Chakrabarti girl needs to watch out, eh? Can't wait to see you on *Question Time*.'

Red Ken wasn't seeing the funny side. He walked towards me. 'Doesn't it piss you off?'

'Don't know enough about it, mate. I'm used to being treated like shit, but I can see these lads get it a whole lot worse.'

Dex came to join us. 'Well done, Red, you got rid of him a lot quicker this time.'

Red Ken wasn't in the mood for praise. 'That's him fucked

off until the airstrip RV. Let's get on with it. Listen in, we got six crates to lift, right?'

We both nodded and I guessed what was coming.

'Well, we're going to have one for ourselves. I don't trust the twat – and, besides, we're here for us. You both OK with that?'

Dex was more than happy, but it wasn't that simple.

'How do we lift it? How do we hide it? I presume we come back later for it?'

'Correct. I got a wagon parked up at the airport among those three thousand vehicles. Me and Chrissie just binned it when we left. We load it up, re-park it, and come back later. Then we melt it down and sell it.'

They'd only agreed with Spag about not having weapons, Red Ken said, because they already had some. 'If it all goes tits up, we ain't rotting in some fucking Arab jail. We're going to get out of this shit, spend the cash – or die trying.' He shared eye to eye with Dex. 'It's do or die, isn't it, mate?'

Dex looked at me and for the first time there wasn't a smile. 'It's our time. Our one chance to change our lives for ever. Make or break. If it doesn't work, we're dead anyway. You OK with that? If not, maybe it's time to rethink, Nick.'

I didn't need time to re-anything. 'No, I'm not OK. This is getting worse by the minute. Have you two really thought about what we're involved with here? Have you approached this job like you would have done anything else we've been involved with?

'Think about what that fat fuck might have up his sleeve. Think about all the details we don't know. I'm here because I'm here, and I'll stay with you two whatever. We're mates, and mates stick together. But think about the risks. We can walk away any time we want to, lads.'

Red Ken climbed into his buggy. 'I'm not walking away from anything, son. I can't. There's too much at stake for me.'

Dex followed. 'Come on, Nick. Let's finish playing golfers, and then we can get to work. You have a lot of recces to do.'

18

Mall of the Emirates
1450 hrs

The mall felt like Monaco with a roof on, only bigger. All the usual international suspects were there, from a Carrefour hypermarket that took up half the ground floor to Asprey, Rolex and hundreds of others in between. To make Brit tourists feel at home, it even had an indoor funfair a few escalators up, complete with bumper cars and fluffy toys.

Most bizarre of all was the world's biggest indoor ski slope. A huge steel cocoon towered over the car park and taxi drop-off point on the roof. Inside, I imagined, Arabs were skiing in *dishdash*es under Versace Puffa jackets, but I hadn't got to see it yet. After the golf game we'd gone to the hotel for a quick shower, then straight out again. Ken and I were now busy keeping up with Dex as he bounced from one perfume shop to another.

We'd had a white Toyota behind us all the way from the hotel to the mall, a good twenty-minute drive. Not unusual on its own, as the mall was one of the city's major venues. But it was three up, all Arab males in Western dress, and they'd stuck to us like glue. We'd soon see if we'd been pinged, and maybe by whom. It could be UAE internal security – or Spag's people keeping tabs on us. Right now, it didn't matter who. What did was confirming that we were targets and then deciding what to do about it.

'Doesn't *anyone* here sell Amouage Homage?'

'They must do – it's the most expensive perfume on the planet. Nick and me'll go and ask at McDonald's.'

I followed Red Ken as Dex disappeared into yet another shop. He shook his head. 'A whole field of rose petals to produce a teardrop of the stuff. They make it in Oman. I bought Chrissie some and she went crazy about it. I think that's where Dickhead got the idea. He's trying to get Cinza back.' Red Ken smiled at me. 'Can you see the one with the checked shirt? He still about?'

We headed for the food court.

'Nope. He could have gone with Dex.'

There had been a young guy, maybe mid-twenties, who hadn't got past Surveillance 101. He was always getting in our eye-line. Either he was bad, or we just happened to share exactly the same shopping preferences.

'We'll soon find out, Nick. Not that it's going to make a difference to me. Fuck 'em, whoever they are.' Red Ken led me past the falafel and vegetarian joints. 'He really is soft in the head, that lad. You can't just bribe women back – and don't I know it.'

We reached the counter and ordered Big Macs. We didn't check for anyone or anything yet. There was no need – we'd soon see if someone had a trigger on us once we sat down. Besides, we didn't even know for sure we were being followed. And if we were, we didn't want to look aware.

'Dex want anything?'

'He won't touch any of this shite. I'll get him an orange juice.'

We carried our trays to the seating area and sat each side of the table to maximize our view of the hall. Three women on the next table were *burqa*'d up in black gear. Each time one of them brought food to her mouth she had to lift the beak and try to post it through without leaving a blob of mayonnaise on the flap of the letterbox.

Beyond them, a table-load of local kids were busier texting than eating. On our other side, two overweight American lads with goatee beards, ball caps and overalls emblazoned with an energy company logo and the Stars and Stripes were making up for them, in supersize.

Women of all races paraded around us in short, strapless dresses. A couple of hours down the road in Saudi it would have been a capital offence. There were a lot of girls down that way with mayo stains round their letterboxes.

I reached for my Pepsi. No Coke here: most of the Middle East seemed to think Coca-Cola was a Jewish company.

As on the aircraft, there was no talking shop while we were around others. 'What made you get out of here so quick, mate?' I was thinking about the abandoned vehicle. 'Just that Chrissie didn't like it?'

He took the top off his drink and rejected the straw I offered. 'The whole expat lifestyle. The way they treat these lads—' He nodded in the direction of the Filipinos sweating at a stir-fry counter. 'Me and Chrissie, we're from shite. Our dads were both down the pit. They had principles. Socialism rubs off, you know. Seeing these people treated so badly pissed us both off. She couldn't handle it.'

He took a bite out of his burger. 'I said we'd bin it – but maybe just another month or two to get some money together.' He over-concentrated on the tabletop all of a sudden. 'She had a breakdown. It wasn't just the being here ... it was a culmination of years of me fucking off working. I was just too engrossed in what I was doing to see it coming.'

He raised his paper napkin to his eye, trying to persuade me that he had a bit of grit in it. 'We left, but it was too late. She binned me. I should have listened to her. I fucked up, mate

– forgot there was another life, something more important.'

He looked at his Big Mac and put it down. He'd lost the taste for it. He sat back with his arms on the table, his hands squeezed together. 'I kidded myself I was doing all my soldiering for them. Creating a family, putting together a nest egg. But guess what? It was all for me, because I loved it. Now it's make or break. My last job – and this time it's for Chrissie. No more bullshit. I'm going to get some of the good stuff and give it the big fuck-off to everyone else – including you and Dex. It's end-ex for me.'

Red Ken couldn't pull off the grit act any more. Tears welled in both eyes. 'From now on, it's going to be about her. I'll go down on my hands and knees at the christening if I have to, if it means she'll have me back.'

I watched a tear dribble down the crags in his cheek. 'Is that why you left everything to the Fat Controller?'

He sort of nodded, and at the same time waved his finger in front of his face. He was right: no work talk. 'Believe me, son, I'm desperate. Without Chrissie, I've got nothing. I want her back. I want my kids and grandkids to have a good life. Not a shite one like I've given to Chrissie. If this doesn't work . . .'

I cut away from it a moment to scan for Checked Shirt. 'What about Dex? Why's he taking the risk?'

'Because he's soft in the head, that's why. You know him. One minute he's here for the fucking juice, and the next – who knows? He's been talking about moving to Scotland and buying a castle, but that was last week.'

Red Ken looked over my shoulder and nodded. I turned to see Dex empty-handed.

'For all that, I'm glad he's here. You too, Nick. I just wish Tenny was too, you know?'

Dex bounced in and sat next to me. He studied Red Ken's face. 'You OK, chap? Nick here been stealing your chips?'

Red Ken wiped his eyes. 'No, you soft twat – just the normal thing.'

'Ah.' Dex pointed at the carton full of juice. 'That mine?'

He gulped it back with relish, then leant forward with that ever-bright smile. 'Guess what? We're being followed. The checked shirt stayed with me. So, what now?'

Red Ken took a swig of his drink. 'Fuck 'em. We're just shopping, aren't we? So we carry on doing what we're here to do – show Nick what he needs to see, and carry on as planned. We finish our drinks, get on with our job, and keep our eyes skinned.'

19

Dex had some bits of orange caught in his straw and was trying to blow them out instead of just taking the top off and drinking normally.

Red Ken thumped his watch. 'We need to go up to the car park.'

Dex gave it some thought. 'I'll bring it with – and I see Checked Shirt. He's sitting to my half-right, outside Starbucks. He's talking with a white shirt, long-sleeved, buttoned-up, jeans. It's a trigger.'

We got up and started walking, ignoring the two of them. We passed through the funfair, where Indian and Filipina girls stared out from behind the stalls. They looked as though they were in prison.

It's best not to look for followers while on the move. It's too obvious and not necessary. The best way is to check things out once you go static. Who was there the last time you stopped? Who just fucked up by jumping into a shop doorway?

We came to a massive floor-to-ceiling glass screen, the other side of which was Switzerland. Acres of blindingly white snow glittered under a brilliant blue sky. Chairlifts carried skiers over snowmen and tall fir trees. You could almost smell the *glühwein*. We stopped and had a quick look at all the Arab lads wrapped up in their hired cold-weather gear. As usual, the women in *burqas* had drawn the short straw. They couldn't get the skiwear on over their other clobber. Their breath hung around them in clouds as they waited at the bottom of the toboggan run for their kids to appear at warp speed. They must have been freezing.

Dex took another suck from his juice container. 'They're still with us, chaps. They really need to sharpen their skills.'

We turned to walk away from the skiers. He was right. The two of them were directly in our eye-line, trying to look normal as they window-shopped for women's clothes.

We took the escalator to the roof and walked out into forty degrees of overwhelming heat. Like any other mall on the planet, a queue of people with shopping bags stretched back from the taxi rank. There must have been space in the car park for at least a thousand cars, but only a third of it was occupied.

'Recession.' Dex shook his head as well as his drink. 'It's everywhere.'

The sun was low in the sky. Red Ken checked his watch. 'Ten past six. Last light in about fifty.'

We moved into the shade of the ski slope. It ran up the side of the mall and above the car park to dominate the skyline. We admired all the massed ranks of sparkling 4x4s and Lamborghinis, and tried to look like we were waiting for someone to join us.

Neither of the shirts made an appearance. Red Ken pulled out his cigarettes and I admired the scenery. 'They can't be that shite. We're up here for one of two reasons. To get a taxi, or meet someone with a vehicle. Bet they've gone back to the Toyota. They'll be staking out the exit.' I turned to the click of a disposable lighter and was met with a cloud of smoke.

'Good. Fuck 'em. Let them wait. Dex, you keep an eye out for them. Nick, look out there.'

From our vantage-point, the area round the mall was littered with patches of barren ground and half-finished buildings draped in scaffolding. Over the constant background rumble of traffic came the rhythmic thud of pile drivers. Little ant-like bodies scurried about in yellow or blue hard hats. It must have been a fucker labouring in Gas Mark Ten.

The whole city was criss-crossed with highways that looked like giant concrete flumes. A monorail was also under construction. We had seen the elevated strip of concrete heading towards the city centre from the airport. The partly built stations looked like golden cocoons wrapped around the track. Red Ken, of course, thought they were shite. I quite liked them.

We could see all the way to the sea. The Burj Al-Arab hotel looked like a giant sail a couple of K away on the coast. The needle-like Burj Dubai was well on its way to being the world's tallest building. In all directions, the rows of dominoes gleamed in the sun. But we weren't there for the view.

He leant against one of the concrete supports for the ski slope and sucked hard on his B&H. 'Dunes. You got it?'

The hotel, like a black glass pyramid, would have looked at home in Las Vegas.

'Got that.'

'OK, that's your axis. Go half right. Five hundred.' He was using a fire-control order format to get me onto the target. I looked half right, scanning the five-hundred area.

'You've got a ten-storey building with an all-black ground floor. Seen?'

'Seen.' The boring ten-storey cube's shop fronts were all black marble.

'OK, go left of the building, into the wasteground, at about a K. You've got a one-storey flat-concrete-roofed building – rectangular, with a wall surrounding it. Seen?'

'Seen.'

'That's the target. The surrounding wall is five metres away from the building. The wall is three metres high and the wall gate and building shutters are facing us. All the damage we do must be within the wall, inside the compound. That way it'll be months, maybe years, before anyone gets to see our handi-work. And when they do, they won't even know what was in the building. The outside wall will not be touched.'

I couldn't see much detail from this distance but I had a visual on what Red Ken and Dex had described to me. We couldn't do a walk-past to soak up more detail. No one walked in this city.

20

The perimeter gate, the only way in and out of the compound, directly faced a doorway set into rolled-steel shutters wide enough to admit a vehicle into the building. Either side of the shutters was a window, the one on the right larger than the one on the left. I couldn't see from this distance, but Red Ken said they were iron-barred. He and Dex had been on-target during their last recce. There were no other entrances or exits.

There was no electricity or water running into the building. It had been left to decay for the past nine years, waiting for Saddam to defeat the Americans and then get down to a bit of DIY on his palace.

'Nick, make a note of the main drag between us and the target. That's our route out. Going left, as we look at it now, it takes us south-west out of the city, following the coast towards Abu Dhabi and the RV. Going right, we take the tunnel under the Creek into the old quarter, the gold souk and markets. You got it?'

'Yep.'

The job was kicking off at last light tomorrow. For Red Ken and me, it would start in a block of public toilets in the old quarter. Dex was going to go local and steal a Tata truck in the same area they'd pinged with a crane attached, much like the ones Jewson's used to deliver bricks and stuff in the UK.

Red Ken and I would keep out of sight as we moved to the target. We'd lift the crates, load them onto the truck, then take a swift detour to Dex's GMC Suburban, parked about six K west of the target. After transferring our little insurance policy, we'd take the Tata and the Suburban back to the airport before catching up with Spag at the strip.

Bingo.

It was perfectly simple. Too fucking simple by half.

I reckoned it was time for one or two awkward questions. 'So, these Gucci gold doors have just been sitting there since the second Gulf War – and nobody knows?'

'They will when the developers move in. Five years ago this was the Empty Quarter. Now look at it.'

A flood of tourists spilt out of the mall, designer bags bulging with stuff they could have bought back home, and probably for less.

'Spag said he found out about the doors just after the war.'

'Yeah, he told me.'

'Did he also tell you he found the lads who made them?'

'No, he fucked me off on questions. Told me to ask you.'

Red Ken nearly choked on his next mouthful of nicotine. 'The guy in charge locked the crates in that building for Saddam to collect as soon as he'd sorted out the Americans.'

'And the others?'

'Two of them, apparently. Spag reckons he binned them – permanently – in case they confused the gold with their pension scheme.'

'Then Spag binned him, and it's been sitting there ever since?'

Red Ken nodded. 'Just waiting for the right time.'

'The right time for Spag, or for some other fucker?'

'Who knows?' He checked his watch again. 'You OK, Nick? Seen enough?'

'Yeah.'

'We'll follow the route backwards to the gold market. See where the weapons are and where Dex will lift the truck.'

We wandered over to the cab rank. Dex jumped into the front of the first available and greeted the driver like an old cricketing companion. We headed down the ramp to meet the white Toyota, three up.

21

We drove towards the Creek about four or five K away. The main drag really was main. Four lanes in both directions cut through the city. It was pointless checking if the Toyota was still behind us. We'd wait until we stopped, just as we did on foot. These guys weren't complete amateurs. They must have had some training or they'd have stayed with us on the mall roof. But if they were internal security, police, whoever, why tag us? Was it because we'd been with Spag this morning? Maybe they'd been following him, seen us meet and decided to find out who we were and what we were doing.

Whatever, I didn't like it. The job felt compromised before we'd even begun. A big part of me wanted to get these lads to call the whole thing off, but I knew that wasn't going to happen.

We fell silent as we thought about the job and the Toyota. Well, maybe just Red Ken and I did. I had no idea what was going on in Dex's head. But then neither did he.

We drove through the tunnel and followed the Creek towards the sea. Knackered old dhows were parked five and six deep all along the harbour front while their crews unloaded fridges and all sorts straight onto the pavement.

Dex gave the driver a tap on the shoulder. 'We'll stop here, chappie. Thank you very much.'

Red Ken and I got out and left Dex to pay. The Toyota passed us and disappeared down a side turning. The lads would be jumping out any minute to keep with us. We both checked to see if any other cars were doing the same. Maybe they had a team with us, or maybe they'd split when we were all pinged together at the golf course this morning. We did the tourist bit, watching the locals work their arses off unloading and then dicing with death as they barrowed everything, including the kitchen sink, to the shops on the other side of the road.

The sun cast long shadows as it began to bin it for the day. Lights were already on in the shops. Street signs flickered into life, and I started to feel the energy of the place. Night-time was when Dubai began to hop. Who but dickhead tourists wanted to wander around in the sun?

Red Ken tapped my shoulder. 'There's the subway. Get into the toilet block and do your stuff. We'll wait here, see if the team have pinged us yet.'

I wandered under the road. As I emerged the other side, I passed an enclosed steel-and-glass bus shelter with an air-conditioning unit on the roof. It must have been nice and cool for all the people who never used it because they all went by car. It was almost space age compared with the place I was going.

I could smell the flat-roofed cube from several metres away. The cars around it looked as though they'd been abandoned rather than parked. The local dudes leant against the wall and smoked.

I went inside.

The place was boiling hot and stank exactly like a shit-hole full of tobacco smoke should. The two sinks were cracked. The taps were broken. There were four cubicles, and only one was being used. I always thought the hole in the ground with a hosepipe to sluice your arse was a better system than ours, apart from the squatting bit. There's quite an art in keeping your jeans and slack belt out of the firing line.

Above my head, to the right of the entrance, was a ledge on which sat an ancient air-conditioning system, a plastic box caked in grime that probably hadn't sparked up since this place was declared open – about twenty years ago, the same time it had last been cleaned.

I watched the shadow under the occupied cubicle door. The bloke was still squatting. I eased myself up against the wall. If anybody came in, I'd stop what I was doing and leg it.

I stood on the tips of my toes, and stretched up my hand as Red Ken had instructed. The ledge was shaped like a tray for the air-con unit. My fingertips brushed the taped-up plastic bag and the hard steel it contained. Red Ken's three pistols were still where they should be. Now I knew precisely where they were we could head towards the old gold market and the wagon Dex would lift tomorrow night.

22

A mountain of sacks, crates and plastic-wrapped white goods covered every square metre of pavement. Indian lads loaded up with cargo ran up and down the line of dhows like they were stepping-stones. As we headed deeper into the old part of town we mostly had to stick to the road.

Once past the main offloading point, we could see the lights of Ye Olde Dubai across the Creek. Swarms of water-taxis waited to ply you over to the purpose-built tourist trap sited right opposite the real deal.

The two shirts were behind us, on the town side of the road.

Red Ken was deep in thought. He fished out his cigarettes and Dex and I took a couple of brisk paces to get ahead of his smoke cloud. 'What are we going to do with them?'

I shrugged. There wasn't much we should do right now. 'They know where we're staying. If they lose us they'll go and wait for us there. We might as well keep playing tourist until tomorrow night. Then we ditch them and get on with the job.'

Dex nodded. 'And then, Red, I think we should consider missing out on the Friday-morning golf. We should get an earlier flight.'

Red Ken took a big drag and, a moment or two later, smoke seemed to curl out of every hole in his head. 'Agreed.'

'I'm going to keep saying it, lads. You sure you still want to go on? We've just picked up another problem, something else we have no control of, and—'

'Save your breath, son.' Red Ken moved forward a little and slapped Dex between the shoulder-blades. 'Right, boy? Still got your eye on that castle?'

Dex turned and grasped his hand. 'Definitely.'

There was a lot going on there that obviously went beyond words. I felt a little jealous, and pissed off with myself at the same time. These two and Tenny had made the effort to stay tight all these years. 'What's all this Monarch of the Glen shit?'

Dex gave a smile that seemed more wistful than his normal don't-give-a-fuck version. 'It's not shit, Nick. I've been thinking a lot about my father lately. The night before I went to Eton, he sat me down and gave me just one piece of advice. It's something I've never forgotten.' The smile faded. He was lost in another world. His voice deepened. ' "Son, the only way for people like us to succeed in this country is by keeping our heads below the parapet. Laugh, be the happy chappie. Don't let anyone see you're cleverer than they are. If you do, you'll become a threat." '

We walked some more. 'And you know what, chaps? He was right. I was the class clown all through school. They called me the Wacky Paki and I crept in under the wire and was top of the class before they knew it.'

We stopped and looked across the hundred metres of Creek. The lights of Ye Olde Dubai danced on the water.

'And then I joined the RAF, just like my dad. He flew Hurricanes, as you know. They called him Curry-in-a-Hurry. He was brilliant at putting on the smiley face, but in his head he was giving everybody the finger. I've done the same, but I'm fed up with smiling now. I've made up my mind. I'm going to become a Scottish laird. I'm going to buy the title. I've got a castle in mind.' He looked at Red Ken. 'Five acres when the tide's out . . .'

He came in on cue: '. . . three when it's in!'

They laughed.

'I'm going to invent a McWacky-Paki tartan and join Gleneagles and the Royal and Ancient. Two fingers up to the lot of them. One for me, one for my father. He'd be proud of what I'm doing here. I'm going to have the last laugh, something he never had the good fortune to have.' Dex put a hand on my shoulder. 'And you, Nick? There has to be something more than just cash.'

'There is – I told you. I'm here to cover your arses.'

Red Ken flicked his butt into the Creek. 'Nearly there. You see the compound?'

Seventy or eighty metres ahead of us stood a construction site that took up the entire centre of the road. Diversions and temporary traffic-lights funnelled the traffic into one lane.

I was the only one who looked. Too many eyes on one point at the same time would prompt the boys behind us to ask, 'What the fuck are they all looking at, and why?'

Red Ken stopped and made a meal of firing up his latest B&H. 'This whole area is being regenerated. They're going to tart up the promenade road like the Corniche the other side, make it all Gucci. And that's where Dex lifts our wagon.'

Above the blue-painted wooden perimeter walls, I could see Portakabins stacked four or five high, linked by wooden staircases. Cranes reached up into the sky. Arrows and strips of yellow-and-white plastic tape guided us away from the Creek and around the construction site.

'That's if the wagon we want is still there, of course. This is our final recce, so it had better be.'

The site entrance was floodlit. A dozen or so lads squatted on their haunches in the dust around a kettle on a propane burner. A hut that looked like a garden shed provided the only security. Its windows and door were open because of the heat. The guard was watching one of the Indian star channels that played Bollywood 24/7. Flies bounced around in the light.

We let Dex check the place out as we passed the fire station on the opposite side of the road.

'Everything's fine, chaps. Three Tatas on parade, present and correct.'

23

The souk was a collection of narrow pedestrian streets covered by a corrugated roof. To create some kind of air flow, domestic fans had been screwed into each of the supporting pillars. It was packed with brightly lit shops, each with five or six bored-looking Indians sitting behind the counters watching TV. Every window was filled with shiny gold headdresses and belts, and the sort of breastplates they used for weddings out here.

Dex pointed excitedly. 'I'm going to pop into this one. Look at the name.' The shop was called Baghdad. That was where Dex had won his DFC, flying into a contact to pick up a wounded American infantryman. The Brits had wanted to bollock him for risking an airframe, but the Americans said if the Queen didn't give him something, they would. That would have been very embarrassing.

Red Ken and I carried on walking. 'See you down by the junction.'

He shook his head. 'He wants to take Cinza to that ridiculous castle. Like I said, soft in the head, that one.'

I caught a glimpse of the checked and white shirts. They had split up, one on each side of the road.

Red Ken had pinged them as well. 'Fuck 'em, Nick. We'll

deal with them when we have to.' He pointed back to Baghdad. 'You know what? She actually likes him. Both of them are nuts. They suit each other.'

'He buying a ring?'

'Been trying since the funeral. He can never find the right one, and then when he does, he forgets her finger size. He's all over the place.'

A group of Indian guys were suddenly all over us like a rash, trying to herd us towards a once-in-a-lifetime bargain. 'Buy watch, very good? OK Rolex, OK Breitling . . .'

'Not today, mate.'

Dex reappeared and they descended on him instead. 'I'm all right for Rolexes, chaps.' He lifted his wrist to show a few thousand quid's worth of chronograph. 'Already got a real one!'

It was all good tourist banter. We were blending in.

The next assault was launched by guys with trays of cold cans and bottles. This time we were buyers. We stood under a fan and swigged our cans of Fanta. White Shirt followed suit beside a pillar about fifty away. Checked Shirt disappeared down one of the alleyways the watch-sellers wanted to lure us along. They weren't doing too bad. They'd learnt a thing or two since the mall.

Red Ken took a couple of gulps and moved his head from side to side in the draught from the fan. 'OK, listen in. We have a walk round, buy some tourist shite and head for a curry before we go back to the hotel. Tomorrow morning we play golf. If these lads stay with us, they'll have a trigger from the clubhouse – they're shite, but not so shite they'll try and follow us round the course. So that'll give me time to leg it, go get my wagon and position it for tomorrow night. Questions?'

I had plenty. But nothing I had said so far had had any effect, so I kept my mouth shut.

Something in a shop window grabbed Dex's attention. 'Now that really is something . . .'

Red Ken groaned.

'No, Red, I mean really – behind the counter ...'

We looked past the mountains of gold to a digital display. It took me a second to realize it was quoting gold prices in a comprehensive range of different currencies. $27,865 USD. That was about 3K lower than the price at Tenny's funeral.

'Fuck me, lads,' Red Ken said. 'We'd better get a move on.'

24

Mall of the Emirates
Thursday, 30 April
1737 hrs

The taxi stopped off by the rank opposite the Virgin Megastore and I jumped out. Under my arm I had a shirt and a pair of flip-flops wrapped up in one of the hotel's plastic laundry bags. The white Toyota peeled away and pulled into the valet-parking area. I leant back in to ask the boys whether they were absolutely sure they wanted to carry on.

Red Ken didn't even wait for me to open my mouth. 'Wheels already turning, son. We're past the point of no return.'

'OK.' I nodded. 'Good luck.'

I closed the cab door and tapped the roof as it drove away.

Harvey Nichols and Debenhams faced each other and took up three storeys of the mall. I headed between them, towards the huge Carrefour hypermarket. I grabbed a trolley and pushed it through the automatic barrier. If it hadn't been for the *burqa*s, I could have been on the outskirts of Paris or Marseille. It was a one-stop shop for everything from milk to laptops.

I played around with the mobiles and Nintendo games

while I waited. It wasn't long before I spotted Checked Shirt, only today he was in plain blue. He mooched along the store front the other side of the barrier, casting down the aisles for his target. I let him get on with it. When I saw him turn back into the throng of people moving up and down the mall I knew he'd pinged me. He knew I wasn't going anywhere. Now that I was in, I could only exit through one of the checkouts. He could sit back and keep the trigger. Maybe somebody else would come in later on to see what I was up to.

We'd been followed from the moment we'd left the hotel. This time it was a two-car team: the Toyota and a dark blue Mazda saloon. Going by the way they operated, I was pretty sure they'd been trained by the Brits. They used the same stake-out procedures and trigger techniques.

This morning we'd played another round of golf at the same club, but instead of a buggy each this time Red Ken and Dex shared. Red Ken left us on the sixth tee, which was out of line-of-sight of the clubhouse. He'd collected the Suburban from the airport, rattled it off to the RV and got back while we were still fucking about on the fifteenth.

Checked Shirt had come into the clubhouse as we signed in, just to see if we were meeting anyone. As soon as he saw it was just us on the greens, he went and sat at a table in the corner. They couldn't come out and follow us round the golf course. All they could do was hole up and put the trigger on where we'd come back.

They'd followed us back to the hotel. If our rooms were bugged, they'd have been disappointed. There was no planning, no talking. We'd done all that on the golf course where nobody could hear us.

I moved further into Carrefour. By now Red Ken would have arrived at the Bur Juman Centre, another of Dubai's fifty-odd malls. They were the only places we were able to walk around and where we were guaranteed crowd cover. The streets were empty apart from Indians or Filipinos on their way to work.

The plan was now to split up and for each of us to lose his tag. Then we'd RV in the old quarter to carry on with the job as planned. Once Red Ken had dropped him off, Dex wasn't heading for a mall. He was going to the street markets. He had clothes to buy so he could make like a local and go and nick the wagon.

I was moving down the aisles of pots and pans when White Shirt made an appearance. He wasn't there long. His job would be to confirm I was still in the store, that I wasn't meeting any-body, and that if I was, to decide whether they had to follow them as well.

25

I moved from pots and pans to bags: schoolbags, shopping bags, suitcases, rucksacks and day-sacks. I picked up a Day-Glo orange one and threw it in the trolley. In the camping-gear section I added a head-torch. Toiletries and first aid were next. I threw in a pack of surgical gloves. White Shirt shadowed me for a while, checking I was doing what I was doing rather than meeting anybody for a brush contact to exchange information.

He didn't follow as I turned past a group of Europeans checking out iPods. He crossed into the next aisle. I carried on to the checkout. I'd lost him by then; I didn't know where he was. There was no need to look. If he had any sense he'd wait within sight of the exit.

I paid cash, put everything in the day-sack and headed out into the mall. Again, there was no need to look. I didn't want to show I was aware.

I headed for the escalator to the first floor. One of them would probably come with me, but not until I was at the top and about to step off. You don't go on an escalator with your target in case they turn around and ping you.

He would wait until I was 'temporary unsighted' – perhaps because I turned a corner and was out of view until he did the same – and if he and his mate had any brain cells, they'd try and get ahead of me via the fire-escape stairs or another escalator. But I wasn't going to let that happen. As soon as I hit the first floor, I moved right and headed for the toilets.

I took a cubicle and locked myself in. There was a gap of about forty centimetres under the door. I sat, feet up, on a very comfortable European toilet seat, surrounded by glossy marble and stainless steel. Everything smelt wonderful. I whipped off my Timberlands and socks and rolled up my cargos then shoved on the flip-flops, put my feet on the floor, and waited.

I hadn't yet made it look like I was trying to lose them. They'd be checking the immediate vicinity for the VDM, my orange day-sack. They'd be looking through the crowds, trying not to make themselves stick out by pushing people out of the way, all the clumsy stuff you see in films. When they didn't find me, they'd check the men's clothing stores, electrical shops and toilets. All they'd see under the door was a pair of white legs and flip-flops. I was now just one of the hundreds of European men in the mall who could be taking a dump in here – and not the one they were looking for.

Soon they'd have to make a decision. I was no longer just temporary unsighted. I was unsighted – and that was a nice way of saying they'd lost me.

Then what? They'd try to lock the place down. They'd need to put triggers on everyone coming out, but that just wasn't possible. There were too many exits to have eyes-on. Maybe they'd go back and check the taxi ranks. But there wouldn't be enough of them to go round. They'd have to go back to known locations – either the hotel or the golf club. They'd have to go themselves, or tell their mates to go and stake them out.

There were other known locations. We'd been cruising round the old quarter; we'd visited the gold souk. Maybe they'd check Baghdad and the Indian place we'd eaten at last night.

I sat right where I was as cisterns flushed either side of me and dads coaxed their kids to wash their hands. You didn't have to be multilingual to understand what was going on out there.

I checked my watch. I'd been there nearly half an hour. It was time to move or I'd miss the RV with Red Ken and Dex. I put my boots back on, replaced my shirt with the dark blue one in the plastic bag and shoved my purchases into my pockets. I put the flip-flops and cream shirt in the day-sack and left it hanging on the back of the door.

I headed for Debenhams without glancing left or right, then down their internal escalator towards the ground-floor exit.

I was surrounded by people getting into cars or cabs, some in *burqa*s, some in European summer dresses with half their tits hanging out.

The sun was sinking but I didn't want to hit the taxi rank yet. The Toyota was still out there. I ducked back towards the building. It was still only one up. The lads inside the mall would have to make their decision soon.

The two shirts emerged. Checked was on his mobile, waving his free hand like a madman. White bollocked the driver, as if it was his fault they'd lost me.

They jumped into the car and took off, and I joined the taxi queue.

26

Last light

I went straight into the toilet block without hanging about. Dex was lifting the Tata. Red Ken would meet me opposite the construction site to back him if things went tits up. A guy in *dishdash* and sandals bent over the sink, a finger blocking each nostril in turn while he snorted snot from the other into a trickle of water. I headed for one of the cubicles. Glossy marble and stainless steel it wasn't, and the smell was indescribable.

With my feet on the porcelain pads each side of the hole, I fished my docs and cash out of the dark blue Rohan trousers I'd chosen to match my long-sleeved shirt. They were wrapped in a hotel laundry bag. As soon as the snorter had left the block, I moved out and reached up to the ledge. My fingers found two more sets of docs up there, and the weapons gone. This was our final RV. We stored our means of escape here so we could go into the job sterile. All I had on me now was about six hundred dollars of on-the-run money.

It didn't matter what I felt about the job now. It was happening. If I let myself think too much about what might go wrong, I'd end up paralysed.

I retraced my steps through the subway towards the Creek.

I turned right as I came out, following exactly the same route as yesterday. Dhows were still tied up along the pavement, half a dozen deep. The Indian lads were still working their arses off in the dark.

I chose the ill-lit side of the road. As soon as the construction-site floodlights came into view I waited for a break in the traffic and crossed back.

Red Ken stood in the shadows by a massive set of roll shutters set into the wall of the fire station, fishing in his day-sack with rubber-gloved hands. 'All right, son?'

I gave him a nod as I put on my surgical gloves and slipped the head-torch around my neck.

'Here.' He handed me a Taurus, a Brazilian version of the Colt .38 Special. 'It's loaded.' He pressed a speed loader into my palm. 'Spare.'

I checked it. When I needed to reload, I would open the Taurus's cylinder, push the bar, and the six empty cases would fall out. The speed loader had six rounds ready to drop into the chamber. All I had to do was press a button and the rounds would drop into position. I'd close the cylinder again and carry on firing. I slid the speed loader into a pocket in my Rohans and the weapon into my waistband. If we needed more than twelve rounds each to get out of the shit, we were really in it.

The lads hanging around by the main gate of the con-struction site didn't look like they'd moved an inch since last night. The one in the guard hut was still watching something loud from Bollywood. Everyone else was busy brewing up.

Dex had been standing off somewhere in the darkness, keep-ing a trigger on Red Ken, waiting for me to arrive. Within the minute, he walked past us without a second glance. He looked like he'd done his clothes shopping in a skip instead of a street market. His short-sleeved shirt was ripped and the brown trousers held up with a plastic belt were caked with dust. His sandals slapped along the pavement. He smelt rancid from ten paces. He'd prepared well. Smells count.

Dex disappeared into the site.

I checked we were still in shadow, and spotted the sign above our heads. The building we were standing outside wasn't just a fire station – it was also the police station and HQ for Civil Defence.

Red Ken saw me reading it. 'Nobody said it would be easy, son.'

As if on cue, there was a blip of a siren and two green-and-whites pulled out of a side road. The police the other side of the tinted glass didn't give us a second glance before turning right and speeding off down the main.

A Tata truck that had seen better days trundled out of the construction site. Not a single head turned as it nosed through the gate.

Red Ken and I started walking. The Tata pulled in about a hundred metres further down the road. A crane was mounted behind the cab, and a thick steel cable was attached to a chunky hook. Ten metres or so of webbing straps were wrapped around the mesh screen protecting the rear window.

I opened the door and eased myself into the footwell. Dex stared straight ahead. Red Ken came in on top of me, trying to lie flat on the passenger seat. His day-sack dug into my back as he passed Dex his revolver and speed loader. 'It's loaded.'

I concentrated on not fucking up the wiring that dangled beneath the steering column. Dex had rigged it up to get this thing started.

We stopped at a set of lights, which glowed red on Dex's face. He wiggled his surgical-gloved fingers. 'Man, rubber gloves and Tata in perfect harmony.'

27

It stank like a derelict house down there in the footwell. The rubber mats had worn through to bare metal, and there was a thick coating of sand.

Dex gave us a running commentary from the driver's seat. If the shit hit the fan we needed to know exactly what was happening and where. 'That's us about to go into the tunnel.' Everything went dark. Strip-lights flickered. 'Coming out.'

All I could see was skyscrapers that blocked out the stars.

'Approaching traffic-lights . . . looks like they're going to be red . . .' He sounded like a bad ventriloquist. He didn't want other drivers to see him talking to himself.

'That's all the traffic in front slowing . . . slowing . . . lights are red. There's a very nice Maserati down there, with a very beautiful woman . . . short skirt, lads . . . I can't believe it, she's not even looking up at me . . .'

'Show her a picture of your castle, son.'

'Lights changing, lights to green . . .'

The Tata shuddered before we moved on.

'Nearly there, chaps.'

My right leg was cramping up. I had to get it straight. 'Red – got to move, mate.'

He wasn't impressed. 'For fuck's sake.' I was treated to a cloud of cigarette breath.

My face ended up just a couple of centimetres from Dex's flip-flops as he worked the pedals. They'd come from a skip as well.

He rumbled along, not speeding, but bumping around to keep his place in the freeway chaos.

I got cramp again. If a job kicks off well, the rest of it seems to flow. If it judders out of the blocks, it often turns into a nightmare.

'Two hundred to go before our first stop.'

Air rushed through the open window and I caught a glimpse of streetlights. There was a bump and then darkness, like someone had thrown a switch.

'Let's see who's with us, shall we?' Dex checked the vehicles that had no choice now but to pass us. 'So far, so good, chaps. No Toyota or Mazda, no one turning off, staking out, or even giving us a second look.'

The Tata shook itself like a wet dog and moved forward once more.

' "Swing, swing to-ge-ther ... With your bo-dies be-tween your knees ..." '

For the next ten minutes we had to put up with his favourite chorus in between snatches of commentary.

'Here we go, up the kerb.'

We'd reached our final stop and check. We bumped up onto the rough ground surrounding the target. The sky went dark and we came to a halt. The engine ticked over as Dex let the traffic zoom past.

'No vehicles that came past last time.' He gave it another thirty seconds. 'That's it, we're clear. No one following and I have no movement or light on target.' He killed the headlights.

28

Red Ken gave me room to stretch. 'OK, that's it. Let's switch on.'

Dex rolled the wagon slowly over the wasteground towards the target. A couple of hundred metres away from it, he started easing up the handbrake instead of using the foot pedal. We didn't want red taillights flashing on derelict ground.

We came to a halt and Red Ken and I jumped out. The lights of the city glowed all round our island of darkness. The ski-slope tower blinked about a K away so the Dexes of this world didn't fly into it. About five hundred metres behind us, hundreds of vehicles flowed along the well-lit main.

We moved forward on foot.

The target wall was maybe a hundred and fifty ahead.

The gates facing the entrance to the building were immediately in front of us. From here on in, that side of the rectangle was White. The left-hand side was Green, the right was Red and the rear section Black. Colour coding prevented confusion: your rear could be someone else's front.

We eased off to the left. Sweat trickled down my neck as we rounded the first corner of White and Green. We did a complete 360 of the compound wall, gradually spiralling in until we came right up against it where Red met White.

There was a constant hum of traffic. Helicopters buzzed from one high-rise to another in the background. We listened for movement inside the compound. We stayed like that for a couple of minutes, just listening and tuning in. The ambient light wasn't strong enough to cast a shadow onto the wall, but now my night vision was kicking in I could see the dust and rubble below our feet. My fingers had pruned inside the surgical gloves, floating in pools of sweat.

Red Ken gave me a tap on the shoulder to check if I'd heard anything.

I shook my head.

We followed the wall on White until we reached the entrance.

29

The gate had once had a coat of paint, but I couldn't tell what colour it had been. The desert wind had sandblasted some patches bare. Wind from the sea had made it rust and peel.

The three big padlocks Red Ken had spotted on their last recce were still in place: massive square things, just the body exposed so you couldn't attack the shanks with a cutter.

Red Ken went down on his knees, scanning the ground for tread marks. The wind would have obliterated anything more than a few days old, so anything visible could be taken as recent. It was one more combat indicator, something that showed the enemy was close – because tonight there were no friendly forces.

A foot-high ridge of sand had built up along the bottom of the gate. If somebody had made entry recently it would have been disturbed. We were going to leave it just as it was.

Red Ken leant his back against the wall, knees bent. He cupped his hands on his lap. I put my right foot into his gloves, steadied myself with my hands on his shoulders, then reached up and grabbed the top of the wall. He stood and guided my feet to his shoulders.

The yard was pitch black. No vehicle lights, no lights from the windows either side of the shutters.

I waited twenty seconds before looking again, so my unconscious had time for everything around it to sink in. I came back down. 'OK. We're on.'

Red Ken moved a little further along the wall towards White and Red to be the marker for the Tata and I moved towards Dex to guide him in. He'd be driving without lights and using only the handbrake and gears.

I pulled my torch up onto my forehead. Its three LEDs shone white or red, as a stable beam or flashes for emergencies. Stable and red would do us fine, but not just yet. I walked until the Tata was almost on top of me and the cab blocked out the city lights behind it. I gripped the sill of the open window to murmur in Dex's ear, 'You can see the wall?'

'Yep.'

'OK, go half right then turn in. Red's your marker.'

Dex kept it at gentle revs as he rolled forward. There was no rush about this bit. The noise wasn't important; not hitting the brakes was. He pulled up the handbrake when he got to his mark and left the engine running.

I scrambled on top of the cab and jumped onto the wall. I dropped into a stretch of finely powdered sand that had had no way of escaping the compound. One hand on my pistol to keep it in my waistband, I ran to Black. All clear.

By the time I got back, Red Ken was checking the shutter. The glow from his head-torch bathed its sides and then its base. He scooped away years of encrusted sand. 'I got fuck-all to get hold of, son. It's got to be electric.'

Whoever had closed this down had done so from the inside and then come out via the door in the shutters. Three Chubbs secured that. We'd be here all night trying to defeat them. 'We'll have to pull out the frame.'

Silhouetted against the city lights, Dex stood astride the cab roof with the crane's control box in his hand. The electric winch whined and the steel cable snaked down our side of the wall. Red Ken grabbed it and started walking towards the right-hand window.

30

I helped Red Ken loop the heavy steel hook round the eight bars and back onto the cable. He turned to Dex. 'All right, mate, let's do it. Nice and slow.'

The winch hauled in the cable until it was taut. Red Ken and I slipped round the corner of White and Red to get out of the way. If the cable snapped under tension, the whiplash would tear up anyone in its path, like shrapnel from a mortar round. Dex lay flat on the cab for the same reason. We heard the strain in the steel strands, and then a loud crack and rumble as the whole section of wall came away. It hit the ground with a thump and sent up a cloud of dust.

There wasn't time to celebrate.

Red Ken undid the hook. I turned on my head-torch to constant red and climbed through the hole. I couldn't see a thing. The red light bounced straight back off the dustcloud, like headlights in fog. The air was hot and musty. It felt like we were breaking into a pyramid. Coughing and spluttering, I began to make out plasterboard walls. I was in an office. I groped for the door. My nose and mouth had filled with grit. I gobbed it onto my shirt. I needed to contain my DNA.

I carried on through the door. My coughs suddenly echoed. I was in the warehouse proper. I turned towards where I thought the shutters should be and my torch beam hit their metal slats. The operating mechanism was mounted on the side wall. I tried pressing the 'open' button just in case. Then I grabbed the chain as high as I could and pulled. It didn't budge. Years of disuse had seized it up.

I jumped up, with arms extended, and hung on, then kicked out from the wall like a kid in an adventure playground to apply some weight and traction from another angle. It gave an inch. I went through the same routine again, jumping up and kicking out, until it gradually relented. I sank to my knees as the slats began to concertina. My sweat-soaked face was coated with sand.

One final wrench and the shutter ascended. I could see Red Ken's boots in the glow of his head-torch. The hook and webbing straps lay beside them. As soon as the gap was big enough, he rolled under and helped me pull. The shutter came to a complete stop as the inset door hit the top of the roll.

Dex was still on the wagon, silhouetted against the starlit sky.

The dust had almost settled. Our torch beams criss-crossed the interior of the building like lasers. The crates lay in the middle of the warehouse. Six feet by four and two feet high, they each stood on an individual pallet. We moved forward. I felt my heart beating faster. I didn't want these two silly fuckers to be here – and I didn't want to be here either.

Red Ken dropped his day-sack on the nearest crate and pulled out a mini-crowbar. We needed to be sure this wasn't just a bulk shipment from the nearest *burqa* factory.

I went out to keep Dex in the loop. 'Found the boxes, just checking – wait out.' I ran back inside.

'You need to have a look at this.' Red Ken was surrounded by tiny white polystyrene balls. They still streamed from the panel he'd wrenched back from the corner of the nearest crate.

I leant down and did as I was told. A few little white balls still clung to the glimmering sheet of engraved yellow metal inside, but not enough to obscure the familiar moustache and smiling face of Saddam Hussein.

He banged the slat back into place. 'This is the one we're going to have. Fuck checking the rest.'

We fed the strapping under the pallet, secured it and worked the hook into the side of the webbing strap.

I ran back out. 'OK, mate. Gently.'

There was nothing gentle about his reaction. 'Pay day, pay day!'

The electric motor whined as the winch took the strain. The pallet groaned and jerked, then started to creep across the concrete floor towards the exit. Soon it was gouging its way over the open ground. We kept either side of it to make sure it didn't tip over. We were just metres from the wall. At this rate we'd be fully loaded and out of here within thirty minutes.

Dex slackened off the cable. We grabbed the hook and moved it to the top of the webbing.

'OK, mate, take it up.'

All he had to do was lift it over the wall, swing left, and lower.

Nothing happened.

I looked up. Dex was on his knees, leaning down towards us. 'Not good, chaps. We have headlights moving towards Black.'

Red Ken had already grabbed the cable and hoisted himself up to join him.

31

I followed Red Ken up onto the cab roof and watched the single set of headlights, maybe two hundred away, career over the wasteground towards us.

Red Ken drew down his weapon and Dex copied.

I gripped Red Ken's arm. 'We've got no blue lights. It's just one vehicle. Could be taking a shortcut.'

'Maybe,' Dex said. 'But it's going to pass really close. Bound to see us.'

'Skyline!'

I had already jumped but Red Ken needed to drag Dex down.

We stayed in the shadow at the corner of White. I could now hear the rumble of tyres over rough ground. The approaching vehicle was hugging the wall on Red, its headlights throwing us into deeper shadow. The vehicle stopped just short of the corner.

Dex looked ready to lunge. I held him back. 'We can contain this. Nobody's got out yet. There's no doors slamming, no shouting.'

The headlights died.

Red Ken was calm. 'Dex, go play local. We'll hold back. Keep whoever it is in the vehicle while we check them out.'

Dex didn't hang around. Red Ken and I kept a few metres back. I moved away from the wall so we could deploy all three weapons without cutting into each other's arcs.

An interior light came on at the rear. The vehicle was big, a 4x4. A dark-coloured Yukon, as big as Red Ken's Suburban. I moved forward, weapon up, both eyes open. Dex orbited round to the rear cab. The wagon's suspension shifted as a body changed position inside. Dex grabbed the door handle and pulled hard.

'Don't hurt me!' The voice was terrified and female.

I closed on Dex as he covered her with a brown, swirly-patterned nylon fur blanket so she couldn't see his face or know he wasn't alone. The rear cab was littered with carrier bags full of clothes and towels, toiletries, packets of food and bottles of water. Whoever this was, the Yukon was her home.

Red Ken worked quietly up front in the glove compartment and under the seats. He found her handbag and pulled out a purse. Our three head-torches bathed the plastic card he produced in a rubber-gloved hand. The Canadian driver's licence told us she was Sherry Capland.

32

She had about five hundred dollars' worth of dirhams in her bag. There were no pictures of kids, just a wedding photo, her in a white veil and him in a tuxedo. She'd had long brown hair back then, permed up. A sob shook the blanket. 'Please, please, don't hurt me. Just take what you want.'

Red Ken tapped Dex on the shoulder and gave him the waffle sign with thumb and fingers.

He understood. 'Shut up!'

Red whispered into Dex's ear.

'Where's your husband?'

'He's in prison. He lost his job and—'

Red Ken sliced his index finger across his own throat.

Dex slapped the blanket. 'Enough!' He slammed the door on her and we got into a huddle.

'She's homeless.' Red Ken spoke quietly. 'It's like I told you, if you get binned from your job and you've got debts you can't cover, you're fucked. You can't leave the country. They fling you in prison. That's why there's all those wagons at the airport and the planes are full. If her old man's locked up, that makes her an illegal.'

Dex nodded. 'But what do we do with her?'

Red Ken turned back to the Yukon and opened the door. 'Sit

up, love. We're not going to hurt you. It's OK, so for fuck's sake shut it, will you? Wrong place, wrong time, that's all.'

She sat cross-legged with the blanket around her shoulders. She was maybe mid-thirties, but looked older. It's difficult not to when your cheeks are tear-stained, you've got snot running from your nose and your hair's plastered all over your face.

Dex pulled us back again, out of earshot. 'We've got a problem. She's seen us now. Why did you do that, Red? How do we keep the job secure?'

'Tell you what.' I put a hand on his shoulder. 'I'll drive her wagon. We'll just keep her with us until we fly out.'

Red Ken nodded. 'Let's get on with it, then.'

I held out my hand for the keys. 'I'll bring the wagon round. You two can get on with the first load.'

I opened the back door. Sherry was curled up on the floor, wanting the world to go away. I couldn't blame her. One eye peeped out from under her arm, like a child's. Scared people have to be gripped. They don't hear what you're saying. They get more confused and more frightened, not less, and more danger to us and to themselves.

'Sherry, listen in. Everything will be OK. You're going to be with us until the morning. Just do what you're told and you'll be fine.'

Her bloodshot eyes fixed on mine. She nodded quickly, wanting to please me.

'But if you try to run away, scream, shout, or do anything we don't tell you to do, then all bets are off. You understand?'

She wiped snot from her nose and nodded some more.

'Climb into the seat behind me. Cover yourself with the blanket.'

She scrambled over.

'Now get in the footwell. Stay down there.'

I went round pulling up all the child locks, slamming and checking the handles wouldn't open. I heard the electric motor kick in once more.

I got in behind the wheel and swung the wagon round so it paralleled the Tata's cab. Dex could keep eyes-on while Red Ken and I worked in the building.

I locked the door behind me just as our crate cleared the wall. Dex manoeuvred it to the rear of the flatbed. Red Ken was already over the wall, heading back in to sort the next load.

Dex beamed at me. 'Only five to go.'

I jumped down into the compound and helped Red Ken rig up the second pallet. 'She secure?'

'Yep, Dex has eyes-on.' I put the hook into the side of the webbing and gave Dex the signal. 'Red, I reckon we keep her all the way to the airport, yeah?'

'Got to, so we know she isn't gobbing off. But I don't think she'll be running to the police. She needs to stay underground and wait for that handsome young husband of hers.'

The second crate inched out of the warehouse and onto the sand.

33

2238 hrs

The city twinkled far behind in my rear-view. The Tata's head-lights carved through the inky darkness in front of us.

Sherry kept her head down and didn't breathe a word.

The Tata's indicators kicked off and it turned to the right. Wooden benches and tables were dotted about the desert. It was some kind of picnic site. The Tata's headlights raked the length of the white GMC Suburban and then stopped beside it. Dex got out and climbed onto the back of the truck to untie our crate. Red Ken opened the two doors at the back of his wagon.

I pulled in behind the truck, so Dex could keep an eye on Sherry, and got out to help.

It wasn't long before our crate, still on its pallet, was being slowly hoisted into the back of the GMC. A set of headlights moved along the main and swept over us. They kept on going.

Dex manoeuvred it to just above the level of the rear sill. Red Ken positioned the roller, a short length of scaffolding pole, and we pushed the suspended crate until about a third of it penetrated the boot space. 'OK, Dex, lower it.'

The suspension groaned as it took Saddam's weight. Dex jumped down to help us push it all the way inside.

Red Ken brought out his cigarettes. 'OK, order of march. Me, Dex, Nick. Nice and slow, keep within the limits.' He turned to Dex. 'Just short of the airport I'll point out where I want you to park and wait out.' He sparked up his lighter. 'Nick, follow Dex and wait out when he parks. I'll come to you. You then drop me off at the Tata and we move to the airstrip.' He moved to the front of his Suburban without waiting for a reply.

34

The air-con in the Yukon was knackered so I had to keep the window open as we headed back towards the bright lights. The wind rattled through the vehicle as I felt around for a bottle of water among all the crap in the footwell. I didn't find one.

Streetlights soon started to glare and traffic-lights held us at every other junction. I continued to follow the five crates on the Tata as we eventually got onto the main drag to the airport. Dex's right indicator flashed once more. He turned off into wasteground between a strip mall and an apartment block that had become a makeshift car park. I closed up behind Red Ken and we were soon on the elevated approach road, channelled towards Departures for the Emirates terminal.

We carried on past the brilliantly lit glass-fronted building. The forecourt was almost deserted apart from a couple of taxis, a white Toyota and a blue Mazda, both one up, in the no-parking zone. I powered up the window and stared ahead. I wondered if Checked and White were inside the terminal. The airport was the last of our known locations. They'd be checking to see if we'd changed flights, or were waiting in the departure lounge. They'd be severely pissed off. Not just about losing their targets and not finding out what they were up to, but about looking like dickheads for losing them at all.

I waited outside the Emirates terminal long-term car park as the Suburban disappeared inside. There was still no noise from Sherry, just movement now and again under the blanket.

Five minutes later he emerged from the concrete multi-storey. He didn't come and jump into the passenger seat but waved for me to get out of the wagon and join him by the stair-well. 'She doesn't need to know this. It's on the first floor, row sixteen. The key is on top of the back box of the exhaust.'

He checked his watch.

'Red, you see the team up at Departures?'

'Fuck 'em. Whatever happens, we've got some of what we came here for. Tell you what, son. I can't wait to get home. There's the christening in a couple of weeks and a lot of straight talking to be done. I'm ready for it. I'm gonna tell her I've been a total arsehole, but that's about to change. No more work. I no longer need to – and, what's more, I don't want to. It's all about her from now on.'

'That's good, mate.' I started heading for the Yukon.

'Nick, listen. I just want to say thanks for coming on the job. Tenny's death really . . . affected us . . . Me and Dex, we were hoping you'd be with us – you know, together again. It wasn't just the job, it—'

'We're mates,' I said. 'I wouldn't let you two down. I'm here because I want to look after you. Never forget that.' I turned back towards the wagon. Any more of this shit and I'd have to start pretending I'd got some grit in my eye.

35

I dropped Red Ken off with Dex and was soon following the Tata again. Within thirty minutes we were out of the city and on the coastal highway. Before we got as far as Abu Dhabi, we were going to chuck a left and head south, as if for Saudi, less than a couple of hours away. The airstrip lay about thirty K down that road.

Above the hum of tyres on tarmac I could hear the odd sniffle from behind me. 'Sherry, sit up. Keep the blanket on your head and sit up.'

She got up slowly. Her muscles would be in shit state after the hours she'd spent down there. In the rear-view she looked like she was wearing a furry brown *burqa*.

I shouted over my shoulder. 'What did your old man get?'

'Nine months.'

'For having debts?'

It was a while before she spoke. 'Bradley has a brain tumour. He's going to die in there.'

The brake-lights on the Tata glowed. We came to a halt off the road.

'Sherry.'

'Yes?'

'Get down and stay down. It's nearly over.'

'You're going to kill me, aren't you? That's what happens.'

'Just keep quiet. You've been watching too much TV.'

Dex killed his lights and I did the same. I climbed out to meet the other two between the wagons.

The wind was picking up. The sky was full of stars, but there was no ambient light on the ground – apart from round Red Ken, who'd lit his three hundredth B&H of the day.

We were about seven hundred short of the airstrip. We'd wait until we heard the aircraft coming in before we moved in to meet up with Spag. He should already be at his stand-off point.

I told them about Bradley.

Red Ken blew out a lungful of smoke. 'What do you reckon?'

'She's not a problem to us. She has enough stuff of her own to worry about. I'll clean her up with the wipes and take her into my room tonight. They'll think she's a hooker.'

Dex checked his watch. 'Twenty minutes.'

We settled cross-legged between the two wagons and waited.

I scooped up handfuls of sand and let it run through my fingers. Dex stretched to ease the tension in his shoulder muscles. 'Chaps, what about us chipping away just a few ounces to take back home? We'll get it through Customs, no problem. I thought I'd get three rings made for us.'

Red Ken lit yet another B&H. 'Soft in the head.'

'I was thinking of inscribing mine with my new motto. *"Saddam gratias tibi ago."*'

I had to ask. 'Which means?'

' "Thank you, Saddam." '

36

The navigation lights were clearly visible in the black sky long before we heard the jets. A few hundred metres ahead of us, the landing-strip lights suddenly fired up and the desert turned into a stretch of the M25.

We climbed on top of the Tata. No other light sources were visible in any direction.

Red Ken flicked his B&H into the sand to join the others. 'Nick, make sure you grip that girl. Keep a bound away and back us.'

'That's what I'm here for, mate.'

Dex held out a hand to each of us. 'Good luck, chaps.'

We jumped down and got to work. Dex and Red Ken were going to drive down to the aircraft in the Tata. I'd follow.

The plane screamed in. The moment it had taxied to a halt, the landing-strip lights were doused. We bounced onto the tarmac. Spag was supposed to be waiting on the link road between the single track and the perimeter fence.

I kept the window up.

'Sherry?'

I got a muffled 'Yes.'

'Stay low. Don't move, no matter what. Help us by keeping out of the way and you could be free in a couple of hours.'

The brake-lights ahead glowed red. I kept a distance of thirty metres, headlights on full beam. The Taurus was under my right thigh. My lights picked out what looked like a white version of Postman Pat's van at the junction with the metalled track. Spag was in the driver's seat.

Red Ken jumped down from the Tata and Spag wriggled out of the Nissan Cube. They waffled for a while. Red Ken waved me up to them and Dex also got out. By the time I'd joined them, Spag was going ballistic about the missing crate.

Red Ken was calm. 'You're lucky we got that many out before we got compromised. You could have lost the lot.'

Spag spun on his heel. 'Jee-sus Christ!'

Red Ken put up an arm. 'You're Mr Fucking Sirloin. You sort it, or go and get it yourself.'

Spag turned back, pointing up at Red Ken's chin. 'If I find you've screwed the deal over—'

'You'll *what*? Listen, crap-hat – if we'd wanted to play silly buggers we'd have taken the lot and wouldn't be here. So let's crack on and get the job done.'

It was Red Ken's turn to do the pointing. 'OK, this is what's going to happen. You're going to stay with me all the way through. If we get stitched up, you'll be the first to get the good news. Dex?'

Dex drew down his weapon.

Spag's finger shook like a battery-operated vibrator. 'We agreed – no weapons!'

Red Ken wanted to move on. 'How many on the aircraft?'

'Two pilots and two or three guys to load up. That's it.'

'OK. I go with you in your car. We load, and then we come back here and we all go our different ways. Until then, you're mine.' He was already heading for the right-hand seat of the Cube. Dex climbed back into the Tata. Seconds later, all three vehicles were paralleling the black strip of tarmac, lights killed.

The aircraft was ahead. A dim glow came from the open cargo door at the rear. It got brighter as we got closer. Soon I could make out four bodies and a long conveyor-belt sloping from the tarmac to the plane's interior.

I held back as the Tata and the Cube pulled up alongside it. The flatbed became a blur of activity.

I got out of the Yukon to the whine of idling jets. These boys were going to turn around as quickly as they could and fuck off again. The markings on the fuselage told me it was a French-made Dassault Falcon business jet. It had three engines at the back. Its registration mark was on the centre engine covering that made up part of the tail. It looked big enough to cross from Europe to the USA without a refuel, so its destination could have been pretty much anywhere. I'd never seen the RF designation before. I hadn't a clue what country it belonged to.

All four crew were in the pool of light spilling from the cargo door. They were all white. The pilots wore crisp white shirts and black ties. The two loadies were in jeans and short-sleeved shirts. Both had short back and sides. The smaller had sideburns that ended below his ears. The larger had a tattoo on the back of his neck, a phoenix surrounded by flames that seemed to rear from his collar. His arms were almost solid black with designs.

The pilots walked back through the cabin and into the cockpit.

There was a whine as the crane began doing its stuff. Dex stood on the ground with the control box. He manoeuvred the hook towards the two in jeans, who were attaching straps in readiness.

I could make out Red Ken's head the other side of the cab. Spag's bobbed into view now and again.

I kept my eyes beyond the activity, checking the periphery for movement, light or sound.

37

The final crate was about to hit the rollers. I watched from just beyond the light. Dex stood on the Tata's flatbed with the control box. Spag and Red Ken were the other side of the cab, just out of sight.

A movement caught my eye from inside the aircraft. A body crossed the front cabin window. My eyes flicked to the cockpit. I could only see part of it, but the pilots were both mincing about with the controls.

Spag had said two or three, plus crew. The body crossed the next window, heading to the rear of the aircraft. It wasn't running.

The last crate disappeared into the hold and the two loadies jumped down to dismantle the conveyor. Dex brought the crane back into the idle.

The face that appeared at the cabin door was Middle Eastern – with a nose like a Roman emperor. The body was tall and angular. He surveyed the scene. He wasn't in uniform or jeans. He wore a tan windcheater and trousers. His eyes scanned the pool of light, like an ageing rock star looking out at his audience. His eyes were hooded, but unforgettable.

As quickly as he'd appeared, he jerked back inside the cabin and the two loadies drew down.

'Gun!'

The first rounds kicked off.

My pistol was out but Dex was already falling. He hit the edge of the flatbed and cartwheeled onto the runway, drilled by Tattoo's semi-automatic.

I broke into a run.

38

At this range, it was going to be difficult to take them down. I closed in. I could now see the second loadie. His muzzle flashes bounced around in the darkness. He was firing into the other two down on the tarmac.

Dex lay very still in a pool of his blood. His face was in lumps.

The other two were covered with blood. It looked like Spag had tried to make a run for it. He was lying a short distance from Red Ken.

Tattoo must have detected movement.

He dropped to his knee in Dex's blood and his head swivelled like a reptile's. His eyes homed in on me. As he pushed the mag-release catch with his thumb, his left hand went behind him. The mag fell onto what was left of Dex's head. Tattoo's left hand returned, clutching a new mag.

I didn't have time to go stable to take my shot. But even ten metres was too far for a revolver on the move. He didn't flinch as I fired. The top slide was back on his weapon, ready to receive the new mag. He was calm and controlled.

I made more ground, weapon up.

I fired the Taurus twice more. Tattoo had a whole magazine – twelve, thirteen, maybe twenty rounds if it had an extension.

I had just three left, and then the speed loader. I hoped he might turn away or fumble the mag change to give me time for a decent close-range shot, but this boy was too good. In almost the same movement he pushed in the fresh mag and released the top slide with his thumb. It flew forward and picked up a round as he brought it up.

The guy behind him went down on his knee and reloaded.

Tattoo had both eyes open as I ran into his sight picture.

I jinked left.

He fired.

I jinked again, and this time I turned. I ran hard, focused on the Yukon, blanking out the gunshots behind me. No evasive action, none of that shit now. I just kept going. The three of them were dead. There was nothing I could do for them.

The firing behind me was more distant. Only a lucky shot would take me down. All he could do was pump out the rounds and hope.

Just metres to the car.

The tiniest movement of the barrel translates into an enormous diversion of the round.

Head down, almost at the door.

No shouts behind me, no confusion, just more shots.

I grabbed the door handle, jumped into the seat and saw both of them running forward, dumping magazines and throwing in new ones.

I took a breath to slow everything down.

Key in, ignition on.

The windscreen took a round top right. It crazed like a spider's web but the toughened glass held. I pushed my foot to the floor and the auto-transmission did its stuff. I steered for the gate on full beam, hit the main road and swung the vehicle left.

There was no follow-up in the rear-view – at least, none using headlights.

Why would they bother? They'd got everything they wanted, apart from one crate.

I fought to contain the emotion that boiled inside me. Anger wasn't going to help get me out of here. First I had to pick up my passport and then get out of Dubai – maybe head east for Oman a couple of hours' north. Once I was safe, I'd call Julian. He'd get me out of the shit.

I was back on the coast road. The city soon glowed on the horizon. A few K more and, as I passed the rest area where we'd loaded the Suburban, I could see the warning lights blink on top of the skyscrapers.

Six K later I was pulling into wasteland just inside the city limits. I jumped out, looking for something hard to do some damage. 'Sherry, it's OK – get up.'

The ground was littered with piles of broken-up concrete blocks and reinforcement rods from the construction sites all around us. A lump of concrete would work for me.

By the time I got back to the wagon she was sitting up with the blanket still over her head. 'You don't need that any more.' I opened the rear door. One look at what I had in my hand confirmed her worst fears. 'God, please, no!'

I headed for the windscreen. 'Shut up and get out!'

I started by giving the bullet hole a couple of hits to disguise it. Sherry stood there, the blanket still in her hand. 'You're safe, Sherry. It's all over. I'm fucking off now and so should you. If you want to see your husband, don't say a word to anyone. If you do, you're in the shit with the UAE.'

I didn't give her time to answer. She just needed gripping. 'Go get the windscreen replaced.' I gave her half the money I had on me. She took the cash and didn't say a word or even draw breath before jumping into the driver's seat and hitting the gas. Fair one.

I watched her rear lights melt into the mass of streetlights and neon before I started walking in the same direction.

39

First light

I asked the driver to drop me off along the Creek, just past the tunnel. I walked along the waterfront towards the toilet block a K away. There were a lot of people about, despite the time of day. Indians and Filipinos, of course. The traffic was constant but not dense.

I stopped short of the toilet block, taking a seat inside one of the space-age bus shelters. I looked and watched, clearing the area around one of our known locations. It would have appeared a long shot to the lads who'd been following us, but one they would have considered.

I'd take the others' passports and cash as well. They had no use for them now.

A couple of old Indian women came and sat down beside me. They ignored the white man in shit state who was waiting for a bus.

I couldn't see a Toyota or Mazda, no one sitting in any vehicle, just the odd guy going in and coming pretty much straight out again. Everything looked normal.

I nodded goodbye to the women and headed down the subway. I turned left as I emerged and went straight into the toilet block. It was empty.

I felt along the shelf. There was nothing.

Shit.

I started running to the door. I was heading out into the market area, anywhere I could make distance and lose myself down alleyways, behind buildings, anywhere to escape.

A body crashed into me in the doorway. I stumbled backwards. There were another two, maybe three, behind him. They flooded me, and as my head hit the wall I caught a flash of blue shirt. The next thing I heard was the crackle of a Tazer. A nanosecond later, my body exploded and I dropped.

PART FOUR

40

I came round feeling like I'd been on a four-day bender. My mouth was as dry as sand and my teeth were coated with fur. I breathed out and the blanket bounced it back at me. It wasn't my best day out.

I forced my eyes open and looked around. I was in an orange jumpsuit. I was in a cell. There weren't any windows, just a fluorescent light with a mesh cover fixed flush with the ceiling. The walls were plain plaster. I could see scrawls in English. There was a familiar institutional smell, a mixture of school dinners and cleaning fluid.

I vaguely remembered being moved and shoved about ... lying on a stretcher ... the horrible feeling of waking up wet because I'd pissed myself.

I rubbed my face. My hands grazed a good two days' worth of stubble.

They definitely had eyes on me. It wasn't more than a minute before I heard boots squeaking down a corridor. I studied the sheet-metal door. There was no peephole or any of that stuff off *The Bill*. There'd be fibre-optics or some sort of shit chased into the walls.

Keys jangled and the lock turned with a heavy clunk. I got my head under my arms, curled up and waited.

The door burst open and boots and blue trousers headed my way. They were black Hi-Tec, high-leg boots. This was feeling more familiar by the second. I ventured an eye upwards to see two Brit policemen in white short-sleeved shirts, one balding, one with a shaven head. Neither looked in much of a mood to fuck about. They grabbed hold of me. The shaven-headed one had ginger-freckled hands. He did the business with issue cuffs, the ones with a rigid link between them. Even the sight of those was comforting.

His massive fist closed around the link and jerked me to my feet. No words, just actions. He tugged the link behind him and I followed as fast as I could to relieve the pain of the steel against my wrists. My legs took a while to spark up and I had to keep my arms horizontal.

Metal doors lined the narrow corridor. Every one of them was closed, and the ID plates bore no name, blood group or religion. Either I was the only one in here, or they were playing mind games.

Were they trying to disorient me? Then why wear watches that agreed with the big wall clock ahead of us? They all said just after three o'clock. A.m. or p.m., what did I care? At least I wasn't lying dead on an airstrip or banged up next to Sherry's old man. Whatever, it was time to buckle up. Things could still get hairy, depending who had brought me here.

They hauled me into an interrogation room. Why they called them interview rooms I hadn't a clue. We all knew what went on inside them.

The steel table in the middle had four tubular legs bolted to the floor. The two bench seats either side were also fixed. The walls were cream. The paint, I could smell, was fresh. I wondered what had happened to the last occupant to prompt a makeover.

Fluorescent lights were set into the ceiling, like in the cell. Nothing to grab, nothing to pull out.

The two handlers' boots squeaked over the polished tiles

and came to a halt. They turned me round and plonked me by the bench furthest from the door. I kept looking down. My bare feet had left a trail of sweaty prints across the floor.

I was allowed to sit myself down, but they attached my cuffs to the retaining chain welded to the table. I was free to move my hands, but I wasn't going anywhere.

They turned and left the room. I was being watched, of course. There weren't any two-way mirrors. This place had cameras in each corner.

I sat there with the strange sense of comfort that came from being somewhere that felt familiar. Red Ken and Dex had been right. There was no way I was going to fester in a Dubai jail.

The squeaks came down the corridor once more, and the door was unbolted. It wasn't Ginger who came in armed with two steaming mugs, but Julian, the Premiership player from the funeral.

He unbuttoned his single-breasted pinstripe. Even though he was dressed like an upmarket estate agent, always had an annoyingly perfect Windsor knot in his tie and an immaculately pressed, double-cuffed shirt, I had him down as one of the good guys from the Security Service.

I'd been hoping this had something to do with him, and couldn't hide my relief. But now that he was in front of me I couldn't be sure if it was going to be good or bad. After all, he still had me chained up.

At least he was smiling. That made me feel a little better.

I smiled weakly back. 'Hello, mate.'

The door closed behind him but it wasn't locked. Ginger and his baldy mate would be hovering just in case I did a Houdini and went for the throat of one of MI5's big cheeses.

He sat down opposite me and passed across a mug of mud-coloured instant. 'I'm not sure if you wanted it, but I added sugar.'

I picked it up between my manacled hands and went to get it down my neck. Old habits die hard. You never know when the next one's coming, or whether they'll whisk this one away just as you take your first sip.

Julian put down his mug. His expression was sympathetic, but his body language was confident and assured. On the phone, he sounded like he'd shared a school desk with Dex. Maybe he had. If I hadn't had to keep this job from the others, I might have asked old Biggles if they'd ever run the 100 metres together.

I got the brew in both hands and did the squaddie trick of testing my tongue against the mug. Gulp straight from a metal mug and you could peel the roof off your mouth. It was too hot. That was a good sign. It meant I was trusted with scalding liquids.

He looked at me with concern. 'It wasn't us who wanted you lifted, Nick. I hope you know that.'

I held up the cuffs. 'What about these, mate?'

'In case you misunderstood why you're here.'

'You got any water? I'm gagging here.'

He looked over my shoulder and nodded.

I shifted on the hard seat. 'They're both dead – so's Spag.'

For a moment, he looked defeated. I knew he wasn't to blame for what had happened. Why would he have compromised the job before the end?

'I guess it made sense for them to drop the four of us after we delivered. The three bar they paid us in advance is peanuts compared to what they've got now.'

I stopped talking shop as the door opened and Ginger delivered two bottles of Tesco's own sparkling and a couple of white plastic cups. Fuck knows why – everything was being recorded and there were plenty of people listening in. 'Where am I, Julian?'

He gave Ginger a nod. He seemed a bit confused, having a white guy in these cells. 'Paddington.'

That made sense. Out came the keys as Ginger was given the go-ahead to unlock.

144

Julian had recruited me immediately after Tenny's death. Up until then, Tenny had been Julian's man on the crew. He'd applied to join the Security Service when he'd finished his time. This was to have been his early entry job. Red Ken and Dex hadn't had a clue what was going on. All they knew was that they were getting fronted by Spag, and it was a commercial job for their own slice of the world's best steak. Then Tenny'd got zapped, and that was why I was here.

I'd accepted the job on the same condition that Tenny had: Red Ken and Dex would never be prosecuted, and they – we – would lose in the Isle of Man whatever cash was left. I had a document tucked away to prove it, signed by the prime minister himself. As I'd told Red Ken at the mall, I was looking out for them both. Mates have to cover each other's back, because no one else will. I just wished I'd done a better job of it.

My task had been simple: follow the gold, find out who handled it, find out what it bought and from whom. Then follow the weapons, drugs, trafficked women or whatever, and find out who planned to use them. Only then would the job be compromised – once Julian could be sure of hitting everybody in the chain. There'd be a terrorist connection somewhere along the line. This job had one for sure – it was just that Julian didn't know who, where, when or how.

Julian had been on Spag's case from the moment he'd come into the UK to recruit Red Ken, who had brought in Dex and Tenny. That was what the Security Service did: they protected the UK. Spag had been making hay while the war on terror's sun was shining. The problem was, since binning the CIA he'd been doing it for the wrong side. No one could claim he wasn't loyal: he'd had a long-running love affair with the greenback.

I'd been part of HMG's revised Counter-terrorism Strategy, CONTEST. It felt strange to be part of a strategy. Its four strands, known as the four Ps, were:

Pursue terrorists wherever they are and stop terrorist attacks;

Prevent people from becoming terrorists or supporting violent extremism;

Protect the UK by strengthening our defence against terrorism; and

Prepare to respond to an attack to lessen its impact.

The first P was where I came in.

Ginger left the room, still looking a bit perplexed. The last time the high-security cells at Paddington Green had played host to white faces, they'd had Irish accents.

With some Tesco's own tipped into the brew I could start getting the muddy liquid down my neck.

Julian sat there, watched and waited. I liked and trusted him, and you didn't get many of those to the pound. In all the dealings I'd had with him so far, he'd played it absolutely straight. He was the one who'd pushed for the MOU, the memorandum of understanding covering their immunity from prosecution. He might just have been an excellent conman who'd fuck me over like the rest of these people always had – but my instincts told me he was a good guy in a world full of bottom-feeders.

I knew what he was waiting for. 'It was a French-built Dassault Falcon. The reg was RF89702.'

He didn't have to write anything down. He had people to do that for him.

'I had to be careful not to piss off Spag or the lads by banging on and asking too much.' I took another sip. 'But, Jules, I saw a face.'

Go on.

I explained everything that had happened on the ground. I went through the whole job, finishing with the face at the cargo door and the shoot-out. I even came close to telling him that not all the gold had left the country, but something held me back. Maybe I sensed he didn't want to know. A man like Julian would always feel he had to do the right thing. The cash might be pissed against a wall via some MP's expense account, but he would have done his duty.

'How did the UAE ping us?'

'Spicciati was flagged up by their internal security. They don't have too many illusions about him. They pinged him playing golf with three Brits and came to us after finding out where you were staying.

'We've done a deal with them. They don't want any adverse publicity or talk of anti-terror operations within their borders. They still have no idea about the gold. They were supposed to lift all three of you so we could bring you back here for questioning. We hoped they wouldn't get you until after the gold had left the country. That would keep the UAE happy, while removing any potential problem and still keeping the operation covert.'

'You going to try and find the lads' bodies?'

He'd known Red Ken and Dex even less well than I knew Sherry, but I could tell he was genuinely upset about them. 'If the bodies were left at the strip they would have been found by now. Anything picked up by UAE will have been made to disappear. They don't want anything to dull their shine. But the guys who killed them probably took them in the aircraft for op sec. I'm afraid I don't think we'll ever see them again.'

'What about next of kin? How are you going to cover it?'

'The normal, I suppose: no knowledge of anything, and if the bodies show up the Foreign Office will put it down to criminal activity.' Julian got to his feet. 'Get yourself cleaned up and into your own clothes. I'll see if we can get the ball rolling for the Canadian couple. I'll be back soon.'

He got up but didn't turn for the door. 'Nick, I'm very sorry about Red and Dex. I know you all went way back.'

'Yep, we did, mate. Let's find these fuckers, yeah?'

147

41

Julian came back into the interview room about two hours later with a pile of blue folders under his arm. 'Nice work, Nick. Nice work.' He dropped them onto the table as he sat down. 'We know who owns the Falcon. Well, which country. It's the Federation.'

I tried not to laugh because he didn't. 'Captain Kirk at the wheel?'

I knew he meant Russia, but I was feeling a lot better now after my shit, shave, shower, and getting back into my own clothes – and, of course, after the full English in the police café upstairs. All my stuff had been packed and brought from the hotel room. My pink golfing shirt looked a bit out of place in the interrogation room, but not as much as Julian's suit and blue striped shirt with white collar and cuffs.

'At the helm, actually, I think you'll find.' He shoved the folder across to me. 'Space, the final frontier . . .'

I leafed through endless pictures of Middle Eastern males – posing, swimming, eating, alone and in family groups. 'I'm looking for the face, right?'

'Correct. We've tracked the Falcon to Tehran. So these—' he slammed his hand onto the folders '– these are Iranians who we believe have connections with the Russians. Russian arms trade, terrorism, you name it. Go through them, see what you come up with.'

He stood up and left.

There must have been a couple of hundred photographs, but it didn't take long to go through them. Just as well. Julian was back within thirty minutes with more. By then I had just a handful of pictures spread out in front of me and the rest were piled up on the table next to my empty coffee cup.

He sat down next to me.

I'd picked out a selection of faded black-and-whites of a man in his twenties with a full head of curly hair. The focus was fuzzy, but the clothes and winged American pimpmobile he was posing against pegged it to the seventies.

'You sure, Nick?'

I nodded. I'd never forget that face – proud cheekbones, a big Roman nose, and those eyes ... 'These must have been taken thirty years ago – I reckon he must be in his sixties now – but the eyes haven't changed. Yeah, this is almost certainly the man I saw ... how many nights ago?'

'You've been in transit two days.'

'So who is he?'

I looked up at the camera. 'Any chance of another brew?' I gave the universal gesture.

Julian stared down at our man. He tapped one of the pictures with a well-manicured finger. 'We don't know his name. We call him Altun. It's Farsi for "golden". Ironic, isn't it?'

'How do you lads come up with them?'

'I blame the computer – it just spews them out. The Americans are using the same codename.' He raised his bottle of Tesco's sparkling. 'Here's to the Special Relationship.

'This is the last known picture of him.' He tapped it with a fingernail. 'Taken in Tehran, just before the Islamic Revolution.'

The cell door opened and Ginger came in with two proper

mugs and a couple of mini-packets of ginger nuts. I was still in a good mood. 'Family recipe?'

He laughed. He was all right. I'd had a brew with him in the canteen over breakfast. He'd even apologized for giving my wrists the good news.

Julian wasn't one for distractions. 'He was a student when Khomeini took power in 'seventy-nine. He spent four years piecing together documents that the Shah had shredded before he fled. Imagine working on the world's biggest jigsaw puzzle, day after day.'

'So what's he doing now, on a Russian aircraft? Doesn't sound good, mate.'

Julian's jaw hardened as he opened one of his new folders. 'He's Iran's backroom negotiator. He makes the deals with the Taliban, Iraqi insurgents, Hezbollah – any extremist group that needs training, support, weapons. In fact, anyone Iran supports against the West.' He passed over the folder. 'We have a big problem, Nick. That aircraft is not just any Russian aircraft. It's Russian government – hence the RF marking. That would be bad enough, but worse still, the plane really belongs to M3C.'

'The rapper? He a mate of yours?'

The most recent folder was brimming with brochures. Like any other company on the planet with something to sell, Moscow Missile Manufacturing Complex didn't hold back on the glossy marketing bumph. The only difference was that M3C wasn't flogging shower units or timeshares by the Black Sea.

We sat there in silence. I was sure we were thinking the same thing. Had Saddam's doors been used as payment for some of this shit? If so, where was it going to end up, and who was going to be on the receiving end?

Julian grimaced. 'Scary thought, isn't it? Can you imagine a C-130 full of troops or an Apache getting shot down over Kandahar? Or missiles coming into this country, taking out commercial flights on their way into Heathrow? The good citizens of Putney won't be too pleased if a giant Airbus comes down their chimney.'

I dunked my ginger nut and gave it a munch. 'Not good, mate, not good. But I'm in north London. I don't think I'm on a flight path.'

He wasn't about to let himself be thrown off course. 'It's becoming increasingly obvious that the US cannot stabilize Afghanistan or Pakistan. This company's activities could result in a mountain of body bags. If domestic pressure made Obama pull out, China would close its borders with Pakistan and establish a Pak-Taliban pact. Iran would then pull out all the stops in Afghanistan, just as it has in Iraq. And nuclear India? They won't just stand by and watch. They'd be forced to take action against a nuclear Pakistan.'

He turned down my offer of a biccie. 'Then we all bunker down and wish we were born two hundred years ago.'

'You'd have been singing "Old Man River".'

I finally got a smile. 'While we're on the subject of slavery, I have a job for you. More CONTEST.'

I didn't reply, but I didn't have to.

'The Falcon landed in Tehran. There were no stopovers, so that's where the gold was taken. There's an arms fair starting there in three days, and M3C is an exhibitor. You're the only one who might be able to make a positive ID of our prime suspect. I want you to find this guy Altun and get me an up-to-date photograph. I want to know who he meets, where and why. Maybe then we can find out what's being sold and to whom.'

Julian went into smile overdrive. 'Today Paddington. Tomorrow Tehran. We'll finish my briefing here, then there's someone across town who needs your full attention.'

'Can't I go home first and get some real gear on?' I tugged at my polo shirt.

'Don't worry about it. Trinny and Susannah won't be there.'

151

42

DIS building, London
Sunday, 3 May
1430 hrs

We walked the three miles from Paddington Green to
Whitehall. After two days of incarceration, Julian thought I'd
want to stretch my legs. While we were at it, he briefed me on
the DIS and Squadron Leader Gavin Kettle.

According to their website, the mission of the Defence
Intelligence Staff was to provide 'timely intelligence products,
assessments and advice to the Ministry of Defence to guide
decisions on policy and commitment and employment of the
UK's armed forces, to inform defence procurement decisions
and to support military operations'. Alongside MI5, MI6 and
GCHQ, it went on, DIS also contributed to the UK's
threat assessment picture at any given time. Despite the
general cutbacks, the DIS still seemed to be relatively well
resourced.

'Just don't mention weapons of mass destruction,' Julian had
said. 'They still can't see the funny side of that particular load
of bollocks.'

If this man ever did make it to the top, the Queen could sleep easy in her bed at night. The security of her dominions would be in good hands.

'You ever had dealings with them?'

I shook my head. Not in ten years with the Regiment, or the same again as a deniable operator.

'Well, they have in excess of four thousand staff on their books. More than six hundred are threat analysts. They're good at what they do.'

Julian didn't spot the box that had been left a couple of feet inside Squadron Leader Kettle's doorway. He only stopped himself falling by shoulder-charging a filing cabinet. A couple of box files crashed to the floor, spilling old aircraft magazines across the well-worn carpet tiles.

I came in behind him. The office, without air-conditioning, smelt like a teenage boy's bedroom, right down to the lingering whiff of illegal nicotine.

A stern-faced man in his early forties knelt to pick up the mags with the reverence of the obsessive collector. He wore a check flannelette shirt and brown tie that reminded me of the bed sheets I used to have as a kid. A half-eaten prawn sandwich lay next to an old-fashioned light box on his desk. Strips of film were scattered across the backlit glass. I'd thought transparencies had gone out with the Ark. Timely intelligence products? Binning the 35mm and going digital would have been a good place to start.

The squadron leader finished gathering up his mags, then retrieved the upturned box and set it on his desk. Using both hands, he carefully removed something resembling a mirror, roughly the size of a jam-pot lid, attached to a random collection of cogs and springs from an ancient grandfather clock.

He held it up to the window and gave it the once-over.

Double-glazing muffled the rumble of traffic and squeals from the excited Italian teenagers we'd passed minutes earlier as they jumped over the lions at the bottom of Nelson's column and posed for each other's camera phones. The stone of the plinths matched the colour of Kettle's classic RAF handlebar moustache.

Thirty seconds had passed without any form of verbal or eye contact between us. Maybe the squadron leader wasn't too happy about being called into the office on a weekend.

Julian tried to break the ice. 'What's that thing?'

Kettle glanced up and peered at us both for the first time. 'That *thing* is the seeker-head of an AA-11 Archer – a Russian air-to-air missile.'

Julian was probably as unmoved as I was, but he was better at disguising it. 'I thought you were a surface-to-air specialist?'

Kettle thawed a little. 'I am. But during the nineties the Serbs adapted the AA-11 to fire from truck-mounted ground-launchers. It was surprisingly effective.' He glanced between the seeker-head and Julian's foot. 'Lucky the Russians built them to last, eh?'

I pointed at the light box. 'Holiday snaps?'

All Julian's good work was undone. Kettle put the seeker-head down and stared at me. 'You must be the chap who's taking my place.'

Once my MoE into Iran had been agreed, somebody senior would have told him the good news: after months of anticipation he wouldn't, after all, be going to Tehran; his place had been taken by someone else.

If Kettle was looking at me the way Dex had examined his plastic glass on the Emirates flight, it was with good reason. Julian had warned me that, for DIS specialists like him, field trips to events like IranEx were the culmination of years of mind-numbing analysis work that would have taken him no further than his office.

Kettle had built up a picture of what the Iranians were up to in the SAM (surface-to-air missile) weapons arena, increasingly vital with the current threat of first strikes by the US and the Israelis against Iranian nuclear facilities. He would have been aware that his meticulously crafted briefing documents on Iranian air defences were required reading within the Firm and the Ministry of Defence, occasionally even landing on a minister's desk. The IranEx trip would have been his reward – a once-in-a-lifetime opportunity now the Iranians, eager for press coverage of their indigenous weapons industry, had decided to throw their doors open to the international media.

Kettle's cover had been prepared long ago. He'd be travelling as a writer for a defence publication called *Aerospace and Defence Technology Monthly* – *ADTM* to those in the trade. His alias: James Manley, ex-RAF, divorced, and trying to make it in the notoriously badly paid world of freelance defence journalism. His passport was ready. His visa was ready. For several years he'd submitted articles under his assumed name to the wholly innocent editor of *ADTM*.

And at the moment he was all set to go – just as he was about to take the Labrador for a walk and pick up the Sundays – he'd had the phone call telling him to get into the office and brief someone who was going to fill his slot. After all that hard work he'd been mugged by some dickhead who didn't know SAM from Samantha and didn't even talk proper.

Julian looked at his watch. 'I'll leave you two to get to know each other. We don't have much time and you have quite a lot to talk about.' He paused by the door. 'Call me as soon as you're through and be as quick as you can. There's a lot more to do before tomorrow.'

Kettle turned and gave me a look like I'd just run over his dog.

43

'Listen, mate.'

There was nothing matey about his tone. The room temperature had dropped several degrees as soon as Julian closed the door. Fair one – in his shoes I'd have been pissed off too.

'There's nothing unusual about DIS posing as a freelance defence journalist. It happens all the time. The Russians know it happens. We know it happens. Bet you a penny to a pound, the Iranians know it happens, too. Defence exhibitions, no matter where they are, end up crawling with spooks. So, mate, whoever you are, at least you've got that going for you.'

Kettle had known better than to ask my name and I hadn't volunteered it. I still hadn't shaken his hand. The only good things were that I no longer noticed the smell and he hadn't offered me a bite of his sandwich.

'Right, so you want the one-oh-one on the fledgling Iranian missile industry so you can be James Manley, eh?' He looked at the clock on the wall. 'How long have we got?'

I hated briefings. And I hated government buildings – especially dust-filled places like this one. They brought back too many bad memories of too many bollockings. Besides, I just needed enough to make my cover story sound like I knew what I was on about. I was there for something more important than geeking up. I couldn't wait to get out.

'No more than two hours.'

Kettle went over to the filing cabinet and pulled open a drawer. He riffled through it, yanking out sheets of paper as he went. They turned out to be magazine articles.

'Take them with you. Don't worry, they're all open-source – some recent pieces from *Jane's Defence Weekly* and *Aviation Week* on the state of the Iranians' air defences. You can bone up on it at your leisure, but here's the short version. Don't make the mistake of dismissing them as a bunch of no-hope, clueless Islamofascist rag-heads – they're not. Since the Shah got deposed, they've built up an incredibly successful aerospace and defence industry. It's in their blood. They've had to, given all the arms embargoes that have been imposed upon them over the years.'

I glanced at the articles. From everything I'd read, the embargoes had proved about as useful as an ashtray on a motorbike. 'They've been getting technical assistance from everyone on Baby Bush's axis-of-evil list, haven't they?'

Kettle shut one drawer and opened another. 'Plus some that aren't even on the list yet. But then again, necessity is the mother of invention.'

'So what invention shit have they been up to?'

'No need for that.' He clearly wasn't a big fan of profanity. Maybe it was because it was Sunday. He threw some more homework my way. 'Take their air-defence network. It's a mish-mash of old Soviet stuff and missiles that the Americans abandoned when the Shah left in a hurry. The Iranians have watched and learnt. They've not only reverse-engineered spare parts but, where necessary, they've improved upon the actual hardware. For the past decade or two, this has been sufficient to ward off any threats they might face, but with the Israelis and the Americans back in sabre-rattling mode, they need something a little more effective. Which is where

157

IranEx enters the equation. Or would have. For me, I mean.'

Kettle gathered a few more articles into an envelope, scrawled 'Russia' across it, and chucked it onto his desk. 'Technology transfer between Russia and Iran has been particularly active – albeit at a covert level. In 1998, UN sanctions were issued against a number of Russian organizations – state research facilities as well as companies – that had supplied technical expertise to Iran's ballistic-missile effort. Not unnaturally, that's where most of the world's attention has been focused. After all, it's the ballistic missiles that will carry the weapons of mass destruction, nuclear and otherwise, that threaten the West. But we know that Russian co-operation with the Iranian state weapons industry goes way beyond that.'

I had a long night ahead of me. 'What do you know about M3C?'

'Moscow Missile Manufacturing Complex. They Anglicized it to M3C. Less of a mouthful on the international circuit, where they compete against the big boys from the US and Europe. M3C used to be three different Soviet-era weapons entities until somebody, somewhere, read a book on market economics and decided it was better to lump all Russia's missile expertise under one roof, like every other country does.

'M3C make everything from anti-tank missiles to space launch vehicles. The way they read the rules, there's nothing wrong with lending assistance to the Iranians as long as it's for defensive purposes or ends up in space. That's not exactly how I'd interpret the rules of the Missile Technology Control Regime, but in Putin's Russia, nobody much seems to care as long as it brings in the bacon – and, trust me, when it comes to hard cash, the Iranians have petro-dollars aplenty to splash about. Have you ever been to a defence exhibition?'

I shook my head, although that wasn't exactly true – I'd once been to the British Army Equipment Exhibition during my time in the Regiment, but I couldn't be arsed to explain. I just wanted him to keep waffling.

'There are a number of elements to any exhibition that are important to journalists. The first is the press centre. Every major defence exhibition has a place set aside for the media, a place the hacks can go to file their stories, meet up and grab a beer.' He laughed. 'Although that clearly won't be an option in Iran.

'The press centre will keep you informed as to whether there are any announcements that day and whether the major news conferences are due to be held in the dedicated conference centre or in one of the chalets of the exhibiting companies.'

'Chalets?' He made it sound like a ski resort.

'An exhibition area is divided into exhibition space, usually in covered areas, where the companies show off their hardware, and chalet areas where their execs do all their hobnobbing.'

'So what are the magic words to get you in?'

'I'm sure Iranian Revolutionary Guards will be on hand to ensure that hacks don't wander where they're not supposed to. But in a Western defence exhibition – Farnborough or Paris or IDEX – they let accredited media into the chalet area. The big companies like to keep the press onside. I don't know how it will be in Iran. You'll just have to play it by ear.'

He glanced at the Russian missile seeker that was now sitting on his desk like some bizarre executive toy.

I followed his gaze. 'You nick that?'

Kettle smiled for the first time. 'Let's just say there's a Russian exhibitions manager who's probably still in the *gulag*, or wherever Russians keep their miscreants these days. Anybody could have nicked anything at that particular show – Farnborough 'ninety-two. It just happened to be me.'

'I hope it was worth it.'

'Certainly was. We hadn't seen this particular variant of the seeker-head before. That's why defence exhibitions are such good value.' He looked at me earnestly. 'I have no idea why you're going in and it's none of my business. I just hope that it's – as you say – worth it.' He looked at the clock. We were out of time. I picked up the envelope and the other material he'd selected for me and headed for the door.

'One other thing . . .'

I turned to see him playing with the seeker-head.

'The new SA-16M. Read about it in your notes. The missile's seeker has some kind of fault. It's important that we know what it is, and what they're doing to correct it. That was my sole reason for going to IranEx. Any information you can find about the 16M is vitally important to DIS.'

The moment I closed the door behind me I pictured him grabbing his Nick Stone voodoo doll from the filing cabinet and jabbing its bollocks with pins.

44

Monday, 4 May
1039 hrs

As the Galaxy people-carrier sped west along the A4 by the Chiswick flyover, I gazed out at the high-rise office construction projects stalled by the credit crunch and wondered how the skyline would look in Tehran.

Julian had handed over all the supporting documentation I'd need – passport and business cards in the name of James Manley, a letter of commission from the editor of *ADTM*, a media visa from the Iranian embassy – and I'd been boning up all night on the country pack and more int on Altun. Sitting next to me, his eyes closed, Julian seemed to be doing some quiet reflection of his own.

The traffic bunched on the Heathrow spur road. I reached down for Kettle's envelope. I'd have a couple of hours at the airport and a good few more *en route* to Tehran, but I had a lifetime of plane-spotting to catch up on.

I pulled out a clutch of papers marked 'Technology' in the squadron leader's spidery handwriting. There was a note attached with a paperclip to some cuttings on an advanced handheld missile.

161

Mate, Anything the Iranians are publishing on the SA-16M is of interest to us. Get whatever you can lay your hands on in the way of brochures and leaflets. Take as many photographs as they'll let you, and a few more if you can. We can never use enough imagery in this place.

M stands for 'modification' in Russian. We know that M3C has developed this missile, but very little information has been released about the improvements. We need to know if the malfunction rumours carry any weight. Get whatever you can; nothing is wasted. And good luck.

I started laughing to myself and Julian opened his eyes. 'What?'

'Kettle's given me some homework.' I handed him the note. If it was going to self-destruct in five seconds I didn't want to be the one holding it.

'Not such a bad idea. Having something to do – something legitimate, I mean – will help you blend in.'

He wasn't wrong. The more I looked like I belonged, the better.

The Galaxy pulled up outside Terminal 3. It was less than a week since I'd been here with Red Ken and Dex. At least this time I wasn't in golfing pink. It was back to Timberlands, jeans and shirt. I'd left all my cover golfing clothes and the cheap and cheerful Tesco's funeral outfit – to down-gear me in the doing-well stakes – in a bin liner outside my local Oxfam.

I pulled my holdall from the boot, and the day-sack containing my Nikon, laptop and briefing notes.

Julian held out his hand.

It was the first time I'd ever shaken any of my bosses by the hand and meant it. They normally coerced me into this shit. But this time? I wanted to go.

'Will you recognize him again?'

'With my mates' blood still wet on his shoes? He could have body doubles, plastic surgery or spent the last few days shoving Mars bars down his neck to become a fat fuck, but nothing will disguise his eyes, Jules. That's what'll tell me I've got him.'

I didn't tell him that for me this wasn't just about taking Altun's picture and sharpening up his CV. But I didn't think he'd be particularly surprised. I headed into the terminal.

I'd put on the jokey fucking-about act for Julian's benefit because I didn't want him to stand me down from the job. I wanted him to use me. I wanted him to think that I was being practical about the situation.

Truth was, there was a bit more to this than revenge. I needed to square away my guilt. I couldn't help feeling that I should have done more for Red Ken and Dex. Maybe I could have tried harder to talk them out of it. Maybe I could have been closer to them on the airstrip. That way, I might have reacted quicker. I knew the two of them would have called me a dickhead for thinking it, but they would also have understood.

They would also have expected me to get payback, and I wouldn't let them down.

The terminal was its normal over-packed nightmare. I dodged the trolleys and manic wheelie-case runners as late passengers ran for their gates.

I wasn't going to stitch up Julian. Why would I do that to the only friend I now had? I allowed myself a rueful smile. I must be going soft. Friendship was an accolade I didn't hand out easily. Especially when I'd only known someone a few weeks.

I'd do what he wanted because there was stuff there that he needed to know. But after that I'd kill as many of the fuckers as I could get my hands on. I knew that wasn't going to save the world but it would make me – and, if they were still keeping an eye on things, Red Ken and Dex – feel a whole lot better.

45

We hit some turbulence as we crossed the Persian Gulf, some rough stuff that toppled the Iranian businessman in the seat next to me headlong into my lap and prompted the lads in the row behind us to grab their Korans and start asking the all-merciful one to give the pilot a helping hand.

I manhandled the Iranian back into his all-too-narrow economy-class seat and got busy with Kettle's crib-sheets – as you do when you're off to work not knowing anything about the subject.

I knew all too well that if the Revolutionary Guards really wanted to grill me on what I ought to know after five years as a defence journalist, I'd be seriously in the shit – unless they were prepared to let me ask the audience or, better still, phone a friend.

The Iranian nuclear issue had demonstrated just how keen they were to stand on their own two feet and trade punches with the big boys. The list of countries suspected of helping Tehran with its reactors, enrichment sites and isotope separation plants was a long one. There wasn't much point in building a nuclear bomb if you didn't have the means to deliver it and the mullahs had been hard at work on that front too.

In 1985, they'd secretly funded North Korea to develop a long-range version of the Scud missile that Saddam had fired at Tel Aviv during the 1991 Gulf War. In exchange for the cash, North Korea gave Iran full access to the technology. Iran had had a long-range version of the Scud by the early nineties, but they had needed something even bigger. By 1998, with a lot of help from the Russians, the North Koreans and some key pieces of Chinese kit, they'd had the Shahab-3, capable of lobbing a 1,000-kilo warhead 1,300 kilometres – far enough not only to hit Israel but also Ankara, capital of NATO-aligned Turkey.

In spite of UN sanctions against companies in Russia, China and North Korea, the missile-building technology had continued to flow into Iran. By 2008, the Shahab-3's range had increased to 2,000 kilometres, enough to threaten much of southern Europe. As Kettle had said, when it came to developing hardware, these guys had it in their blood. They weren't just a bunch of goatherds who'd wandered out of the desert.

What the Iranians had achieved with their nuclear- and ballistic-missile programmes they'd repeated across other parts of their defence industry. The US had even given them a helping hand. In 1985, Oliver North had hopped on a plane to Tehran and cut a covert deal to supply spare parts for Iranian HAWK and TOW missile systems via Israeli intermediaries in return for a good few suitcases full of readies and the release of US hostages in Lebanon. The cash helped fund another illegal CIA operation – against the Sandinista government of Nicaragua. The Iran-Contra scandal worked its way into the press the following year. If Julian's intel was right, it was what had given Altun his first taste of international power and money-broking. He'd been one of the young bloods in the background, learning everything he could – not only from his Iranian bosses, but from the Pentagon as well.

Once the Iranians had worked out how to build spare parts for their inventory of US fighter jets and missiles, they'd then set about creating their own platforms. Within the past five years they'd unveiled their own domestically produced combat aircraft, helicopters, tanks and submarines. These lads really were the region's superpower.

I glanced at the guy now slobbering away happily in the next-door seat, and tried to square what I saw with what I read. I decided that whatever shortcomings he might have on the etiquette front, these people were on a roll.

I picked up the M3C file again and started to leaf through it.

The conglomerate's breadth of capabilities was huge. It was literally a one-stop shop for any weapon you could think of.

In 1991, with the collapse of the Soviet Union, Russia's state-owned weapons industry had been made up of multiple companies, many of which were competing against each other for the same business at home and abroad. This state of affairs clearly made no sense at all, but had continued – for almost two decades – until a couple of years ago when an ex-KGB oligarch who'd developed interests right across the sector had persuaded his government to put the nation's entire missile industry under one roof. His roof, naturally.

Even the Russian state media, which almost always toed the party line, had cried foul. Not that it had made any difference. Every oligarch knew his continued wellbeing depended on two things: where he happened to be sitting when the Soviet Union reverted to good old Mother Russia; and who he happened to know in the corridors of power.

Like most of his oligarch mates, this particular boy had been in the right place at the right time in 1991 – so much so that after the initial flurry of interest in the deal, the Russian media gave him and his business projects a wide berth. There wasn't even a name check or picture of him.

M3C had offices in Moscow and production facilities along the river Volga between Moscow and Rybinsk. It also had its own weapons proving ground, a closed-off area inside a military training ground the size of Wales, to the east of a place called Vologda, about five hundred K to the north-east.

My next-door neighbour started to fart like a trooper. I reached up and adjusted the air-conditioner.

PART FIVE

46

The Airbus's first encounter with the Imam Khomeini International Airport runway wasn't its last – it continued to bounce for several hundred metres before the pilot slammed on the reverse thrust. The fun and games were all lost on my neighbour. He jolted awake with a final snort, shot to his feet before the plane had even turned off the runway and started rummaging around in the overhead locker.

I stared out of the window. The Imam Khomeini International Airport had been built to commemorate the mastermind of 1979's Islamic Revolution. The blurb in the seat pocket in front of me said it had opened officially in May 2004 and was designed to take over from Mehrabad as Tehran's main airport for foreign air travel. Mehrabad, in the meantime, had been designated as Tehran's principal domestic airport. Gripping stuff. Kettle would have been on the edge of his seat.

From my brief sweep of our surroundings as the plane trundled along the taxiway it was clear that IKIA was only half finished, whatever it said on the tin. Much of it was still a building site. Diggers tore along the perimeter fence, sending up clouds of dust behind them. Men with hod-loads of bricks over their shoulders stared at the plane as it bumped past them. The skeletons of half-completed buildings rose from the dirt on either side of the runway.

Beyond the fence, I could see nothing but scrub and rubble. Nobody was ever going to contest the building of another runway here; it might only have been twenty miles south of Tehran, but in reality it was in the middle of nowhere.

In the distance, half hidden by shit kicked up by the construction work, were rows of military transport aircraft – a hallmark of the developing-world welcome. There, among them, parked in front of a modern, single-storey building, was a gleaming white Dassault Falcon 7X.

As soon as the aircraft rocked to a stop, everybody sprang to their feet to follow the example of my farting friend, who was already elbowing his way down the aisle and powering up his mobile. I waited until the plane was three-quarters empty before I got out of my seat and pulled down my day-sack.

As soon as I stepped off the jetway into the terminal I could see big brother was watching me. There were CCTV cameras everywhere. I tucked behind a group of passengers from my flight and scanned the faces coming the other way. All I got back was a shed-load of gawping from suspicious-looking Iranians. I hadn't seen a Westerner since we'd stopped off at Dubai.

The inside of the terminal was as modern as anything I'd ever been in. My Timberlands squeaked on the polished marble as I followed the signs in Farsi and English to Immigration.

The military presence was low-key until I got to Passport Control. Iranians and Arabs were directed one way; I was sent the other. I followed a roped-off walkway until eventually I ended up facing a stern-looking woman in her twenties seated in a glass booth. It was flanked by two AKs, each with a green-uniformed squaddie firmly attached. I glanced over my shoulder. The welcome was exclusively for me. I knew the best way to deal with situations like this was to look intimidated. People in booths like to wield power over others. It makes them feel good.

172

The woman adjusted the arms of her thick black specs beneath her thick black head covering and beckoned me towards her. 'Passport.'

I handed it over. Now I was closer I could see her face was more Cindy Crawford than Ugly Betty. She had smooth skin, a small, slightly upturned nose, and gleaming white, perfectly uniform teeth. She looked so perfect she could have been chiselled. And, coming from Tehran, she might very well have been. More plastic-surgery and sex-change operations were performed here than in LA or Bangkok – another useless nugget I'd picked up among the stuff I'd learnt last night from Julian's int pack.

She looked up from my passport. No smile, just disdain. 'Your business, Mr Manley?'

First trick question. She was already holding my passport: the London media visa stated exactly what I was here for.

'I'm here for IranEx – the aerospace and defence exhibition. I'm a journalist.'

She seemed to take it in her stride. She slid the passport under a scanner and stared into space while her computer crunched away at the data.

The two AK-holders glared at me as if I was George W himself. But that was OK: they got as much bullshit fed to them about us as we did about them. I just carried on playing dumb, not getting too smart, and looking a little bit scared.

Bang, bang.

I glanced down. She was stamping my passport.

'Enjoy your stay in the Islamic Republic. Now I need your fingerprints.' She pointed to a small box covered with a green rag. They used the same system in the US: place a finger on the glass tray and she'd take a picture. The only difference here was the absence of wipes, just the same bit of rag for everyone.

47

Like Iran's defence industry, my little light reading in Tufnell Park last night had told me, its internal security apparatus shouldn't be underestimated. Not much was known about Tehran's counter-intelligence set-up, but what was, wasn't good. No single organization appeared to have complete control. That was good to hear: it meant there were gaps in the system. The problem was, I didn't know where the gaps were.

There were three groups I had to worry about. The first was MoIS, the Ministry of Intelligence and Security, or Vevak, as it was known in Farsi. It had around fifteen thousand full-time members all doing their meanest for the Republic. It had lost some of its powers in the 1990s following a scandal in which a truckload of Iranian dissidents, mainly Sunni Kurds, had ended up very dead – a fact that made even the lapdog Iranian press sit up and complain. Perhaps it had occurred to them that they might be next in the queue. To show it was still on the side of the people, the Iranian government drummed up some charges against what it called 'rogue elements' in Vevak and, after some ritual bloodletting, everybody went away happy. Except the rogue elements. They'd ended up facing Mecca, but six feet under.

In the meantime, the power of the second mob, the Iranian

Revolutionary Guards Corps Intelligence Branch, had increased. Much smaller than Vevak, the IRGC Intelligence Branch were fearsome in their loyalty to the state – they were the Iranian equivalent of the Gestapo, in effect, and swore death to the enemies of the Islamic Revolution. I decided to try to give them a wide berth.

Then there was the Basij Resistance Force, a volunteer army of around a million people, mostly old men, who had volunteered after completing their military service, or others too young to join the army. A bit like the Hitler Youth, I supposed.

The Basij had a history of martyr-style suicide attacks dating back to the Iran–Iraq war, which had claimed a million lives on both sides during the 1980s. These lads were the ultimate guided weapon. They'd run across enemy minefields to clear them, or load up with explosives and detonate themselves on top of an Iraqi tank or trench.

Like the Stasi in East Germany, the Basij were also the 'eyes and ears' of the revolution. Put a foot wrong or badmouth the government and, chances were, someone, somewhere would tell the Basij. The next thing you knew, the lynch mob would be at your door.

The police force comprised around forty thousand regulars under the control of the Ministry of the Interior, but compared to Vevak, the IRGC and the Basij, these guys were pushovers. And even though the mullahs appeared to view women with complete contempt, it didn't stop them recruiting tens of thousands into the ranks of the secret police.

I wondered where Ms Perfect fitted into this picture. Perhaps the Tourist Board corps.

My bag was the only one left on the carousel by the time I reached the baggage hall. It didn't look as if it had been tampered with, but of course it had. Otherwise they would have let me take it on board as hand luggage, as I'd planned to.

I walked out into the arrivals hall and spotted a tall guy in

175

his early thirties, in a very shiny black leather jacket, holding up a placard. He had a neatly groomed goatee and was so thin his Adam's apple looked as though it was fighting to get out of his neck. A pair of round, wire-framed glasses perched on the end of his incongruously bulbous nose. The scrawl on the placard read: 'Jame Munley – travel from Dubai'.

48

Majid Forsheh was from the Ministry of Information. He'd been assigned to me at the personal behest of the minister, he proudly informed me, to attend to my every need for the duration of my stay in the Islamic Republic.

One look at Majid, with his white shirt buttoned all the way up and no tie – an evil Western invention – told me he wasn't just here to help me on and off the buses. Everything about him reeked of security. But what had I expected? If it was an open secret that defence exhibitions were crawling with spooks, then it was a foregone conclusion that I was going to get a minder. But that was OK, because I had no choice. Getting what Julian wanted – and, more importantly, what I wanted – was what I was here for. I'd just have to work around him.

Majid insisted on carrying my case as we walked to his car. 'Did you have a pleasant trip, Mr Munley?'

'Why don't you call me Jim?' I gave him a five-hundred-watt smile. 'Fantastic, mate. Great passengers, good food and first-rate in-flight entertainment. I'll never be touching British Airways again.'

Majid beamed like a lottery winner. 'And what do you think of our new Imam Khomeini International Airport?'

'I think the Ayatollah would have approved. Beats our Terminal Five hands down.'

'Yes, it is most impressive, is it not, Mr Munley?'

We'd established, then, that Majid didn't do sarcasm – and that he didn't like the name Jim. Maybe I should have kept it more formal.

We stopped by a Mercedes E-class that had pulled over in a bus lane. A guy in a short-sleeved white shirt – buttoned up, of course – had been pretending to read a newspaper as he sat behind the wheel. He awoke with a start when Majid sprang the boot and shot out to help with my bags long after the moment had passed. He was in his sixties and balding, but had forearms the size of logs and shoulder muscles that rippled under his shirt. Wrestling was a big thing here, and this old boy looked like he could still go a few rounds.

Majid sat in the passenger seat. I got in the back. The airport's public-address system called the faithful to prayer just as the sun began to set over the distant mountains.

'I expect you are tired, Mr Munley, so we will go straight to your hotel. You are booked into the Bandar, are you not? Three stars. A very nice hotel, very central. Your people chose well.' I caught his smile in the rear-view mirror. 'This is your first time in Iran?'

My first time, I acknowledged. But on the basis of what I'd seen so far, it certainly wouldn't be my last.

He turned around and shook my hand. 'Then welcome. I hope you will enjoy your stay here very much.'

The wrestler pulled out of the bus lane and almost ran into a taxi. There was a screech of brakes and a sudden whiff of bubbling rubber, then an angry exchange between the two drivers. But one glance at Majid and the other guy got right back into his box.

That told me just about everything I needed to know. I'd been placed very firmly in the tender loving care of the IRGC's Intelligence Branch.

49

'The one and only difficulty with our new airport, Mr Munley, is its distance from the city centre. It will take us more than an hour to reach the hotel. No doubt you have heard about our traffic, Mr Munley.'

And the pollution, I felt like telling him, but thought better of it. Not that Majid took my silence as an invitation to shut up. I was getting the full Thomas Cook treatment.

'Fortunately, we have a very good modern metro system. There are three different types of taxi, too. The yellow metered ones are best. There are also white non-metered taxis that ply certain routes, almost like a bus. And then there are private cars run as taxis, mostly by people in their spare time to supplement their income . . .'

He waved a hand theatrically. 'But you don't need to worry about any of this, Mr Munley, because for as long as you are here you are our guest and all your travel needs will be taken care of. The driver and I will pick you up at your hotel in the morning, I will be your escort at IranEx, and if you have any desire to see our city, then we will be only too happy to take you anywhere you please. My government wants your stay in Iran to be a memorable one.'

'That's great, Majid, thank you.'

These lads are OK, nine times out of ten. They're very much like me in a way, victims of circumstance. Most think differently from what they say about the place they live because they have to live there. Most just toe the line and try to get by as best they can. The nutters who believe all the bullshit can normally be sniffed out very quickly. And even they eventually get to realize it's all bollocks, no matter what side you're on.

'It is important to us that you see Iran in its true light. As a man of words, Mr Munley, I am sure you will already know that Iran is not the place it is characterized to be by certain sections of the West's media. We are an open, democratic society and our only interest is in fostering peace.'

Try telling that, I thought, to the relatives of almost a hundred dissidents killed by Iranian assassins outside Iran in the thirty years since the revolution – or of the victims of the two hundred or so terrorist attacks around the world that had supposedly been given the backing of Altun and his mates.

Shia militias had been supplied by Iran, via Altun, with highly advanced IED technology, specifically to target our troops in southern Iraq. Missile technology was supplied on a regular basis to Hamas and Hezbollah. The list was endless. The missiles for Hamas and Hezbollah were aimed at Israel, even though there were tens of thousands of Iranian Jews, some of whom were in the Iranian parliament. They saw Israel as Zionist, not Jewish.

I treated Majid to another broad smile and turned my head towards the window. That's just the way it is. If this lot weren't the bad guys, then someone else would be. And I wasn't looking for a cuddle.

We left the airport approach and drove past a hotel decorated with dozens of flags, not one of which I recognized. As we joined the newly tarmacked road for Tehran, I noticed some bodies standing on the roof of a brand-new multi-storey car park at the airport perimeter. They looked like soldiers or police, some kind of security presence. One was wearing a peaked cap.

There were three of them. The one with the cap had what looked like a radio pressed to his ear. Another was talking into a mobile phone, and the third was using binoculars to scan the runway.

Majid followed my gaze and shook his head. 'Do you have these people in your country, Mr Munley?'

'Sure. We have security everywhere. Brits are the most spied-on citizens in the world.'

The corners of Majid's eyes creased in confusion. He looked almost hurt. 'Mr Munley, I am not talking about surveillance. The people on this roof are interested in the aircraft that take off and land from this airport. It is their – how do you say? Their hobby?'

50

We hit the traffic in the southern suburbs and ground to a complete standstill. With petrol at about 5p a gallon, why would anyone bother to walk?

The road signs were in Farsi and English, and everywhere I looked I saw Paykans – the Iranian-built copy of the Hillman Hunter, a car that went out of production in Britain forty years ago. My dad used to have one when I was a kid. They only stopped making these things here in 2005. Not a moment too soon, judging by the shit coming out of their exhaust and adding to the thick smog. They looked like dustbins on wheels alongside the brand-new Renaults, Volvos, VWs and all the latest Japanese models on display.

As we trickled along, Tehran became more and more of a contradiction. One moment we were passing modern glass-and-steel office blocks that could have come straight from Dubai, the next I was staring into decrepit alleyways or at water-streaked concrete tenements that could have been designed by Stalin. And ten seconds later I could almost have been back in the Mall of the Emirates. Posters for Levis, iPods and Sanyo TVs were everywhere. Britney and Hannah Montana filled CD-shop windows.

Fast-food outlets sold Thai and Chinese on plastic trays.

Young men wore Western clothes and shared hookahs at outdoor restaurants. Outsiders might have expected angry crowds ready to stone any woman who showed a bit of ankle, but I saw plenty with their headscarves pushed back – a trick that must have kept them within the rules laid down by the ayatollahs, but only just.

If I was ever in any doubt about exactly where I was, the giant murals of Iran's leaders, past and present, were constantly there to remind me. Top of the pops was Khomeini, whose face scowled back at me from the sides of buildings in every square we inched through. Next in the popularity stakes was the present Supreme Leader, Ayatollah Khamenei, and behind him the president, Ahmadinejad – the lad who had made windcheaters the must-have clothing item in this neck of the woods, and who'd threatened to wipe Israel and the West right off the map. The only way I remembered his name was by pronouncing it 'Armoured-dinner-jacket', but I didn't tell Majid.

'You like what you see, Mr Munley?'

'It's different.'

'Oh? I have never been to London. Tell me.'

'You don't see murals of Margaret Thatcher or Tony Blair on the sides of buildings in London – but nobody liked them very much.'

Majid laughed.

We passed a billboard that displayed an evil-looking Bush, blood running from his pointed teeth. '*Marg bar amrika*,' it said. I knew that one: 'Death to America'.

Majid felt the need to explain. 'You have to remember that in Iran our president answers directly to our Supreme Leader and the Supreme Leader is God's chosen representative – a descendant of the Prophet Muhammad, peace be upon him. We note with amusement that it is Mr Ahmadinejad, our elected president, who receives a most unfavourable press in the West, but what your colleagues appear to forget,

Mr Munley, is that it is the Supreme Leader who wields all the power. And the Supreme Leader, our spiritual guide, is given his mandate by God . . .'

There were also lots of posters in shop windows and pasted on walls showing the two main faces fighting the presidential election in June. Hard-liner Armoured-dinner-jacket and the reformist and former prime minister Mousavi. I'd lay money on who Majid was going to vote for.

Almost two hours after we left the airport, we finally arrived at a hotel that seemed to offer the best of both worlds – a tall glass-and-concrete number that looked like Stalin had designed it after a night on the piss at the Burj Al-Arab.

Majid handed me his business card and told me to call him if I had any problems. 'Day or night, Mr Munley. I am here to help. May I suggest that you do not walk around the city? This is a free country, but Tehran has its darker side, like all capital cities, and the traffic can be dangerous. By now you will know that it can come at you from any direction. If you would like to go anywhere, see anything of our great city, Mr Munley, the driver and I will take you. It would be our pleasure. And please, Mr Munley, always have your passport with you at all times. For your own safety, you understand.'

As we walked towards the lobby, Majid pointed down the street to a busy junction. 'We are on Mofateh Street. The big road that crosses it there is Taleqani Avenue. The Alborz Mountains – the range you saw as we drove in, and will see from your room – lie to the north of the city.'

He smiled again and this time I noticed a row of chipped white teeth. 'Mr Munley, you have me as your guide. As I say, you can call me day or night. No problem too large or too small.' He pointed to the card he'd given me. 'What time do you want to arrive at the exhibition?'

'How about as soon as it opens? I always like to be one of the first. Get to know the ground, that sort of thing.'

'The exhibition centre is some way to the north. I will be here at six thirty. We have to allow for the traffic. Do you need any help checking in?'

'No, you're all right, mate. I'll be fine.'

I bent down to get a view of the driver and gave him a wave. 'See you later, mate.'

51

My room was on the seventh floor. It wasn't much bigger than my cell at Paddington Green and stank of old cigarettes, but there was no point asking them to change from the one Majid had picked for me. How else would he have known what I could see from my window?

All the foreigners' rooms would be crawling with surveillance devices. Even looking for the mikes and their transmitters would flag up things about me I didn't want them to know. After all, I was just a geek journalist.

The view from the window made up for everything. I moved the plastic garden chair and got comfortable. Set between high-rise hotels and office buildings I picked out the spindly outline of the Milad Tower, the fourth tallest in the world, Majid had told me with some excitement, and the glowing minarets and dome of Khomeini's shrine, another landmark he had proudly pointed out to me on the drive in.

I wondered what Altun was doing right now. Something more interesting than counting cars and minarets, I was sure. If his picture was anything to go by, he'd followed the Shah's example and embraced all the trappings of the American Dream. Come the revolution, he'd slipped seamlessly into the new way of life. Maybe he was like the

KGB guys before the Wall had come down, just someone who saw what was coming and adapted to make the best of it.

From then on, Julian reckoned, he'd been climbing the greasy pole. First as a back-room boy during the Iran-Contra scandal. He was still a back-room boy, by the sound of it, but one who'd helped Armoured-dinner-jacket into power – and was still the main broker when it came to deals between Iran and anyone who had a beef with the West. I bet that made him a very busy man.

The trouble was, Julian had no information on where he might be. It was reasonable to assume he still lived in the city, but that wasn't going to help me get a cab to his place.

There was no getting away from the fact that this city was the capital of the most powerful and stable country in the Middle East. The lads buzzing about in their cars below me knew it wasn't called the Persian Gulf for nothing. They were busy riding the Islamic fundamentalist wave and wiping out the last vestiges of a secular Middle East.

They weren't doing the mad-mullah thing, though. They were cleverer than that. Armoured-dinner-jacket and his pals pursued Iran's interests coldly, rationally and methodically. They were fighting an asymmetric war. Why take on the West militarily when they'd lose? Better to back a bunch of other nutters and let them do the fighting.

Everything boiled down to one central objective: clearing out the old Sunni order, the foundation stone of American interests in the Middle East. With Saddam – a Sunni – gone, they had a very friendly Shia government in Baghdad. They were backing the Taliban in Afghanistan and Pakistan, both Sunni power bases. How long could they last? The Af-Pak situation was a nightmare, and a fight Obama might very well lose. Then there was US-friendly Saudi Arabia with a Sunni royal family to sort out – and Altun tucked away in the shadows, keeping the pot on the boil by supplying weapons

187

and the means to fight the *jihad* without Iran having to commit a single soldier.

I turned my back on the view and started to sort myself out.

There was a single bed, a fridge containing a jug of iced water, a wardrobe, a phone, a table and two plastic chairs. There was also a Koran, a prayer mat and slippers, and an old twelve-inch TV. A notice on the table in English and Farsi proudly announced that the Bandar Hotel had 'why-fi'. The motel we'd stayed at in Dubai had had nothing on the Bandar.

The TV was even older than I'd thought. It didn't have a remote. I hit the 'on' button. It took an age to warm up. As the speaker mushed away, I slung my clothes into the cupboard.

I pulled the laptop out onto the bed and fired it up as the TV behind me finally swung into gear. A slightly fuzzy Oprah was talking to a big-haired woman about losing her home in the recession. I pushed the channel button to see David Hasselhoff saving the world in fluent Farsi and Columbo tripping up yet another bad guy who was too clever for his own good. I didn't bother trying to find the BBC Persian channel. Aimed at the hundred million Persian speakers in Iran, Afghanistan and Tajikistan, it was sponsored by our Foreign and Commonwealth Office – so it wasn't top of the pops in a government-approved hotel.

This place really was a mosaic. They watched our films and TV, and listened to our music. They wore our clothes and ate burgers. But they had no problem strapping on an explosive vest and taking on a tank or foot patrol. Not because Allah wanted them to, but because it was seen as the only way to win. One thing was certain: we needed to sort our shit out and prepare for what might be coming our way.

Everything on the laptop Julian had provided was seriously geeked up for Jim Manley's world. There were articles penned by Manley for a whole string of defence journals, email correspondence with his ex-wife about how the property was going to be sold and the cash divvied up.

188

The system's history was everything you'd expect it to be. I flicked through email traffic with editors, public-relations consultants, sources within Britain's defence industry, even plane-spotters.

Plane-spotters.

The guys on the roof of the multi-storey.

I wondered.

I logged on to the hotel's free why-fi network. These lads had taken to technology obsessively, just like us. Farsi is the most common language on the Internet after English and Mandarin Chinese. Armoured-dinner-jacket even wrote his own blog.

The grindingly slow speed made me feel right at home. Access details eventually came up on my screen. I tapped 'aircraft enthusiasts', 'plane-spotters' and 'Iran' into the search-engine and hit 'enter'. This would have been Manley's porn channel for the night. Up popped a website called www.iranianmetalbird.net. Magic. The little fuckers got everywhere, even in a dictatorship. Though the West was poring over every aspect of Iran's infrastructure, the mullahs hadn't thought to shut the Internet door.

The website tracked civil and military aircraft that had taken off and landed at most of Iran's major airports, and was bursting with photos – lots of photos. I didn't expect to see Altun waving at the camera, but I clearly had a long night ahead of me.

I started by doing what Jim Manley would do pretty much as soon as he arrived. I sent an email to my editor, telling him that I was in the city and going to work tomorrow. I added a note about my new best mate Majid and what a nice, helpful guy he was. Someone in a Tehran basement would be poring over this any minute now, and I wanted to give those lads something to smile about.

I went back to plane-spotting at IKIA as Oprah put the world to rights.

The first clutch of pictures was of C-130s departing IKIA, and a Chinese copy of the MiG-21 landing at Mehrabad. There was even an email address for the guy who'd taken this last one and posted his comments – in English: 'A Chengdu F-7M used for training flights, tail number 3-7714, taking off from Mehrabad Airport. For more information contact Ali on ali@iranianmetalbird.net'.

There was a knock on the door.

'Mr Munley?'

I pulled back the bolts and found myself staring at the unblinking eyes of my new best mate. Maybe he'd already read my email and was here to thank me for my kind words.

'I am sorry, Mr Munley. I hope I do not disturb you, but I forgot to give you this. My profound apologies.' He handed me a bubble-wrap envelope. 'It is the press pass for the show and vouchers for food here in the hotel, a gift from Iran. They have no restaurant but will bring whatever you care for so there is no need to go out and face the traffic. Have you tried your mobile yet, Mr Munley?'

'No, I just emailed my editor.'

'Your mobile, unfortunately, Mr Munley, will not work. We are taking great steps to update our systems. So you have another gift, a mobile phone for the duration of your stay.'

He smiled and I smiled, both knowing it was all to do with keeping tabs on my calls – and, of course, being able to track me with it once I'd tucked it into my pocket.

'Thank you very much, Majid. Very helpful.'

'I will see you in the lobby at six thirty tomorrow morning. I wish you a pleasant evening.'

52

Tuesday, 5 May
0820 hrs

The traffic was bumper to bumper, just as Majid had predicted. It gave me some thinking time. I hadn't bothered placing tell-tales in the room to check if it had been investigated while I was out. I was sure it would have been and didn't want to flag myself up as aware.

When we finally arrived Majid came good. The area around the conference centre was chaotic. We glided through the crowd and past Registration with little more than a wave of his papers. A giant white banner ahead of us didn't fuck around. It announced in two-foot-high red letters: '*IranEx 2009 – The Achievements of the Islamic Republic that Will Make America Suffer a Severe Defeat*'.

The tools of my new trade were proudly on display and I looked the part. My name badge was pinned to my shirt, my Nikon hung round my neck, and I had my laptop, tons of reading material and three thousand dollars in cash in my day-sack. The war on terror and the US trade embargo meant credit cards were a no-no.

I had another two thousand in fifty- and hundred-dollar bills and my Samsung satellite phone, all tucked far enough down both my Timberlands for me to fold the tops of my socks over them. An ordinary mobile was out of the question. I needed something secure to call Julian on, and to yell for help if I was in the shit. Anything but a satellite phone would be tracked and listened in to, which was why the Iranians wouldn't allow them into the country. I'd only use it when I had to. The Iranians wouldn't be able to listen in, but they would still see its transmission footprint. They'd come looking to find out who was using it and why.

Finally, my passport was in a neck wallet where it should be, around my neck. If I had to drop everything and run, I had the important stuff physically attached to me.

A few metres further on, surrounded by a crowd of admirers, were a tank and a fighter aircraft. The plane was set on a giant plinth; the tank on a mound of plastic rock. Both had been sprinkled with flower petals. The Third World War had collided with the Chelsea Flower Show.

Majid was looking at the aircraft the way most of the young guys I'd come across studied *Zoo* and *Nuts*. 'You will know, of course, what this aircraft is – a Saegheh 80. "Saegheh" means thunderbolt, Mr Munley. As you can imagine, we are very proud of this achievement, because it is living proof that Iran can stand on her own two feet.'

I'd never given a whole lot of thought to aircraft, other than when I'd been jumping out of them or measuring the threat they represented. But I'd done my homework on the flight and recognized Iran's first attempt to build an indigenous combat jet. I decided not to tell him that it was little more than a half-arsed improvement of the F-5E, an American fighter designed in the 1950s that had been supplied in quantity to the Iranian Air Force during the reign of the Shah.

Majid droned on as we circled the plinth. For the first time since I'd arrived in Iran, I saw something above the crowd that could only have been worn by a Westerner. Who else would walk about in a green floppy jungle hat covered with badges? As we got closer a tall guy with wavy light brown hair and a matching safari vest came into view. He was armed with a notepad and an impressive camera and set about photographing the Thunderbolt from every angle. He looked more spook than journalist. The other onlookers included an Iranian cleric and, judging by the medals and scrambled egg on display, a North Korean Army mega-general.

'The Saegheh 80 is a joint project between the Islamic Republic of Iran Air Force and the Iranian Ministry of Defence. The first prototype flew in 2004 and the first production variant entered service two years later. It is a multi-role fighter, every bit as good as the F-15 or the F/A-18 built in America . . .'

I nodded enthusiastically and took a few polite pictures before we moved on to a large exhibition hall that had been transformed into a one-stop shop for Armageddon. Most of the stands were given over to Iranian companies displaying models of aircraft, unmanned aerial vehicles – Iranian copies of the drones the Americans used to hunt for bin Laden on the Af-Pak border – and every kind of weapon imaginable.

Majid stood with his hands on his hips gazing at the hardware. 'Well, Mr Munley, what do you think? So much to see and so little time. It must be hard for someone like yourself to know where to begin.'

It was, though not for the reasons he suspected. I had to play the game for a while to bed myself in before trying to move on from the Iranian gear to the Russian. M3C was all I cared about. It was my only link to Altun.

I needed to remain as far as possible on ground Mr Munley was familiar with. 'I'd like to see what Iran is doing in my field – surface-to-air missile systems.'

'Of course. Then we should visit the stand of the Shahid Kazemi Industrial Complex. The managing director would make a good interview subject for your journal. He can tell you – honestly and openly – about all the great strides that Iran is making to achieve technological independence in this area. And he can tell you, too, how our defensive weapons are more than capable of defeating threats from potential aggressors to our nation.'

We stepped onto a stand whose centrepiece was a badly made model of a SAM battery. It looked a lot like the American Patriot system, with the missiles housed in vertical tubes on a mobile launcher, supported by two other vehicles: a launch-control cabin and a radar unit.

A tall, thin man with piercing brown eyes, a buttoned-up shirt and no tie stood centre-stage. His windcheater was probably on a hook behind the brochure rack. He was explaining to a South East Asian general, via an interpreter, how the system worked. As I leant forward to look more closely at the model I could see his badge. He was from Burma. The man holding court was the MD, Majid whispered in my ear, so we would have to wait.

The system was totally automatic and could engage as many as a hundred targets at once, the MD told his guest. 'It can track, target and destroy threats at low, medium and high altitudes from as far as a hundred and fifty kilometres.' And it was one hundred per cent made in Iran . . .

The Burmese listened politely to the MD's sales pitch for a few moments more before wandering off as if he was in a street market and a lad was trying to harass him into buying yet more bin liners.

Majid stepped in and introduced me. I told the MD that I was preparing an article on man-portable air-defence systems and was interested to know what Iran was doing in this important field. My editor had promised ample page-space.

They conferred for a minute and, while it was all in Farsi, from the tone I pretty much knew how the conversation was going – Mr MD was wondering how much he could reveal to a Western technical journalist, and Majid was reminding him that this was a showcase of Iranian capabilities so he shouldn't hold back.

Whatever passed between them, Mr MD relaxed. He started to tell me about a new shoulder-launched missile called the Misagh-3, which he claimed was even better than the latest versions of the American Stinger.

I jotted some notes and stuffed the brochure he gave me into my day-sack. If nothing else, it made me look like I knew what I was doing while I worked out how to get to M3C instead of listening endlessly to what the Iranians were doing in the name of the Great Republic.

53

Majid took me into a room constructed from three adjacent Portakabins. It looked like it had been air-dropped into Iran from the 1972 Ideal Home Exhibition, and the cigarette smoke hovering at face level gave it that extra stamp of authenticity. The work surface running around its edge was covered with brown Formica. The floor was covered with red and black marbled lino tiles that did their best to camouflage the burn marks from stubbed-out butts. Air-conditioning units were built into the wall, but none was switched on. They probably didn't work.

On the left-hand side, some local journalists typed away on desk-top computers that Alan Sugar would have fired immediately. The light grey plastic had been turned black in places by years of handling, and the air vents looked like coked-up exhaust pipes. Several more journos jabbered into Bakelite telephones set up alongside them.

On the far side of the room two or three foreign journalists pounded away on their laptops. One was the guy with the jungle hat and long lens I'd spotted earlier. A TV in the corner was belting out Iran's version of *Sunrise*. Same colour scheme, same rolling news at the bottom of the screen. The only thing missing was Eamonn Holmes. And his tie.

Majid waved his arm to clear some of the smoke from an Iranian journalist standing next to us. 'This is the press centre. From here, Mr Munley, you can file your stories to your editor, check the latest announcements from companies at the show or simply relax. You will find everything that you need here, including free Internet access. Know that all your editorial needs can be met in this room. And if there is anything we haven't thought of, then all you have to do is ask.'

Only part of me was listening. The rest was tracking a girl who'd just walked into the room. The scarf on her head didn't quite cover her hair, which was so naturally blonde I knew she couldn't be Iranian. She looked a whole lot like the one from Abba I'd fancied big-time as a teenager. I used to sit in the NAAFI as a sixteen-year-old boy soldier with my pint of Vimto and a steak and kidney pie, waiting for *Top of the Pops* to come on. 'Dancing Queen' had been number one for what seemed five years, and this boy soldier always hoped her reign would be extended one more week.

As she manoeuvred past us and sat down under the TV, it was like having Cinza walk by at the funeral. The Red Sea parted. I studied her face. And why not? Every other man in the room was. The high cheekbones gave her away. She was Ukrainian or Russian; eastern European, for sure.

The bit of me that wasn't tracking her and listening to Majid was trying to work out how I could access the chalet line that Kettle had told me about – the VIP area where the execs hung out away from prying eyes; the place where the real deals were done and maybe Altun would be. I needed to head over to M3C and get an invite.

'Majid, I need to do a comparison of the missile system I've just seen with what the Russians are developing in the same field. Are M3C exhibiting here?'

Majid riffled through the show guide. 'They are in Hall Two, at Stand Three E – next door, in fact, to the Shahid Hemmat

Industrial Complex. You know this company, I suspect, James
... Do you mind if I call you by this?'

'No problem, mate.' I knew I should have said James at the
airport. Never mind, he was coming around.

Majid inclined his head in a mock-bow. 'After you have
visited the Russian stand, I can take you to see the director of
Shahid Hemmat. You will like this company very much, James.
It represents the very best of our Iranian technology. Doubtless
you heard of the rocket that Iran put into orbit last year? The
company that built it was Shahid Hemmat. You will be able to
give your editor a real exclusive, believe me.'

You had to hand it to him. When his days in the
Revolutionary Guard ended, he could always become a salesman for Iran plc.

54

In the middle of the M3C stand was the SA-16M, the missile that Kettle had asked me to look out for. It was spotlit from above and the placard beneath it was printed in Farsi, Russian and English. A number of salesmen in mega-smart suits tried to get eye-to-eye as Majid and I studied the latest addition to their company's product range. I wondered how much of a discount they offered for gold.

For once, Majid was out of his depth. M3C wasn't Iranian and he had no authority here. What he really wanted to do was to haul me next door, so I could big it up with the guys who'd pitched Iran into the ballistic-missile club – or, as he put it, 'The peaceful pursuit of the commercial space business.'

The Russian stand was among the biggest and slickest at the show. Behind the weapons and the display boards, there was a reception area staffed by two heavily made-up girls with orange electric-beach tans, their heads covered with red scarves. Their eyelashes fluttered like electrocuted daddy long-legs. Just beyond them was a row of office windows. Shadows moved behind half-closed blinds. A squat Russian with a shaved head came out and barked at the salesmen, then disappeared.

I stepped up onto the stand and approached one of the mega-suits. 'Do you speak English?'

'Leetle . . .'

'Jim Manley, *ADTM*.' I handed over one of my business cards.

One of the other suits stepped forward. He'd gone to the trouble of Anglicizing the name on his card. It read: 'Paul (not Pavel) Sergeyev, Media Relations'. Great, the company spin-doctor.

'Hello, how can I help you?'

I explained who I was and what I was after. The mega-suit and Paul (not Pavel) went into a huddle with one of the girls who began hitting her keyboard.

I turned to see Majid deep in discussion with a little guy in a white turban and brown robe at Rockets R Us across the way. He must have been warming him up for me.

Paul (not Pavel) reappeared by my side. 'Mr Manley, please forgive me for taking so long with my colleague. We just wished to check your magazine. Of course.'

His flawless English carried a hint of an American accent. 'Now, please let me show you our wonderful SA-16M.' He pointed towards the missile with an open hand, like a game-show host introducing tonight's star prize.

55

I followed Paul (not Pavel) the few steps to the missile. 'Mr Manley. Your magazine, it's a good publication. I have just seen that we have our people translate it for our technical staff.' He smiled. 'They learn much from it. What do you need to know about the SA-16M?'

'You could start, I guess, by telling me something about its status. Is it in production yet?'

'Yes, yes, it's in production.'

'And what's so special about it? The SA-16 has been around for years.'

He nodded. 'It remains a favourite with our customers.'

I didn't remind him that a whole load of those customers were terrorists. 'So, talk me through it.'

Paul (not Pavel) lifted the green tube off its stand. He stood with it on his shoulder. 'The SA-16, as I'm sure you know, Mr Manley, has no IFF interrogator. The SA-16M – the improved version you see here – retains the simplicity and robustness of the original design but adds the IFF interrogator. We are conscious that customers demand high levels of safety and assurance from the weapons that we sell them and so we have provided Identify Friend or Foe technology in our product. Nobody wants to be responsible for . . . What do you British call it? A blue-on-blue? A friendly-fire incident, anyhow . . .'

'Is that it?'

'Well, there are some further modifications, but it would be wrong of me to discuss them in any depth.'

'Countermeasures? It's got to be. It's all about getting the missile past the aircraft's defences, isn't it?'

'You know your subject, Mr Manley. You look like you were once a military man . . .'

'I was in the British Army. Way back. We used to fire the Blowpipe system. Not the easiest of man-portable weapons to use.'

Paul (not Pavel) laughed sympathetically. He was right. Blowpipe was a heap of shit. 'I, too, was in the army, for many years. That is why I know this is an excellent piece of engineering for the man on the ground.' He shrugged a little to adjust the weapon still on his shoulder. 'It is completely fire-and-forget. It is so simple, a child could use it. And, with the SA-16M, the added bonus is that it is effectively immune to all the very latest countermeasure systems.'

I pointed at the missile. 'I hear the seeker's faulty.'

He laughed again, but uncomfortably this time. He took it almost as a personal insult. 'No, these rumours are just that, rumours. We have been improving the seeker's capability. It has been a period of development, not repair.'

'Could you knock down an Apache with one of these?'

He paused. 'Mr Manley, you are drawing me into a technical discussion that I would prefer not to have. So let's just say that with the SA-16M and even the non-IFF version, the SA-16, we have found an ingenious way of combating dark flares. That took some time to perfect. But if you know how to discriminate against dark flares, then you can defeat all countermeasure systems. You understand what I mean?'

I nodded. I did.

'I expect you would like a simulation, yes?'

He handed me the missile launch tube. It felt pretty much

the same weight as the Stingers I'd used in Afghanistan – against the Mi-24 Hinds these lads had flown in the eighties. Paul (not Pavel) looked the right sort of age to have been there. I threw it onto my right shoulder.

Paul (not Pavel) directed me to look through the sight. 'First thing you must do is position the aircraft within the range ring – you need to keep it positioned there throughout the engagement sequence. The SA-16M is an all-aspect missile, which means you can engage the target from any angle. You understand?'

I nodded.

'Next, you must interrogate the aircraft to see if it is friendly or not. The IFF interrogation switch is on the left-hand side of the gripstock. Here. You've got it?'

I felt for the switch with my thumb.

'If the aircraft is friendly, it will transmit a coded signal back to the IFF interrogation system within the launcher. The system emits an audible signal that tells you whether the aircraft is confirmed friendly, possible friendly or unknown.' He flicked a switch on the simulator console.

I heard a succession of short electronic beeps coming from the missile by my ear.

'You hear that? That tells you the aircraft is a confirmed friendly.'

The beeps changed into a succession of longer signals.

'This means possible friendly . . .'

The longer beeps changed into one continuous signal – a high-pitched *wiiiiiiiiiiiiiiii.*

'And this means the aircraft is unknown – for our purposes, therefore, it is the enemy. Clear so far?'

Clear, I told him. It was very much like a Stinger, but easier. Like he said, a child's toy.

'So, now you must select the arming switch, here on the other side of the gripstock. Feel it?' He directed my forefinger to the switch. 'Now, push it forward. This readies the weapon for firing – super-cooling the seeker to allow it to lock onto the target's primary heat-source, most likely its engine. When enough infrared energy is detected, you will once more notice a high-pitched signal – there, you hear it?'

Wiiiiiiiiiiiiiiiiiiiiiiiii . . .

Like before, only louder.

'That tells you the seeker has a firm lock and is tracking the heat-source.'

Once the missile was tracking the target, there was precious little its pilot could do, Paul (not Pavel) said. The missile operator just had to flick a switch forward of the gripstock from safety to armed, then pull the trigger. Provided the aircraft was below 10,000 feet, its destruction was 99.9 per cent guaranteed.

Where the SA-16M differed from any other system on the market – certainly one this affordable, Paul (not Pavel) added, with a smile you'd normally get from a car salesman – was that it defeated all known countermeasures. He didn't mention those mysterious dark flares again, but I had already lodged the term and Kettle could translate when I was back in London.

I couldn't quite see why the Taliban or a group of head jobs on the Heathrow flight-path would need Identify Friend or Foe technology: as far as they were concerned, everything up there was the enemy. But what worried me most was that Saddam's doors could buy a shed-load of this shit.

I heard raised voices coming from the neighbouring stand. The Shahid Hemmat Industrial Complex had been invaded by the Iranian press corps. Photographers, reporters and film cameramen were jostling for position. Some even seemed to be coming to blows as they tracked an entourage a dozen strong, some wearing military uniform, moving between the ballistic-missile and space-launcher models. At the centre of the entourage, in the glare of the film camera lights, was the guy in the white turban and brown robe.

I turned to Paul (not Pavel). 'What's happening, mate?'

The Russian looked at his watch. 'It's Mohammad Kermanshahi, the leader of Iran's Supreme National Security Council. He's here for the press conference.'

'What about?'

'We are making a joint announcement with the Iranians.' He glanced nervously at his watch again. 'You will have to excuse me, Mr Manley. I need to make my way to the conference hall.'

When I turned back to Rockets R Us, I could see that Majid was being swept along by the crowd, against his will, towards one of the exits.

56

I slipped off the M3C stand and made my way to the exit furthest from the one I'd seen Majid jostled through. I pulled out the map of the exhibition centre and took a second to orient myself. The chalets were on the far side of the facility. A hatched line on the map indicated that they were segregated from the rest of the site by another level of security. The head shed didn't want any Tom, Dick or Abdul invading their space as they talked business away from the prying eyes and ears of the exhibition halls. I wouldn't even want to mix with people like me. If Altun was here, he'd want to be tucked away somewhere like that.

I passed through an exhibition hall filled with artillery pieces, rocket launchers and mortars, crossed the open area with the petal-strewn tank and fighter aircraft, and reached a barrier manned by a couple of AK-carriers. One was checking a pass by the driver's window of a Toyota pick-up laden with bottles of mineral water and Zam Zam, Iran's answer to Coca-Cola. I'd guzzled gallons of it in Afghanistan and got to quite like the stuff. It reminded me of the Strike Cola my mum used to buy in the Co-op to keep the dentist busy.

The guard returned the driver's papers, raised the barrier and waved the truck through.

I flashed my press pass with the confidence that said, 'Here it is, look at it, and fuck off,' and kept moving. I ducked under the barrier and kept walking. Ahead of me was a row of single-storey executive Portakabins, with flags fluttering out front.

I pretended I knew where I was going and pressed on.

I found myself in a kind of avenue. The corporate hospitality suites stretched away to either side of me. There were clearly big bucks to be made here if you were in the mood to trade arms with the pariah state.

It was mid-morning and the sun was already high in the sky. The avenue was filled with people making their way to and from the chalets. Cars with blacked-out windows rolled past me. Crates of food and drink were off-loaded into kitchens. The aroma of spicy food hung in the air.

It was hardly the Excel Centre, but it was busy. Among the Russians, Ukrainians, Moldovans and a dozen other dodgy former members of the Soviet Good Lads Club, I was just another white face. No one paid me the slightest attention.

I pressed on, turning to give the M3C chalet the once-over as I did a walk-past. It was much like their stand, bigger and slicker than the competition. The M3C logo, a stylized arrow bisecting a circle with a red star in it, fluttered on the company flag. A couple of BG straight out of Central Casting flanked the glass entrance. They were wearing sun-gigs and suits that couldn't hide the weapons beneath their jackets. Five feet beyond them, engines running, were three very shiny black Mercedes saloons.

I'd walked past the chalet when I heard a crackle.

I turned.

One BG had a radio up to his ear. He brought it down and waffled back.

The other half snapped to attention and pulled open the door.

A third BG waited in the front passenger seat of the middle Merc.

A moment later, a man with slicked-back hair, sun-gigs and a khaki windcheater stepped out into the sunshine. He paused, as if to smell the air, and looked about him. He seemed particularly pleased with himself. Then, escorted by one of the BG who'd been on the door, he walked slowly down the steps and slid into the Mercedes.

I had a possible.

57

I dropped onto one knee and made like I was tying a shoelace. I tried to get my Nikon up. Too late. The Mercedes pulled out of its parking slot and headed in the direction I'd just come from.

I doubled back as quick as I could against the flow of people.

It was an E-class, straight from the showroom. I scanned it quickly for a VDM (visual distinguishing mark). The plate meant nothing to me: it was in Farsi. I needed something to pull it from a sea of other vehicles. It had four doors, tinted windows and five-pointed, star-shaped aluminium wheel hubs; all bog-standard, which was how Altun would have liked it. The only thing that distinguished it from any other brand-new black E-class 350 was a mobile phone antenna mounted on the roof with its left-hand blade bent slightly upwards. A set of chintzy green curtains was drawn across the rear window to provide that extra little touch of anonymity.

Every now and again the driver encouraged pedestrians to move out of the way with a blast of the horn. As the crowd parted, the car surged forward ten metres or so. It reached the Zam Zam barrier. I kept on fighting my way through the crowd.

The barrier lifted and the Merc rolled forward. It manoeuvred its way around the petal-strewn tank and the fighter, still heading for the exit. Maybe if I ran through one of the exhibition halls I could get to the head of the taxi line and intercept the wagon as it drove off-site. It picked up speed as the crowd thinned. Fuck it, I was going to lose him. I fired off about six or seven shots of the rear of the Merc. I'd learn the plate script.

But Altun wasn't leaving after all. The driver turned down an alley to the side of the conference hall, the entrance to which was blocked by an armed sentry.

The two BG stepped out of the car and did their job, covering their principal against a shoot from both ends of the alley.

He darted into the building.

I ran across the road and muscled my way to the front of the crowd surging through the large glass doors.

A cordon of men clutching AKs to their chests directed us towards a huge staircase that curved up to the first floor. As I climbed, I spotted some of the journalists who'd been in the press centre and slipped in behind them. A Brit and a French guy were speculating on trade-fair gossip. I overtook them at the entrance to the conference room. There was another log-jam. A phalanx of flustered media-relations people, some Iranian, some Russian, staffed a table to the right of the door. A woman in a headscarf was signing journalists in. The lad with the badges on his hat argued the toss with her in German. I could just hear her above the din. We all had to hand in our cameras. 'The Ministry of Information will provide the pictures.' She took his and gave him a numbered ticket.

Fair one. The Afghan warlord, Ahmad Shah Masood, had been assassinated two days before 9/11 by Al-Qaeda posing as journalists. They'd detonated a bomb rigged inside their TV camera.

More journalists milled around us and had a good honk. I was too busy deleting the Merc's registration-plate pictures. I had to. If they had any sense they would check the cameras while they had the chance, and half a dozen hits

210

of a VIP number-plate wouldn't be good for business.

An extended hand almost hit my face. 'Aha, James Manley, *ADTM*. We meet at last!' The Brit I'd passed on the stairs looked up from my badge and we shook. 'I've been reading your stuff for years. Some of us thought you didn't exist, dear boy.'

I managed my best smile as the pissed-off German disappeared inside without his big lens.

He kept on shaking. 'Collier. *Military Systems and Components Quarterly*.' In his other hand, he was clutching a pipe.

This wasn't the time for pleasantries. 'Collier,' I said. 'Fuck off.'

He stood there trying to work out if he'd heard me right.

The woman was asking me to open my day-sack. She removed the Nikon and gave me a ticket. 'If you have a mobile phone, Mr Manley, you need to keep it switched off while you are in the conference room. If you do not, it will be taken from you. You can collect your camera from here when the conference is concluded.' She gave me a badge and waved me on.

58

The conference hall was built like a theatre. There were banked seats – around two hundred of them – leading down to a stage. Whole blocks near the front were filled with Iranians, all with the same red badges. The front row itself had been reserved.

The noise was deafening. Near the front, photographers jostled each other for a good view. The stage was bare except for a long table covered with a bright red cloth. Ten matching red chairs were ranged behind it. On the table there were two jugs of water, a glass for each seat, and three evenly spaced microphones. To keep the theme going, a single vase of flowers sat in the centre of the table.

Name-plates were arranged in front of each chair, but I was too far away to read them.

The only clue to the imminent announcement was a PowerPoint slide that erupted on a screen behind the table: *Towards A New Era of Space Collaboration*. It looked like *Military Systems* and his French mate had been right.

I flipped down one of the seats near the back and played about with my boot, trying to extract the mobile without looking like I was drawing a weapon. I got up again and made my way to the aisle, then down towards the mêlée of photographers. "Scuse me, coming through, sorry, 'scuse me . . .'

The lights went down, leaving just the stage illuminated.

59

The auditorium fell silent as White Turban walked onto the stage. All the red badges jumped up and stood to attention. They stayed on their feet while more dignitaries filed in. Some went on to the stage, others to the VIP seats.

Then came my possible. He took the furthest seat on the right, not far from an emergency exit. His size, face shape and nose were all familiar. One of his BG kept the exit clear. The other stood behind his left shoulder.

I had to get much closer to make a positive ID and take a decent picture. I elbowed my way down towards him. I felt a tap on my shoulder and breath in my ear. 'I have been looking for you everywhere,' Majid whispered. He made it sound like an act of complete betrayal.

I turned to him as the waffle sparked up on stage. 'Sorry, mate, I got lost trying to find you so I thought I'd just crack on.'

'Please, James, do not get lost again. This will be a very important announcement. Something positive for you to write about. We listen now.'

Up at the table, White Turban leant closer to a microphone.

Majid nudged me. 'This is Minister Kermanshahi, a very important man – a very powerful man.'

'What's he saying?'

'One of my colleagues will provide a translation.'

On cue, someone at the end of the table started to interpret, first in Russian, then in English. The announcement concerned the teaming of Iran's illustrious rocket industry with Russia's foremost rocket-manufacturing company, M3C. Nobody was actually calling a spade a spade and mentioning the word 'missile'. The purpose of the teaming arrangement between Shahid Hemmat and M3C, explained the interpreter, was to help establish Iran as a true presence in the commercial space launch business. Using its long-standing experience, M3C would help Iran adapt its existing two-stage rockets to launch micro-satellites into space. At this point, there was a loud ripple of applause from the red-badge brigade. White Turban subdued them with a wave of his hand.

The presentations from the stage went on for the best part of an hour. My eyes never left my target. I was just too far away for a picture, and with Majid at my elbow I had no chance anyway. That didn't matter just now. What did was that I'd found him. His eyes confirmed it.

The interpreter announced that the formalities were over, but the minister would be happy to take some questions.

Altun turned in his seat and gestured towards the emergency exit. The BG stepped forward. As the lights came on for questions he bent down to take his instructions. On the back of his neck a tattoo linked his collar to his hairline. I couldn't see the pattern. I didn't need to.

Altun moved swiftly to the emergency exit with Tattoo and the other BG.

I started to get up. I'd catch them outside.

A hand grabbed me.

'I'm sorry, Majid, I need the toilet.'

'No, James, we have to wait until the important men leave. It is very impolite. You must stay.'

A woman's voice, clear, loud and confident, fired the first question. Her accent was Russian. 'Minister Kermanshahi . . . I

215

would like you to tell us about the military implications of this deal . . .'

It was Agnetha from the press centre.

Kermanshahi looked like he'd been hit by a tank round. He raised his eyes, shielding them against the lights that shone down on the stage.

Everybody turned to look at her, including Altun and Tattoo.

On the stage, the interpreter whispered something into Kermanshahi's ear. His face tightened with anger. The interpreter picked up the microphone. 'There are no military implications. Now, if you please—'

'In particular, Minister Kermanshahi, I would like you to explain why Iran is acting as a broker in the supply of weapons built by M3C to—'

There was a howl of indignation from the red badges but my eyes were on the emergency exit. It was closed. Altun had disappeared.

'Sorry, mate, got to go.'

I jumped out of my seat and ran up the steps. Majid called my name, but I wasn't stopping for anyone.

As I reached the back of the auditorium, I collided with Agnetha. Two plain-clothes security men were dragging her out, kicking and shouting. I pushed back at her. 'Out the fucking way.'

The security men stumbled back a pace, and I was gone.

60

I burst outside and raced around to the alleyway.

The gate was padlocked and the sentry had gone.

No time to stop and think. I had two known locations for him. Locations where I knew he'd been.

The first was M3C's chalet.

I ran back to the avenue. My throat was dry and sore as I pushed through the crowds. Sweat streamed down my face and stuck my shirt to my back under the day-sack.

I looked right. No Merc.

Gulping air, I showed my press pass to the heavies at the M3C door and told the girl I was there to interview Paul (not Pavel), the media guy.

She was ice-cold, unsmiling. 'Everyone has gone for all day. You are Mr . . . ?'

But I was already running again, back towards the auditorium. What now? Back to Majid to get a bollocking for not being able to control my bladder, and lose the target? Or just fuck him off and keep looking?

It was an easy choice. The target was more important than Majid's annual report.

The second known location was the Falcon, and I'd need the Nikon if I was going to do my bit for Julian.

61

I rushed outside the exhibition centre and flagged down a knackered eighties Peugeot taxi, one of the yellow metered ones Majid had gone on about. 'Airport, mate – the airport. You understand?'

The driver wore a dirty T-shirt and dragged on a cigarette as we crawled down the road. A curtain of brown haze hung across the city. I inhaled a lungful of diesel and chemicals the moment I wound down the grime-covered window to scan for the Merc's VDM. At least Altun, wherever he was heading, would be stuck in the same mid-afternoon traffic. Limo or not, it didn't matter – Tehran's jams didn't discriminate.

I tapped the driver on the shoulder and told him I'd pay double if he got me to IKIA fast.

He shrugged his shoulders and pushed his hands towards the nightmare outside.

He spoke basic English and was determined to tell me about Tehran's night life. 'You want plenty drink, my friend. You like to party, mister?'

I looked up and caught his expression in the mirror. I was a breath away from being offered his daughter. I got out my mobile and checked the pictures.

'Signal very bad Tehran, my friend, very bad. Ahmadinejad

very bad. Mullahs very bad.' He drew a finger, knife-style, across his neck.

They were crap: too distant and too dark. The mobile went back into my sock and Majid's went out of the window.

By the time we got out of the city and the traffic began to thin, I'd learnt more than I'd ever wanted to know about what this man got up to on his nights off. And still no Merc.

Anyone caught with alcohol was looking at a public flogging or a prison sentence so they drank at private parties. 'You like come my house tonight, mister, for drinking and girls?' By now, we were on a long, straight dual carriageway that cut through the sand-salt desert towards the airport.

I shielded my eyes against the glare, searching in vain for any sign of a black vehicle ahead. The surface reflected the sunlight like a mirror. The temperature in the back of the taxi was unbearable, even with the window open.

Fifteen minutes later, I caught sight of the control tower in the haze. Ten minutes after that, we entered the airport perimeter. I looked at my watch. It had taken two hours to get there. The Merc would have warp-speeded it as soon as it was out of the city, but there was still a chance – unless the aircraft had been on the pan, engines turning. Unless he'd gone somewhere else entirely.

I reached for my cash and prepared to hand over a ten-dollar bill. Then I remembered it wasn't my money but Julian's and doubled it. My friend, the pimp, thanked me over and over as I jumped out of the Peugeot and looked up to the sound of aircraft engines crackling in the late-afternoon sky.

A white Falcon was climbing like a rocket, banking towards Tehran and, half masked by its pollution, those fucking Alborz Mountains where it would disappear from sight.

62

I tracked the Dassault until I lost it in the heat haze. Part of me was thinking about the phone call I'd have to make to Julian; part of me was wondering what I'd tell Red Ken and Dex when we met up at the final RV.

'You very late, my friend?'

I glanced down. The pimp was watching me in the rear-view mirror.

'We go Tehran, yes?' Having seen the colour of my money, he clearly thought he must be on to a good thing.

Going back to Tehran to regroup, get a bollocking from Majid and probably get binned from the country seemed like a good idea. I'd get Julian to task me to carry on with the job and find him the Falcon's destination.

But then I saw something glint on the roof of the multi-storey ahead of us. Somebody was up there with a pair of binoculars. I shook my head. 'Nah, I'll wait here.'

The driver shrugged, giving me the universal sign for what-ever, and drove off.

I slung my day-sack onto my back and headed for the multi-storey. The sun burnt my face and I had to squint. A gust of wind blew in from the airfield, bringing with it the smell of jet fuel. I was dripping with sweat and my shirt was soaked.

It was a lot cooler in the stairwell – and, like the rest of the airport, the multi-storey was over-specified and under-used. Only one in ten parking spaces on the ground floor of this polished concrete building were occupied.

I began climbing the stairs. The sound of my footsteps was drowned by the roar of another aircraft taking off. The smell of aviation fuel was rapidly replaced by the stink of urine from a men's toilet on the second floor. Busy or not, car parks are the same the world over.

The stairs finally led to a door on the fifth level. I waited for the sound of the aircraft to recede, then put my ear against it. I heard the murmur of young voices on the other side. I turned the handle and pushed.

The roof level didn't have a single car parked on it – at least, none that was visible from my viewpoint. Half a kilometre beyond a waist-high wall around the edge of the building, the metal-and-glass roof of the airport terminal shimmered in the heat. To the right of it, I could make out the control tower and a revolving radar dish.

I could also hear the male voices very clearly now.

I stepped out onto the roof and closed the door behind me. Pressing my back against the wall of the stairwell, I stuck my head slowly around the corner.

There were three of them leaning on the wall, their backs to me. One was pointing across the airfield. Another was listening to a radio. The third guy was using a pair of binoculars to track whatever the first lad was pointing at. They were dressed in jeans, T-shirts and, despite the heat, thin windcheaters from the Ahmadinejad spring collection.

What I'd taken yesterday to be a military-style hat on the head of the guy with the binos, I now realized was nothing more than a baseball cap. He gobbed off excitedly to his mates, giving a running commentary of what he could see.

I started towards them, a big smile on my face, one hand up

221

in a wave and the other shielding my eyes. 'Hello, any of you guys speak English?'

The one with the radio turned and stared dumbly, then nudged his two mates in the ribs.

63

Foreigners weren't a common sight for these lads – even at what was supposed to pass for an international airport. The guy with the baseball cap was the only one who sparked up – he seemed generally more confident than his mates.

'Hello, who are you?' He spoke, of course, with a slight American accent. They were all around the same age; somewhere in their early twenties.

I told them the truth – well, sort of. I flashed my IranEx badge at them. 'James Manley, British aerospace and defence journal – *Aerospace and Defence Technology Monthly.*' They exchanged doubtful glances with each other until I handed over my business card.

The guy with the baseball cap studied it, then looked at me. 'You work for *ADTM*?'

'You know it?'

'Sure.' He took a step forward and shook my hand.

I missed the names of his mates, but I caught his loud and clear.

'Ali.'

Under the peak were two very clear and excited brown eyes. He kept smiling, like he was waiting for something from me as he held onto my hand and kept shaking. 'Iranianmetalbird.net, you know it, yes? That is why you are here?'

One of Ali's mates, a beanpole around six-four, spoke to him in rapid-fire Farsi. He didn't like me at all.

'There a problem?'

'He wants to know what a foreign-defence reporter is doing at IKIA – a civilian airport.'

'Not entirely civilian.' I pointed to the military-transport aircraft I'd seen alongside the northern perimeter fence when I landed. I could still see them there, way in the distance. As a piece of point-scoring, it wasn't up to much but it bought me a few seconds. 'I came here to find you. '

He took a step backwards. 'Me?'

'Your website. It's pretty well known in defence publishing circles back home. My magazine has been meaning to approach you for a while. IranEx gave me the opportunity to look you up. I take it that you'd be happy, Ali, if we could agree the right terms, for us to reprint some of the pictures that you post on the web, maybe even write some articles for the magazine?'

Ali looked at his mates, then at me. 'You are offering me a job?'

'A contract, possibly. But let's see how good you are.' I gave him a smile. It wasn't going to be much of a test. 'An aircraft, white private jet, took off from here a short while ago. Do you know what make it was?'

I liked his enthusiasm a lot more than the scowling glances I got from his mates.

'Sure. A Dassault Falcon 7X.'

'What can you tell me about it? Does it have a history here?'

Again, the beanpole interrupted him. This time, the conversation between the three got heated. Whatever was being said, Ali was clearly in the minority.

'Is there another problem?'

Ali pulled a face.

I pointed at the beanpole. 'What's up with him?'

'He wants to know why a foreign-defence journalist is interested in a commercial aircraft. A corporate jet, of all things. This has nothing to do with the military, he says. Perhaps he is right.'

'I'm interested because it's registered to a Russian aerospace company that's exhibiting at the show – at IranEx.'

Ali smiled. 'You mean, a Russian *missile* company that's exhibiting at IranEx.'

'You know about this company?'

'There's not much I don't know about the aerospace business, Mr Manley.' He beamed. 'It's my hobby. You could say it's my life. Why else would I be up here?' He flung his arm around the expanse of tarmac and desert as another 747 rumbled down the runway.

He stopped playing helicopters and pointed towards a low building faintly visible through the dust of the construction work on the other side of the airport; the building I'd seen the Dassault parked in front of when I'd touched down yesterday. 'That's M3C's own private terminal. From the air-traffic movements of its corporate jet fleet, it is very obvious to us that M3C is doing a lot of business with my country. We are not stupid. If we posted the movements of M3C aircraft on our website, we'd find ourselves in a lot of trouble.'

'You have data?'

He smiled. 'We see everything that flies in and out of this country.'

The other two shifted uncomfortably.

'I'm doing a story on this company, Ali. Aircraft and the weapons that can take them out the sky, that sort of thing. I need to know where that jet has been over the past few days. It gives the article a bit of excitement – you know, international company jetting around the world, that sort of thing. Did you see any of the people who boarded the plane?'

Ali shook his head slowly. 'No, it was on a pan the other side of their terminal.' His voice went up an octave. 'But isn't the 7X a great bird? It only entered service in 2007. This is the very first one we have seen in Iran.'

It was still as hot as an oven and we'd been standing out here long enough.

'Ali, I'd like you to show me everything you've got on that jet.'

'I can show you its flight paths on my computer at home.'

'Let's go, then. Where do you live? The magazine will pay you, of course.'

He smiled again. 'That's good, Mr Manley, because I drive for a living. And, to be honest, it's not much of a living right now.'

64

He lived in a southern district of Tehran; a journey, he said, that would take us around an hour from the airport. We drove there in his sparkling white Paykan. He told me proudly that it was nearly fifteen years old, but it looked almost new. His father had lovingly maintained it. The taxi really belonged to his dad, but now he was ill and Ali had had to interrupt his studies at Tehran University to drive it and help make ends meet.

He seemed like a decent enough lad. As we left the airport behind, I apologized for the trouble I'd caused him with his mates. They'd gone one way in the car park and we'd gone another. When they'd parted, you could have cut the atmosphere with a knife.

As we drove through the desert on the southern approaches to Tehran the rift still seemed to hang in the air like smog.

After a long silence, Ali finally sparked up. 'Do not feel bad, Mr Manley. The thing that unites us is our mutual interest – planes, aerospace, technology. We get on, but they are not like me. There are – how do I say? – differences between us.'

'You're all geeks like the rest of us, aren't you? What's not to like?'

'I am a Kurd, Mr Manley.'

'A Kurd and so a Sunni, eh?'

With both hands on the wheel he shrugged and smiled.

'Not much going for you here, is there?'

He shook his head slowly. 'A minority in my own country, Mr Manley. Qasim and Adel, on the roof, do not feel this way themselves, but their families certainly do. Their fathers do not like them to spend time with me.'

'Know the feeling, mate.'

'I do not feel Kurdish. I consider myself an Iranian, a proud Iranian. But not everyone looks on me the same way.'

'Know that feeling too, Ali. Almost like being invisible sometimes, yeah? They want to get in your taxi because they want a lift, but don't really want to be seen with you . . .'

We passed another poster of Bush with vampire teeth. Ali kept his eyes on the road, glancing occasionally in the rear-view. 'Do you believe Iran will go to war with the West?'

It was already, but in a cleverer way than he was thinking. 'Dunno, mate. You?'

'Our economy, Mr Manley, is deteriorating and unemployment is a disease. I believe it is one of the key reasons why our rulers are spoiling for a fight with the West. When your world is falling apart, it is always preferable, is it not, to blame someone else? Especially Great Britain.' He looked across to me for some encouragement.

'Always. It's what people do.'

He liked that. 'My father always says that if you trip over a stone you can be sure the British man put it in your way.'

It was a fair one. The Brits had been the main colonial power in the region for two hundred years. There was bound to be a lot of resentment. I'd be pissed off too.

'My father says that you are more cunning than the Americans and you use them as glove puppets. That's why Bush is on all posters and no British man.'

'I don't think we're that clever, mate.'

'Maybe, but I believe that our government is determined to

228

have a war with the West and that there is very little that ordinary Iranians can do about it.'

'Sounds like you're not much of a fan.'

'We Iranians lost over six hundred thousand people in eight years of war with Iraq, and millions more were injured. The war was not started by Iran – it was Saddam Hussein. He invaded Khuzestan province. In the name of Allah, in the name of Holy War, the mullahs sent millions of Iranians to the front.

'I studied history at university, Mr Manley. I know about conflict – trench warfare, poison gas, wave upon wave of young men cut down by machine-gun fire. So I think Iranians should have had enough of it, but the lessons of the past are easily forgotten. I am not afraid of you, Mr Manley, but Qasim and Adel are. They believe what they are told – that Israel and the West want Iran's destruction. When they see a foreigner, it frightens them. They think foreigners bring trouble for them. You're not going to bring trouble for us, are you?' He turned to me.

'No, mate. I've got enough of my own.'

He smiled. 'That's good, Mr Manley, because my father was a warrior in the war and I would fight also for my country. I may not be a fan of my government but I would never do any-thing to hurt Iran.'

'Call me Jim.'

We pulled off a main drag and manoeuvred our way down a cobbled alleyway, narrowly avoiding the people walking on both sides of us. This wasn't the London-, New York- or Paris-priced part of town. There was no pavement. Waste water ran in an open channel along the middle of the street. Tall houses with shuttered windows cut out most of the light.

It was coming up to six o'clock. The modern supermarkets and malls I'd seen in the north of the city had been replaced by holes in the wall – dark, dingy shops that seemed to sell every-thing from car batteries to carpets.

The people we passed were dressed more traditionally than

the Iranians I'd seen in the central and northern part of the city. There were lots of turbans and women in *chadors*. But I wasn't getting the stares I'd expected. Just like the housing estate I'd lived on as a kid, it didn't matter what colour you were or where you came from. The one thing that bonded people here was that we were all in the shit.

'Where are we?'

'Bazaar Mahfouz. It is part of the Tehran bazaar. It has ten kilometres of covered stores and alleyways. It is, I believe, what you call a maze and where we live is just a tiny part of it. Jim, you have nothing to fear.'

I wasn't worried. I felt quite at home in any low-rent area.

He smiled and turned into a narrow cul-de-sac. He parked alongside a wall and switched off the engine. 'From here, we walk.' He opened the boot and removed a canvas cover for the Paykan. 'This is the Kurdish-Sunni part of town. Everyone leaves us alone here.'

That made my day. With luck it would keep Majid off my back.

I helped him pull the cover over the roof, then followed him out of the cul-de-sac and into a covered alleyway lined with yet more shops.

65

As we walked past the concrete blocks, turning left, then right every few metres or so, we passed all kinds of traders. On one street they sold nothing but carpets; on another, books were all the rage, including a lot of English textbooks.

The election posters in the shop windows round here were all of Mousavi, greyer hair and beard than Armoured-dinner-jacket, and with a steady gaze behind wire-framed glasses instead of the president's squint. Green rubber wristbands in support of him were on sale everywhere.

'Like I said, this is the Sunni part of town. Our president does not get any support from here.'

'Who do you think will win?'

Ali just shrugged. 'Even if my sister's vote makes the difference and Mr Mousavi wins, it will not matter. The president will be re-elected, of course. No election will change anything. That can only be done by the Supreme Leader. He decides everything.' He smiled and pointed at one of the posters. 'Even who can stand for election.'

I started off trying to memorize the route, but soon knew I'd be in trouble if the shit hit the fan. After several more twists in the journey, I was completely lost. Traders at every corner tried to sell me a hundred and one things I didn't want, from flip-flops to melons.

We ducked into another tiny alleyway and passed a café with a handful of tables spread under a patched awning. The lads were all linked up to a hubble-bubble. There was hardly room to pass by and my nostrils filled with applewood smoke.

An old man sweeping shit out from under the chairs caught Ali's eye and waved. Ali waved back. They gave each other a burst of Farsi.

We walked on. I glanced back over my shoulder. 'What's he on about? Me?'

'No, just chit-chat, but a little bit formal. We have to be formal – respectful – with people older than we are. He is my father's friend. We used to come here to meet him for a breakfast of fried egg and meatballs in the days before my father became ill.'

Talk of food made me hungry all of a sudden. I hadn't eaten since about six this morning.

'When I could eat no more, my father would drive me to Mehrabad airport in the Paykan so we could watch the planes taking off and landing. This, for me, was the perfect day.'

Ali told me that his family had lived in the bazaar ever since his great-grandfather had crossed the border from Iraqi Kurdistan. He'd made a fortune trading sugar. The family had built a large house in the bazaar on the proceeds and Ali was old enough to remember what it had been like when his grandfather had still owned the entire building.

The Shah had tried to break the power of the *bazaris* by building roads through the district. He'd failed, because the bazaar was too big in every sense of the word. At the time of the Shah, almost half of the country's retail economy had pumped through its streets and alleyways and over the years the *bazaris* had branched out into new disciplines, like money-lending and banking.

After the revolution the mullahs had decided the *bazaris*

were getting above themselves so they encouraged the growth of shops, supermarkets and banks in the central and northern part of the city. That way they'd fucked up the *bazaris'* power base and managed to achieve what the Shah had failed to do.

Under Ali's grandfather, the family business had collapsed. To pay off his debts, the old boy had converted their home into apartments, selling off every floor except the top one, which was where Ali now lived with his father and his sister. Life, clearly, wasn't easy.

We emerged into a courtyard and Ali pointed to the large, red-brick house opposite. It had an ornate double door for an entrance and big balconies with carved stone pillars rising to the fifth floor. It looked like a Venetian palace. 'This is where we live, Jim. Come.'

He pushed open the door. Inside, dim electric light fizzed from a bare bulb hanging from the flaking painted ceiling. Rubbish littered the cracked marble floor. There was a rank, putrid smell – either the rotting rubbish in the bins I could see under the stairs, or perhaps something had died.

There was an ancient lift, too, but it had jammed fast between two floors and looked like it had been there since the time of the Shah. The lift well, as we passed, seemed to be the main source of the stench.

Ali climbed the stairs ahead of me, our footsteps echoing off the walls as we made our way to the fifth floor.

'Jim, it would please me greatly to work on your magazine.' He started taking the steps two at a time. 'And my sister Aisha would be so happy!'

Halfway up, Ali's mobile beeped. He pulled it out of his pocket and flipped it open. 'The signal is so bad here that I only pick up messages when I am on the second floor.' He stopped to read the message, swore under his breath, then broke into a run.

I called after him, but he was already half a floor ahead of

233

me, taking the steps in threes. I didn't catch up with him until we reached the apartment door. 'Ali?'

He was breathing hard and fumbling in his pocket for his keys. 'It's my sister, I—'

The door was opened by a girl in her late twenties, with heavy kohl-laden eyes and long dark hair. She wore frayed jeans and a T-shirt with a photograph of Bono just about to swallow a mike.

She glanced at me and cut away just as quickly to focus on Ali. She spoke fast, pulling him into the apartment as she did so. There was a look on her face – one that I knew from years of soldiering and a whole lot more of shitty times.

Somebody was either dead or dying.

66

I followed them along a dark corridor into a room with tall French windows. Dirty full-length net curtains blew into the room. There was a double bed with a large carved headboard set against the far wall. A ceiling fan that wobbled on its axis above it pressed the sheets against the outline of a body. Despite the open window and the fan, the room remained sweltering. Voices drifted up from the street below. The melons and flip-flops were still on special offer.

Ali jumped onto the bed and pulled back the sheets. His father was curled in the foetal position, a bag of bones in a pair of stained pyjama bottoms. Every inch of his sweat-covered skin seemed to be scarred with short, angry red welts, like someone had turned a sandblaster on him years ago.

The girl knelt by the pillow and mopped his face with a flannel. The fact that he was shivering was the only way you could tell that he was still alive.

The girl lifted one of his eyelids. From where I was, just behind her, I could see that the pupil was as small as a pinhead. His breathing was painfully shallow.

Ali felt for a pulse. His sister stood up and put her ear to their father's chest. Their eyes met and she gave a small shake of the head before turning to a chest of drawers.

'Ali, you need help? I am—'

The girl raised a hand to me as he moved back towards the bed. 'No, but thank you. We know what to do.'

Ali manoeuvred his father into the recovery position.

The girl held a syringe to the light, flicked it with her finger to work the air up, and squirted a small jet of the fluid from the needle.

Ali took hold of his father's wrist and tried to find a vein. He looked at his sister and shook his head. She just shoved the needle into his arm, below the shoulder joint, and depressed the plunger.

I picked up the box from the top of the chest. The drug was American: Naloxone. They used it for acute cases of heroin overdose. Ali's sister knew they didn't need to get a vein up: straight into the muscle would do just as well. They'd been here before.

67

I turned back to see the two of them stroking their father's wet grey hair away from his forehead. Ali checked his cheap market Casio as he and his sister murmured to each other. If the Naloxone worked, Dad's pulse would become stronger and his breathing more regular in about five minutes. If there was no visible improvement within ten, there'd better be a doctor in the neighbourhood.

Right now I didn't exist to them. It wasn't the time to push them for what I wanted. I shut up and looked out over the broken rooftops, cluttered terraces, telephone wires and washing-lines stretching away into the middle distance. There was a thick forest of TV aerials and satellite dishes as far as the eye could see. The dishes weren't allowed by law, but this was Iran. Another contradiction – and I bet there were plenty of viewers sitting down in front of their TV with a plate of kebabs to watch the BBC.

It was fifteen minutes or so since we'd stepped into the apartment and the Naloxone was doing what it said on the tin. Some colour had returned to their father's skin. His breathing was stable.

The girl looked at her brother and gave him a faltering smile. The danger appeared to be over – for now.

Ali got to his feet. 'Jim, this is my sister, Aisha. Aisha, this is James Manley, an English journalist here for the defence exhibition.'

She got to her feet. She brushed her dark hair away from her eyes. 'Mr Manley . . .' Like Ali, she spoke excellent English with a trace of an American accent, and a tone that betrayed the fact she wasn't too pleased to see me.

Ali beckoned me towards the door. 'We will need to keep my father under close observation for the next two to three hours. After that, God willing, he should make a full recovery. Aisha will watch first. You and I, meanwhile, can talk.' He gestured towards the bedroom door. 'Please . . .'

68

I followed Ali through the room and out onto a balcony. The sun had just slipped below the horizon. Night was falling fast and with it came the chorus of wailing. We seemed to be hemmed in on all sides by minarets.

Ali leant on the balustrade and stared at the street below. 'I'm sorry you had to see my father like this. He is a good man, but he suffers.'

'What happened to him – the scars? The war?' That type of shrapnel injury does things to a man. I'd seen it.

'Would you like a drink? I don't drink myself, but my father always has whisky – black market.'

'No, mate, I'm all right.'

'Aisha will bring us something. Some *chay*, perhaps – tea.'

I asked him again.

He shrugged. 'When Aisha and I were little, we used to ask him about the scars. He always used to tell us that he'd fought off a fire-breathing dragon.' He gave a bad dragon roar and then a smile. 'He used to breathe on us just like that, holding his hands up like claws, and making this noise – the noise that the dragon made when it breathed fire at him. We used to run away, squealing and laughing . . .' His voice tailed away.

'What happened to him, Ali? In the war?'

Ali beckoned me to a carved table in the corner of the balcony and invited me to sit down. He pulled up a chair next to me. For a moment, he stared out over the rooftops, a faraway look in his eyes. Then he reached into his pocket. He produced an object wrapped in an ornate, gold-embroidered cloth, the kind of thing I'd been dodging during my walk through the market. He started to unwrap it, but was disturbed by a noise inside the apartment – the sound of a door closing. He rewrapped it quickly and placed it back in his pocket just as Aisha walked in. He smiled at her. 'How is Father?'

Out of some kind of respect thing for me, perhaps, he spoke in English.

'Resting.'

While there was something childlike and innocent about Ali, Aisha was every inch the big sister. She still wasn't impressed with me.

I held her gaze. 'How often does this happen, Aisha?'

'Often enough, Mr Manley. But we will cope, we need no help. '

Fair one, keep my nose out. It was clear she didn't want me here. Except that I'd been dragged headlong into the apartment of an overdosing heroin addict, it was none of my business.

'Would you like some tea, Mr Manley?'

'Tea would be good.'

As soon as she had left the room, Ali retrieved the object from his pocket. He set it on the table and unwrapped it again. 'I am sorry, Jim, but my sister doesn't like me talking about certain things, things that interest me, but are of no interest to her – and especially in front of strangers. But, if you will allow me to say so, you do not feel like a stranger to me. I have always wanted to do what you are doing – writing about military technology, aircraft . . . hardware, I think you call it. And that you

240

were looking for me is such a compliment. I feel very privileged.'

With a final flourish, he unfolded the cloth and produced a military medal inscribed in Farsi.

69

He passed it to me. 'My father joined a Basij Battalion – a volunteer battalion. They ended up in a village in the desert somewhere west of Khorramabad.'

The decoration was thin and tinny, but those things didn't matter to any soldier from any country the world over.

'The Iraqis attacked and our forces counter-attacked. The village changed hands many times. My father was a lieutenant, in charge of a platoon of young Basij. Most of them were just fourteen or fifteen.'

I passed the medal back and he polished it with the rag.

'My father was ordered to carry out a first-wave assault on the village. They had to attack across the minefields, using their own bodies in the name of *jihad* to clear them so that the main force of Revolutionary Guards could follow through and wipe out the Iraqis. He did not hesitate. He and his men assaulted the enemy across the minefield. That was when my father was injured. A mine blew him up, but he and his soldiers who survived the minefield still fought on and took the village. The Revolutionary Guard were not needed. And he received this for his bravery.' He held up the newly gleaming disc. 'A martyrdom medal. The highest award you could receive. The Supreme Leader himself presented it. War is a terrible thing,

James, but for my father to have been decorated in this way, for what he did, is a very big honour. It is one of the many reasons I love my father so . . . and why I forgive him for what he has done.' He wrapped the medal back in the rag.

'The drugs? That could happen to—'

'No, Jim. My mother, he was a terrible man to her. He beat her – sometimes I would come home from school and she would be lying just there.' He pointed under my chair. 'In her own blood. My father would then cry and beg forgiveness, and she would give it.' He stood up and put the martyrdom medal back into his jeans. 'I keep it with me. Always.'

'You should be very proud, Ali.'

He stood up. 'I am, Jim – very much. Now let me show you what I know about the Falcon.'

70

I'd never been able to understand what made grown men stand at railway stations or airports writing down numbers – or play golf, come to that.

Ali's bedroom shelves were lined with books, some in English. There were hefty volumes on engineering and reference books by the yard on all kinds of aircraft. Maybe this subject and this room were where he'd retreated when the trouble started at home.

Ali opened an antique desk. Inside was a laptop. He fired it up, snatching the odd glance at his father through the adjoining door as he waited for it to come online. I sat and got on with my glass of very sweet black tea. Through the open door, I had a good view of his dad. He was sleeping soundly now, as the fan battered his bedding once more.

Ali kept his voice low. 'First, I need to log on to iranianmetalbird.net to see if there have been any unusual movements . . .' He tapped some keys and his home page came up. He traced his finger across a table. 'Both main airports, Jim – IKIA and Mehrabad. From this time column I can see which aircraft have landed and departed.'

'In real time?'

'Let me show you.'

He typed in further instructions and the screen changed. This time a digital map of the entire Gulf region appeared. Moving across it were hundreds of letters, numbers and what I'd always known as 'tracks' – dotted lines that charted an aircraft's speed and heading.

I checked the time in the corner of the screen against my watch. Everything was happening live. 'How do you get into data like this?'

He looked at me and smiled because he knew something Mr Manley didn't. 'IKIA is my country's pride and joy. The government bills it as a modern airport comparable with the best in the world – Singapore, Dubai, Denver . . . It's not, of course, but one of the things they upgraded at the time they built the airport was an air-traffic reporting centre for the Tehran region and, unlike the airport itself, it's pretty good.'

'You hack into the air-traffic-control computer?'

Ali was now in full-on geek mode. 'I wouldn't put it quite like that. A commercial aircraft, as I'm sure you know, Jim, will transmit a constant stream of data to centres like these – where it is, where it's heading, lots of different information. The data is transmitted essentially in the form of an email. The emails are encoded into radio signals, and if you have a good scanner, you can intercept and receive those signals.'

His smile turned into a big grin. 'A member of our group has a scanner linked to his laptop and some decoding software that allows him to see the position and heading of any aircraft in the region. What you are looking at is the result. We post it on a secure site to which a handful of us have access. In any other country, this wouldn't be illegal – in fact, the scanner and the software are standard equipment for spotters in most parts of the world. But this, my friend, is Iran. We have to exercise some care . . .'

He hit some more keys and the screen changed. I checked the digital clock. This time, we were looking at a representation of the air-traffic picture as seen by a controller at the Tehran reporting centre a little after five o'clock local time – pretty much the moment at which the Falcon climbed away towards the mountains.

Ali peered at the screen. 'Now, let's see . . .' He used the tip of a biro to point at a dot that was slowly tracking away from Tehran.

I got into geek mode too. 'That's our bird?'

He nodded.

'What can you tell me about it?'

He hit the keys again and a small panel appeared next to the slowly tracking dot. 'This tells me almost everything I need to know. Type of aircraft: Dassault Falcon 7X. Fuel status: full. Destination: Quetta, Pakistan . . .'

'Does it give a passenger manifest?'

'It flew out empty. There were no passengers.'

I looked at him to check he wasn't taking the piss. 'You're sure no one was on board?'

He was busy on the keyboard. 'Sure, the catering company only delivered meals for the pilots.' He pointed at the screen. 'See? It says so right there. Two different menus in case one man gets food poisoning. Just two sets of meals, Jim. It's going to Quetta empty. Maybe to pick someone up or something. Who knows?'

'Are you able to track back?'

He gave another of his little smiles. 'You mean, review the historical air-traffic picture? Sure. How far do you want to go?'

'I'd like to know the aircraft's status when it first flew into IKIA.'

'Two days ago, correct?'

I nodded.

Ali started to type. A few seconds later, the screen changed. He leant forward, said something under his breath, and rekeyed the data.

'What is it?'

'I don't know. You don't often see this . . .'

'See what?'

'The aircraft did not file a flight plan. Do you know where it flew in from?'

'The UAE.'

He flicked open a notepad and leafed through. When he found the page he needed he ran his finger down a set of letters and numbers next to the margin.

'What are those?'

'Registration numbers.' He flicked to another page and typed in some more data. He leant forward. 'Ah, OK . . .'

'What?'

'I made the mistake of thinking that this is a commercially owned aircraft. It isn't.'

'No, it's an RF registration. It's almost a military aircraft.'

He pointed to the dots and tracks criss-crossing the Persian Gulf, before picking one of them out with the tip of his biro and following it – a track heading north out of Dubai.

'The software "sees" all commercial air traffic along with all the details of a particular flight. Take this one, for example. From the data on the screen I know that it's an Emirates flight out of Dubai, that its registration number is A6-ZDA, that it's *en route* to London and that it's at fifteen thousand feet and climbing.' He then pointed to some untagged dots within Iranian airspace. 'You see these? These are all uncorrelated tracks. The system registers their *presence* – it has to know where they are for it to operate safely – but the tracks themselves carry little if any data. Some do not even carry call-signs.'

'And those are military flights?'

'Yes. The Falcon effectively fell into this category when it flew out of UAE two days ago, but reverted to a civilian mode of operation inside Iran. That is very odd. They must have been keen to hide something.'

He geeked about the screen a bit more. 'Would you like to see the photographs?'

I couldn't help sitting upright.

'I told you, Jim. Nothing flies in and out of the country that we don't know about. We had never seen a Falcon 7X before. It is a very rare bird. When it was on the ground we photographed it from every angle we could.'

'Yeah, OK, then. Let's have a look. Why weren't they on your website?'

'I have to work, Jim. I haven't had time to unload.'

I didn't want to sound too full-on about it. 'If they're any good, I'll buy them right now.'

71

'Even though it's a big jet, the Falcon has a short take-off and landing capability.' He scrolled down a list of files. 'It was one of the few large corporate aircraft to have been cleared for service at London City – as you know, Jim, an airport that's renowned for stringent regulations governing the aircraft that use it.'

I nodded. If you needed STOL capability to get you in and out of London City, the airstrip RV would have been a piece of piss. That was why it had been used. It could carry the weight, get in and out, and didn't look military.

He opened a file and up came hundreds of aircraft thumbnails. 'Found them.'

The first few were of the Falcon coming in, nose high, flaps dangling, over the perimeter fence at IKIA just hours after Red Ken and Dex got dropped. I wondered if their bodies were on board, or whether they'd been burnt or cut up and fed to animals – anything to ensure they'd never be seen again. There was a good picture of the Falcon as it hit the tarmac – you could see little puffs of white smoke coming up from the wheels. There were several of it taxiing and many more of it parked up in front of M3C's very own terminal, the building tucked away on the far side of the airport.

We were getting closer to what I hoped was going to be gravy time. With his long lens, Ali had snapped several clear pictures of the aircraft's passengers as they disembarked. First off was Tattoo, still wearing the clothes he'd had on when he'd dropped Dex: short-sleeved blue shirt, tail hanging out over jeans. One snap had him putting his sun-gigs on, exposing his ink-covered arms.

And then, in the next shot, there was my target: standing at the top of the air-stairs, sniffing the breeze. The picture was an improvement on the black-and-white, but not by much.

'You know who any of these people are?'

'Just M3C people, I suppose.'

There was another shot of Altun as he made his way down the steps and then, finally, the money shot: staring out over the airport, his face turned to the camera, almost as if he was posing, one hand smoothing back hair that had been ruffled by the wind . . .

'Ali, they're excellent. The magazine will love them.'

'Really? You are sure these are good enough for you?' He was a happy man.

'More than sure, Ali. I'll take all of them. I'm sure my editor would agree for me to pay, say, a thousand dollars.' I didn't want to fuck about. That would have been more than he made in a couple of months behind the wheel of the Paykan. And the three of them could do with it. I would have liked to give them more, but I still had a job to do and no idea what it would end up costing.

'I have more!' His fingers darted across the keyboard.

I found myself staring at several good clear shots of a fork-lift truck offloading the wooden crates. The second loadie from the airstrip was in charge. There was nothing that looked like a couple of freshly wrapped bodies.

72

I needed to get them out of my possession and into Julian's as fast as I could. Majid would be going ape and I might find myself hung upside down and searched with rubber gloves.

I couldn't send them from Ali's apartment: Vevak would pick it up. I didn't want this rebounding on him or his family.

There were internet cafés, of course, but they were definitely monitored.

There was the press-centre at IranEx. In among the images of boring take-offs and landings, people standing next to an undercarriage wheel and all that shit, my editor would be getting the Falcon, the gold and the faces that accompanied it. By the time Vevak cottoned on to what I'd sent – if they ever did – I would be away from IranEx and hiding in the city, trying to find Altun and the loadies. With the Falcon now in Pakistan, I only had one known location for Altun and that was IranEx. There were two more days of the exhibition, so that was where I'd wait. I still had more to do for Julian, then for Red Ken and Dex.

I checked my watch. It was already past midnight. Majid would have staked out the room after searching it, and getting his lads to check for me in all the Western hotspots.

'Ali, any chance of me staying the night? It's a waste of time going back to the hotel now. And if you want a job in that taxi of yours, you could take me to IranEx in the morning and work with me for the next couple of days. I'll pay you another five hundred.'

His eyes lit up. 'It would be a pleasure. What time do you need to be there?'

'Soon as it opens.'

73

We ate dinner cross-legged on the carpet – a meal that Aisha had prepared that was a cross between soup, and potato, tomato, chickpea and mutton stew. She was a busy girl. As well as looking after these two she was a medical student at the university, and had joined Mousavi's green movement for reform. She had the wristband to prove it.

Ali was munching away like a good 'un, his pockets stuffed with the wad of oners I'd just given him.

Aisha, however, didn't seem too pleased to have the extra income in the house. She was almost ignoring me. Ali was either too blind to see it or chose not to notice.

Every so often one of them would get up to check on their dad, but the Naloxone had worked its magic and he was no longer in any danger. It wasn't the first time he'd overdosed, Ali said. He'd done it so many times, in fact, that when their mother left and they were just kids, they had become experts on what to do. Some days, the two of them would come home to their dad crying in a corner of the bathroom, clutching his knees, shaking with fear – or just throwing a wobbler and smashing the place up.

'Have you two heard of post-traumatic stress disorder?'

They looked at each other for any recognition.

'It's an illness that some people can develop after having experienced one or more traumatic events – like fighting a war, like getting blown up, like seeing fourteen-year-old boys being blown to bits beside you. It affects some people hard. There's no telling who. Maybe your dad . . .'

Aisha acknowledged me at last. Well, sort of. At least she was listening.

'Guys with PTSD can have problems with alcohol and drugs. Sometimes they can't communicate with family and can get violent against them.'

They both stopped eating and listened. 'Does he have nightmares – you know, shout out in his sleep?'

Aisha stifled a sob, which I took as a yes. 'It's OK, he can be helped. Your dad needs treatment.'

Ali comforted her as she cried into his shoulder. I tried to lighten it up a bit. 'Even the great Satan has a general who suffers from it because of his time in Iraq. Can you imagine that?'

Aisha pulled herself off Ali, her hair now pasted to her face. 'How do we help him? What does the American general's family do?'

It was a tough one. I wasn't sure Iran was known for its mental-health record. 'He needs to see someone who can treat psychiatric conditions, someone who understands what he's going through and knows how to help. Tell them you think he may have PTSD – look it up online. He doesn't have to be like this.'

74

Wednesday, 6 May
0555 hrs

The muezzin had sounded like he was right outside my window when he started calling the faithful to prayer half an hour ago. I'd spent the night on the floor in Ali's room. I didn't get much sleep. His dad woke me several times as he cried into his sheets. Aisha had plodded past our door to tend him.

Ali was in the kitchen. Incredibly, he looked as bright as a button. Maybe it was the thought of going to Air Geek City. 'Would you like something to eat, Jim?' He was tucking into a pitta-bread sandwich that had bits of salad hanging out of it.

I nodded away and looked for a kettle or teapot. Ali got the idea. '*Chay*? Or *ghahve*?'

'*Ghahve* would be great.'

Ali poured some into a cup while I threw some goat's cheese and lettuce into some bread.

Aisha walked in. She had never got out of her jeans and Bono T-shirt, and her hair didn't look so perfect after her intensive-care night-shift. She acknowledged me with a nod, then spoke to Ali in Farsi as she poured herself a coffee as well.

Ali picked up another cup and followed suit. 'I will go and check on Father.'

When he'd left the room, she placed the fifteen hundred dollars on the table in front of me. I gave my full attention to the remains of my sandwich. 'Mr Manley – thank you, but we do not need charity.'

'It's payment for your brother's pictures and the time I've spent with him. He drove me from the airport and he's driving me for the next two days. Thinking about it, maybe it isn't enough.'

She cupped her mug with both hands and brought it up to hide her smile. She slowly shook her head. 'You know it is a small fortune. And now I am embarrassed.' She took a sip then pulled a pack of Camel from her pocket. She offered me one.

My turn to shake my head. 'The money is yours. He's earned it.'

I pushed the notes back at her but she focused on lighting her cigarette. She took the smoke down deep. 'Thank you for explaining about my father. I have been online most of the night. I think I have found someone who understands these things, a doctor at the university.'

'That's great, Aisha. I'm sure everything will work out.' There must have been millions here suffering after that war. No wonder the place had become Heroin Central.

Aisha sank into one of the three knackered wooden chairs, her cigarette held high so I didn't get a face full of it as I sat down opposite her. I watched her as I sipped my coffee, so sweet it was almost sticky. There was a lot more going on in that head of hers.

'Ali . . .' She finally broke the silence. 'He is a dreamer. He always has been. He idolizes his father. They have a special bond. Ali does not think about himself, so I have to, Mr Manley. You know, if he could ask for any job, any job in the world, it would be yours. Do you really

256

think you will be able to get him work from your magazine?'

I hated this part of the job when it involved real people. But it had to be done. I still needed Ali. 'I can't promise anything. I have to talk to my editor. But, yes, of course. I think he'd be excellent.'

'I understand, but please do that, Mr Manley. And maybe ask him if Ali could come to England and work. That would be good, wouldn't it?'

'But what about you and your dad?'

She blew another cloud of smoke into the air and showed me her wrist. 'Do you know what this means?'

I nodded.

'I will work with the party to bring reform to our country, Mr Manley, our green movement, our green revolution. Looking after my father will be easy compared to looking after my country. Ahmadinejad will win no matter how many votes he gets, and that means there will be blood on the streets after the election.'

She took another drag and picked some tobacco from her lips. She spent more time than was necessary removing it from her fingertip.

'We students, the young, we need to show our people that we can change, but still be a Muslim country. I do not know if our green revolution will end like the Berlin Wall coming down, or with a slaughter like Tiananmen Square.'

She drank and then smoked, her eyes burning into mine so I understood the seriousness of what she was saying.

'But it is a struggle that I do not want Ali to be part of. He deserves better. I am going to make sure he gets it.'

Ali was coming back down the corridor.

As if I didn't feel enough of an arsehole already, she pushed the money back at me. 'Here is his airfare. Please, look after him, won't you?'

He reappeared with an empty cup and a big smile as I shoved the notes into my pocket.

257

'We should leave now, Jim.'

'Can you get me a mobile in the market? You know, just a cheap pay-as-you-go?'

75

It was too early for any but the local press to be up and about, and I was able to take my pick of the desktops in the media centre. I worked quickly. Nobody paid me any attention. There was no sign of Majid. I had left $3,500 in the drawer next to the Naloxone, somewhere they were sure to find it. I'd been hoping it would make me feel better about bullshitting Ali and Aisha, but it hadn't. In fact, it had made me feel worse. They were real people, who deserved much better than crossing paths with the likes of me.

I'd kept the last $1,500 for myself. I wasn't out of the country yet and might need some in-the-shit money. The cash would still come in useful in Dubai. I planned to stay there a while. There was a Suburban at the airport that needed attention.

I opened up the file and hit the email option. I typed in my editor's address, shoved in the USB stick Ali had downloaded the pictures onto, attached them along with some others to disguise them a bit, and hit send.

Then I dragged the mobile out of my sock and went just outside the door to get a signal from whoever's satellite was up there. The two bars were enough for a call to my editor.

'Morning, mate. I've sent some photos for the next edition. Can you text me to say you've got them?'

It was four and a half hours earlier where he was but Julian was a very happy boy.

'Will do. Any movement on Altun? Found out where he lives, his contacts – anything?'

I could hear him rushing about now, probably heading for his computer. It was OK for him to use clear speech as he didn't have bodies walking past every couple of seconds.

'Not yet, but working on it. Soon as I have anything for you, I'll call.'

'Excellent.'

Behind me, just inside the door, I was aware of an argument kicking off.

'All right, mate, see you soon.'

I cut the call and turned to see the big German guy in the jungle hat leaning over the reception desk, clutching a steaming cup of whatever and having a go at the girl about the milk. Our eyes met and he wandered through the door. 'Morning.' He checked my badge. 'James.' He held out a tanned hand.

I checked his. 'Morning, Stefan.'

He towered over me, and had that world-weary look of been-there-done-it about him. Sixty-odd years ago that square jaw and mass of hair would have been sticking out of the turret of a panzer. He was here for *Die Welt*, according to his badge, but no way was Stefan Wissenbach a reporter for any German weekly. Maybe he'd come in my direction because he could smell a fellow fraud.

He took a sip of his brew and still didn't like it black. He offered it to me. 'Never one to say no to a brew, so thanks.' I glanced at my mobile. Nothing yet from Julian. I took a sip. I quite liked instant.

As we leant against the Portakabin, Stefan rubbed the couple of days' growth on his chin. 'Just the same old stage-managed bullshit?' He had a clipped German accent.

'It's my first.'

He laughed, then stretched and yawned at the same time.

'Well, you won't have another press conference like yesterday's. Anna had fire in her belly yesterday, for sure. She is one *Hitzkopfig*, that girl.'

That bit of German wasn't in my squaddie vocab. It certainly didn't sound like food or beer. 'The blonde one, going on about missiles?'

His eyes darted about, sizing up a couple of good-looking women who'd come past us to lay out trays of dodgy sandwiches for the morning media frenzy. 'The new SA-16M – probably the only thing worth coming here to see.'

There had been quite a buzz about these things. The Brits, Iranians, Russians, and now Germans. Maybe they were the new must-have.

I checked my mobile again. Still nothing. I wondered about Majid picking up the email and knowing where I was. Not even GCHQ was that quick. It would take a couple of days. 'The guy at the M3C stand told me they can defeat dark flares. That explains the rumour the missile had a fault. It didn't. They were redeveloping it to defeat the flares.'

His eyes shot from the women to me. I suddenly had his full and undivided attention.

76

'But, like I said, this is my first time. What are they?'

He laughed. 'You Brits!' A heavy hand slapped my back and pushed the bottom half of the coffee from the cup. 'You invented them.'

'I'm more an infantry-weapon guy.'

His hand left my back with a smile that said he had smelt a little more about me. 'I'm sure you are.' Both hands went up into the air, as if he was framing something up there. 'When an aircraft is targeted, it could be by using laser or radar. So the aircraft has countermeasures to stop that happening. But with a handheld SAM, the system for detecting the target is best described as a passive device that emits no signal. These things . . .' He turned to me and pulled down his lower right eyelid. 'The Mark 1 Eyeball.'

He paused. 'You with me so far?'

I knew the theory. These things were just like a Stinger. I let Stefan waffle on as I checked the phone.

'It's the same with the missile itself. It has a passive seeker that homes on heat – the engine, usually – and so, traditionally, the first time you ever know you have a missile coming up at you is when it hits.

'You remember the order for all NATO aircraft to stay above

fifteen thousand feet during the Kosovo conflict because the low-level threat from the handheld SAM was too great? Were you there?'

I nodded.

'Me, too. Fucking slaughter.'

He took a couple of seconds as his head churned up whatever nightmare he'd been part of.

Julian was back. He'd got them. I closed down.

'It is the same today. If you want to stay alive when you go low-level, then you need to chuck out flares – lots of them. But you can't dispense flares all the time. You don't have enough of them.

'Since the Balkans, the Russians have designed a missile able to discriminate between the flares that aircraft dispense and the heat-source – the engine. Instead of being seduced away from the aircraft towards the flare, the missile examines the flare, rejects it, and looks for a darker heat-source, if you like, less intense – the aircraft itself.'

Stefan's hands were up in the air once more.

'The missile literally climbs a "ladder", rejecting flares, locking back onto the aircraft, rejecting another flare and so on – until it hits the aircraft. That's why the black flare was developed.'

'So they burst out of the aircraft a different colour?'

'No, they look the same as normal flares, but they have a different temperature range – they don't burn like magnesium flares, they mimic the heat signature of an aircraft much more accurately. So now, when the missile rejects the regular flare and goes looking for the darker heat-source, it sees the black flare and goes for that instead.'

'Could it take down an Apache?'

He knew where I meant. His hands were down and the smile had disappeared. 'If they weren't bullshitting you, it would be able to take down anything that is out there below ten thousand feet.'

263

'Nice talking with you, mate.'

We shook.

Ali and the Paykan were waiting for me outside.

On my way out, I broke open the USB stick and swallowed the memory. If these lads had spent years putting shredded bits of paper back together, finding out what was on a smashed stick would be a piece of piss.

Stefan Wissenbach would be making sure his people, not *Die Welt*, knew what we both did. They, too, had people out there. If an Apache or fast jet was taken out, we could no longer assume control of the air. Worse still, if a C-130 full of troops got dropped, the people back home would go ape-shit. It could all be over by Christmas. Then the dramas would really start to kick off.

I powered up my local mobile as I walked towards the exit. 'Hello, mate. You get the car parked up where I showed you?'

I didn't want Ali to have a call from my sat mobile registered on his. Better to use local – and how much more local could you get than his dad's machine? It wasn't as if he'd need it today, unless he had an urgent appointment with his dealer.

77

We sat in the front of the taxi in what looked like a bus lay-by but had become an overstuffed car park. Anywhere vehicles could stop in this town, they did.

IranEx was just under a hundred away, right in front of us. That was why we were here, to have a trigger on the entrance and wait for the Merc. With baseball caps tilted over our eyes and leaning well back in our seats we looked like loads of others, just getting our heads down for a moment or two before grappling with the challenges of the day.

I'd told Ali I was doing an M3C story. I was going to follow the management, find out where they were staying and try for an interview. They'd turned me down yesterday, but that wasn't unusual in our neck of the woods.

He nodded as if it all made sense, but I could almost hear that mind of his ticking over. He was going along with it because I seemed to be offering him a future.

Ali stared through the windscreen, concentrating on the traffic as I watched the entrance. People and vehicles streamed in and out.

'Jim, you will email me about the job when you get back to England? Do you think your editor will like my work?'

I couldn't work out if he was questioning his own capabilities or doubting me.

'I will take classes to become a good journalist. Will you tell your editor that? I will work very hard.'

'I will, mate, don't worry. I'm sure everything will be OK.'

Now I was doing the worrying. Giving a guy a glimpse of the light at the end of the tunnel only to snatch it away was an arsehole's trick. I knew what it felt like, waiting on a promise that never came good. My step-dad was always promising us a trip to Margate or to the fun fair. I'd wait for the day to arrive, my heart racing, excited to be doing stuff that other kids did all the time, but nothing ever happened. I'd start to doubt myself, checking I had the right day, waiting for him to come back from the pub, but he never did.

'Highway To The Danger Zone', the theme tune to *Top Gun*, erupted beside me. Ali flushed pink with embarrassment. 'Sorry, Jim – I cannot seem to erase it.' He flipped open his mobile. He sounded guarded at first, but there was a rapid thaw. He was soon waffling away. Whoever it was, they'd called with good news.

I spotted the wrestler's vehicle, held in traffic, trying to cut across the road to IranEx. Majid was up front and looking very pissed off. He, too, was waffling away at warp speed into his mobile. His spare hand jabbed into space, as though he wanted to hit whoever was on the other end.

Ali closed down. 'Qasim and Adel. They say the Dassault is back, Jim. It's just landed.'

'Let's head towards the airport. Can they get any pictures?'

On second thoughts, that would be a mistake. 'No, no, don't ask them.' I didn't want to get them thinking too hard. 'You're all mates again, are you?'

He tucked his phone into his pocket. 'It is good that it has come back, Jim, no?'

'Very good, mate. They'll call if something happens?'

We could be anything up to two hours away.

We were fighting through the southbound traffic when *Top Gun* kicked off again.

'*Salam?*' He listened, jabbered away for a few seconds, then turned to me. 'The Dassault has been met by a car. A black Mercedes. It has already left.'

78

The taxi sat in the shadow of a small avenue of trees on the city outskirts. Behind us, a scrapyard was surrounded by a rusty barbed-wire fence. Piles of old cars were stacked on top of each other next to mountains of worn-out tyres. Either the place was abandoned or the people who worked there had decided to stay out of the sun. Even the dogs were lying low. The birds chirping in the branches above us were the only sign of life. A couple had taken a dump on our car's windscreen.

Ahead of us the heat haze shimmered over the only road into Tehran from IKIA.

I sat behind the wheel, with Ali's ball cap still on my head and his aeroplane-geek binos on my lap. My eyes were glued to the steady stream of cars heading north.

The contrast between the bright, reflected sunlight on the white desert sand and the shade beneath the trees made it almost impossible to see us from the road. It was the perfect trigger point.

Ali sat beside me, flapping but not saying so. He now knew for sure that this wasn't anything to do with journalism.

'It's not just about taking pictures of planes. It's about finding out what people are doing with them.'

He nodded, but I could see last night's dreams fading and

fear taking their place. 'Don't worry. I'll show you the ropes. My editor already knows I couldn't crack this story without you.' I studied another blob of black coming our way.

The less he knew the better, for his own good. He was staying with me for now anyway, whether he liked it or not. I needed him and his car. If he sparked up and said he didn't like it, he was going to spend the next few hours in the boot.

Gold, Altun, M3C, dark flares and now something, or more likely someone, arriving from Pakistan. I didn't know what these fuckers were up to yet, but it looked increasingly like it had to do with Brit, US and even German blood staining the Afghan desert.

I adjusted the focus. The black blob had become a Merc. Its side windows were blacked out. 'Here we go, mate. I got a possible.'

I fired up the engine. The Merc was two up in front, both with gigs on. I couldn't make out who they were, just the silhouettes and shades.

As it drove past the trees, I prepared to follow. 'Got it. That's ours.'

I slid my sun-gigs on and pulled out.

The Paykan's wheels hit the tarmac and I pushed my foot down as far as the fifteen-year-old pedal would let me. There was no reason to talk to Ali. I had more important things to do now.

The traffic slowed and thickened as we entered the city. I could see the Merc four vehicles in front. Its green curtains and bent mobile antenna were as clearly in view as they had been in the binos.

We juddered up the road. Traffic-lights somewhere up ahead were letting no more than three cars through at a time. Mopeds whizzed in and out through the smallest of gaps.

With vehicles between us and his rear-view blocked by the chintzy green curtains, we were hidden. We'd have a problem if he turned and I was held, but that's just how it goes. I was more concerned right now about keeping my head down to help the ball cap and gigs do their job – hiding my face.

We edged forward. The jam wasn't a problem for me. Out on the open road with just four gears and an old Paykan engine would have been far worse.

Up ahead, the traffic went from bunched to more or less gridlocked. Horns honking, engines revving, it moved forward a few feet, then ground to a halt again for minutes on end. Cars peeled off left and right to try their luck down side roads. I gradually ended up right behind the Merc.

I eased forward until I was just about kissing his boot. If I couldn't see his wing mirrors, then the driver couldn't see me.

Ali strained forward in his seat. 'Bobby Sands must be a very important man in the UK, yes?'

'Bobby Sands?'

'My father said the Supreme Leader changed the name of this street in his honour.'

'What did it used to be called?'

'Winston Churchill.'

79

'Death to America' and 'Burn the US Den of Espionage' were scrawled across the only stretch of wall that hadn't been covered by Mousavi's green revolution posters.

About a hundred beyond the long-abandoned US embassy, the Merc took a sudden left, no indicators. I couldn't go with him. It would be too obvious. They would ping me immediately.

'Jim, he has turned . . .'

'Can I get down the next left?' It was approaching fast. 'Hurry up, Ali, think – can I go down? Is it a dead end?'

Too late; I turned.

I kept checking the junction about seventy ahead and pressed the pedal to the metal. No Merc had crossed it left to right by the time I got up there.

'Jim, it is lost. I think I should drive now and—'

'Shut up.'

I stopped at the junction and checked left. No sign of it moving away from me or parked. It must have gone straight on. Swinging the car left, I hit the gas. I needed to make distance before turning into the target's road.

'Jim, please. My father's car! Please, Jim, we will get into a lot of trouble. I want to go home.'

I slowed to turn right. I had to take it calmly on the corner in case the Merc had parked up just past it.

No sign of it.

'Jim, please – I really, really want to go home.'

I carried on down the road, avoiding the swarm of wheelbarrow-pushing construction workers buzzing around the concrete skeleton to my right. I checked each junction. The Merc must have parked. It had to have done, unless he'd pinged me. Why else would it come down here?

'Jim—'

'Shut up and check down the roads your side.'

At the far end, about two hundred further on, we emerged into a square. Stalinesque concrete office buildings were ranged round a patch of dusty ground with a couple of park benches and a moth-eaten palm tree in the middle.

The Merc nosed into view on the far side.

I watched the green curtain and bent antenna pull up at a set of iron gates set into an archway. The driver lowered his window and stuck out his ink-covered arm to punch some numbers into an entry-pad.

I carried on around the square as the gates swung closed behind the target. I took the first road out of sight and pulled over. I leant across and opened his door for him. 'Go and see if the Merc comes out again. Walk around the square, just act normal. Don't look directly at the house, or the Merc, the driver, anything, anyone. Just walk . . . '

'Jim, I don't think . . .'

'Just do it, Ali!'

He climbed out reluctantly onto the pavement.

'Walk slowly past. Tell me what you see. Does the building have a name, a number, anything? I need to know if the Merc stays or leaves. I'll meet you further down this road. Now go!'

I drove off, watching him walk back towards the square, shoulders down and scared. Fuck it, I'd had no choice. There's no time for debate when this stuff happens. All you can do is

272

grip the body and make it do what you want. Only afterwards can you give it a hug and make up.

I was able to turn back towards the square at the next junction and park up – a tactical bound, which meant the Paykan was out of line-of-sight from the square. I kept my head down and sun-gigs on.

I glanced at the construction site two hundred further down. A cloud of dust billowed around the base of some rickety scaffolding that framed a couple of minarets. They looked for a moment like a couple of missiles taking off.

Ten minutes later Ali slumped his way towards me. He couldn't even look me in the eye as he got back in. 'The car has gone. It was coming out as I got to the square. The building has no number or name.'

He collapsed into his seat, close to tears, as I hit the ignition. I needed to get a trigger on the target. I still had to find out who was inside that building, and why. 'It's all right, mate. You'll get the car back and everything will be OK. Not long now.'

I knew he didn't believe a word of it.

80

1905 hrs

Last light would be with us in less than an hour.

With the brown PVC seat of the Paykan tilted back, I could see straight through the windscreen towards the target. It was a two-floor, drab concrete cube, an office building, much like the rest around the patch of dirt and dust, surrounded by high walls. CCTV covered the gate, walls and even the building itself.

No one else had left or entered it since I'd stagged on. But there was at least one body inside. A couple of minutes after we'd moved into position, a ceiling fan had started to turn in a first-floor room. I'd scanned the place through Ali's binos but couldn't see who'd switched it on. With the wall so high and me so low, my perspective was limited.

There had been a great deal of coming and going. Trucks piled high with rubble had pulled out of the construction site every few minutes. The last one had left more than an hour ago. About fifteen others loaded with steel reinforcing rods were now parked up in the square. An old guy in a leather jerkin and flat Afghan-style hat had done his best to direct them but the drivers totally ignored him and did their own thing. Even Ali managed a smile as we watched them moving through the gate, oblivious to the old boy's complaints, with their rolled-up blankets tucked beneath their arms.

Young women had paraded constantly through the square all afternoon. Some were in Western dress, some a mixture, some totally covered. Those in *burqa*s had trainers and jeans on underneath.

The construction site had already achieved iconic significance for the local population. It was an extension of the campus for what the mullahs intended to become the Islamic world's foremost seat of learning. Aisha studied medicine here; there were more mosques and classrooms on the far side of the plot.

The cicadas were going ape above the distant drone of traffic. A slight breeze rustled the dry leaves of the near-dead palms. I glanced across at Ali. He was feeling more of a prisoner now than a friend. He was scared of leaving his dad's car with me, but even more scared of staying.

It was time to let him off the hook. 'Listen, mate, you can go soon – and with the car. OK?'

He sat up slowly, eyes straight ahead, hardly daring to believe what I'd just said. 'Thank you, Jim, thank you. I will not say anything to—'

'It's all right, mate. Listen, I need you to know something. I'm not going to bullshit you. I'll do my best with the job. But it's a long shot . . .'

He turned very slowly towards me. His eyes bored into me. 'You are not a journalist, are you, Jim?'

'No, mate. But you've helped me do something important. I'm not exactly sure where it's going to lead yet, but we're doing our best to stop what happened to your dad happening to a whole lot of others.'

He nodded, but I knew he was far from convinced.

'I'm sorry, Ali.'

He raised his hands and slowly massaged his temples. It was some time before he spoke. 'Can I go home now?'

'Yes, mate.' I paused. 'But I need one last favour.'

81

This area didn't have streetlighting. I wasn't complaining – I always felt safer in the dark. I stood against the fence, trying to get some pitta bread down my neck. There was no curtain across the target window, and the fan kept going. Somebody had turned the light on but I still hadn't been able to see who.

Another light came on, somewhere on the ground floor this time. Weak light spilled over the wall.

I now understood how difficult it must have been for the women in the Emirates food hall to hoover up their Big Macs. Getting anything through the hole in Ali's mum's old *burqa* was proving very difficult indeed. Most of it seemed to miss and tumble down the black material.

No way could I have got away with what I wanted to do tonight without some sort of cover. *Burqa*'d up, I passed for a very chunky university girl. If Arab men could cover up and get through airport security on their sisters' passports, I should be able to mince about at night in this kit to my heart's content. If not, I'd soon find out.

Snatches of waffle and banter filtered through from the far side of the tall plywood sheets that encircled the building site. I looked through the gap where two sheets didn't quite meet. Blankets were spread out round a fire, with pots and pans rigged over the flickering flames. The wood spat and split, completing the western campfire effect. It could have been a scene from a John Wayne movie – except that these boys, truck drivers, I guessed, were in *dishdash*es and had a TV perched on top of a pile of concrete blocks, next to a fat extension reel. The other end of the lead disappeared in the direction of a genny I could hear ticking away in the distance.

A couple of students walked hand in hand across the far side of the square, giving the odd giggle along the way. I stayed in the shadows and thought about Ali. I wondered what he was going to do. Tell the police? Tell his sister, and she'd tell the police? She was going to be really pissed off with me. I didn't know, and I tried not to care. Whatever, it was out of my hands. All I could do was what I was doing now – keeping eyes on the target and trying to identify whoever was in there.

I'd had no choice in my treatment of Ali, but that didn't stop me feeling sorry for him. First his dad's illness had screwed up his university plans, and now I'd done the same with his dreams of a journalistic career.

Fuck it, there was nothing I could do but cut away from all that and get on with the job.

I needed to get a trigger on the target and find out who was in there. Altun had to be somewhere with the Pakistan delivery. Whether he was sitting under that ceiling fan or not, I still needed to find a way of making entry on target tonight. Short of bursting straight into M3C's airport HQ, I had nowhere else to go.

I needed to find a good OP, ideally high up in an unoccupied building that was still under construction and looked right down on the target. The closer of the two minarets fitted the bill. My only problem would be getting into it. I couldn't just sashay past the lads round the campfire – it wasn't that kind of party. Nor could I get over the fence. I'd checked. It wouldn't happen. The only way was to head for the uni and see how I could make my way from there.

Before I did anything, I had to finish getting some more bread and water down my neck – instead of down my *burqa*. I didn't know how long I was going to have to be up there, or the next time I'd get a chance to eat or drink.

I was finally done. I brushed the crumbs off the black material and moved onto the pavement, day-sack over one shoulder. I blended in pretty well, I thought, apart from being a foot taller than the rest of the girls. I just hoped my size-ten Timberlands wouldn't stick out too much, and that nobody stopped me to sympathize about how badly the diet was going.

I went back into the square and followed the other students down to the right of the target, trying to avoid taking long paces or looking like I was about to enter a boxing ring. Paralleling the road that led to the university via the construction site, I lost eyes on target. I wouldn't have it again until I got into my OP, but it was worth the risk. If I stayed at ground level I wouldn't see jack.

A hundred metres or so past the square, the students were starting to bunch. By two hundred, they were crossing the road and coming in from all directions, bottlenecking at what I assumed must be the entrance. I joined the mob.

We surged through the gates into a big, brightly lit open space with marble flooring. A mosque reared up on the far side, another couple of hundred metres away. Its huge square façade and minarets towered above us, floodlit from the ground like something from Cape Canaveral. The spotlights were harsh enough to make God blink.

The square was humming with chat and ring tones. The girls laughed, glanced at their homework and munched peanuts or other stuff out of bags. It could have been almost any university campus, almost anywhere in the world.

I worked my way to the right of the mosque, where a tree-lined border had been planted to give the square some shade. I kept moving, making sure I didn't bump into anybody or

279

anything and draw attention to myself. It was easier said than done, when the hole I had to look through was smaller than a Warrior's letterbox. I wanted to move through this lot like oil, not giving a single person cause to stop, stare and wonder what class the big bird was in.

I headed beyond the trees and into the stretch of shadow where the floodlights between the old and the new part of the campus didn't meet. I picked my way over mounds of earth and rubble for about twenty metres until I was in total darkness. I took off the *burqa*, folded it up and shoved it into my day-sack. I'd need it again to get out.

82

As my eyes adjusted to the ambient light, blurred shapes slowly took on recognizable outlines. I picked my way past a cement mixer, and piles of wood, concrete blocks and steel. Soon I could see the bubble of orange light from the campfire and hear the mush of the TV they were shouting at.

As I moved closer to the carcass of the new mosque I could see the drivers from earlier quite clearly. The TV was side-on to me but I caught the odd bit of frenzy. '*Rooney ... Giggs ... Rooney, Rooney ...*' They suddenly roared at the screen, rose as one from their blankets, then sank back, disappointed. I knew that feeling all too well.

The old man in the hat offered round cigarettes to console them. Then they got back to the job in hand. Tin plates glinted in the firelight as they scooped more rice and sauce from pots over the fire.

I half crept, half crawled to the opening that would one day house the tall white mosque doors. I slipped inside as the truckers threw down their plates and sparked up again about something involving Ronaldo.

Windows had already been fitted into the walls, but the stars shone through a big empty hole in the central dome forty metres above me. I picked my way carefully around endless piles of cement bags, wheelbarrows and scaffold towers that reached skywards towards nothing in particular. I headed for the far left-hand corner, the minaret closest to the target.

A cool breeze blew down the spiral stairwell as I started to climb. Twenty steps up, I passed a narrow slit window – the kind Robin Hood's mates fired arrows from in Crusader castles. It looked out over the back of the mosque. I had a bird's-eye view of the lads and Man U. The noise from the TV gradually faded. When I reached the muezzin's chamber, it was like entering the Tardis. The room was wider than I'd expected – the concrete floor was eight to ten metres across – and perfectly circular.

The smell of cement filled my nostrils. On the far side, just visible in the half-light, were stacks of boxes, concrete blocks and a pile of sand. Stark white light flooded in from four narrow, dust-coated windows that extended from waist-level to the roof. A door led out to the muezzin's balcony. It would bristle with loudspeakers by the time the thing was finished.

I tried the handle, but it was locked. No problem. I still had a good field of view down into the target from the window to its left. It was a bit fuzzy because of the shit on the glass but I could see the lights were still on. I checked my watch. It was coming up to nine.

The panoramic view was even better than my hotel room's. The square directly below was a big dark patch, but to my right, the floodlighting around the university mosque picked out hundreds of ant-like students milling about in the court-yard. I was prepared to bet that every one of them would be sporting a green wristband. A few blocks away to the left, traffic streamed along the main.

I moved closer to the window overlooking the target and wiped a bit of cement dust off the glass with my shirt-sleeve. Binos are an excellent night viewing-aid when there's ambient light. I raised one of Ali's lenses to it, scanned along the second storey, then focused on the still-lit window.

I could now see a wooden floor, a white leather settee and, next to it, a small rectangular glass side-table holding a tray of half-eaten meat and rice. Only one plate, one glass and a half-empty water jug. The room on the ground floor to the left of the building's entrance was clearly a kitchen. The arched gateway was the only way in or out of the courtyard. The double glass doors at the front opened into a reception area. The target was some kind of business premises.

Movement at the top window caught my eye.

I swept the binos upwards with one hand and tried to undo the flap on my day-sack to get at my Nikon with the other. A picture would make Julian a happy boy.

Tattoo was in mid-bend. As he picked up a tray, his heavily inked biceps slid out of his short-sleeved white shirt. He stood with his back to the window, treating me to a grandstand view of the artwork on his neck as he talked in the direction of the dead ground on the other side of the room. His body language was respectful. He was almost standing to attention, tray held out in front of him. He nodded, turned and disappeared.

Whoever was also in there would move at some stage. I didn't know if I'd get a picture from here in this light but, fuck it, I'd try. Why not? I had the kit.

As I straightened up with the Nikon, I spotted another freshly cleared patch of window, directly under mine. I couldn't believe I hadn't seen it before.

I put the camera down slowly on the day-sack and stood up, my full attention still on the window. Then I turned and launched myself into the dead ground behind the building shit on the other side of the room.

83

The shadowy figure shifted on its hands and knees, trying to scuttle for cover. I kicked hard into the centre of the mass. There was a dull scream. The figure surged towards me, arms straight out like battering rams, and thrust me back against the wall. Then it kicked and punched like a mad thing before breaking away and running for the stairs.

I followed and jabbed my Timberland against a running leg. The body crashed to the floor. There was a moan, and hands started to flail. I pinned an arm to the ground with one foot then kicked hard with the other, two, three times into the centre mass, then reached down and found the back of a neck. I jammed my hand around a throat, squeezing the windpipe, and rammed the head against the concrete blocks. Fingers scrabbled their way upwards and gripped my wrist. I heard lungs fighting for air. I ran my free hand down the body for a weapon and brushed against a woman's breast.

Keeping a firm grip on the girl's throat, I shifted my free hand to the base of her skull, raised both my arms and started to lift her back across the chamber. She was level with me, but facing away. All she could do was stumble backwards, trying to keep up with me, trying to keep on tiptoe to minimize the pressure on her throat.

I reached my porthole and jammed her face against the wall to its right. I still had a job to do. I still had to keep trigger on the target.

Nothing was happening. Light but no movement.

I scanned down, trying to see into the kitchen. Again, nothing.

Then I turned my attention back to the girl. 'What the fuck are you doing here?'

Her blonde hair hung limply over her face as she begged for oxygen. She didn't look too much like Agnetha from Abba right now.

84

The call to prayer kicked off big-time in the mega-mosque over the way. I checked the drivers, hoping that Ronaldo and his mates would have covered any noise that might have worked its way down there. But they were otherwise engaged. The TV had been turned off and they were shifting their blankets to face east.

I kept my hand tight around her windpipe.

I couldn't see her face clearly in the gloom but I knew it would be bright red by now. She'd be dizzy soon from lack of oxygen and that was good. It would control her.

I looked back towards the target. A man had begun to pray below the fan. He was on his knees, pointing in the same direction as the truckers. His forehead was pressed against the floor.

Agnetha's hands worked their way up to my wrist again, but she didn't struggle. She couldn't: she was starting to die.

I let go of her throat, pushed her to the floor and kicked her up against the wall. She gave a gut-wrenching gasp. 'Get your face down! Face down!' I stuck my boot on the back of her neck. She could breathe, but she wasn't going anywhere fast. I picked up the camera and fired it up, checked the flash wasn't on, pointed and shot. I clicked the shutter three times in quick succession and checked the screen. All I'd got was a burst of light from the window that turned everything around it dark.

There was a choke and a mumble from under my boot. 'There's not enough light . . . I've already tried . . .'

I rotated the ball of my foot, like I was stubbing out a cigarette. 'Shut it!'

A sermon of some kind was being banged out over the speakers at the top of the uni mosque. Using my camera zoom, I watched the body beneath the fan continue to pray. He was in his early thirties with neatly cut, side-parted hair and a well-trimmed beard, and dressed in a plain dark suit, white buttoned-up shirt, no collar. He looked like he'd just stepped out of a Bollywood movie poster.

I put the camera down on my day-sack and grabbed a serious handful of hair. 'Get up! Up!' I needed her to know who was in control here. That way she had no choice, no power, no voice. I slid her up the wall, my knee pressed between her shoulder-blades, until her face was level with the bit of window she'd cleaned. I rammed her face against the glass. 'Can you see him? Who is he?'

'Taliban,' she rasped.

'He got a name?'

'I don't know it.' There was no fear in her voice. She was angry, a bit like she'd sounded at the press conference. 'Please let go. I'm not going to run. I'm not going to shout. I'm not going to do anything. I'll do what you say.'

'Why is he here?' I shoved her face back against the glass.

'To buy ground-to-air missiles. SA-16s.'

'Who from?' I wanted to know everything she knew.

'M3C, of course. That's why he's in the Neptun building. Look, I can help you. Tell me what you want to know. Just fucking let me go.'

'What's Neptun?' I stood directly behind her, forcing her back against the wall. I twisted my hand further into her hair. Her skin tightened like a bad facelift. 'What's Neptun?'

'The building – the office. The company's called Neptun. It's one of the companies M3C absorbed when it went multi-national. It produces handheld surface-to-air missiles. That's what you're here for, isn't it? That's what we're both here for.'

'The Taliban buying 16s?'

'Well, you're British, aren't you? You're here about the missiles, trying to stop them getting into Taliban hands, yes? Look, I can help you. Just let me go. I'm not going to do any-thing. We're both here for the same reasons, for God's sake. What do you think I'm going to do?'

'Spark up like yesterday. How are they being paid for? Is there a middleman? They dealing direct?'

'Heroin cash – and direct, of course. Why would he be at Neptun if not? Either drugs direct or cash from the sales – I don't know exactly which and I don't really care. All I want to do is expose the deal – maybe even stop it in its tracks. Why don't you let me help you? We want the same things, don't we?'

The Taliban had stopped praying and was back on his feet. He started rolling up his mat, then stopped and dug a cell phone out of his jacket. Headlights rolled into the square and the Neptun gates swung open. The Taliban put the phone to his ear as the Merc pulled in.

I let go of her hair. 'Pick up the binos. Tell me who you recognize.'

She nodded and did as she was told. The reception lights were now on. I zoomed the Nikon in on the white-marble-floored hallway. A large French-style three-seater settee with mahogany arms stood on the right-hand side of the foyer, opposite an ornate desk complete with repro Bakelite telephone and a couple of high-backed chairs. Tattoo and the Taliban waited just inside the glass entrance.

'You know the guy with the Taliban?'

She took a couple of seconds to check him out. 'No. '

The Merc swept round the forecourt. The rear door opened

before it had come to a standstill. Out jumped Altun, arms at full stretch. He and the Taliban embraced and lavished multiple kisses on each other's cheeks. Tattoo skirted round them and kept eyes on the square.

'Do you know him? You know the lad who's just got out?'

She scoped him for another few seconds and shook her head. I could feel her disappointment. 'He was at the press conference, but I don't know him, no. Who is he?'

'That's one of the things I aim to find out. Who were you expecting?'

'Brin.'

The name didn't register with me.

'He owns M3C. That's why I'm here. If I can prove the deal is going ahead, I can shine a light on some high-level corruption. I may also help prevent your planes and helicopters, and America's and Pakistan's, getting blown out of the sky by my country's missiles . . .' She took a deep breath. 'I keep telling you, I can help you. Isn't it about time you started to believe me?'

The three of them piled into the Merc and they drove back out of the gate.

Agnetha rested her head against the window, her eyes closed as the headlights disappeared towards the main. Either she didn't know as much about what was happening as she'd claimed or she was bullshitting. It didn't really matter which. We probably did want some of the same things, but I doubted she had the solutions in mind that I did.

There were plenty of people like her out there who were bent on saving the world, and a conscience was a good thing, I supposed – except that in situations like this it could easily get you killed. Crusaders for truth look great under the studio lights. But in the real world they get swatted like flies.

85

I thought about pushing her back down onto the floor and giving her the Timberland treatment while I packed my day-sack, in case she made the mistake of thinking we were new best mates.

'M3C are trying to hide the SA-16 deal by using Iran as the broker. That probably explains the guy in the Mercedes.' She gestured towards the Neptun building. 'Look, I can't prove it yet, but Brin is where all this shit begins. The Taliban may fire the guns and Iran may think it's pulling their strings, but M3C loads the bullets. If we can close Brin down, that's where it ends.'

'Until some other fucker takes his place.' I pulled the cord to close my day-sack and spotted a nylon shopping bag close by where I'd found her.

'It's not just the military who are killed by these things. People who have no say, who are just trying to get on with their lives – the ones everybody forgets. That's why I'm here. We have to stop—'

'For fuck's sake, shut up. Here . . .' Her bag contained the same sort of stuff I had in mine: cash, passport, camera, *burqa*. No weapon. I threw it at her. 'You come in via the university?'

She nodded and pulled out her *burqa*.

'We'd better get out the same way.'

'Where are we going?'

'Your hotel.'

Her eyes narrowed. 'You throttle the life out of me, treat me like a silly little girl who doesn't know shit, and then expect me to invite you back to my room?' She gave a soft laugh. 'They moved me out to the airport. I'm getting thrown out of the country tomorrow. They want me on the first flight out. I'm on the seven thirty to Astana, then Moscow – they're in such a hurry to get rid of me they're not even sending me back to Russia. They put security in the lobby so I just took the rear exit. What's the worst they could do if they catch me sneaking back in with you? Threaten to throw me out in the morning?'

The worst they could do was a whole lot worse than that, but I didn't think now was the right time to mention it.

86

We sat in the back of the cab in our *burqas*, me playing the big, ugly sister. There wouldn't have been a lot to talk about even if we'd both sounded local. We were on the outskirts of the city, in the glow of cheap orange streetlights and what looked like a shanty town thrown together with cardboard, wriggly tin, mud and straw. Dogs skulked and pissed on the pavement. Kids in rags played in the doorways.

Agnetha wore a plain band of gold on the third finger of her right hand. In Russia, that meant she was married. If she'd worn it on the same finger of the left, it would have sent a clear signal that she was divorced or widowed. Either her husband was at home doing a little light housework or she wanted people like me to stop bothering her.

It hadn't taken us long to get out of the minaret and sneak past the drivers. They were now focused on the Iranian answer to *Friday Night with Jonathan Ross*. All we could hear was canned laughter, punctuated from time to time by giggles beneath the blankets.

The square was teeming again as women poured out of the mosque. We dusted ourselves down as best we could before taking our places in the crowd. We headed up to the main and jumped into a taxi – a Peugeot 305 with a sunroof, air-conditioning and a nice blue digital dash. Just right for the ladies.

Agnetha gave directions. Her Arabic was really good. These lads weren't Arabs, but they understood her. After all, their religion was inseparable from the language. They'd known it since they were kids.

I felt my eyes beginning to droop in the comfort of the rear seat and the cocoon-like security of the *burqa*. I shook myself awake and tried to make sense of the M3C/Iran/Taliban triangle.

The Taliban had the drugs and the cash to pay for the weapons.

It didn't add up.

Why did Altun need the gold?

Why would a guy who was so high up the food chain organize a robbery and use a Russian plane to cart away the proceeds? Why would the mullahs turn a blind eye? They weren't that mad.

And then I realized that the deal wasn't being brokered by the Iranians at all. Agnetha was wrong. They had nothing to do with it.

So what was Altun up to? And why did he need the gold?

I was going round in circles. I had to cut away. The answer didn't matter. It didn't do anything for me right now, and it couldn't affect what I was going to do.

87

We were approaching the airport road. Red and white lights blinked on top of the towers. The terminal glowed brilliant white. It looked like a recently landed UFO.

The Peugeot drove towards Agnetha's hotel. Beyond the flags in the driveway, the lobby was another beacon of white neon. A bored-looking guy in a uniform slouched at the reception desk. Agnetha asked the driver to go round to the back. I checked my watch. It was coming up to eleven.

She paid off the driver and pretended to look for her car. The blue glow of the dash faded into the night.

She led me to the steel fire escape. I took off my *burqa* and bundled it into my day-sack but she kept hers on. I was quite pleased about that. The bruises on her neck would be developing nicely. She was halfway up the stairs before she realized I wasn't following. 'Aren't you coming up?'

I shook my head. 'The room's probably bugged.'

'But I—'

'You online?'

'Yes.'

'Whatever I find out, I'll let you know. What name am I looking for?'

'Anna Ludmilova. Shall I spell it?'

'I'll find you.'

I headed out of the car park, my day-sack on my back. I broke into a jog to get out of the light and make some distance. Being alone had never been a big deal for me. It was simpler than surrounding yourself with people the whole time, and I'd sometimes confused it with a kind of freedom. But I'd have given almost anything just then to have Lord Dex of Cards and his Hallowe'en torch beside me, and to be able to take the piss out of Lord Ken of t'Pit for firing up his thousandth roll-up of the day.

This might be a crusade for Agnetha, but it was a whole lot more than that for me. I reckoned I'd already discovered enough to keep Julian happy for a day or two. I'd done what I'd been asked to do. Now I was going to find Altun and his mates again. And then I was going to kill them.

It wouldn't stop any missile deal; it might not even delay it. It wouldn't get the Taliban flapping or make the world start smelling of flowers. But it would make me feel a fucking sight better.

88

I was pumping the Timberlands as fast as I could, but the Air France 747 overtook me with ease as it taxied down to the bottom of the strip about two hundred to my left and prepared for take-off.

I'd kept on the Imam Khomeini International Airport approach road so that I could move faster. I was soaked with sweat, but my head was clear. The M3C terminal was on the far side of the complex. Behind me, a never-ending stream of traffic roared along the main.

The 747 lumbered down the runway and climbed into the air. I turned off the tarmac and stumbled across a stretch of rubble-strewn sand, keeping out of the stark white light that separated the airport from the desert.

I picked my way past a spaghetti junction of rusty metal pipes and interconnecting valves that were due to bring water into or take waste out of IKIA at some point in Majid's glorious future. A single-track road curved around the edge of the airfield. I turned onto it and speeded up again. My throat was dry. My hair was plastered against my face. The day-sack pounded my back with every step. I felt like a squaddie again, on a tab. Switch off, head down and make distance. It's what you do once you're there that counts, so get there fast.

Two more airliners took off as earthworks, bulldozers and heavy plant sprang up around me. Three hundred metres of concrete and wasteground separated me from the perimeter fence as I skirted the end of the runway.

I stopped and got out Ali's binos as another jet taxied down towards me. Either there wasn't a night-flying ban in Iran, or nobody gave a shit. I focused for a moment on the taxiing jet. A line of passengers settled into their window seats and reached for their safety instructions or gazed in silent wonder at the monument to the '79 revolution. Then I panned right until I found the M3C hangar in the semi-darkness opposite. It was around two hundred metres away.

The Dassault was on the pan. No lights, no generator on the go. But there was a dull glow from the centre of the building. I scanned the windows, but the blinds were down.

Still keeping to the shadows, I made my way round towards the turning circle outside the front entrance and raised the binos again. There was no visible security; no barriers, no checkpoints and no vehicles.

I could see a darkened reception area, accessible via big glass front doors. The building straddled the perimeter fence. The only way to get airside was to go through it.

I cut across the wasteground, past a seemingly random scattering of abandoned concrete sewage pipes, sections of rusted fencing and deep caterpillar tracks. I needed a good OP, close enough to see anyone who arrived; close enough to grip them before they had any time to react.

I slowed. I didn't have to gulp great lungfuls of air any more, but the sweat started to pour big-time now I was cooling down. I hated this bit. Every stitch of my clothing was starting to stick to me. I knew the sand would, too, once I'd found somewhere to hide up.

I was about a hundred away from the M3C set-up. It was as close as I could go. There was no cover from here on in. I crawled into one of the sewage-pipe sections to sort myself out.

I eased off the day-sack and leant my wet back against the concrete. All sorts of grit and giant spider's webs immediately found their way down my neck and into my shirt. I took a couple of deep breaths and hoped my body heat would dry everything off before dawn.

Using the ambient light from the main terminal, flashing tower beacons and yet another aircraft taxiing down the runway, I got out the mobile and powered it up. It was just after 0300.

Julian needed to know about the missile deal and the dark flares, but my finger hesitated over the keys. It didn't want to call. Right now I was in control. If I talked to him there was a strong chance I'd have to disobey a direct order. I was a hundred per cent sure his way of dealing with this situation wasn't going to be the same as mine. I'd fucked over enough people on this job already. I didn't want to add him to the list.

I started to put together a text. I didn't want to give him the opportunity to call me in, but I needed to let him know what was happening, just in case I fucked up and joined Red Ken and Dex a whole lot earlier than I'd planned.

SA-16 seeker has NO fault.
It now has ANTI-DARK FLARE CAPABILITY.

I also told him about the Taliban, M3C, Altun and their deal.

But don't know where the gold fits in.

I felt a gentle breeze as I crawled out of the pipe in search of a satellite signal and a weapon. Minutes later my fingers closed around a metre-long section of steel tubing that was just what I'd had in mind.

89

Thursday, 7 May
0535 hrs

A sliver of sunlight edged above the eastern horizon. It wouldn't be long before the rest of it burst through. Birds sparked up and punctuated the quiet moments between take-offs and landings. If Altun turned up I'd wait until he'd dropped off his new best Taliban mate, then take him and his BG on with the steel. The BG would be first: I wanted his weapon. Then I'd drop Altun with it. With any luck he'd take some time to die. If he didn't turn up, I'd take the BG and persuade him to tell me where Altun was. It wasn't much of a plan, but it would do. And when it came to choices, I was running on empty.

I never thought too much about dying. My most philo-sophical view on the matter had always been: fuck it. If I was too slow or too unlucky today I was dead, so anything else was a bonus. It had always been that way. Maybe that was why I'd always been the one to put my hand up and volunteer. *Fuck it, so what? It'll be a laugh . . .*

Laughs had always been in pretty short supply where I came from, and I guess the situation I was facing right now wasn't so funny. But I'd treat myself to a good one when Red Ken and Dex gave me the thumbs-up from whatever cloud they were hanging around on.

There was movement at the rear of M3C. Three guys in dark blue boiler-suits headed for the Falcon and hooked up the generator. Its engine kicked in and lights flickered on inside the aircraft. A set of steps unfolded, linking the cabin to the concrete so the ground crew could jump inside and do whatever ground crews did at times like this.

Two guys in short-sleeved white shirts and ties, each carrying a black air-crew case, strolled up to the 7X and disappeared inside. Shouldn't be long now.

The sun heaved itself over the horizon to my right and threw the mountains on the other side of the city into sharp relief. A pair of headlights came up the road, fast. I raised the binos. It was a Merc, trailing a dust-cloud, covering the distance in a few short minutes that I'd taken hours to cross.

I steadied the binos. The sky was still too dark and the car too far away for me to be able to see whether or not its antenna was bent, but I knew where I was placing my money. It pulled into the turning circle and the passenger door began to open.

I pulled the steel tube from behind me.

It was two-up in front. This was going to be hairy.

As the vehicle stopped, the BGs jumped out. Both were in sleeveless white shirts with weapons on their belts. Tattoo had been in the passenger seat. I couldn't be totally sure, but the driver looked like the second loadie from the Dubai airstrip. They opened a rear door each.

Altun and the Taliban stepped out onto the concrete and fastened their jackets. They didn't talk, or give the muscle a second glance. They headed towards the terminal. Tattoo went for the boot and his mate rushed past them to hold open one of the big glass doors. The Taliban was still dressed in last night's suit. Altun's was grey, and the shirt had a buttoned-down collar. They disappeared inside. Tattoo followed with two

300

small overnight bags and a prayer mat, and the door closed behind him.

Time to move. I gripped the steel rod and crawled out of the concrete pipe. Get to the terminal, wait to see who came out, and go for it. My head was completely clear, my heart-rate even.

Another vehicle approached the M3C terminal from my right. It was also a Merc. These boys hadn't spent too much time at the Paykan dealership. I eased myself back into the pipe as it pulled up alongside the first. This time no one jumped out to open the rear door. It did that by itself, and a pair of short dumpy legs appeared.

Spag's light cargos and blue fleece strained at the waist as he clambered out. There was no mistaking the fat fuck.

A thousand thoughts raced through my head in a nano-second, none of them good.

90

The Dassault's engines had started to whine as soon as the second Merc had spat out its passenger and he'd waddled into the terminal.

I wrenched the Nikon out of my day-sack. I still couldn't believe it.

Spag was dead – I'd seen him killed.

No, I hadn't. I'd just seen his body. I never actually saw him go down . . .

I'd seen Red Ken and Dex go down; seen them take a whole mag each. I thought I'd seen Spag get the same treatment, but he'd never been directly in my line of vision. There had been a gap of a few metres between Red Ken's body and his. As soon as he saw Spag run out of the arc of fire, Red Ken must have realized it was a stitch-up and tried to drop him.

Four bodies came out of the terminal airside and headed for the Falcon.

I rattled off a series of pictures of Altun, the Taliban and Spag sharing a joke, then some more as they walked up the aircraft steps. Tattoo's sidekick checked the bags were on board before joining them. The stairs were sucked into the fuselage and the aircraft headed off down the runway.

I scrolled back through the pictures. They were all in focus, and I knew without a doubt that I was looking at Spag and the second loadie, the one who had hosed Red Ken down.

I got out the sat comm and powered it up. 'Jules, stand by, get a pen.'

'Nick, listen, I want—'

'In a minute. You ready?'

'Nick—'

'Mate, listen to me . . .'

The roar of the three engines drowned whatever he was trying to say.

'That's the Falcon, Jules. It's just left IKIA. Altun is on board. So is the Taliban and Spag. Spicciati is alive. The fuck is part of the deal. Track it, tell me where it's going and I'll get there, find out what's happening. Just find out where it's going for me.'

There was a pause.

The Falcon's engine noise faded.

Finally Julian spoke. 'I know.'

'Know what?'

'I know that Spicciati is alive.'

This was not a good day out for Julian. I could feel his pain.

'I'm sorry, Nick. This is where it ends. I've been ordered to stand you down. It's been taken away from us. Stand down – acknowledge that, Nick.'

'You pissed or what? We don't know if the gear is in-country yet. And if it isn't, we don't know where it is or how they're getting to it. I'll find that out, mate. Follow the plane and I'll get there and stop this shit. What if our lads get dropped out of the sky tomorrow? That's all right, is it?'

'No, it's not.' Julian sounded as pissed off as I was. 'Nick, I can do nothing here. It's not just you being stood down. It's both of us.'

'He still CIA? You telling me it was some fucked-up Ollie North-style double-dealing CIA bullshit that got Dex and Ken killed?'

The line stayed dead for a few seconds.

'Jules! Is he?'

'Roger that. He never got out. He's been undercover for years. I'm sorry. We didn't know. No one knew.'

I felt like I'd been hit by a sledge-hammer. 'You didn't know?'

'Nick, if you decide to go ahead and do whatever it is you plan to do, it's against my direct order. I will no longer answer your calls and I will track your sat comm. Do you understand what I'm saying?'

'Acknowledged, I'm stood down.'

'Correct. Good luck.'

I powered down. Fuck it. I didn't trust our Firm. I didn't trust the US Firm. Or any other fucker's Firm, come to that. The whole fucking lot of them only gave a shit about one thing. Themselves. Well, not quite all of them. There was still Julian.

I checked my watch: 06.10.

I leapt out of the pipe and bundled my kit into my day-sack as I ran. I left the steel tube behind. I didn't want to make too much of a mess of Tattoo. I needed clean clothes.

This was my start line. Nothing else mattered now apart from getting to Tattoo. He was going to die first, simple as that.

My head was crowded with images of Dex falling to the ground as Tattoo pumped rounds into him. And now he was just metres away from me. I wasn't going to hang around.

I sprinted past the Merc, checking that there was no one inside it. It was parked less than a couple of metres from the entrance. The keys were in the ignition.

I pulled the peak of my ball cap down low, walked up to the door and rapped on the glass. Tattoo looked up from behind the desk, put down his drink and gave me a curl of the lip, half in sheer bloody-minded irritation, half in disdain. I wasn't that surprised. I'd caught my reflection in the glass – a day's stubble and filthy clothes. I wouldn't have invited me in.

I banged harder.

Tattoo sprang up and powered towards me, his arms

304

swinging like an RSM's on the drill square. He had a holstered Makarov on his belt, along with three mags in holders.

I turned towards the Merc, gesticulating and waving.

He was nearly at the door.

I kept moving towards the car, pointing to the back of it as if there wasn't a moment to lose.

I heard the buzz of the door-release mechanism. He started gobbing off at me in Russian.

I gripped the mobile in my right fist like a dagger. There was no time to answer him, to look up – no time to do anything. Head down, arm bent and solid, I spun around and rammed the top end of it into his gut.

He dropped, but only to his knees. He went for his pistol.

I slid behind him, totally focused on the weapon. I grabbed it and wrenched it downwards.

As it bounced off the tarmac, I lifted his chin with my left hand and jammed the top of the mobile into his throat with my right, just below the Adam's apple. I pulled back with all my strength, trying to bury the thing in his neck.

His hands reached up to mine, fingers scrabbling, trying to pull them away. I dragged him out of line-of-sight of the entrance to the building and dropped to my knees. He came down with me, his legs splayed out in front of him.

I pressed my chest down on the back of his head, keeping maximum pressure on his throat. I pulled the mobile towards me as if I was trying to thrust it right through his throat and stab myself between the ribs. The more he struggled, the harder I leant against him.

He kicked and bucked like an animal until his windpipe was finally crushed. Snot and saliva frothed at his nose and mouth and his brain started to close down. His hands flapped weakly at my arms.

Hypoxia had him in its grasp. He collapsed, but it wasn't over yet. I counted off another sixty seconds before I wrenched us both to our feet and starting dragging him towards the Merc.

I dumped him on the back seat and gave his shirt a wipe. There was no blood, but a good few nostrils-ful of snot. I pulled his coat off its hanger, checked its pockets, found what I was looking for and laid it neatly on the front passenger seat.

I jumped in behind the wheel, twisted the key in the ignition and slipped it into drive. I rolled slowly out of the turning circle, then accelerated towards the multi-storey car park.

91

The car park was as empty as the last time I'd been here. It seemed more like a century ago than a couple of days. I peeled off the ramp at the second floor. I wondered whether Qasim and Adel were up on the roof, not a care in the world, getting their rocks off as another airliner took to the air.

I opened the back door and started to undress Tattoo. He was bigger than me so there'd be no drama getting into his kit. I unbuttoned his shirt and pulled it over his shoulders. His chest and back were covered with tattoos. He'd obviously done some time. The pictures of bears shagging women and rats with numbers above them would tell anyone in the know what detention centres he'd been to, and why.

He had stars tattoo'd onto his kneecaps. In gang language, he was going to kneel for no man.

With Tattoo tucked safely into the boot, and none of his ID in the car, I emptied a couple of bottles of mineral water over my face and hair. I dried myself off with my own shirt before putting on his, brushed as much sand and shit off his trousers as I could, then finally slid on his jacket.

I binned the mobile as I legged it towards the terminal.

It was 06.45.

Inside, it was busier than I'd expected, a lot busier than

when I'd flown in. I looked up and scanned the departures board. The Moscow flight stopped off first in Astana. I headed towards the ticket-sales counter. The girl standing behind it looked as though she'd just come off the high-cheekbones-and-perfect-teeth production line.

I took some deep breaths as I went to slow everything down inside my body and my head. I got into the zone. I'd always known that people like Red Ken, Dex and I were lucky to be able to do that. I didn't know if it was genetic or acquired or a combination of the two, but when everything went to rat shit, thinking clearly just sort of happened. It had nothing to do with being brave or, in Dex's case, certifiably insane. It had to do with mastering the stress when it would be natural to flap big-time.

Stress improves performance. Your heart-rate is governed by adrenalin levels. That's all good stuff when you need flight, fight or bluff, but there is an optimum state – when it's hammering away at between 115 and 145 beats per minute. Anything above that and your body stops being able to control what it's doing and you get killed because you fuck up. Or in this case it arouses suspicion and encourages the uniformed automaton in the driving seat to check everything about you more closely, starting with your passport.

She finished her call as I reached the counter. She looked up and switched on her brilliant white smile. I tried my best to match it.

'The seven thirty for Moscow via Astana. I'd like a seat, please.'

She tapped away at her computer keyboard as I flipped Tattoo's passport out of his jacket pocket and got extra busy looking down and fucking about in my day-sack.

She scanned it and passed it back to me with just a cursory glance at the personal details. She certainly didn't see anything odd about a guy with a British accent presenting with Russian travel docs. I know people who've travelled the world on their wife's passport. You just have to show a bit of front.

'How would you like to pay, Mr Sinitsin?'

'US dollars, please.'

She checked her tariff. 'That will be ninety.'

She gave the keyboard a really good hammering and a ticket eventually clattered out of the printer beside her. She passed it across the counter, giving me the opportunity to admire her green wristband and immaculate manicure.

'You are boarding at gate ten. Air Astana do not allocate seats, but that is no problem – the flight is nearly empty. Please hurry. The gate is closing in fifteen minutes.'

Immigration and security were a piece of piss. They were there to tag foreigners coming in and nationals going out, not the other way round. The camera had lost its memory card; it was now in my mouth. My James Manley passport was in Tattoo's wallet.

A stewardess looked at my boarding pass and waved towards the hundred or so empty seats. As I moved down the aisle I heard the door close behind me. I spat the memory card into my hand.

The aircraft was relatively new, much better than the ropy gear that former Soviet Union countries used to fly. There were three seats either side of the aisle. I spotted Anna about three-quarters of the way back, on the right-hand side, hunched over her netbook. Judging by the expression on her face, she was using the last few minutes before take-off to spit teeth and feathers at her readers about the misdeeds of M3C. She had a silk scarf tied loosely around her neck. I knew she was going to be wearing it for a good few days.

I didn't know where the Falcon was headed, and Julian wasn't going to be of any help. I had to get out of the country. So here I was, with the only person who could help me find out what the fuck was going on.

I carried on down the aisle and took the seat next to her.

92

Anna looked up, eyes like saucers. She opened her mouth to speak, but I silenced her with a finger to my lips. My other hand swivelled the netbook towards me. I hit the keys with my two middle fingers.

talk like this

Nowhere is safe from surveillance, especially on an aircraft. Even the toilets can be bugged. State-of-the-art systems can screen out the sound of running water.

falcon left with the 2 players onboard – do you know where?

no

People were still thronging the aisles and waffling away on their mobiles, but the plane had started to taxi.

I slotted in the memory card. Spag's picture filled the screen.

know him?

She shook her head and typed.

who is he?

dont know

I didn't need to tell her anything that didn't help me.

he with the other two?

I nodded.

how did you know about neptun building and the meet?

She smiled.

a source
who?
She smiled again.
go fuck yourself ☺
I tried again.
can you find out where the falcon is going?

There was a commotion behind us. The stewardess had started bollocking people big-time. She spotted the netbook so we got a verbal slapping as well.

Anna turned and nodded.

We touched down in Astana at 12.15 local. Once we'd left the plane, Anna scrabbled around in her day-sack and pulled out a mobile and battery. Good drills: no tracing. Once she'd reunited them and found a signal, she started dialling. It wasn't long before she was mumbling away, her hand covering her mouth to hide the sound.

It took no more than a minute. As she closed down and removed the battery again, we exchanged our first words since I'd sat down next to her.

'Well?'

'He will help us.' She raised a finger and tugged her scarf far enough down her neck for me to glimpse a bruise that was pretty much the same colour as Tattoo's prize tattoo. 'At least until he sees this, you bastard.'

We transited through for the 13.25 flight to Moscow.

93

Astana airport

IKIA had been a palace compared to this dump. The transit lounge was old-school Communism back with a vengeance – drab, dirty, full of cigarette smoke and people lying on top of crushed cardboard boxes because there weren't any seats.

Anna toyed with her plastic coffee cup and looked at the empty tables all around us. I asked her the question again. 'Why are you so fixated on just one man?'

She took a big pull on her cigarette.

'Br-in . . .' She almost choked on the word. 'Brin was one of those people who found themselves in the right place at the right time the day the Soviet Union ceased to exist – the first of January 1992. He was in his mid-thirties, an ardent Communist and, until Gorbachev and Yeltsin pulled the plug on the old system, a man at the very height of his career – or so he believed. Back then, even he couldn't have guessed quite how big and successful he would eventually become. None of Russia's oligarchs could . . .

'Brin was extremely ambitious. He came to Moscow from the fourth largest city in Russia – Gorky, which is now known as Nizhny Novgorod. During the Communist era, Gorky was a closed city – the reason many dissidents were sent there. Once you arrived in Gorky, it was almost impossible to leave, such was the ring of security the KGB placed around it. And for good reason: Gorky was a strategic industrial centre for weapons production, something Brin knew a great deal about.'

She paused and gazed into the middle distance for a few moments, watching the smoke she exhaled blending with the grey wall of the cafeteria.

'Brin was not an engineer. He was an administrator, and he was KGB. He was responsible for the production of a large part of the programme. And by all accounts he was good at it. Russians build weapons differently from the way they are built in the West.

'In the USSR we had bureaux, as we called them, places where the weapons were conceived, designed and prototyped. The bureaux were usually in Moscow or Leningrad and the production facilities were almost always in areas very far removed from the centre – places like Gorky.

'Brin did such a brilliant administrative job at the production centre that he was transferred before long to the design bureau in Moscow. He was only thirty-eight and already a KGB colonel, and assigned to one of the most important defence projects in the USSR – a strategic missile system that, when built, would have had the power to wipe America off the map. It never came to that, thank God, because soon after he arrived in Moscow the Soviet Union ceased to exist and the Cold War ended.'

She looked into my eyes. 'You have to imagine what it was like on that January morning – the day Russians returned to work after the country that they had known and sworn allegiance to for more than seventy years had effectively evaporated. For some, the phones stopped ringing, orders stopped coming in, and they simply went home. Brin was not one of them. With his friends in the KGB – soon to become the FSB – he was able to purchase stock in the company.

'Within a very short space of time, he had complete control of it. Many Russians who worked in the defence industry thought that it would go into a terminal decline as the Cold War ended. Not Brin. With the liberalization of the Russian economy, he soon started to acquire other missile companies, some for next to nothing. By 2003, with the blessing of Putin's government, he had built M3C into what it is today: a one-stop shop for anyone needing anything from the smallest handheld weapon to a nuclear missile. The nuclear variety were not on sale outside Russia, of course, but that never stopped Brin selling the *technology* within them to pariah states that had the money to pay – under-the-table deals that were allowed to proceed because they had the blessing of Putin and his cronies in the FSB.'

'How did you get involved?'

'Chechnya . . .' She was lost to me again for a few seconds. 'Chechnya was good for M3C. War has been good for M3C, full stop. The conflict saw the Russian government pour billions of roubles into weapon systems devoted to the systematic eradication of the Chechen people. I was in Chechnya as a reporter for *Novaya Gazeta*.' She sighed. 'At first, it was the humanitarian narrative that pulled me in. Later, I realized that the corruption that sustained it – fuelled it, in fact – was the story I was supposed to tell.'

'What do you mean?'

'Putin started the Chechen war. It suited his purposes to have a conflict on our doorstep – to get ordinary Russians focused on an external enemy, rather than the real enemy, the corruption that lies at the heart of Russia itself. Corruption in our country is a cancer, fostered by alliances between powerful figures in our government, oligarchs who control our economy and criminals – *mafiosi*. Having started it, Putin and his government needed to sustain the war in Chechnya.'

'So why single out Brin?'

'Chechnya made Brin a billionaire many times over and he,

in turn, made sure that the people who were keeping the war going were also very well rewarded. I can't get them all.'

'This is the story you want to tell?'

'It's the story I'm *compelled* to tell. The trouble is, ordinary Russians are bored – they think they've heard it all before. They have become anaesthetized to scandal. But they haven't heard *this* story – not by a long chalk . . .'

She smiled fleetingly. 'I am lucky. My source told me about the Tehran meeting. The Cold War may have ended, but there is little affection in the upper echelons of the Russian government for the West. Nor, as you can imagine, do Russian defence companies care particularly about the fate of the average NATO soldier.'

I took a taste of muddy coffee and changed tack. 'Is Brin normally involved in heroin?'

She smiled again, but bleakly this time. 'Defence is a declining market. With George Bush gone and Barack Obama in power, the amount of money that the Americans are due to set aside for their defence and intelligence expenditure is declining dramatically. It is the same in Russia. Apart from anything else, few people in the grip of the current economic crisis can afford highly sophisticated weapons. The Russian government certainly can't. It is raiding any budget it can to pay for the current debt crisis. And that isn't going to change any time soon.

'Brin is not a fool. Quite the opposite – he remains a driven, highly ambitious man. He needs to look for new sources of revenue, and yields do not come any bigger than those to be found in the opium and heroin market. The Taliban want highly sophisticated missiles? They pay for them with heroin – and Brin cements another part of his developing trade.

'That is the picture that I went to Tehran to capture. I needed to see an employee of Brin dealing directly with the Taliban. I needed a photograph of the meeting that would make those responsible for that transaction completely transparent. The

315

evidence would be published and it would lead to Brin. The story is ninety per cent written, I just need that picture. Then you can do whatever you have to do . . .'

Anna didn't have quite as much of the story as she thought. She didn't have the bit I had – and that bit was Altun. I suddenly saw a whole lot more – more, even, than I'd tumbled to in the past twenty-four hours. The only thing I didn't understand was where Spag fitted in.

Did I care about Brin? He was Anna's demon, not mine. My attention remained fixed on Altun and Spag – and it would stay there until I'd got payback for Red Ken and Dex. No – that wasn't true. I wanted every fucker on the trail to get what was coming to them for what had happened in Dubai. Brin had just been added to the list.

'Anna, why are you telling me all this?'

She looked at her watch and stubbed out her cigarette. 'Because you need to understand.'

94

**Moscow Sheremetyevo
1730 hrs**

The seatbelts sign was still illuminated, but the engines were winding down. That was good enough for most of the locals. They were up and out of their seats as if the first to the exit got a free bottle of vodka.

Anna and I let the initial wave scramble for the door.

If I'd been able to speak the language, we'd have disembarked separately, but my Russian didn't stretch any further than *da, niet, spasibo* and *dasvidaniya*, and that wasn't going to get me to the bottom of the steps. I needed Anna. Only with her help could I remain the grey man.

She zipped her camera and laptop into her day-sack and looked out of the window. 'In Moscow we have only two seasons, summer and winter. The snow has melted and the sun is out. It must be summer.' She smiled, waiting. It must have been a joke.

All the same, it wasn't going to be as hot as Tehran. I wished Tattoo's jacket was a little thicker.

We eventually joined the scrum – I didn't want us to be the last off. We reached the galley area, turned left and shuffled towards the door. I'd slung my day-sack over my shoulder. On the ramp there were three guys in fluorescent jackets – normal airport staff manning the air-bridge. No men in black leather waiting to push us back onto the plane until the real people had gone.

We walked up the ramp and joined the spur that led to the main terminal. People milled about at gates or drifted in and out of shops that seemed to sell nothing apart from chunky watches and bottles of vodka shaped like AK-47s. I finally spotted a pharmacy.

I'd briefed Anna. She went in, and came out again with a pack of tissues and a jar of stuff that stank of eucalyptus. I looked at her with obvious gratitude and rubbed a handful round my throat. It made my eyes water. I opened the tissues and had a good blow. The airport was bound to be crawling with CCTV. Untold pairs of eyes would already be watching us. This was no time to look furtive or guilty, or anything other than a passenger with two days' growth and a bad cold.

We came to the end of the walkway and took a down escalator, following the signs for Passport Control and Baggage Reclaim. I could see the Immigration hall straight ahead of us when we were only halfway down the escalator. This was where Igor Sinitsin would stand or fall. It all depended on whether the body had been found. Unlikely until it started to smell. Then it would need to be identified, and the only ID was the Merc's number-plate. It should give me a few days, but you never knew.

There were four or five people queuing at each of the desks. I blew my nose to give myself something to do. At the same time I reddened my face by holding my nose and trying to breathe out.

We waited in line. I still had my day-sack on my right shoulder. Anna had hers on with both straps fastened, and a small blue plastic wheelie-case by her side. She was a pro: no hold luggage to lose control of or delay you. We exchanged a smile, but there was no excessive eye contact. For those watching on monitors and from behind two-way mirrors, that would add up to suspicious behaviour.

The suit in front of us went through with not much more than a nod and a wave to the official. It was Anna's turn to approach the booth. She looked back and pointed. I saw her gripping her throat and miming a cough.

The Immigration guy signalled me to join them. He was mid-thirties and looked as if he spent every hour he wasn't in his booth pumping iron, shaving his head and taking misery pills. He also looked much more interested in her than me, that was for sure.

I handed over my passport. He asked me something.

I made a sound as if to speak, then brought a fistful of tissues up to my face and croaked. My throat was agony.

Anna answered for me.

His eyes flicked up and down as he studied first the picture, then my face. He put the passport down below the level of the desk and I saw the tell-tale glow of ultraviolet light. Something troubled him. He looked back into my eyes and muttered another question. I guessed it wasn't to ask me why I was so much more handsome in the flesh than on camera.

I gave a weak smile and Anna gobbed off. He grunted something but he didn't hand back the passport. There was a bit of a lull, like he was waiting for me to fill the silence with a confession.

Then Anna made another comment and he smiled. He put the document back on the desktop. As I took it, his attention had already returned to the line.

I started to walk. We were nearly there.

The sliding doors opened into the arrivals hall and we ran the gauntlet of taxi drivers holding up bits of cardboard and people clutching bunches of flowers. Nobody gave us a second glance.

Anna pointed towards an exit. I was still apprehensive.

Being dependent on others gave me the same feeling as knocking on a strange door without knowing who or what was on the other side.

95

We set off across the huge concourse. Judging by the signs, we were either heading for the car-rental desks, the platform for the Moscow express or the car park.

We came out of the terminal and took a left. Definitely the car park. As we rounded the corner of the building and entered the walkway into the multi-storey, we turned left again. We were at the bottom of a stairwell.

A guy in his late sixties was standing waiting, a black woollen coat over his arm. His hair was grey and well-cut, like the suit he was wearing under his open black raincoat and the woollen scarf around his neck.

Anna flew into his arms and it was full-on hugs all round. They kissed each other five or six times on the cheek then drew back and gobbed off to each other in Russian for several seconds. He ignored me and made her put the coat on. I'd started to appreciate her joke. It might have been summer in Moscow, but there was a chill in the air.

She thanked him for his kindness, gave him a beaming smile and fed an arm through his.

I took the chance to look around. I mostly noticed what was missing. There were no CCTV cameras trained where we were standing. This boy was switched on.

They talked some more. He spoke quietly and warmly, his pale grey eyes fixed on hers. They were slightly rheumy with age, and made him look kind, like everyone's favourite granddad.

She finally turned to me. 'Semyon was alarmed after my call. He wasn't expecting me back for another two days.'

'And Semyon is . . . ?'

She translated for him and he looked at me and smiled. His teeth were yellowing, but at least they were still his. He offered us both a cigarette from a light blue pack. Anna took one. He said something that seemed to have nothing to do with cigarettes and she answered.

'What's he saying?'

He sparked up a plastic disposable and she cupped her hands round his as he offered her the flame.

'He's asking me about you. I said we can trust you.'

'Can you?'

'I've spent my working life around bad people. I can smell them. And why would you risk everything to be here with us now?'

'Risk everything?'

Now it was my turn for the smile. 'When he sees what you did to my neck, Semyon will probably want to kill you.'

The old boy spoke again and her brow creased. The waffle bounced back and forth a couple of times.

She turned back to me. 'It's not good, I'm afraid. The Falcon came back here, to Moscow.'

'No – that's good. Tell him that's good.'

Anna didn't bother. 'He says it's due to go to the proving ground tomorrow. Assuming everyone is still together, that can mean only one thing. They will test fire. There were rumours that it was faulty, but—'

Semyon gobbed off some more.

'You know about dark flares? You know the importance of them? You know that the SA-16 can defeat—'

322

I dredged a name out of my briefing notes. 'Vologda?'

She nodded. 'It's in the middle of a military training area.'

'I know.' I undid my day-sack and took out the Nikon. 'How long will it take to get there?'

'Maybe six hours by road.'

'There's no train?'

'The line goes from St Petersburg only, and the area is north of the city. No internal flights either.'

Semyon said something else.

'The weather forecast is cloudy until the afternoon. They will want a clear sky.'

With the camera powered up, I opened the side to replace the memory card. There was something I wanted to show Semyon. 'Does he know where the people in the Falcon are now? They in Moscow?'

They waffled away, but it wasn't sounding hopeful.

'Can he try and find out where they are? It's really important.' I didn't give a shit what Anna had in mind for them after she had her photos. 'Where is the Falcon?' If I could get to it before they took off tomorrow, maybe I'd be able to get the job done without leaving the city.

She didn't have to ask Semyon. 'No good. M3C have their own hangar in a military air base on the other side of the city.'

I passed him the Nikon. 'Ask if he knows him.'

Semyon pulled a pair of cheap reading glasses from an alloy tube and focused on the back screen.

'The little fat one, tell him.'

He zoomed in until Spag's face filled the screen.

The accompanying shrug and shake of his head said it all. As he handed the Nikon back his eyes fixed on mine. He seemed to be apologizing.

'If he doesn't know where they are, I need to get into the proving ground. Can he help?'

His eyes bounced between the two of us and he gobbed off some more.

323

'OK. We will go to his apartment later tonight and he may have more information.'

I realized I had their relationship all wrong. It wasn't *their* apartment. But they'd said a lot more to each other than she was translating. 'I don't want to go to his place. I want to meet outside.'

'No.' Anna protected him. 'He may be able to get maps, papers, find out where everyone is in the city. If he is stopped in possession . . .' She searched my face. 'No matter where they are, you will take me.'

Semyon asked something.

Anna turned to me. 'We do not know your name.'

'Manley. James Manley.' I'd always wanted to say that. 'But you can call me Jim.'

'Jim, we need to help each other. We get what we want, the pictures that prove the story, then you can do whatever you have been sent to do.'

Semyon stepped forward, his hand extended, but his eyes burnt into mine. There were several messages there, none of them good.

96

Izmailovsky Park, Moscow
1930 hrs

We followed the crowd out of the ornate, almost Victorian-looking metro station. The thirty-minute non-stop express ride from Sheremetyevo had given me time to check out the others in the carriage.

Once up at street level, Anna fumbled about in her day-sack for a pack of cigarettes. It gave me time to study the twenty or so who'd come up with us.

We headed down a tree-lined avenue littered with empty bottles and rusty cans. Anna's wheelie-case squeaked over the paving-stones. At the end, set in a large park of patchy grass, was a mock-Russian fortress with bell towers and onion domes. We could have been in Disneyland, if it hadn't been for the slogans and graffiti daubed on the walls and the methers sparked out beneath them.

We manoeuvred round a group that had gathered to watch and applaud a fire-breather and passed through a pillared gateway topped off with balloons. The Izmailovsky flea-market was huge. You could lose yourself in it – and anyone you needed to.

Anna had chosen well. I wanted somewhere we could disappear for a few hours, that had constant movement and faces that changed quickly. She knew the score. She'd been doing it herself for years. Campaigning journalists weren't exactly in the Good Lads Club in this country.

Her flat was routinely watched. A hotel was out of the question – they'd want to see our passports. So, it was hang-about time until we went to Semyon's. After that, the plan was for her to go and collect her car. If Semyon didn't know where the targets were in Moscow, or if he discovered that they'd already left the city, we'd need to get to the proving ground as fast as we could. The area was the size of Wales, the brochure had said. Finding it was one thing; finding out where exactly the test firing was going to happen was quite another.

Straight ahead there was a long run of stalls. The flea-market was a tourist attraction and kept long hours. A group of Japanese camcorded each other buying tat. Cold War chess sets, brass busts of Lenin, and Russian dolls with Putin and Obama painted on them were flying off the stall. So was the cheap padded coat I asked her to buy me, the sort any respectable granddad would wear. Del was very happy with the US dollars she handed him.

I steered her down an alley that opened up on our right. As we moved behind a rail of hanging T-shirts, I turned and had a quick browse. Nobody was following or taking the slightest interest. I decided I didn't want a Putin T-shirt after all and we moved on. If someone's behind you innocently, they might follow you the first time you take a turn. At a push, they might take the second. But nobody follows you round the third side of a square without a fucking good reason.

Anna caught on fast and didn't need to ask. She pointed to things, smiled and laughed. Sometimes she took my arm. Worst case, I was a foreigner with a girl I had out on appro from the Russian-brides catalogue.

The third right had brought us into the flea-market's very

own B&Q district: rows of stalls covered with all your needs if you were building a house or knocking one down, from second-hand screwdriver sets to petrol-powered Kango hammers. I looked at my watch. It was nearly eight and coming to last light. The first stars were out. The temperature had dipped. We still had three or four hours to kill.

We crossed into a place filled with counterfeit DVDs and CDs and Russian rock memorabilia. Techno thumped from a speaker. A guy with a head-load of stubble-length bleached hair tried to get Anna to buy a Prodigy mug. Instead he got back the short, sharp Stalin daughter's stare and bollocking. We moved on a bit, but not far. The deafening music was good – it made it impossible for anyone to hear our conversation.

She drew my head down and moved her mouth against my ear. 'Would you like a drink?' I could feel her breath. I wasn't going to complain about that.

I pointed to a café at the end of the alleyway instead. Embers glowed in an open fire. A guy was cutting neat slices off something roasting over it. I started to head towards it.

'No, not there.' She pulled me in the opposite direction.

'What's wrong?'

'Somewhere else. Anywhere but there.'

97

We sat in a bar filled with people, smoke and music. It doubled as a kebab shop, and that was what she bought me to eat. I filled my face and lifted the Pepsi Max can to my mouth. She gunned down Baltika beer from the bottle. I was sure I'd never seen Agnetha do that.

'Remember, we got a busy time ahead.'

She put down the bottle and picked up her cigarette. She blew the smoke towards the ceiling, as if that was going to stop the nicotine getting anywhere near me. 'Do not patronize me. If I want a drink I'll have one. You are not my father.'

'Is Semyon?'

The cigarette went down and the beer came up. 'No, he is not. But he is special – perhaps more so, even, than my own father.'

I looked at the ring on her right hand. 'What about your husband?'

The beer bottle smacked down on the tabletop. 'Do I ask anything from you? I don't even know if James Manley is your real name. IranEx is full of people with unreal names. Are you a spy, Jim? I imagine you are.'

I couldn't help laughing. She didn't know how much I wished I was. I'd been brought up on old Bond films. 'No.'

'I don't believe you. But that's OK.' She nodded at the two remaining kebabs. 'They will get cold.'

As I kept eating she drank and smoked, deep in her own world. She ordered more drinks and tapped another stick from the pack.

'What about you? Are you a spy?' I wiped grease from my mouth. 'Your Arabic's good. And your English is better than mine.'

'I am what I say I am. I like languages, that's all. Besides, Arabic pretty much came with the territory.'

'Chechnya?'

'Yes, and Bosnia, and Afghanistan . . .'

'I thought your thing was anti-corruption.'

'It is. Where do you think M3C sells its weaponry?'

'Does your source work for them?'

'Semyon . . . Semyon is a very trusted friend.' She spoke the words slowly to emphasize just how much she meant them.

I picked up a piece of pitta bread and got stuck into the last kebab. 'How do you know him? I mean, M3C are the enemy, aren't they?'

She didn't answer. Neither did she fire up another cigarette as I ate. She just stared at me, her mind buzzing. 'OK, Jim, we'll talk . . .' She sat back and took a deep breath. 'I'm not married.' She lifted her right hand. 'I wear it to keep men out of my way. This is Russia, after all. But it is also there to remind me that I was going to marry once, years ago. Semyon was going to be my father-in-law. I love him deeply. He is the only family I have now.'

Her hand came down and played with the cigarette packet.

'My boyfriend was older than me. My father didn't approve.'

'What was his name?'

'Grisha. We used to go to that place you were aiming for, to escape the eyes of my family. It's a young person's hang-out –

329

always has been. He always said it served the best *shashlik* in Moscow.'

'What happened?'

'It was 1987. We were young. We were in love. And then he went to Afghanistan. I waved goodbye to him at the station . . . and the next time I saw him he was in a coffin. Now Semyon and I have only pictures of Grisha to remind us of what he was like.'

I watched a tear form and trickle down her cheek. She fumbled to get another cigarette out of the pack. I took it from her and helped.

She sniffed. 'I still go there sometimes when I want to remember him.'

The firebrand who'd gobbed off at the press conference didn't square with the person I was with now. In Tehran she'd seemed utterly driven. The girl in front of me was vulnerable. But if you'd lost the love of your life in a war? The picture was steadying a little. 'Grisha's death still drives you.'

She looked at me. Her eyes narrowed. 'Yes. But not, I suspect, for the reasons you think.'

I passed her the cigarette and she took it and lit up. 'Grisha used to write a lot when he was in Afghanistan. Then, one day, February 'eighty-nine, the letters stopped. They told us he was missing, presumed dead. We wrote requesting further information, but the army never replied. It was like he'd never existed.'

In the wake of the Chechen war, I'd helped a number of families who'd tried to find out what had happened to their dead or missing sons. But during the Soviet era it would have been dangerous even asking the question.

'It must have been – must still be – difficult.'

'What?'

'Not knowing what happened.'

'But we do.'

98

Anna toyed awkwardly with her Baltika. 'Almost a year after we lost the war, Semyon got a call from a man who claimed to be the colonel of the military forensic medical laboratory that had performed an autopsy on Grisha's body.'

She saw something in my face. 'You're thinking the army didn't carry out autopsies on ordinary soldiers? Sometimes they did. In certain circumstances.'

I didn't need to ask her what they were. I knew she was going to tell me soon enough.

She took a swig. 'The colonel told Semyon that he wanted to meet, that there was something he needed to ask. But Grisha's father was scared to meet him.'

'Why?'

'This was Soviet Russia.'

'So you said you'd go.'

'I had nothing to lose. I'd left school and was waiting to go to university. I met this man – this colonel – at a café. He told me about himself – told me that he had served in Afghanistan and what an utter, godforsaken waste of life it had been. People like Grisha, he said, deserved better. It was then that he showed me the pictures.

'The autopsy had been carried out at a military medical

laboratory in Kazan. They'd flown the bodies there, the bodies of everybody who'd been in Grisha's armoured personnel carrier. The first picture showed him almost as I remembered him: he was face up, eyes closed, like he was sleeping.'

The tears were really flowing now. She didn't even bother wiping them away.

'I asked the colonel what had happened and he told me Grisha's armoured personnel carrier had been hit by an anti-tank rocket. A fragment had pierced his eye, hit bone and tumbled, removing the back of his skull. In the next picture, I saw the exit wound. There was nothing left of the back of his head – just a big black congealed mass of blood, brains, bone fragments and matted hair.'

She steadied herself.

'The fragment that had killed Grisha had come from an anti-tank missile that had only just entered service with the Soviet Army. It was effectively brand new. Someone had sold it to the *mujahideen*. Never mind that it would kill Russians. To the people who'd done the deal, the only thing that was important was the money.'

'So why did this pathologist approach Semyon?'

'Oh, that bit was easy. In exchange for the information, he wanted a job.'

Caught in the pool of light cast by the street-lamp outside, a couple of peaked caps and heavy trench coats walked past the window. They stopped to look through the glass. She watched and waited until they moved on.

The stub of her cigarette joined the others in the ashtray. 'Jim, we should go.'

99

We were on a main drag – a long *prospekt* heading westwards, the direction we needed to go. Traffic streamed in both directions. I turned to Anna as she took my arm. 'Tell me about Grisha.'

'What do you want to know?'

'As much as you want to tell.'

She wrapped her coat more tightly around her against the wind that was blowing along the *prospekt*. With it came a few spots of rain.

'Grisha was an idealist. He loved poetry. That's how we met. His family lived in the same apartment block as mine. One evening, when I came back from school, I found him sitting on the front steps. He was reading Pushkin. I loved Pushkin. We got talking. He wanted to go to university to study literature, but his family didn't have the money or the influence to send him – in those days you couldn't do it any other way. That's why he joined the army.

'He would have been conscripted anyway to fight in Afghanistan, so why not get a university education from the army as well as fight for them? It meant signing up for five years, but then he'd be free of it. He wanted to become a teacher. But to do that he first had to become a soldier.'

'What was he? An engineer, an officer?'

'No, he was nothing special. Just a normal infantry soldier. One of the thousands our government sent to be slaughtered out there.'

'I had a friend, a British soldier. He's just been killed in Afghanistan.'

'Did you love him?'

I had to think about that one. 'There were four of us who were close – we'd done a lot together. I'm the only one left now. You know what? I think I cared for all three of them. I miss them very much.'

She looked away. Her tear-stained cheeks glistened in the glow of a street-lamp.

I'd surprised myself talking about Tenny, Dex and Red Ken like that. I decided to cut away before it happened again. I didn't like not being in control. 'So, how much older than you was Grisha when you met? Was he old-enough-to-be-your-dad sort of old?'

'No, no.' She gave a giggle, which surprised her even more than it surprised me. 'We'd started dating when I was just sixteen – a schoolgirl. He was almost nineteen. Like I said, my father did not approve of the relationship. But by then my father did not approve of anything much.'

She paused.

'He was an alcoholic. The Soviet system killed his love of life. He worked in a factory that made machine tools. He hated it. My mother was scared of him. I was his only child. He wanted me to make something of my life, and study, study, study, he said, was the only way to achieve it. Grisha and I had to see each other in secret. Thank God he had a motorbike, a Ural, so we could escape every so often for a few hours on our own.'

For a second she seemed lost. 'When he joined the army Grisha went away for almost a year. In that time I saw him only once. He didn't talk about his training, but I could see that it

334

had affected him deeply. It was only years later, through my work, that I found out what they do to recruits. Systematic abuse. Punishments have nothing to do with your performance. If the officers and the NCOs in charge are having a bad day, they beat you. If they are bored, they beat you. When Grisha came home that summer, he was a changed person. He didn't want to talk about the army, just kept telling me that it wouldn't be long – another four years – and then he'd be free of it. I had just turned eighteen so we decided to hand in our application.'

'For what?'

'To get married. Russians do not have engagements and rings. We just apply to ZAGS, the department of registration. They furnish a date when you can marry.'

The rain was falling harder now. She unwrapped the scarf from her neck and tied it round her head. 'It was stupid – I was so young – but I wanted to let him know that I would wait for him. I couldn't tell my father. But Semyon was very supportive. He became like a father to me, too. It was he who bought the Ural, a beat-up old thing from the Great Patriotic War, and restored it for Grisha. The only times I saw Grisha happy that summer – his old self – was when he and his father worked on that bike and when we were out riding on it.'

I didn't say it, but Grisha was lucky to have had her – and Semyon. I'd never had a dad who cared enough about me to buy me a skateboard, let alone restore a motorbike.

'We bought the rings . . .' She gently played with hers, twisting it around her finger. 'But the wedding never happened. He was sent to Afghanistan before ZAGS would give us a date . . .'

Her tears returned, and I thought about the three I'd lost. I'd never dwelt on how much those fuckers meant to me. It wasn't as if we'd lived in each other's pockets but just being with them again, even fleetingly, had made me feel good. They were my family, or as close as I was ever likely to get.

'Anna, you still have family. There is still someone who . . .'

335

Ahead of us, lit by a flickering street-lamp, was a bus shelter. Anna stepped into it and I followed. The shelter stank of the things bus stops normally stink of. The rain drummed on the roof.

She smiled sadly and removed her scarf as I reached out and touched the ragged bruise on her neck.

An image filled my mind – of a twenty-one-year-old kid lying on a mortuary slab with the back of his head removed by a tumbling missile fragment. 'So Semyon works for M3C. He was working in one of the companies sucked up by Brin? Weapons that Semyon had helped to build killed his son?'

She gave a shallow nod. 'That's why Semyon and I do what we do.' She checked her watch. 'Come, time to go and see him.'

Her wheelie-case bounced behind her as we carried on towards the station in silence. I could see the lights of the metro up ahead. I'd been keeping one eye on it. In the couple of minutes since I'd last looked, the crowd outside had almost doubled in size. Anna had noticed it too. In the harsh light of the entrance, over the heads of the people waiting to get in, I could see two grey peaked caps. Police were checking everyone returning from the flea-market as they passed through the turnstiles.

'What's going on?'

'I don't know. Maybe they are searching for drugs. It happens sometimes . . .'

'Let's walk to another station, yeah?'

We edged around the back of the crowd and onto a main drag.

At the time Grisha was killed, everything was still for sale. Now it was more organized, and that made it more dangerous. It was easy to see why she was a woman with a mission.

But I had one too.

And if Semyon had found out where they were staying in the city, I could be done and out of here by the morning.

100

Grey apartment blocks loomed either side of us. We kept in their shadows while holding the trigger on Semyon's equally drab concrete building. Lights pushed through net curtains on two of the five windows that made up his second-floor flat.

An old diesel truck, a product of some ancient Soviet factory, belched fumes as it trundled past. We were about eight K away from the Gucci and Prada stores off Red Square. The tarmac was cracked and potholed. Areas of hard-packed mud that had once been turf were covered with a layer of dogshit and rubbish.

'It's a company apartment, Jim. He has done very well. The higher he has gone, the more information he has been able to discover.' Anna told me this was a middle-class area, but it was like the old USSR had never gone away. Communism had produced generations that couldn't have cared less about public areas. Why should they? The Party told them they'd take care of everything. Anything the other side of their own front door meant nothing to them. They weren't even allowed to feel any responsibility for it.

337

'Do you two have any tell-tales? You know – a sign to show it's OK to go up?'

'Yes – it's always at night, so he has the kitchen light on, the one to the far right.'

I checked again to see if anyone else was watching his windows. 'You sure that's the only way in and out?'

'Yes, Jim, it's an apartment block. Just the one entrance and exit. And before you ask, those are the only windows. He has none facing the back of the building.'

She was getting a little bit crisp, but so what? Questions like these kept you alive.

'He got a car? You see his car out here?'

'No. He uses Grisha's motorbike. It will be in the garage.'

She dug about in her pocket and replaced the battery. 'Let me call him.' She started pressing away.

'How come you use a mobile if you two need to be so disconnected?'

'It's a pay-as-you-go. We both bought them for cash and only use them between us.' She closed down the mobile. 'His isn't on.'

I took a breath and started to move.

'No, Jim, it's OK. He often forgets. He is getting old, that's all. Come, we'll check if his bike is there. Will that make you happy?'

I took her arm and we walked down an alleyway. The long, one-level strip of concertina garage doors ahead was covered with graffiti.

She led me to one about two-thirds of the way down, stood on tiptoe and pulled out a piece of broken concrete to retrieve a key. We lifted the door together. The smell of petrol and oily rags hit my nostrils.

Once inside and the door was down again she hit the power. A dull orange bulb hanging from a dodgy wire sparked up in the middle of the ceiling. Anna walked over to the bike. As she ran her hand over the metal it was as if her memories returned.

I knew about Urals. I'd blown a few up in Afghanistan with our IEDs. They were big, clunky pieces of Soviet engineering, a little underpowered but solid, and ideal over rough terrain, which was why the Red Army had bought them in their tens of thousands. This one still had its bullet-shaped sidecar fixed on the right-hand side, and was a mass of immaculate, gleaming chrome and black gloss – Semyon's mobile shrine to his dead son.

Anna walked around the machine, reliving old times. 'I come here by myself sometimes . . . birthdays, anniversaries . . .'

I felt the working parts while she sat in an old cane chair pouring her heart out. They were warm. Semyon had been using the Ural less than an hour ago.

'I know this is stupid, but we called this old thing "Cuckoo", after a song we loved. It was a hit when we met. Everyone used to sing it and . . .' She stared into the sidecar for a few more seconds, before reluctantly getting up. We closed down the garage and headed for the apartment.

101

We walked into the lobby through a set of wooden doors with Victorian-wired glass panels. The harsh white light from the overhead fluorescents did the cleaners no favours. Hastily swished mop marks showed as plain as day across the black marble floor.

Sweet, flowery disinfectant did battle with the stench of boiled cabbage. There was no lift, so we climbed the stairs to the first floor. Anna pointed down the corridor. I counted four doors. 'Last one on the right.'

I signalled to her to carry her wheelie. It was making too much noise.

None of the doors had a bell or a knocker. They didn't even have numbers. Each was just a plain sheet of veneered ply-wood with a fake brass knob, dulled from decades of use.

We reached Semyon's apartment. Anna's hand was poised to rap against the veneer. I heard a dull thud inside and knew exactly what it was. I pushed Anna clear as the lock turned.

I rammed my full weight against the opening door. It only travelled a foot. I burst through to see the body behind it stumbling back into the hallway. Tattoo's mate staggered to his feet, one hand tugging his leather jacket away from his waist. I focused on the other and jumped on him, pinning him to the floor. I grabbed his fingers a nanosecond before they could make contact with the pistol-grip in his waistband. His cologne matched the building's disinfectant. I felt my eyes water and my throat constrict. With him in the room, the boiled cabbage didn't stand a chance.

He bucked and kicked, trying to head-butt me off him. His stubble rasped at my neck and face.

I pushed my hands down on his, determined to keep the weapon where it was. My knuckles sank into his stomach. I felt the hammer of the revolver and found my way to its grip. We rolled about on the carpet, each scrabbling for some kind of advantage. His fist thumped into the side of my head. I tried to sink my teeth into his face or neck to cause him enough pain to disorient him.

I thrust my right hand between the weapon and his skin, searching for the trigger. At the precise moment my middle finger found the guard he raised his knee to push me away. I used the distance between us to jab my finger onto the trigger.

There was a dull thud.

The suppressed barrel put a round into his lower gut, bollocks, cock or leg. I didn't know which and didn't much care. I shoved my left hand over his mouth to muffle the scream.

I suddenly had enough space to draw down the weapon. I jammed the long fat barrel against his head and fired again.

I rolled off his corpse and allowed myself a couple of deep breaths before moving on. I knew there wasn't time for more. 'Anna?' I got up and closed the front door.

Low-level bookcases ran the length of the corridor. Books and magazines lay strewn across the floor. The brown, swirly-patterned carpet at the entrance to the living room was wet with blood. Anna knelt, sobbing, beside Semyon's body. He lay half in, half out of the doorway, still in his raincoat and scarf. He'd thrown up his right arm in a vain attempt to protect him-self. He must have known what was coming. There was no mistaking the exit wound on the left side of his forehead, slap in the middle of his frontal lobe. It wasn't the only one. His left arm and both legs were stained crimson where he had taken rounds.

I checked the weapon. The chamber was empty. I ran my hands over the second loadie's body for spares. He was carrying no extra ammunition. I guess he must have brought just enough to torture and kill an old man.

I ran into the kitchen and grabbed a bread knife. Two sets of bike gear lay on the floor, along with the rest of the room's contents. They were old waxies, 1980s-style jackets. The pockets had been turned out.

The kettle had boiled dry on the stove. Semyon must have put it on as soon as he came in. The loadie had been waiting for him, or maybe he'd just knocked on the door. Semyon had known we were due any minute.

If anybody else had been here, they'd have done their stuff by now. All the same, I had to make sure. I cleared the two bedrooms, living room and bathroom. They'd all been ransacked. Drawers had been emptied, stuff torn apart – even in Grisha's room, another shrine, still with his teenage football teams and pop-star posters on the wall.

I checked the loadie's pockets and pulled off his fashionably pointed shoes. I couldn't stop thinking about Red Ken lying on the tarmac, having taken a mag from this man. It made me feel good that the front of the bastard's head now looked like Semyon's. I just wished I'd been able to cause him the same amount of pain.

He had nothing on him at all. He'd come to the job sterile, and there was no sign of whatever he'd hoped to find in Semyon's apartment.

The old boy must have kept whatever he was going to tell us in his head. That was why he'd been tortured. The leg wounds were kneecappings. The one in his arm had gone through his elbow. The grey woollen scarf that hung loosely round his neck was soaked with saliva. The loadie must have shoved it against his mouth to muffle the screams as he pumped in another round.

There was more blood on the living-room sofa and two or three separate trails across the floor. Semyon had been one hell of a guy: he must have used every ounce of his dwindling strength trying to crawl into the hallway and warn us. The loadie had head-jobbed him on his way to the front door.

Semyon had probably been pinged at M3C as he'd tried to find out where the targets were staying – or to get details of tomorrow's test firing. He must have held out and said jack shit. The loadie had decided to sit tight and wait for us to arrive.

Anna's car was now a no-no. They'd see us coming a mile off.

I snatched the jackets, leggings, gloves and helmets off the kitchen floor. The keys were by the cooker.

I went back to Anna. Her sobs were turning into a wail and it was getting far too loud. I grabbed her under the arm and pulled. 'There's nothing we can do for him.'

'No, not yet . . .' She stroked what was left of his head.

'Anna.' I bent down and took her face in my hands, trying to get eye contact. 'Anna, I need you to get me to the proving ground.'

She turned and grabbed me. She pulled me into a desperate hug, sobbing into my shoulder. I held her for a while, stroking her hair, comforting her. I knew it didn't mean anything. She was just clinging to the wreckage. The muffled sobs continued as I gently prised her away from me. 'Anna, you can't help him here.'

She nodded slowly and her body sagged. Her arms fell away from me.

I helped her to her feet and we both stood there, knowing there was nothing we could do for Semyon but not wanting to leave him untended. I looked again at his head wound, the outstretched arm. My eyes were drawn to the magazine beneath his pointing hand.

I suddenly realized what he'd been trying to do.

He hadn't crawled into the corridor to warn us, or thrown out his arm in a last vain attempt to protect himself. He'd been giving us another kind of message.

The magazine cover shot was a group photo, a row of suits in front of a shiny new glass building. I picked it up and jammed it into the bike jacket. I'd try to make sense of it later. Right now we had to get as far away from here as possible. 'Let's go.'

I grabbed her case under my arm and closed the front door behind us.

102

We drove along the not-so-deserted streets. Anna was riding. I was in the sidecar. She knew the bike and she knew the city. I couldn't stop thinking about Semyon. I knew I should cut away – I'd always managed to do that in the past. Sometimes my survival had depended on it. Sometimes I'd just used it as an excuse not to look at myself too carefully in the mirror. Whatever, it wasn't working any more.

I finally managed to grip myself. Even if I did know why he'd got zapped, it didn't change anything. I still had no control over what Altun and Brin and the Taliban did or didn't know. The most important thing was that they didn't have us. I was still moving on. I still had a job to do. I still had my mission.

After ten minutes we were a good tactical bound away from the flat. I tapped her leg and pointed down a side-street. Two or three clapped-out cars parked in front of a line of locked-up Spar-type shops were intermittently floodlit by a flashing neon bar sign. She pulled in and stopped and I passed her the magazine.

345

She took off the black full-face helmet and shook her head to unstick her hair from her skin. She was still in a bad way, but comfort wasn't what either of us needed right now. We needed to crack on.

I hoisted myself out of the sidecar and we examined the magazine cover together. Semyon was on the far right, in the back row. I pointed at the egg-shaped guy in the centre of the group.

Her face turned to stone. 'That's Brin.'

'First name Vladislav? Is he Vladislav Brin?'

The wind was getting up. She wrapped the waxed jacket more tightly around her. It must have been Grisha's: it was in far better condition than mine.

'Yes,' she said finally. 'He is the CEO of M3C.' She cupped her hands to light a cigarette, took a deep drag and, without taking it out of her mouth, pulled her wheelie-case from between my legs. She undid it and retrieved a pashmina, which she wrapped round her neck. I'd been cold in the sidecar; she must have been freezing.

She stared at the magazine cover, transfixed. I couldn't tell whose face she was concentrating on. The one she hated or the one she loved.

'I know Brin.' I zipped the case up and shoved it back into the footwell. 'The last time I saw him was in 'eighty-eight. He was selling technology to the US in East Germany.'

She jerked her head round. '*What?*' Her eyes blazed.

There was no need to bullshit her any longer. We had less than a day to do what we needed to do. I told her everything I'd been keeping from her. I told her who I was. I told her about how Dex, Red Ken and I had lifted the gold. I told her what had happened when we were loading it. I told her about Tenny, Altun and Spag. I told her why I'd been in Iran, working for Julian, and about getting binned from the job as soon as I knew that Spag was involved, and that he was still CIA. I told her who had killed Semyon. And finally I told her I was there for one reason and one reason only – to avenge my mates' deaths.

She stared at me, taking it all in as I continued.

'I still don't understand where the four of us fitted in. I know Altun is the middleman between Brin and the Taliban. I know the Taliban can pay for the missiles with heroin or heroin money – it doesn't really matter which. I can't understand how Spag and the gold are involved. Or what cements him to Altun and Brin.'

'Nick?' She thought for a while. 'I don't know, and I don't care.'

That was good enough for me. 'You're right. The story, the pictures, so what? They won't bring Grisha or Semyon back. These people –' I pointed at the magazine '– these people will survive anything you do and then they'll kill you for it. It's just the way of the world. So fuck 'em. I'm going to kill them. I don't care that the CIA are involved and I don't care about the gold, the heroin or any of that shit. I'm here for Red Ken, Dex and Tenny. They were all I had left. And now I'm here for Semyon and Grisha too. I'm here for revenge. What about you? You want some?'

Her whole demeanour had changed. 'Yes – no more story. I want revenge.'

'Good – you get me to the proving ground and I'll do the rest.'

She took the cigarette from her mouth, flicked away the ash, and considered the burning tip. 'How?'

'I don't know yet. We'll share the riding – get us both out of the city and I'll work something out.'

103

Outskirts of Vologda
0648 hrs

The night ride along the endless ribbon of pitted tarmac had been dank and miserable, and so was the truckers' stop we'd pulled into. A strip of ancient wooden shacks was attached to each side of a filling station. Poor-quality light spilled from their windows and dribbled away into the forest. Power lines drooped between their poles and branched off over the parking area. If it hadn't been for the Cyrillic signs, I could almost have been in the American Midwest.

I sat on Cuckoo, wet, cold and hungry – all the things I hated – waiting for Anna to come back.

A convoy of military trucks made their way down the other side of the road. Each set of headlights caught the rooster tail of spray thrown up by the one in front. As they drew closer, they slowed and stopped. I heard boots on tarmac before I saw soldiers run into the shops.

I made myself look busy, double-checking all our gear was well strapped down. The first filling station we'd come to must have thought they'd won the state lottery. Besides fuel cans, a small bubble compass and a roll of Sellotape, we'd bought them out of food, water and maps, and even their stock of towing kits.

The maps had been OK for getting us here, but the training area was just shown as a massive stretch of grey. No roads, buildings or even water-courses were marked, and there was no sign in the middle of it saying 'Proving Ground'. But I had a plan.

I looked up. The convoy would have come from the naval air base Anna said was located about forty K further up the road. That was the direction we were heading when we left here.

The thunder of turboprops rumbled somewhere above the low cloud. Anna had said the base was where long-range aircraft took off to patrol the Atlantic. I knew the ones she was talking about – Antonovs with wingspans as big as B-52s, but props instead of jets. The papers had reported that the Russian crews held up boards with their email addresses on so the Brit interceptors could drop them a line and join their Facebook page.

Anna came out of the nearest shack carrying two paper bags and a couple of large steaming cups. She wasn't short of admirers, even here. Five or six soldier boys followed close behind. They whistled appreciatively, zipped up their jackets and headed reluctantly for their wagon.

The bag she passed me contained a small loaf of brown bread and a jar of strawberry jam. I broke the loaf in half and scooped jam into it with two fingers. 'Did you find out where we can get it?'

'About ten kilometres further up the road.'

I wolfed down the bread and jam between gulps of strong, sweet black tea, then climbed back onto the saddle. Getting aboard Cuckoo was just like straddling a regular bike, except you had to manoeuvre your right leg just ahead of the metal bars connecting it to the sidecar and just behind the air intake for the right cylinder. I liked to be able to move my leg around, and it felt hemmed in by the hardware.

Another invisible aircraft laboured above us as I kick-started the Ural. I hoped the cloud cover hung in there. We needed all the help we could get.

104

We soon found ourselves paralleling a four-metre-high chain-link fence. The fir trees the far side of it seemed to advance and recede as we continued, and in a few places crossed the wire in an attempt to overwhelm us.

It doesn't matter what flag you're flying or what uniform you're wearing, every army in the world has certain things in common. The chain-link fence is one of them. The high command can't seem to get enough of them. They don't stop anyone getting in, but they're great for hanging warning signs on. Red ones emblazoned with a skull and crossbones were pinned to it every twenty-five metres or so. I couldn't read the Russian writing beneath, but the message was clear.

We throbbed away at the Ural's top speed of 100 k.p.h. Its basic 750cc twin-cylinder sounded like a diesel truck. These machines hadn't changed a bit since the Russians reverse-engineered the German Army's BMW in 1939 – and Cuckoo was the real deal, one of the originals. It was designed to go to war, take a pounding and still come back for more.

Like most of the really good squaddies I knew, it was also a pain in the arse. Taking orders was not what it was about, and

I rather liked that. There was plenty of feedback from the handlebars. It had its own way of doing things, and it didn't care who knew.

It wanted to turn right whenever I accelerated, so I began steering left to counteract the pull. But easing off the throttle for a shift of gear made the bike yaw back to its original axis. I had to learn to feather my steering according to throttle input in order to keep the thing heading in the direction we needed to go.

Braking and turning were also no picnic. Hitting the front brakes pulled the Ural to the left, whether or not you wanted to go there. Right turns were even more hair-raising. If the change of direction was too sudden, the bike would start to lift.

We passed a barrack block overlooking a wet parade-ground. An endless line of wooden shacks stretched along its furthest edge, probably selling everything from beer to women. Neat lines of trucks and APCs glistened in the rain. Soldiers drilled or ran around at the double, all the normal business. It could have been any fortified military compound anywhere on the planet. It was exactly what I'd been hoping for.

We cracked on. I checked the odometer, watching it move up to the ten K mark. Anna slapped my left leg. We'd reached the truck stop she'd been told about. I pulled in.

This one had a hardware store. There were rows of shovels and picks lined up against a wall in some kind of display, next to knackered tractors that had probably left the production line in Stalin's time.

I waited outside in the rain while Anna went in. I took off the helmet to get some air. My whole body felt grimy and stiff, like I'd spent the night in a trench. For some reason, a night in the open always feels worse after first light. It was the bit I'd hated most about being a squaddie.

Anna came out twenty minutes later, laden with gear. 'Shall we fill it up at the pump?'

352

'Not here. Let's get on target.'

I put the helmet back on and we rode for another thirty K along the fence line. The skull and crossbones still made regular appearances every twenty-five metres or so. The occasional building materialized out of the drizzle beyond the wire. I didn't have a problem with the bad weather. There would be no test firing until it cleared.

At the thirty-five K mark we reached the guts of the air base, and barrack block after barrack block, all drab concrete and flat-roofed, interspersed with semi-circular huts made of corrugated iron. The whole place was heaving with lads in uniform trying to look as though they were on the way to somewhere important.

We passed the main gates. A MiG fighter and a Hind helicopter gunship were mounted on plinths either side of them. Two sentries in fur hats and camouflage waterproofs stood to attention beneath them, AKs across their chests. Their pissed-off expressions reminded me that there was something about being a squaddie that I'd hated even more than waking up after a night in the open.

Runway lights throbbed in the gloom behind them, fading away into the distance. Several massive Antonovs were lined up on a concrete apron alongside jets and helicopters. Jeeps buzzed between them. I slowed down as much as I could without drawing attention to us. I gave my visor a wipe and scanned the place for a smaller white jet among the grey.

Nothing.

We pushed on, passing armoured fighting vehicles and general military traffic.

About a K further on, a dense block of trees came right up to the fence line and crossed over it. The chain link disappeared among its branches.

I braked and shouted down to Anna. 'What do those signs mean? They saying the place is mined?'

'No – just that you'll be shot if you trespass into the training area.'

I slowed some more and checked behind us for possible observers. There were none. The road was deserted. I swung Cuckoo to the right, across a thin strip of wet grass, then manoeuvred between the trunks of the firs until we reached cover up against the fence. I turned off the engine, dismounted and pulled off my helmet. 'Now you can fill it.'

I lifted a whole lot of gear off her legs and undid the rope clamping the full petrol cans to the rear parcel rack. As she tried to haul herself out, I dropped one of the cans by the side-car and left her to it.

The fence was easy enough to climb. I used one of the pickets as support. I wasn't worried about sensors. This thing stretched for hundreds of miles.

From the top, all I could hear was the gentle glug of fuel into our new Chinese chainsaw. I couldn't see anything of the runway through the trees. That was good: it meant they couldn't see us.

I jumped back down and grabbed the other can. We'd topped up the bike at every filling station we'd come across over the last six hours, even if the tank was three-quarters full. If we had to leg it, the last thing we needed was a fuel gauge on zero.

Anna was done. She screwed the filler cap tight. 'What are we going to do now, Nick?'

'They're going to shoot down drones, right?'

She nodded. 'When the clouds clear. They'll want to do it at near maximum altitude.'

A MiG screamed off the runway to our right.

'Maybe they're going to take off from here. It's the main base and the only airstrip we know about so far. We should penetrate as far as we can into the area, and check out where the drones are heading.'

'Is that it?'

'No, we've got to keep on pushing forward. The more we do that, the more we can find out – and the more chance we have of getting on target.'

I pointed to the clear plastic bubble on the side of the chainsaw. 'Pump that thing until it fills with fuel.'

I went and tied everything back onto the bike. It was beginning to look like a really bad Cub Scout's rucksack – all we were missing was a frying-pan and a bunch of tin mugs. 'OK, on the bike. You're going to ride through the hole.'

I picked up the chainsaw and after ten or twelve wrenches on the starter cord, and finally working out how the choke operated, the thing sparked up. I stuck the eighteen-inch blade against the chain link to the right of the steel post I'd just used to climb up, and throttled up to full revs. It was pointless worrying about the noise. If we were heard, we were heard. There was nothing I could do about it. What I could do was cut the fence and keep cracking on.

The thing didn't cut that well – they never do at first. The chain bounced and snagged, but we got there. By stretching my arms as far as I could above my head, I cut a strip about two and a half metres high.

I turned off the saw and handed it to Anna. 'Lash everything down – even the helmets. We have to look as normal as possible when we get back on the road.'

She nodded. We were definitely going to do this job and then escape. Everything would go like clockwork. That was part of the forward-momentum thing. You did your best to make yourself sound as if it was going to work, as if the job was going to be done. With luck, it became a self-fulfilling prophecy.

I laced my fingers through the bottom of the fence and tried to drag it upwards.

105

It resisted at first, but came up easily once I'd wrenched the lower links clear of the undergrowth that had twisted its way through them. We were left with a gap like a badly drawn, inverted V.

Anna revved and pushed Cuckoo through, gouging its beautiful paintwork right down to the bare metal in places. She brushed her fingers lightly across the scars as she made way for me to replace her on the saddle. I knew what she was thinking, but I reckoned both Semyon and Grisha would have thought it was all in a good cause.

We worked our way through the trees and bounced onto a four-metre-wide gravel track that cut through the forestry like a firebreak. Puddles stretched across its rutted and pot-holed surface as far as the eye could see. The Ural bucked and reared and sent up sheets of muddy water, but kept ploughing on just like it was built to do.

I could hear the props of a reconnaissance aircraft taking off a couple of hundred metres to our right.

I just wanted to keep moving forward, try to find something – *anything* – that might give us a clue as to where we were, and where we should be going. I was working on the assumption that the most secure area, the proving ground, would be in the middle of the site rather than at the edge.

For a moment I was back in Brecon, in the training area where I seemed to have spent half of my squaddie life – a maze of forestry blocks, tracks and firebreaks just like this, and just as wet.

The cloud hung low overhead, and mist filled the gap between it and the treetops. There wasn't a breath of wind and the drizzle fell in a fine sheet. Give me proper pouring rain every time – but this stuff would do just fine. Low cloud meant no drones.

The little bubble compass was taped onto the speedo lens. The ball inside it pitched and yawed with every pothole, but I could see we were heading roughly north-north-east. I tried to keep the air base to my right. We were moving in more or less the same direction as the runway, towards the centre of the site. We emerged from the firebreak after another two hundred metres. I stopped when the track and the tarmac converged.

Most of the activity seemed to be at least seven or eight hundred away, the other side of the runway. I pulled the Nikon out of my day-sack and scanned what I could see of the air base. I checked the lines of aircraft for drones and the Falcon and found neither.

We carried on until we hit a junction from which five different gravel tracks headed back into the trees.

Numbered arrows in a riot of different colours were nailed to picket stumps. This was good news if you'd just been told to follow the yellow route to the RV point, but not much help otherwise.

Military training areas are plastered with signs and markers because head sheds the world over assume every squaddie is as thick as shit, and needs every message to be delivered as simply as possible. Don't drive your tank here. Don't dig your trench there. We don't want this whole place to be full of flattened buildings and fucking great holes. A training area might look rough and ready, but there are more restrictions than a national park.

I could see another sign a bit further down one of the tracks – a wooden panel on a metal pole, with faded lettering beneath a smaller version of our old mate the skull and crossbones.

The Ural's valves clattered as I bounced us down to it.

'What does it say?'

'Nothing much, Nick. Ranges. Shooting ranges.'

'How far?'

'It doesn't say, just down this road.'

As we headed onwards, another Antonov thundered overhead on its way to fuck about over the North Sea and hassle Scotland.

Anna looked up at me from the sidecar. 'Why are we going to the ranges?'

'They'll be restricted areas. That means there'll be checkpoints to stop unauthorized traffic moving through them. And where there are checkpoints, there's a good chance there might be maps or information on their exact positions. We're going to get ourselves a map.'

'What about the sentries?'

'They'll be the ones with the maps.'

I checked my watch. It was ten thirty-seven. I opened the throttle.

106

We bumped down the track at 40 k.p.h., only easing off at the bends. I slowed for each one and exited on the outside of the curve to give me more of a view of what lay ahead. I didn't want to sail round a corner and straight into a checkpoint without warning.

Fir trees towered on both sides of us. The mist cut visibility to a hundred metres. The ranges might have been three minutes away, or three hours.

I drove another couple of K, shut down the engine and listened for the crack of supersonic rounds.

I didn't hear any gunfire. But I did hear the rumble of wagons coming towards us.

'Nick, we've got to hide.'

'Where?'

The forestry block was too close and too dense. There were no firebreaks. We had been channelled down the track.

I restarted the engine. 'Give them a wave. Show confidence. You belong here. We'll carry on as if nothing's the matter. No looking back.'

'But what if—'

'Fuck it. Let's see what happens.'

I opened up the throttle. There was no more time for

discussion. I wanted us to pass them on the move, not give them an excuse to stop and ask questions.

We were doing a very bouncy 50 k.p.h. as the first set of headlights cut through the gloom. There were four of five of them, closing fast. I had to swerve off to the left to let them keep their momentum.

The trucks were green and canvas-backed. The driver of the first looked as though his face had been carved out of stone. Anna gave him something close to a salute and the lad didn't even bother acknowledging. The next four rumbled past. I checked in the mirror as I wrestled Cuckoo back on the track and saw soldiers on benches in the rear, leaning forward and resting their heads on their rifles. They looked very wet and very knackered.

That was a good sign. With luck they'd just had an early morning on the range.

We came to another sign at a T-junction a couple of K further on. This time, when I stopped and closed down, I could hear weapons in the distance. Single shots: high-velocity cracks as the rounds came out of the muzzle so fast they broke the sound barrier.

'Anna, we're nearly there.' I leant down towards the sidecar. 'There will be troops, but just sit tight and do what I say when I say it, OK?'

She nodded slowly. She didn't like it one bit. 'Do you have a plan?'

'Sure.' I gave her a lopsided smile. 'My plan is just to get on with it. If we fuck up, we fuck up, and they've won – but at least we'll have tried.'

I fired up the Ural again and we lurched in the direction of the shots.

107

One K further on a red flag hung limply at the roadside, a big old cotton thing weighed down with rain – a warning that the ranges were active. Even the most rough and ready set-up of this kind has worked out its safety templates. They cater for the rounds going down the range at the target, with a safety margin each side to cover fuck-ups. Templates normally look like big, open fans, at the base of which are the firing positions. Anywhere inside that fan is the danger area.

Another hundred down, we came across a second red flag and, soon afterwards, a red and white barrier across the road, next to a small shed. I really was back in Brecon.

I could see movement inside. Whoever the sentry was, he'd be bored out of his skull spending all day on stag. I knew the feeling. I'd done range-sentry duty a million times.

He came out reluctantly to see what the deal was with this bike and sidecar. The look on his face said he was already getting ready to turn us back or fuck me off onto another route.

He noticed the civvy clothes and all the gear hanging off the Ural, like we were on some kind of eccentric cross-country rally. He didn't have a weapon, but why should he? He was just a lad on stag. He'd drawn the short straw. Or, in this weather, maybe not. At least he was nice and dry.

He didn't have a clue who we were, but he didn't look overly concerned. Nine times out of ten, the deeper you are inside an area, the safer you feel.

I dismounted nonchalantly and treated him to a five-hundred-watt smile. 'Hello, mate, how's it going? Fucking wet, eh?'

His brow creased. He was in his early twenties and had goofy teeth. I could see the sides of a crew-cut under his helmet, which he wore tipped back. I could almost hear the cogs turning.

Was that English?

He pointed behind me and spun his hand.

'Yes, mate, that's right. Anna – give me a helmet.'

She reached into the nose of the sidecar and passed it up to me. I showed him the helmet in my right hand as I walked towards him. He stared at me from behind the barrier, inquisitive more than intimidated.

I kept on talking. 'Listen, mate . . .' His eyes were bloodshot. He'd probably been hitting the vodka bottle in one of those shacks opposite the camp. 'I'm going to fuck you over. I'm sorry.'

I focused on his eyes.

And then I swung my helmet hard at the centre of everything I could see that was flesh rather than metal.

He didn't have time to react. He took the full force of the blow and he buckled. I threw myself on top of him as he went down, my knees in his chest. I pounded the bike helmet a couple more times into the side of his face, once hitting the ridge of his helmet and missing, once connecting. I didn't want to hurt him badly. All I wanted to do was keep him out of it for a while. I yanked his helmet off and gave him one more good whack.

Anna went ape-shit. She tried to drag me off. 'Nick, stop! You'll kill him. What's he done? Stop it!'

I stood up. 'Look for a map in his hut. Go, go!'

362

Of course I wasn't going to kill him. I just needed to control him. I had to be short, sharp and aggressive – there's no other way to do this sort of thing. If you hesitate, he might turn out to be Russia's cage-fighting king. If you don't control him straight away, you could land up in a prolonged fight, with the only way out being to kill or be killed.

So, short, sharp and aggressive it had been. Anna wasn't going to understand this right now – all she could see was another poor bloody squaddie at the sharp end of a fight he hadn't asked for – but it was the best way to get what I wanted and still keep him alive.

He had a big lump on his head, but he'd be back having a few bevvies with his mates in no time at all.

108

I was dragging him towards the sidecar when Anna came out of the shed. She had two maps in her hands. One was a folded sheet, the other fixed to a board and covered with plastic film.

The sentry wasn't fully conscious, but he was compliant. I half slapped, half pushed him down into the seat. I shoved his head between his legs and held it there. I didn't have to use much force. The lad's survival instincts had kicked in now and he knew which side his bread was buttered. 'Anna, I need his helmet.'

She handed it to me, concern etched all over her face.

'Don't worry, he's coming with us.' I tossed it into the sidecar, along with Semyon's bloodstained one. 'You ride, OK? We need somewhere off the track.'

I climbed on behind her with the board in my left hand. My right stayed on the sentry's head. He needed to know somebody was controlling him. It would make him feel safer, and therefore more obedient. It didn't mean he wouldn't be scared. He'd know by now that if he tried anything he'd be on the receiving end of a lot more pain.

We carried on to the next junction. Anna turned right, out of line-of-sight of the road the trucks had careered down. She found another firebreak and started down it. I stopped her before we'd gone ten paces. We couldn't risk running into deep mud. We were off the track; that would do.

I jumped off and undid all the gear on the back. I needed the rope. I got the sentry to sit up and looped it round his neck. It was too much for him. His chest heaved and he gave a couple of loud sobs. Tears started to run down his face, to join the rain and the blood. The poor fucker thought I was going to hang him. 'Anna, tell him to shut up. I'm not going to hurt him – but if he fucks about I will kill him.'

The colour drained from her face. 'Nick, I—'

'We don't have a choice. I have to keep control. I have to let him know who's boss.'

She gobbed off to him. Her message seemed to be a whole lot longer than mine. I guessed it didn't really matter, as long as she managed to calm him down.

'OK, now ask him if he knows where the testing ground is. The restricted area, the proving ground, whatever you want to call it – does he know where it is?'

She gobbed off some more, while I fastened his hands to his ankles and brought the rope back up and around his neck. I tied it off to one of the connecting rods between the bike and the sidecar. I put his helmet back on his head to protect him as we bounced around.

By now he was sobbing big-time.

'He doesn't know, Nick. He hasn't got a clue. Look at him, he's just a boy. What would he know?'

I tucked the chainsaw down beside him and secured it with another length of rope, then turned my attention to the maps. There were a lot of fan-shaped areas outlined in red but none of them stretched more than a couple of kilometres. They were everyday, bog-standard rifle ranges. They weren't big fuck-off testing grounds. A couple of much larger, irregular-shaped areas were outlined in blue. One looked big enough to be Wales.

'What does this say?' I jabbed my finger at a heap of Cyrillic.

365

The boy let out another agonized plea from the footwell. I slapped a hand on his back. 'Shut up, mate. You're all right.'

It was going to be a nightmare for him. It was something he would remember for the rest of his life. He'd probably have bad dreams about this day – the day he'd thought he was going to die – but he would be alive. He stood more chance of getting shot by his own troops in a compromise than of me doing him any permanent damage.

Anna finished reading. 'The whole of that area is restricted – it's got to be the proving ground.'

I held the folding version open in front of me. 'So we've found the haystack. Now where's the fucking needle?' I scoured the area. There were bits and bobs of markings, no more than the major tracks. But then I spotted a short, isolated line, too straight to be a track. 'That's got to be a runway . . .' The board map showed us the shed we'd nicked it from. There was a big red 'You are here' blob for the sentry to show people.

I looked back to my folding map. 'OK, line-of-sight, it's about a hundred and forty K from here to the proving ground.'

'You sure that's it?'

'Of course I'm not sure. I just don't know. But neither do you, and he doesn't either – or he's not telling. And where else could it be? You've got a proving ground, you've got a private company coming in – they're going to use their own airfield. We've got a possible – let's go for it. On the way we might find something we prefer the look of.'

'And what about him?'

'He's coming with – it'll reduce the temptation to let the world know exactly where we are and where we're headed. Get on the back.'

I binned the board map and had a last quick look at the folding one before shoving it inside my jacket. I checked the compass and drove back down to the five-way junction.

I took the track that headed north.

366

109

I cut my way through yet another chain-link fence. It felt as though I was making progress. It was our third since we'd entered the training area. We'd used the forestry tracks, going cross-country when the ground opened up. We'd got bogged down once. I'd had to get the squaddie out to help. His name was Zar – a great name and an enthusiastic pusher before I tied him up again.

This had to be the proving ground. The other fences hadn't carried any signs, but this one did. Instead of being red with the usual 'Fuck off or we'll shoot you' warning, this one was yellow. It looked civilian even before Anna translated: 'Private property – no military allowed without a permit.'

We were in the inner sanctum.

We'd done just over 160 K to get there. If I'd got this right, the airstrip should be about forty K further north. And if the maps were to be believed, the drones could only take off from the main air base to our south or the airstrip itself. And the same went for the Falcon. It didn't matter where they took off. I had no control over that. But the drones would still have to get up in the air, and they would still have to do a fly-past to get shot down.

367

I pulled back the link for Anna to squeeze the bike through. Zar kept his head down. He was switched on. He was a good lad.

Once through, I got back on the driving seat, checked the compass and then the sky. The cloud was starting to lift. A breeze was moving things along. Ominously, shafts of light broke through in the distance, like someone up there had a fucking great torch.

The ground had been getting boggier so there'd be no more cross-country. I took the first track I found running north, up to higher ground. From there, we'd be able to get better eyes on the target ground.

There were no signs or coloured markers on this track. We climbed through forestry blocks and undulating grassland. The valves chattered but Cuckoo plugged on gamely. I stopped to watch the sky and listen, but saw and heard nothing.

We'd been going about an hour since the last fence when I checked the fuel gauge and pulled off to one side to top up the tank.

The cloud was almost gone. The wet fir trees glinted in the unexpected light, and steam rose from the leaf litter on the ground. Shadows appeared at the roadside as the sun burnt through the mist.

Anna dismounted and drank direct from a stream. 'I'll untie Zar and let him stretch his legs.'

'No. Too much time. I'll make sure he—' I held up my hand. 'Listen . . .'

It wasn't the thunder of an Antonov. It was the sound of something much smaller, coming from behind us, from the south. I couldn't see it. The fir trees blocked the view.

I screwed up the cap and threw the can back at Zar's feet. 'That's it – it's started.'

Anna leapt on the bike behind me. I kick-started it and pointed to the sky. 'Keep looking up, keep looking up.'

We bounced back the way we'd come, heading south, as I

368

dodged and wove among the potholes. I stopped about ten metres short of the edge of the forest and rolled the Ural the rest of the way to the tree-line.

110

Two aircraft were approaching from the south. The second was flying about four hundred metres behind the first. It was hard to judge the altitude, but I knew it couldn't be any higher than ten thousand feet. That was the limit of the 16's effective range.

The gap between them suddenly increased. The lead aircraft had cut away the drone. It banked left, orbiting back towards the air base. Almost simultaneously, the drone's jet engine sparked up, creating a heat signature as it surged towards us. It passed over us, heading north, its engine giving out a deep, throaty roar. Sunlight glinted off its wings.

All of a sudden, flares burst out either side of the fuselage – brilliant, blindingly white balls of magnesium that decorated the sky like a Roman candle.

The white smoke trail from the SA-16's power pack streaked across the tree canopy about two K to my half-right. Then it screamed up into the air and towards the balls of light.

The missile jinked left and right.

It locked onto a flare, rejected it, moved onto the next, rejected that too, moved on up, defeating the dark flares like they weren't even there.

The explosion, when it came, wasn't massive. Ground-to-air

missiles rely on kinetic energy as much as their warhead to down an aircraft. The rear of the drone disintegrated. Splinters of it showered from the sky as the main body started to spin towards earth.

I started running. 'Back to the bike. We carry on down the track.'

Zar must have been flapping about the explosion, but he didn't budge.

I kick-started and we were off. The back wheel lost a bit of traction, and slid out. I corrected, and the whole bike shuddered as the sidecar wheel hit a rut. I stood up on the foot pegs to get a better view. I had to keep the power on to keep that back wheel spinning, and I had to keep looking the way I wanted to go – not pointing, but looking. Start worrying about where you're putting your wheels and the bike stops doing the thinking for you.

The track opened up from the forestry a couple of hundred metres ahead. I could see clear sky.

Legs and arms still straight, I eased back on the throttle. We were close to the end of the firs. I trickled forward another ten metres and nosed it as far into the trees on the right as it would go, then closed down.

Zar didn't take much coaxing to climb out.

'Anna, bring the cameras.'

She gripped the kit while I dragged Zar to the nearest tree and retied him. He looked happy just to be breathing.

I waved to Anna. 'Give me your scarf.'

I stuffed one end of it into his mouth to fill the cavity and make sure he couldn't develop any sort of sound. I tied the free end round his eyes. Then I grabbed one of the cameras from Anna and we moved forward. When we reached the end of the firs, I stopped and listened. I could hear the buzz of another aircraft. I started running. I wasn't going to wait for her and I didn't have to – she had done her bit. Now it was time to do mine.

I hit the next tree-line after twenty metres and slowed. I was sweating big-time under the heavy bike gear but I didn't give a shit. We were nearly there.

111

I got down on my hands and knees and crept to the edge of the trees. I could make out bodies about three hundred metres away. They stood on the middle of an expanse of tarmac that began where the firs ended. There was another little strip of forestry to the far side of them. The runway disappeared off to the right.

The tarmac dried in a steamy haze around their feet as they chatted. A table and chairs had been set up beneath a small gazebo beside them. It was like a fucking garden party.

I motioned Anna forward. All she could hear was their laughter. She couldn't make out what they were saying.

I got out my camera and zoomed in on the two eggs on legs. I could hear Anna doing the same.

Spag and Brin stood next to each other in identical light cargos and blue fleeces. It was like one of them was holding up a mirror to the other. They covered their eyes with their hands as they heard the buzz of another prop engine, high up and behind us. Altun and the Taliban were still dressed for the boardroom.

I picked out movement in the trees beyond them. A fifth body stepped out of the shadows with a launcher on his shoulder. Almost immediately, he seemed to change his mind.

He swapped it for a fresh one from the back of a people-carrier parked behind him.

He took a couple of steps towards the picnickers, who were now toasting each other. The Taliban watched the others gun a shot glass down their necks. I felt my face flush with anger. I'd have given anything for a weapon to help their party really go with a swing.

A jet engine sparked up above me.

All heads turned to the sky as the second drone came into view.

Altun offered the Taliban a baseball cap but he refused. He'd be used to the sun and, besides, he'd want an unimpeded view. Altun continued his sales pitch as the Taliban looked over at the firing station, then back up at the sky. He nodded slowly as the flares kicked off.

There was a deafening roar as the 16 left its tube. A cloud of smoke erupted beside the people-carrier and a white trail streaked up into the sky. Like its predecessor, it jinked left and right, up and down as it interrogated the flares and sniffed out the correct target.

Two more seconds and it made contact.

Three of them clapped gently as the remaining fragments of the drone cascaded downwards. The Taliban stared open-mouthed at the hole in the sky where there had recently been a plane. He was probably thinking he should have bought more.

I checked the people-carrier. The guy was already pulling out another missile.

I got to my feet.

'Nick – where you going?'

'To do what we came here for.'

She nodded.

I turned and ran back towards the bike.

374

112

I didn't have time to tell Zar how lucky he was. If he'd been in the sidecar he'd have been coming with me.

I kick-started the Ural and bounced back onto the track, screaming over ruts and potholes towards the open tarmac. The chainsaw, helmets, wheelie-case, all the shit in the sidecar jumped and jolted as I rode out onto the pan.

I had to screw up my eyes. The sun glared off the wet tarmac. I squinted to see the bodies the other side.

The people-carrier was still stationary. The four men beside the gazebo spun towards the overworked motorbike. They didn't know what it was, but they'd have guessed it wasn't bringing dessert.

They started hesitantly towards the people-carrier. Before they could get there the lad who'd test-fired the missiles jumped into the wagon and it lurched towards me.

The four players melted into the trees.

Full revs, I aimed at the point where they'd disappeared, trying to outrun the wagon.

I knew immediately it wasn't going to happen.

The Ural splashed into a puddle the size of a small lake and aquaplaned. I kept the revs up, kept looking the way I wanted to go.

The wagon was gaining on me. Within seconds it was all I could see in my mirrors.

I jinked the handlebars and swung left. The wheel of the sidecar lifted. I had to throttle back before we flipped.

The wagon closed tight up behind me.

Less than a hundred and I'd be in among the foliage.

The sidecar jerked and was suddenly in front of me. The bike was spinning. The fucker had kicked me up the arse.

I had to jump. If I didn't get off, it was going to take me off. My right leg was hemmed in by the sidecar bars and air intake. If I didn't go now, I might have to leave it behind.

Hands over my head, chin tucked in, I launched myself sideways. All I could do was curl up, fly, and accept the landing.

I hit the tarmac hard. The air was punched from my lungs. I skidded across the ground. All that lay between me and a severe cheese-grating was the set of 1980s waxies. My elbows and hands took the pain as I rolled and tumbled.

I flipped over onto my back and my head met the cheese-grater. The asphalt ground through hair and skin down to the bone. I was slowing down. I spread my arms and legs to create more friction.

When I finally came to a stop I couldn't seem to function. I tried to get to my feet. I couldn't. My vision was blurred. The back of my head felt like a blowtorch was trained on it.

I could see the blurry shape of the van. I saw the door open. The body behind the wheel began to get out.

All I could do was stagger towards it.

113

I hurled myself at the driver's door and rammed it as it opened. There was a pistol in his left hand. His arm was extended. The metal frame banged against it. I held it there, slapping him like a drunk.

It wasn't working. He screamed at me through the window as I pulled the door open and he started to launch himself out. I slammed my weight against it and rammed his head back against the trim. His arm came down. I tried to kick the pistol away. He screamed as I held him there, kicking again and again at his hand, sometimes hitting, sometimes missing.

The pistol finally dropped. I yanked open the door again and slammed it hard into the side of his head. He collapsed into his seat. His head crashed into the steering-wheel, then slumped towards the footwell. His jaw came to rest on the door-sill. I raised my foot and kicked down. There was a loud crunch as his jaw gave way and the top of his head carried on four or five inches more towards the tarmac.

The rest of him poured out of the wagon and hit the deck. He wasn't going anywhere. My head was still spinning. I tried to take deep breaths.

The whine of jet engines sparked up on the other side of the firs.

I stumbled over to the weapon and picked it up. It was a Makarov. I slipped it into what was left of my jacket pocket as the Falcon's engines got louder. It was still the other side of the tree-line but definitely on the move.

I looked through the windows of the wagon. The seats were down and there was a stack of long green plastic containers in the back. I pulled up the tail hatch and grabbed the handles of the top two. They were light. They'd already been fired. I pulled them out and chucked them down beside their owner.

The next two were heavy.

The nose of the Falcon emerged from the far corner of the tree-line, about four hundred away, turning slightly left, then right again as it positioned itself for take-off.

I spun back to the container and took a long, deep breath. I had to be in control.

My heart-rate slowed, and so did everything around me.

I knew what I wanted to do. I knew how to do it.

I mustn't rush. If I rushed, I'd fuck up.

The four catches along the side of the tube flipped open easily. I lifted the lid. The 16 and its two-kilogram warhead nestled in a solid-foam cut-out.

The engines screamed as the Falcon developed the thrust to rattle down the runway and take off.

I pulled the weapon from its housing and hefted it onto my shoulder.

I was calm. I was in control.

The sun glinted on the clean white fuselage, still wet from the rain. I just hoped they were looking out of their windows and could see what was about to happen.

I turned on the power pack and heard the gentle whine of the electrics sparking up.

Everything was self-testing. It completed in seconds. As the Falcon's engines reached take-off power, I took my final deep breath.

114

The aircraft rolled, and was soon roaring down the tarmac, piercing the heat haze and throwing up a huge plume of mist.

I positioned the range ring of the sight on my target. I'd need to keep it there throughout the engagement sequence. Like Paul (not Pavel) had said, the SA-16 was an all-aspect missile. You could engage the target from any angle.

There was no IFF on this one. The Taliban didn't need it. Neither did I. I felt with my forefinger for the arming switch on the right of the grip stock. The Falcon was halfway down the runway. I pushed the switch forward from safety to armed. The weapon readied itself for firing, super-cooling the seeker to allow it to lock onto the target's primary heat-source, those three engines on the back. When enough infrared energy was detected, I would hear a high-pitched signal.

It was too easy. The electronics buzzed loud into my ear as it locked on.

The front wheel lifted from the tarmac.

My right ear filled with a high-pitched whine.

The seeker had a firm lock and was tracking the heat-source. We were ready to rock and roll.

I pulled the trigger just as the rest of the aircraft left the tarmac and tried to gain height.

Paul (not Pavel)'s words echoed in my head: *provided the aircraft was below 10,000 feet, its destruction was 99.9 per cent guaranteed.*

The missile made me wobble as it exploded from its tube. The white smoke trail was almost perfectly horizontal. It created a little white circle as it rolled over to the left, corrected itself, then jinked a little to the right as it locked on.

The aircraft was no more than a hundred metres from the ground when the missile struck. There was a small explosion. No big fireball, just debris falling away from the rear of the target.

The Falcon seemed almost to hesitate, and then dropped back down in a slow clockwise spin. It impacted beyond the end of the runway, throwing up walls of mud around its final resting-place.

A few pieces of wreckage fluttered from the sky like industrial-strength confetti.

As I threw down the tube and staggered towards the driver's seat of the people-carrier, the third drone scudded across the sky, chucking out flares as it went.

The back of my head felt like it had been dunked in acid. I got into the wagon and hit the ignition. The bike was lying on its side, engine still throbbing. The chainsaw lay about fifteen metres away.

I picked it up. This wasn't finished.

115

I sped along the runway towards the crash site as hundred-dollar bills fluttered out of the sky. Thousands of the things papered the wet tarmac – it looked like Broadway after a ticker-tape parade.

In the distance, the Falcon looked like a broken toy in a lake of mud. The back third of the fuselage had snapped clean off and lay about a hundred metres from the main section.

I swerved round another chunk of twisted aluminium. The last thing I wanted was a puncture. We still had to get out of this fucking place and I reckoned the Ural had already done its bit.

Brin was moving – staggering – across the tarmac. I swung the wheel towards him. He took another couple of steps, turned and looked me in the eye. His face and hands were charred, his clothes tattered.

My foot hit the accelerator. The people-carrier must have been doing at least forty when it hit him. It didn't connect with the same explosive force as one of his 16s, but it was the best I could do.

He flew backwards three or four metres. I hoped he'd have massive internal damage. I wanted him to know the meaning of pain before I killed him. I turned back and came to a halt a couple of metres from his burnt and shattered body. I pulled myself out of the wagon. He was face down on the tarmac. His back heaved a couple of times, but each breath sounded like a death rattle.

I pulled him over onto his front and stood above him. Brin's eyes stared at me. His brow furrowed. Maybe he was trying to work out where he knew me from. He was welcome to try, but it wasn't going to happen.

He gasped and jerked as I raised the weapon. I didn't care if he was about to die anyway, I wanted to make sure the job was done – and I wanted to make sure it was me who did it. I had some promises to keep.

I flicked off safety and aimed at his head. I fired just once. I was going to need every round I had.

He lay completely still. His eyes stayed open.

I turned away, leaving him lying in a fast-spreading pool of his own blood, just like he'd left Dex and Red Ken.

I surveyed the wreckage five hundred away. Smoke curled from the gaping hole at the back of the Dassault, but there were no flames.

Neither was there any movement.

Fuck that. I needed to take a closer look. I climbed back into the wagon and drove.

116

The rear section lay on its side, minus the right-hand engine and tail wing. I could see now where the cash had come from. The cargo hold was below the two side engines. The missile's kinetic energy had ripped apart the alloy boxes inside.

I didn't want to fuck about with the doors and emergency hatches. If anyone was alive in there it would give them time to think and react. The only way I was going in was via the mess of wires, panelling, seats and jagged metal where the back section had once been attached. From the noise I'd be making, they might even mistake me for a rescuer.

I stopped the wagon at the end of the runway. I was going to have to walk the rest of the way through ankle-deep mud.

I grabbed the chainsaw off the back seat and checked the mag on the Makarov.

I started walking. I was on auto-pilot. This was my time. Nothing was going to stop me. Nothing. I was doing what was right.

With the chainsaw on full revs, I sliced through the twisted wreckage in my path. As soon as there was enough room for me to squeeze through, I dumped it in the mud. I drew down the Makarov and stepped into what was left of the plane.

The smoke-filled cabin was in shit state. Yellow oxygen

masks dangled from the ceiling. Seats had become grotesquely distorted. The fuselage had buckled. The dark leather sofas round a fixed coffee-table were upended. Sparks jumped from severed wiring and at least four different warning alarms were going off. They were so loud I could no longer hear the chain-saw still chugging away behind me. I could smell burning electrics, cigar smoke and alcohol.

The crew door swung open and the two pilots saw me. Then they saw the pistol. The door cannoned shut again and I heard bolts slamming home.

Altun was sprawled on the floor to my left, nursing an arm that flopped like a broken wing. It was covered with blood. A champagne bottle was emptying itself onto the thick pile carpet next to him.

His eyes were glued on my weapon. He opened his mouth, but I spared him the indignity of begging. 'This is for Red.' I double-tapped him in the head.

Another one down.

I moved along the cabin. Everything was still in slow motion. I was floating.

The Taliban was on the right, hiding behind a section of brown leather. His eyes met mine. He knew what was coming. He didn't even flinch as the weapon came up. He stared, and waited.

'This is for Tenny.'

I fired.

One more to go.

I moved deeper into the cabin, clearing a path through the oxygen masks with my Makarov'd right hand.

He was in the far right-hand corner, struggling to get up. His lap was wet. Either it was champagne or he'd pissed himself. There was a cigar on the floor, still smouldering. 'Nick! Is that you, Nick? You're supposed to be stood down!' A cut that started just above his right ear ran all the way to his neck. 'We've got to get away out this shit. Come on, let's go.'

He staggered to his feet. 'It's been a total fuck-up. They should have called you off. They were told to.'

He took a couple of paces but I pushed him back. He toppled into one of the leather chairs. His eyes never left the weapon. He looked up at me, his arms outstretched. 'Nick, what are you doing? I'm on your side here, that's why they should have pulled you out. What's the deal?' He saw my head. 'You OK?'

'Why aren't you dead?'

His hands came up in mock surrender. 'Dubai? I didn't know that was going to happen. I took a round myself.' He pointed to his side. 'Luckily it didn't hit anything vital. I'm not carrying, by the way. I'm going to show you.'

He lifted his fleece and the polo shirt beneath to show a dent in the side of his overflowing gut. 'I didn't know. I swear.' He shook his head. 'Your people were told to back off. Now they've really fucked up.'

'I'm afraid I'm going to have to take all the credit for that. What were you up to, Spag? Doing your Ollie North impression again?'

He pointed beyond the gap in the tail section. 'You see that shit out there?' He meant the carpet of dollar bills. 'That's the money we're going to use to fight fucks like him.' His podgy finger moved to the Taliban. 'That fucking Obama and his new fucking broom . . . He's cutting our budgets left, right and centre . . . He's fucking up our world, Nick. My world and your world. But we're putting that right.' He gave me his trademark leer. 'Damn right we are!'

I kept quiet. Neither of us had anywhere to go right now.

'I used the gold to buy the missiles from Vladislav. You remember him?' He didn't wait for an answer. 'Then I geared up by trading the missiles to the Taliban for heroin, via that fuck Altun.'

His hands finally came down. 'Iran's having an election soon, Nick. The Taliban paid us way over the odds to get their hands on the missiles. We're going to flood the country with

385

their heroin and pocket the proceeds. Double whammy! The CIA needs black money to finance guys like me and you.' He reached out a hand for me to help him up.

I stared along the barrel. 'Not me, Spag. I was stood down. But you know why I'm here. You were there when it happened.'

His jaw dropped. 'This whole thing – for two guys? You're kidding, right?'

I was almost in a trance. I just looked at him, wondering when I was going to pull the trigger. 'Not just two. There's Tenny, and all the others like him.'

'Big boys' rules, Nick. They knew what they signed up for. This is bigger than them.'

'Wrong.'

As I brought the weapon up he sprang towards me, slapping my hand off to the left.

The weapon spun and he started running for the gap.

It was OK. I had five or six metres. I wanted to take my time, get it right, savour the moment.

I turned, brought the weapon back up – even thought about my stance. Nice stable position with the feet; weapon solid in the right hand; web of the thumb and forefinger tight into the back of the grip. Nice straight right arm; left now bent, fingers closing over the right wrist.

Both eyes open, fixed on the foresight so it was clear and sharp, I took aim in the centre of the big, now out-of-focus mass dodging the oxygen masks and debris.

The pad of my right forefinger rested on the trigger.

'Nick! Nick!'

She stood in the opening, right in my arc of fire.

'Out of the way!'

He saw his chance. The gap between them closed.

I started to run.

The chainsaw engine roared, but it was drowned almost immediately by Spag's high-pitched scream.

Red stuff exploded over the rear cabin as he fell to his side, the chainsaw still embedded in his chest.

Drenched in his blood, Anna dropped to her knees and vomited.

I jumped over the American's body and put my arm around her shoulders.

117

Spag's eyes were fixed wide open, like he was watching with amazement as the blood dribbled from his nose and mouth and his intestines spewed out over a rack of his own ribs. The motor idled, making it pulse from side to side.

I dragged Anna to her feet and out of the cabin. Out on the tarmac, I kept her upright. Once people are on the ground they flap even more. It's all to do with the body language of surrender.

'Anna – switch on!'

I shook her. I squeezed her face with my hand, trying to force her to focus. 'Look at me! It isn't over yet!'

It took her a while. 'Yes, yes.' She swallowed hard and I smelt strawberries again. 'Yes, Nick, you're right.'

She wiped hair from her face and I let her go. 'Now listen to me. I want you to take the wagon . . .' I kept my voice slow and low. 'Take the wagon, and go and untie Zar. Don't bring him here. He can do that himself. Tell him it's steak time for him and the lads.'

'What?'

'Tell him to take as much money as he can carry and bury the rest. He can come back for it later. Do you understand?'

She nodded.

'Deep breaths, Anna, it's all right.' I kept an eye out for the crew, but if they had any sense they were going to stay where they were until the dust had settled.

'Then get the bags and all our kit from the bike. We don't want to leave anything here that can be connected to us. Do you understand?'

'Grisha's bike . . . we can't . . .'

'Just leave it, Anna. We're taking the wagon. You got what you wanted. It's time to let go.'

She looked dazed. She needed gripping.

'Anna! Switch on!'

'Yes, yes – Zar, I'll go to Zar.'

She turned away and I went back into the aircraft. I tipped half a dozen immaculately pressed shirts from a Louis Vuitton bag and started stuffing it with muddy hundred-dollar bills. When it was full I found another, and then another. I'd filled four by the time the wagon came back down the runway. The tailgate was still open.

I threw the bags into the back and climbed into the passenger seat.

Anna was recovering. 'I heard him shouting at you. What did he tell you, Nick?'

'Nothing we didn't already know. Everybody's got their face in the trough and the ones who pay the price are lads like Grisha . . . my mates . . . and the rest of us at the shit end of the stick. So fuck it, let's go.'

We passed the missile-launcher. He hadn't moved anywhere fast, and was going to need a lot of work on that jaw of his. She was more concerned about me. 'Nick – your head . . .'

'Don't worry about me.' The pain was excruciating, but I managed a smile. 'I'm still breathing. So I'm still winning.'

A fourth drone cut across the sky, not realizing this particular show was over.

She drove fast. We were just about to enter the trees when Zar burst out onto the tarmac, staring wild-eyed at the wreckage at the end of the runway. Anna smiled as she watched him run towards the Ural. 'I told him to take Cuckoo. It's his now.'

118

Saturday, 18 July
1456 hrs
London City airport

Late-afternoon sunlight streamed in through the big plate-glass windows as I strolled through the automatic doors.

Through half-closed eyes, London City airport on a Saturday afternoon was how air travel must have been forty years ago. The building was almost deserted. A couple with small kids were making their way up an escalator towards the departure lounge. Some punters ambled from the shop, magazines in hand, to one of the two short check-in queues. An announcement encouraged last passengers for a flight to Geneva to make their way to the departure gate.

The person I'd come here to meet wasn't where he'd said he would be, but I'd half expected that. We were at an airport, after all. I turned around and headed back towards the car park. It should have been the first place I'd looked.

A couple of vehicles came and went in the unloading bay. An overweight woman with a bad case of sunburn lugged a heavy suitcase on wheels across a pedestrian crossing, shouting at her overweight kids to keep up.

I heard the roar of engines behind me as a commuter jet pulled into the sky.

I stepped out of the bright sunlight, and scanned the cars. I picked him out of the background clutter, his face angled sky-wards, one hand shielding his eyes from the glare. I hadn't a clue what the plane was – I didn't care – but I knew this was where his attention would be. Once a geek, always a geek . . .

'Oi, Ali.'

He lowered his arm and dropped his gaze. 'Jim!'

That was a bridge we had yet to cross. He rushed up and I held out my hand. 'Good to see you, mate.'

'You, too.' His eyes flicked from my face to my head. The scabs had gone and the skin was starting to lose its red-ness, but there was still a rather obvious lack of hair on one side.

I bent down so he could have a good look. 'Came off a motorbike.' I showed off the little stubby hairs trying to push through. 'But I can see the green shoots of recovery.' I stood up again, feeling quite pleased with my joke.

He didn't get it.

We were supposed to meet in the café – the airport being a handy halfway house between my place and his. He looked at his watch. 'I'm sorry. Have you been here long?'

I shook my head. 'No drama, mate. Settling in OK?'

'Yes, thank you. The weather is not like they told me it would be.'

'Better or worse?'

'Better!' He raised his eyes. It was another of those cloudless days that convinced us for a moment that we might have a really good summer this year. The papers had been full of phew-what-a-scorcher headlines.

Ali had been at summer school at the University of East London for the past month – on a lead-in English course before he kicked off his degree in journalism in September.

'How's Aisha?'

'She's well. I owe her so much. If it hadn't been for her . . .'
He didn't need to say any more.

As far as Ali was concerned, it was Aisha, researching online, who'd found the course as well as the bursary that had paid his tuition fees and living expenses. It was how she and I had agreed it.

Coming up with the cash had been the easy bit. Julian had played his part by pulling strings at the UK Border Agency to ensure that the fast-track student visa went through, no questions asked – not easy, when the subject in question was an Iranian with an encyclopedic knowledge of the world's aerospace and defence industry.

'And the old man, how is he?'

'Better. He has – how do you say? – turned the bend.'

I already knew because Aisha had told me but, Oscars all round, I had to look surprised.

'It was like you said. My father has been living with a pain in his heart for many years. But he is leaving the past behind . . .'

'And Aisha? Things calming down after the election?'

He shrugged. 'It happened just like I said, Jim, yes?'

Ahmadinejad had won. But he was never going to be allowed to lose.

'Aisha still believes in the green revolution. She still struggles.'

People like Aisha were the cinders under the ashes. This time it looked like it was going to turn into a baby Tiananmen Square. But next time maybe it would be an action replay of the Berlin Wall.

Ali stood there beaming at me like an idiot, but I could see he was itching to get back to some more plane-spotting. He had my email address.

We shook hands.

'I just wanted to make sure you're all right, mate.'

We both smiled and I made to leave.

'Jim?'

I turned back.

'What I helped you with . . . It was a good thing we did, yes?'

'Not just a good thing, Ali. The best thing.'

This time I kept walking.

SA-16s would still reach Afghanistan, of course. They'd just take a while longer. Heroin would continue to flood the Iranian market. Another Ollie North lookalike was probably already making cash that Obama didn't know about to spend on a war he wouldn't want to know about.

I pulled my keys from my pocket and pressed the fob. Twenty metres away, the rear hazards of a gun-metal Porsche 911 flashed into life.

I clambered in and shut the door. I hadn't had it long enough yet to stop appreciating the sound of that reassuringly expensive clunk or the smell of new seat-leather.

As I eased the car out of the airport onto the North Woolwich Road, sunlight glinted off the gold ring on my left pinky.

I'd found the sixth crate exactly where Red Ken had left it. The tricky bit had been finding a patch of desert where I wouldn't be overlooked melting down Saddam's face, but it's amazing what you can do with a few uninterrupted hours and a propane burner if you put your mind to it.

If the guy in the souk had had any inkling of where the gold had come from, he didn't show it. He'd got a good deal, so why rock the boat?

As for the CIA's muddy dollars, Anna had most of them. Getting them ready for circulation must have given a whole new meaning to money laundering. I'd only kept enough to buy me a beanie to cover my head, to clean and feed myself up, and to get on the train with her to St Petersburg, then on to Narva, on the border with Estonia. The river that separated the former Soviet satellite from Russia was a piece of piss to deal with. Then it was on to Dubai.

Five days later, I was home again – just in time for the

christening of Red Ken's granddaughter. At a break in the proceedings, I gave his widow her gold ring and told her I'd opened an account for her with five hundred grand in it. She knew better than to ask where the money had come from. The code was the code, and she knew that he was gone for ever even before I told her. His seat was occupied by a large, framed picture of him in uniform. I liked to think Red Ken would have done the same for me, but maybe I was getting soft in my old age. I must have been, because Tenny's widow had got the same amount.

Cinza? I have a feeling she's already made other arrangements, but she got the biggest bottle of Amouage Homage I could find to help her on her way.

After that I'd decided I'd had enough of *The Secret Millionaire* routine and headed for the Porsche showroom. Well, it was about time I had the odd mouthful of steak as well.

I'd never been much good at keeping score. Did it go some way towards compensating for Dex and Red Ken getting zapped? Julian reckoned it did – but then he always was a big softy.

Not only did he pull strings for Ali. During the Iranian election riots, there'd been a low-key news story that a certain Bradley Capland, banged up in the UAE as a bad debtor, had been allowed to go back to spend his final days in Canada with his beloved wife Sherry by his side. Several commentators expressed their surprise at the UAE authorities – not known for their touchy-feely side – letting him go. The story was a welcome antidote to the bad news that had been flooding out of the Gulf state as the Dubai dream continued to turn sour.

Julian wanted me to work for him and I told him I might. But not just yet – I had some things to do.

It took me ten minutes to reach the basement car park of my docklands apartment block – a glass-and-steel monolith that had had its final lick of paint, the estate agent told me, the day Lehman Brothers went to rat shit. Their crunch had been my gain. If you've got cash in your back pocket, recessions are a great time to clean up, the experts say. Since in every other recession I'd ever lived through I'd been penniless, I was only just beginning to find out.

My biggest problem was not really knowing what furniture I needed for the penthouse two hundred feet above my head. But help was at hand. Anna was arriving tomorrow and staying over – as long as she only ever smoked on the balcony.

I had two outings planned: a trip to IKEA, followed by a night out at *Mamma Mia*. She was a smart girl, but I doubted that even she would get the connection.

Andy McNab joined the infantry as a boy soldier. In 1984 he was 'badged' as a member of 22 SAS Regiment and was involved in both covert and overt special operations worldwide.

During the Gulf War he commanded Bravo Two Zero, a patrol that, in the words of his commanding officer, 'will remain in regimental history for ever'. Awarded both the Distinguished Conduct Medal (DCM) and Military Medal (MM) during his military career, McNab was the British Army's most highly decorated serving soldier when he finally left the SAS in February 1993. He wrote about his experiences in three books: the phenomenal bestseller *Bravo Two Zero*, *Immediate Action* and *Seven Troop*.

He is the author of the bestselling Nick Stone thrillers. Besides his writing work, he lectures to security and intelligence agencies in both the USA and UK. He is patron of the Help for Heroes campaign.